A Wiley Poynter Mystery

A BAD GAME
for
AMATEURS

By
Jeff Ridenour

Publisher: Karlsbad Middleford Press **KMP**
Charleston, South Carolina

Now the hacienda's dark, the town is sleeping.
Now the time has come to part, the time for weeping.
Via con Dios, my darling,
Via con Dios, my love.

— "Vaya con Dios"
Written by Larry Russell, Inez James, & Buddy Pepper
Popularized by Les Paul and Mary Ford

Deception is [a] bad game for amateurs.

— Charlie Chan
Shadows Over Chinatown
Monogram Pictures, 1946

for

Wayne and Marilyn

*for all their hospitality
while the gears were grinding*

Acknowledgements

I would like to thank John Blunt, Norm Storns, and the late, great Tony Strong Maynard for their useful comments on early and late drafts; more than thank my editor and wife, Ronda Lynn, she with a keen eye for errors, despite a marked repugnance for the sundry sleazy characters she was obliged to endure. Any remaining errors are mine alone.

1

Saturday

Despite his name, Sigmund was neurotic as hell. At the first whiff of blood, Siggy raced along the cart path toward the pungent smell, leaving his mistress to whine futilely for him to come back. The three-year-old Schnauzer was sure he would be punished for his disobedience. But half the time faithful compliance earned him a rebuke for tardiness anyway. He never knew whether he would garner a treat or a swat for good behavior. So, in this instance, screw obedience, screw unconditional canine love, Siggy thought. Even if the complexities of the scent told him that what he was smelling was not fresh blood. Still, blood is blood.

Gwen Dupree slowed to a walk. The cool late-April morning air made the perspiration on her forehead feel chill and she stopped to mop her face with the towel she wore around her neck whenever she jogged. She saw Siggy disappear from the cart path where a row of spidery mesquite trees lined the bank of Scorpion Wash to the right of the fairway bunker at the dogleg of the 14th fairway of Diablo Verde Country Club. So she pressed on. She had begun her regular morning jog from the back porch of her ranch-style home, which faced the 8th green. The pedometer attached to her gym shorts registered 1.2 miles. Of a sudden that distance seemed longer to her.

"Siggy, where are you? What have you found?" she called out.

The dog barked and Gwen hastened her pace, now walking on the asphalt path. She began to jog again as Siggy's barking became more frenzied. She was startled when a pair of large crows flew up from the dry wash and began cawing as they alighted on scraggly tree branches. Beyond a white out-of-bounds stake, through a ragged hedge of creosote, she saw her dog barking and bowing at a prone object partially shaded by overhanging limbs of the two mesquite trees.

"Come here, Siggy. Come. Come. Get over here right this instant."

But Siggy stayed and barked. He knew his mistress was no better than one of the neighborhood mothers whose habitual beckoning, warning, and scolding of her toddler amounted to a feckless, "Johnny, if you don't shape up by the time I count to a million, I'm going to –" – followed by the mother's favorite idle threat of the moment. Sigmund Dupree was not about to be cowed by that kind of pathetic intimidation.

"Arf! Arf! Arf!"

Gwen looked behind her and saw a groundskeeper riding a lawnmower, the blades of the machine folded upward, as the man in coveralls drove the mower in the direction of the green. Then she turned, parted the creosote, watching for snakes and lizards, and stepped gingerly to the edge of the dry wash.

When she saw the object of Siggy's attention she let out a scream. And then another, causing the crows to take flight. She pulled her cell phone from a pocket in her jogging shorts and dialed 911. Between deep breaths, she reported her finding and her location. Then, after easing herself down the crumbly bank, Gwen knelt and beckoned for her dog. "Come, Siggy. Momma's not angry with you. Really I'm not. How about a little treat? That's a good boy."

Gwen pulled a baggy full of miniature biscuits from another pants pocket and held one out for the dog. "That's my sweetie." When Sigmund took the biscuit from her palm, Gwen grabbed him by the collar with her other hand and snapped his leash to the collar ring. "Let's get away from here, baby. This is an awful place."

As she stood, she gasped as she saw a pair of eyes watching her from behind a tangle of purple buckhorn cholla on the far side of the wash. Siggy sensed another presence, too, turned his head to look, and began to bark again. Gwen stared until she realized the greenish eyes belonged to a coyote.

Giving a tug at the leash, she said, "Let's go, Siggy. Back onto the fairway." She stumbled in the soft sand, regained her footing, and, as she tugged on her dog's leash, she saw Siggy looking up. He barked again. Gwen followed the dog's gaze and saw three turkey vultures, wings spread, floating on updrafts, circling.

Again on the cart path, Gwen began waving an arm in the air at the groundskeeper, who was now criss-crossing the distant green. Just then she heard another motorized sound behind her and turned to see a golf cart driven by a young man she recognized as the boy who inserted the flags into the holes on the greens each morning.

When the young man stopped in front of her, she dramatically pointed toward the dry wash and explained to him what her dog had discovered.

"Shall I call the police, ma'am?"

"I've already done that. Now we just have to wait. Would you mind waiting with me? I'm afraid the shock of what I've seen is starting to set in."

"Yes, ma'am. Come sit in the cart. I'll take your dog's leash, if you like."

"Thank you. Oh, God! I can't believe what I saw." Gwen Dupree put her face in her hands and began to sob.

2

Arroyo Arenoso's police chief, Roland Morton, parked his black and white on the far side of the dry wash, across from the golf course. Before he even climbed out he could see the corpse, face down in the sand. Two of his deputies were standing guard nearby, the younger one, Mike Logary, shifting from one foot to the other, looking away from the body. The chief wondered if this might be the first stiff Mikey had ever seen. Probably.

After crossing the wash, the chief exchanged nods with his deputies. In his best church-usher whisper, the older deputy, Ed Phillips, said, "It's Bobby Shane Hollsworth, Chief."

"So I see. You boys go up and join Charlie in keeping those folks at a good distance. And don't tell 'em a damned thing. Nothin'. You understand?"

Both men nodded and climbed up the loose soil that formed the western bank of Scorpion Wash. Beyond them a crowd had gathered near their squad car, parked in the middle of the 14th fairway. Some stood in bathrobes and slippers; early-bird golfers sat in golf carts. The sun was barely above the telescope dome atop Mt. Hopkins in the nearby Santa Rita Mountains.

Kneeling beside the boy, Chief Morton touched the young man's arm, gauging its coolness. "You've plucked your last guitar string, Bobby Shane. I hope whoever did this to you didn't do this because he hated your goddamned music as much as I did."

That prospect struck the chief as unlikely. Bobby was clad only in a pair of blood-stained jockey shorts. His back was dotted with what appeared to be cigarette burns and knife cuts. Rising from the teenager's cropped, bleach-blond punk hair was a blue and purple lump the size of a golf ball.

"Did you die here, Bobby? Or were you dumped here afterwards?" the Chief said aloud. "Never mind. I'll figure it out for myself."

Scorpion Wash was a small stretch of drainage in the larger scheme of water funnels in the region surrounding the town of Arroyo Arenoso. Draws, arroyos, gulches, and washes aplenty served as conduits for rain water, mostly from the brief-but-violent summer storms that pummeled the Sonoran Desert in July and August.

The wash that ran beside the Diablo Verde golf course fed into the larger arroyo for which the town of Arroyo Arenoso was named. That stream fed the northward-flowing Santa Cruz River, which meandered through the west side of Tucson and continued its path paralleling Interstate 10 until it petered out in the Santa Cruz Flats, just before reaching the Gila River, which, before the Gadsden Purchase, had served as the boundary between Mexico and the pre-Civil War United States.

The chief spoke into his should microphone. "Betty, is the Coroner's wagon on its way yet?"

The static-filled reply came. "I show it passing Sahuarita on the interstate as we speak, Chief."

Chief Morton forced himself to take a long, hard look at the young man's face, what he could see of it, then waited for the sudden spasms in his stomach and throat to pass. He closed his eyes for a moment, hoping that would help suppress what kids like Bobby laughing called the urge to regurge. The chief thought, it's not so funny now, is it, Bobby Shane? For either of us.

In the Sonoran Desert critters anxious to feed on the flesh of the dead gather quickly. Whether the carrion is fish, fowl, or mammal makes no difference to hungry scavengers. Either crows or turkey buzzards had already plucked Bobby's eyes. One or more coyotes had chewed at his exposed flesh. The chief imagined that, though unseen, fire ants and other crawly creatures were gathering. All around flies buzzed. Dust to dust is too poetic and symmetrical for what really happens, Chief Morton knew.

So who wanted you dead, Bobby Shane? Rollie Morton knew the torture-murder scene gave some suggestion of a drug-cartel execution. The border was less than sixty miles away. And, despite the nearby checkpoint and Border Patrol vehicles zipping about the local landscape, busy as bats at sundown, everyone knew I-19 was a pipeline more profitable than the gasoline and natural gas lines that came from El Paso.

But more often, the chief supposed, a bullet to the back of the head would be a cartel's style. After all, these days Latino drug kingpins owned more guns than the Chinese army. The fact that many of the guns were bought in Arizona was another matter.

And what are the burns all about, Bobby? What did you know? And why wouldn't you tell them? Drugs? Even a little drug-related knowledge was a dangerous thing in these parts. Were you buying? Selling? The chief knew that drug-deal-gone-wrong was a regular and deadly event in the Southwest.

Chief Morton made a mental note to ask his daughter what she knew about Bobby. Even though she is a freshman and he was a senior, as lead guitar in a local rock band he was known in the area to every kid old enough to tap two sticks on a piece of hide or pretend to strum a three-foot piece of lumber. Or, in his daughter's case, screech like a banshee in response to the obscene shimmying by the producers of the resultant clamor.

Who found you like this, Bobby? Oh, yes. The Dupree woman. Or rather, her yappy little terrier. Christ! Sunrise joggers. That's a piece of a larger lifestyle I'll never understand, the chief told himself. Not that he was a couch potato. He set a healthy example for his staff. Ate right, drank little, smoked not at all. But running just for the sake of running? No thanks. That makes no more sense than eating for the sake of eating.

As he was driving through the front gate of the country club the chief had instructed Deputy Phillips to see that Mrs. Dupree was escorted to the club house where she could wait more comfortably to be questioned. He then called in to have a female officer, Candy Rogers, come down from the police station to sit with Mrs. Dupree. He did not want the woman left alone; did not want her to return to her house. He also decided that Candy could take a preliminary statement from Mrs. Dupree.

He began composing a mental list of suspects, starting with the other boys in the band, Prickly Pear Jam, in which Bobby Shane Hollsworth played lead guitar and lead vocalist. The chief had heard a rumor the band members had been quarreling. Over what he was not sure. Music? Women? Money? Probably all three. Even at their age.

When he looked toward the noises he heard coming from the direction of the growing crowd of onlookers, he saw the mayor, Pete Kemper, and the chairman of the country club's board, Lyle Ehrhausen, barging their way past an I'm-tellin'-you-that-you-can't-go-over-there Deputy Mike. The chief took off his hat and wiped several beads of sweat from the band of his white Cattleman Stetson. It was going to be a long day.

3

"I do wish you would change your mind and stay at least through the remainder of the weekend, Wiley."

"I can't," I said, as I finished drying the last of the breakfast dishes. I felt as though I had already outstayed my welcome. Dearly as I loved my older sister – and knew she reciprocated the love – I also knew she was scarcely tolerant of my lifestyle, which included some rather slovenly personal habits, at least by her ultra-fastidious school teacher standards.

She said, "I don't understand what you see in detective work. It's dangerous, the pay is poor, and you spend all your time dealing with unsavory people. How can it be satisfying?"

"It's a game, Sis. A puzzle-solving game. I like doing puzzles. Mysterious murders and missing persons are fun kinds of puzzles to try to unravel. You know. Was it Colonel Mustard in the library with the lead pipe? Professor Plum in the kitchen with the wrench? Miss Scarlet in the billiard room with the candlestick?"

"Silly games, if you ask me. In any case, what do you have to return to so urgently?" she said, putting away the cups and saucers and picking non-existent toast crumbs from her bathrobe. Though I was dressed, packed, and prepared to leave for the hours-long drive back to Las Vegas, Adelle remained dressed in her jammies and robe, a concession to Saturday morning. No school today.

She could lollygag in her pj's all day long for all I cared, though such garb scarcely flattered her. I had noted the first morning we had breakfast together, a week earlier, that, *sans* makeup and a smart outfit, she looked her age. Her odometer had clicked over to forty a couple miles back. But, made up and togged up in a well-cut dress, she could mask five or six of those years.

"I have an empty office to return to," I finally said. "I don't want the resident cockroaches to begin thinking they can take over my desk, chair, and filing cabinet during daylight hours as well. The cheeky little bastards have probably given thought to the notion already."

She winced. "Let them have your dingy little office. I hate to be a harpy, but I must state again that I deem your occupation unworthy of your talents and wish you would set about trying to find useful and respectable employment."

Though she was not one to read detective stories, except for Conan Doyle, Adelle thought she knew just enough about the profession of being a private detective to suppose my kind were as seedy as we actually are. For Holmes, of course, she made an exception.

"Dear sister, I have no talents. We both know that. As for useful and respectable work, that kind of thinking has no place where I live. Las Vegas imports all its talent from Hollywood and Nashville."

"All the more reason you should decamp from that wretched state and move closer to me."

"I'm afraid Arizona has its own issues. We both know that."

"I want you where I can keep an eye on you more frequently."

"Ah! The deeper, darker motivation emerges from the closet. I require a shorter leash, do I?"

"You do. And you know it."

"Eager to clean the ring around my bathtub daily, all year round, are you?" I said.

Adelle was compulsive-obsessive about bathroom cleanliness, to the point of –. Well, the example I just gave will do for a small start. My sister was the epitome of that ideal, virtuous woman described in the last chapter of Proverbs by Lemuel's mother, at least insofar as: *She looketh well to the ways of her household, and eateth not the bread of idleness.*

"Now don't get me started on –," Adelle started to say.

She was interrupted by the doorbell.

Adelle looked at herself, then at me. I knew she considered her present state of dishabille much too indecorous for her to confront a visitor. After all, the caller might be the Queen of England or – more threatening to my sister's reputation and standing – her school district superintendent.

The bell ringer turned out to be her scandal-mongering neighbor, Mrs. Fortunato. "Where's Adelle? Tell her to come quickly. I have news."

News. Likely not about an earthquake in Nepal or of a politician's indictment in Chicago. No. This would be *Local Headline News at 9 a. m.*, featuring the faux-Pulitzer-Prize-winning Gertrude Fortunato.

"Come in, Gertrude. Adelle is still getting dressed. What's up?" I said, beckoning her into the living room.

She came in quickly, rubbing her hands together in that age-old gesture humans bursting with juicy tales to tell have used at least since Miriam began spreading tales about Moses. I quickly suppressed my hope that, akin to Miriam's penalty for such mischief, God would inflict leprosy on Mrs. Fortunato. I told the old woman I would go and try to hasten my sister's appearance. I gestured for her to make herself comfortable on the sofa as I excused myself to knock on Adelle's bedroom door.

Six minutes later Adelle emerged from her bedroom looking as impeccably dressed as if she were on her way to have tea with the Queen. She had even applied lipstick – and one dab too much of whatever perfume she favored.

I picked my own imaginary toast crumb from her dress collar and told her, "Gertrude is here to announce tomorrow's local newspaper headline." As it turned out, I was right about that.

4

After Mrs. Fortunato had delivered her news and departed to ring other doorbells, Adelle sat at the kitchen table and wept while I made a fresh pot of coffee. She had her head down on the table, so I added a dash of Wild Turkey to hers when I poured it. She probably did not even know I knew where she kept the bourbon, at the back of the top shelf of a corner cupboard.

My sister was not a closet tippler. The level of the booze in the bottle had not declined so much as a finger's worth since my last visit, eight months earlier. I have no idea why she even owned any hard liquor. Another instance of the many just-in-case items she kept on hand. She was never very clear when trying to explain exactly what the cases might be that required her to maintain a liquor collection, Scotch, bourbon, and vodka. But then I knew she also maintained a boxful of recipes for dishes she would never think of preparing for herself, or even for any guests who might appear on her doorstep minutes before dinnertime. And she owned enough bath towels to supply several Olympic swim teams.

When I handed her the coffee, she took a sip, but made no mention of an odd taste. She simply looked up at me, her eyes watery and swollen. "I can't believe it. He was such a bright and promising young man. He earned a B-plus in my American history class last year and I know he didn't crack open the textbook very often."

Adelle taught classes in American history to juniors, along with government and economics to seniors at Arroyo Arenoso High School. She loved to teach and, from all reports, she was an excellent teacher who adored her students. And they apparently adored her back.

"Murdered, for chrissake," she said. That was about as profane as my sister ever allowed herself to be.

"Are the local police competent to deal with murder?" I said, perhaps a tad too casually.

She took another sip of her coffee, then held the cup closer to her nose and sniffed at it, cracked a faint smile, but refrained from commenting on my unsolicited enhancement. Without looking at me, she said, "You're planning to stay now, aren't you?"

"Why not?"

"Rollie Morton won't like it."

"And he is –."

"Our chief of police."

"I'll be discreet."

"Like hell you will."

I withdraw my remark about Adelle's eschewing profanity, although I sincerely believed that, with her last remark, she had dipped into her next year's quota of expressing naughty words or even thinking them. But murder will do that, even to the most careful and respectful speakers, among which I counted my sister. As she did herself.

And so began my inquiry into the grisly and mysterious death of Robert Shane Hollsworth.

As most of Adelle's female pupils could have told her, even a few drops of hard liquor, when applied timely, will undo a lady's inhibitions significantly, in many a young woman's case frequently leading to the undoing of her bra hook and her jeans' zipper as well.

Several wet tissues later, Adelle agreed to tell me what she knew about Bobby Shane. I'm afraid she began badly by telling me, "Bobby was such a nice boy."

"Nice." I repeated with a clear implication of disbelief. Along with a touch of disgust even.

"He was, Wiley. I mean it. He was well-mannered, soft-spoken, gentle, kind –."

"And no doubt loved puppies. But I must tell you, Adelle, I'm calling bullshit on 'nice'. It's crap. Trust me. I never met the lad but I know it's crap. Every eighteen-year-old American male is little more than a bundle of sex-crazed appetites. Priapism is their natural state. A permanent erection. The rest of their nature is nothing but smoke and mirrors."

"My God, Wiley. Recall that you were once eighteen and I don't remember you as being any such thing."

"Then either you misremember or else I was far cleverer than even I give myself credit for. Smoke and mirrors. My thoughts, fantasies, delusions were one hundred percent carnal one hundred percent of the time. And that in no way made me aberrant."

"I can't believe you are telling me this poppycock."

"I can't either, only it's not poppycock. There's nothing poppy about it."

"No need to be crude. I get your point," she said, clearly disappointed in both the tone and content of my remarks.

We looked up the Hollsworth's address in the phone book and Adelle explained that Cochise Avenue lay on the other side of the interstate from where Bobby's body had been found. My sister knew that his mother was a clerk at the Arroyo Arenoso post office and that his father was a town firefighter. Bobby was an only child.

"Who were Bobby's girlfriends?" I said, before she could continue focusing on my shortcomings and reflecting on how badly I might have deviated from the image she bore of me in my youth.

"He only had one. Kristy Serling. Well, that I know of. She, too, is such a –." She started to say "nice", but then thought better of it. "— a genuinely wholesome young woman." She might as well have said "nice". *Wholesome* made for a distinction without a difference.

"What can you tell me about Kristy? Facts, rather than character estimates," I said.

"Kristy is a honor student. She received all A's in my class last year and is achieving the same this year. She's in the band. Plays flute. Had a minor role in last year's theater department play. Oh, and she even holds down a part-time job. She's a cashier, hostess, or some such at Graciela's."

"What and where is Graciela's?"

"It's a Mexican restaurant. Downtown. On the main drag through Arroyo Arenoso. I've only eaten there once. The food is quite good, but I abhor the ambience."

"How long has she been Bobby Shane's girlfriend?"

"They started last year as I recall. Both of them were Homecoming attendants," Adelle said.

"Attendants?" I'd been out of high school a long time.

"That means they were runners-up in the voting. Came in second or third. So they went as a couple to all the Homecoming events."

"And have been trading spit ever since, I gather."

Adelle gave me her stop-being-so-crude look. Sometimes I'm uncouth just to bug her. Other times my rudeness simply rolls off my tongue unprovoked, like slobber from a Great Pyrenees. *Spit* was to bug her. I hate fawning descriptions, even when they accurately portray bright, pretty girls. Especially then. Unlike a Great Pyrenees, I'm not allowed to slobber. Only fantasize – without letting my colorful imagination – read: impure thoughts – show.

Adelle shifted to ticking off the names of Bobby's friends, including fellow members of the hard rock group Bobby had formed. Perry Crisp, rhythm guitar, Jason Altheiser, bassist, and Richie Maldonado, drummer. Bobby was lead vocalist and lead guitar.

Adelle wrote down a list of other folks she deemed to have been friends of Bobby Shane. All of them were students.

"No adults?" I said after examining her list.

"Well, maybe Mr. Sechrest, our director of music. He tried very hard to befriend Bobby," she said, making an odd face when she said it.

"Bobby didn't reciprocate Mr. Sechrest's feelings?"

"Not very much, that I could tell."

"Is Sechrest gay?" I said.

Adelle's jaw dropped. "Not that I'm aware."

"And how aware is that?" I said. I had formed an opinion even as a pre-teen that my older sister's grasp of people's sexual proclivities and identities could be classified in terms of what kids these days call *clueless*.

"Well, Mr. Sechrest has never mentioned anything about his being a gay person."

"Well, there you have it then. Definitive proof."

"I suppose so."

"Shit O'Dear, Dell. I was mocking you, for chrissakes."

"You were?"

Duh. What was I saying about her being clueless? "I guess I'll have to meet Herr Sechrest myself."

"What for?" she said.

"To size the man up. Draw my own conclusions regarding his Queer Factor. See if he might have been harboring any prurient notions of wanting to play a game of Priests and Acolytes with Bobby."

"I do know Sebastian kept trying to convince Bobby he should switch instruments, give up the guitar."

"Take up the skin flute, I suppose."

That earned me a puzzled look, but I was hardly going to elaborate.

"What instrument does Mr. Sechrest play?" I said, to prevent a follow up question on flutes.

"Oh, Sebastian plays a fine cello."

Cello. Perfect. An instrument he can put between his legs and stroke with a bow string. I could scarcely wait to meet Sebastian Sechrest.

Adelle, consistent with her cluelessness, had no idea what a groupie was. "No, Sis. The fish is called a grouper." But I did manage to pry out of her a list of secondary females Bobby Shane might have befriended in some form or another. No other adults struck Adelle as possible candidates for friendship with Mr. Lead Guitar. Bobby apparently wasn't into adult relationships.

"Did Bobby have a job?"

"You mean besides the band?"

"Yes."

"His band was a full-time obsession. He had no time for anything else. Again, as far as I know."

"He had time for Kristy.'

"Well, I think… know… that was a source of contention between them."

"She resented his giving too little time and attention to her."

"Exactly."

"Any conflicts between Bobby and his fellow musicians?"

Adelle hesitated.

"Well?"

"Jason Altheiser, the nice young man who plays bass, came out of the closet just before Christmas. Bobby was infuriated. Clearly, Bobby's tolerance for…for that sort of thing… is, was, I gather, um, shall I say…limited."

"Limited. Right. And how did Jason respond to Bobby's… limited tolerance?"

"I heard and saw them screaming at each other as I walked by the band room one day a couple weeks ago."

At last. My sister had paid attention to something that was perhaps relevant to Bobby's demise.

5

By early afternoon my sister announced she felt uncommonly drowsy and was going to take a nap. I had mistakenly supposed the caffeinated bourbon would have put her down by noon. I left her asleep on the couch and drove to the Country Club to see what I could see for myself.

The gated was blocked off by a squad car. The cop leaning against the car's hood told me golf had been cancelled for the rest of the day. Not even members were allowed onto the premises. Undaunted, I outflanked the cop by driving around to the back of the club by way of the desert, following a perimeter service road that years of summer storms had turned into a washboard.

I assumed correctly that forensic people had swarmed all over the scene and nearby environs. A medieval philosopher-friar named William Occham proposed one of the first keep-it-simple principles. The rule is famous now and makes sense in most contexts, but cops habitually disrespect it. By the time I crept slowly up to where Bobby Shane's body had been found, the crime scene was easy to identify. The entire 14th hole had been decorated with yellow keep-your-asses-out tape. That's an instance of what I mean by cops' dissing Occham. The real crime scene was no bigger than a backyard swimming pool. It took in the dry wash, the bank of the wash, the mesquite trees above where the body lay, as well as the creosote and ground as far back as, and including, the cart path.

Maybe Bobby's method of arrival, dead or alive, at the site where he was found had been via a vehicle too large to fit on the cart path, in which case some of the fairway was fair ground for those who had put up the yellow police cordon. But not the whole damned fairway, from tee to green. The cops might as well have put tape around the entire premises of the club, which included several dozen homes and their backyard swimming holes.

But, these days, cops are given to expanding the boundaries of everything they can mark off as exclusive cop territory. In that regard they are like male dogs pissing on fence posts and trees. Maybe that is why crime-scene tape is always yellow.

Staring at the place where some woman and her dog discovered Bobby's body – which may or may not be identical with the scene of a crime – told me no more than I would learn from watching the evening news on Tucson stations and reading the Sunday morning *Arizona Daily Star*, Tucson's quaint notion of a big city newspaper. Each of the local TV channels granted the murder three minutes, having a sent a reporter with a broad smile and silky voice to tell audiences where the murder took place and who the victim was. The remaining two minutes and forty-five seconds consisted of interviews with citizens on the streets of Arroyo Arenoso, all of whom were as clueless as my sister and were shocked that such a horrible act could have been committed in their quiet, friendly town.

The next day *The Star* gave the murder even less publicity, two column inches on page two of section B. Even by then no more information had been provided by the police. The newspaper merely announced that a high school senior named Bobby Hollsworth had been found dead in a dry wash in the town of Arroyo Arenoso. No mention of the weapon involved. And the powers-that-be had managed by then to keep the country club where the body had been found out of the paper. Those who boast that advances in technology guarantee advances in public knowledge are full of shit.

6

Sunday

After Adelle and I finished a brunch of omelets, scones, and bacon, I drove to the Country Club again. A sign now had been posted just to the left of the gate announcing that, by order of the chief of police, no golf would be permitted until further notice. I was sure that gave many of the club's members a taste of what heroin detox and cold-turkey cigarette withdrawal felt like.

I parked across the street from the main gate and watched the cop on duty consult what I assumed to be a street map of the club grounds and check it against the driver's license of each supplicant wanting to enter the club. Finally I walked over and asked him who was and who wasn't allowed in. He explained that only bona fide residents of the club were allowed in or out of the club grounds until Chief Morton said otherwise.

So much for my hope of gaining an easy interview with the woman who had discovered Bobby Shane's corpse. TV reporters had given her name as Gwen Dupree, but none of them had succeeded in getting her to speak with them, let alone talking her into appearing on camera, either live or taped. Good for her. Or maybe the police chief had warned her not to give out media interviews. I wasn't a news medium, but then perhaps his warning, suggestion, or whatever to her had been to shun all interviews period – as if such a remark by a cop to a witness would stop me from trying my damnedest to question the lady. Paparazzi and stalkers have nothing on me when it comes to persistence. And stealth.

"Mrs. Dupree?"

I had parked next to a tall brick fence along what turned out to be the 6th hole and climbed over the bricks with the help of a palo verde tree. The fence was meant to separate club residents from the riff-raff, but there I was, standing on the upscale side, trying to get my bearings. Several minutes later I found the house I wanted and rang the doorbell.

"Do I know you?"

She was a tall brunette. Attractive for sure. She was dressed in Sunday casual: a loose white blouse that showed off the edges of a well-filled pink bra, slacks that stopped just below her knees. The lenses of her glasses were the size and shape of little gum packets, set in red frames. I guessed they were strictly for show, to give her perceived IQ a boost.

The rock on her wedding band stood out. It was the size of a mini-Gibraltar. Maybe her husband was deeply insecure. I wondered about that only because I had had a friend in college who swore a married woman's availability to other men is an inverse function of the size of the diamond in her wedding band. The smaller the diamond, the less she would be inclined toward fidelity. So a man gave a woman a large diamond on their wedding day either in the hope it would be an incentive not to stray or else as a confirmation of his faith she wouldn't. I doubted the theory. On the other hand, I had never tested it. And my friend who put it forward was such a handsome, charming, and relentless ladies' man, he had no need of his theory.

Mrs. Dupree wore no shoes. She had copper polish on her fingers and her toes. I don't know when copper nails coupled with pink undies came into fashion and I wasn't about to ask. I'm neither a fashion maven nor a critic. I tried to ignore her clothes. I tried even harder not to imagine what lay beneath them. But on that score I failed.

I soldiered on anyway.

"My name is Wiley Poynter and I'm working on behalf of friends of the unfortunate young man whose body you came across yesterday morning."

"I gave my information to the police already."

"I know. But Bobby's friends asked me see what I could find out – in order to aide the police investigation. Not that they don't trust Chief Morton and his staff. But additional minds at work may come up with some tidbit or other the police might not get around to considering for a while. And we're all anxious to find out who committed this dreadful crime, don't you agree?"

Always structure opening remarks in such a way that the listener can't help but agree with you. I had learned that long ago from a shyster insurance salesman whose job it was to fleece retirees by selling them long-term care and disability policies by inundating them with horror stories spun from whole cloth. I had helped put a stop to his misrepresentations, but I had to admit I liked some of the methodology behind his sales pitch – the getting listeners to agree part, not his tall tales of woeful suffering by uninsured phantoms.

"Come in, Mr. Poynter. I was just reading the morning paper. I'm afraid I overslept and am just getting my day started."

"I appreciate your time, Mrs. Dupree. It is Mrs., am I right?"

"Yes."

"Surely Sunday mornings are meant for oversleeping, unless –." I looked about and didn't see any religious memorabilia or icons. "Unless you're a regular churchgoer."

"Ha! The last time I was inside a church was at my cousin Nora's wedding. Years ago."

"May I sit down? I only have a few questions," I said.

A dog appeared from the hallway, stopped, and stared at me. I remembered the woman's having a dog from hearing about it on the television news.

"Is that the dog who discovered the body?"

She snapped her fingers. "Yes. Come, Sigmund. Say hello to the nice man."

Sigmund stood his ground.

"Siggy, don't be rude. Go over and greet our guest. His name is Mr. Poynter."

"Wiley," I added.

"Oh no, Mr. Poynter. Sigmund isn't sly at all. He's pretty dumb actually."

I had to explain that I had repeated my first name, rather than made a comment on the canine's cunning. I figured it was a good thing Sigmund's grasp of English didn't include *pretty dumb*. Otherwise, one or both of Mrs. Dupree's lovely exposed ankles might have suffered from two rows of canine dental indentation. I was beginning to think Mrs. Dupree herself was not very cunning. Or wily.

The dog continued to stand and stare. I stared back but couldn't get a read on the beast. Having never owned a dog, I felt I was at a disadvantage. Siggy had clearly spent considerable time figuring out humans.

"I'm sorry, Mr. Poynter. How rude of *me*. May I offer you some refreshment? Coffee? Tea? Beer? Wine? Something stronger?"

"No thank you. I'm fine."

"Do you mind if I fix myself a thirst quencher?"

"Not at all."

She went to a far cupboard and pulled out a fifth of Old Grand Dad. Why the distiller had chosen to spell it that way escaped me. In any event, I had expected a member of the country-club set to swill a classier brand of bourbon. Maybe that meant she and her husband poured Two Buck Chuck to accompany their filet mignon. It took me aback. Nearly all lah-dee-dah people I knew insisted on wearing their alcohol snobbery on their tuxedo lapels and ball-gown sleeves. Brand-slumming, when it came to booze, was strictly déclassé.

I began to suspect that the Duprees were *nouveau riche* and hadn't been around long enough to get the message. While Mrs. Dupree waffled between ice and no-ice, I glanced around to see what else among the household appointments and tchotchkes might have been purchased from Sears or Wal-Mart.

Most items struck me as second rate, except for the stereo system. An acquaintance of mine in Las Vegas owned an Outlaw Audio system with Infinity Classia speakers. I'm not an audiophile, but I was impressed when he demoed it for me with as much pride as if he were taking me for a spin in a new Corvette. I thought it odd that a drinker of K-Mart quality liquor owned Neiman-Marcus class audio components. But I guess maybe even the upper classes have to limit themselves in what luxuries they indulge themselves in these days. At the current price of gold, I imagine the rich sometimes might feel obliged to settle for porcelain crowns – on their teeth at least, but probably not on their heads.

But the Duprees were sham nobility. I guessed they had risen from proletarian roots only a cut or two above trailer trash to their current status of ticky-tacky strivers who had achieved some modest success. A garish semi-respectable-rags-to-semi-respectable-riches story. My own plebian status made me no more envious of them than a bulldog is resentful of not being a rat terrier-poodle-mix mutt.

Gwen Dupree plopped down languidly in her queen's chair, while I sat on her cheap-but-serviceable sofa. She had finally come down on the side of chilling her bourbon and now stirred the cubes with an index finger. She clearly hadn't gotten around to perusing Miss Manners' must-read guides to correct social behavior either. The use of index-finger swizzle sticks ranked as uncouth conduct.

Or perhaps she was engaging in a bit of reverse snobbery. A my-house-my-rules sort of gesture. I was in no position to throw a penalty flag. I suppose, in that regard, she could flaunt convention by lolling about in her own home in her birthday suit. I mentally slapped myself for letting that thought pop up, then decided: Why be so hard on myself?

After listening to her recap her previous morning's experience beside the 14th fairway in a mode that practically portrayed her, not Bobby Shane Hollsworth, as the most damaged party, I asked, "Did you know Bobby Shane?"

"Not personally, but I knew who he was."

I waited for elaboration.

She sucked on an ice cube until it melted, then said, "The band thing. I saw a poster up at the clubhouse sometime around the beginning of the school year advertising a gig they were doing at the high school. And, oh, there was an article about the band in our local weekly newspaper. That was maybe a year ago."

"Did you ever hear him play?"

"No." She waved vaguely in the direction of the cabinet that held the stereo system. "Boyd didn't buy that hoity-toity music equipment just to listen to racket and roll."

"Are you familiar with any other members of his band?"

She shook her head. "I only knew about the dead... about Bobby Hollsworth because he was the bandleader. Or whatever a rock group's *numero uno* is called. Lead guitar? I don't know."

"You jog around part of the golf course every morning, do you?"

"Except for the two days a year it rains here."

"Did you notice anything unusual along the area where you found Bobby?" I said.

"No. But then keep in mind that I'm not out there to take in the scenery. I'm pretty much in a zen-like trance when I jog. That's to keep my mind off how boring jogging really is. And off the little aches and pains I feel these days to remind me I'm not eighteen any more."

I didn't dare ask how old she was. I guessed twice eighteen. "Does your dog always join you on your jogs?"

"Oh, yeah. Siggy loves to run."

"Off-leash is acceptable to your neighbors?"

"Oh, sure. Siggy's not an ankle biter."

"I believe you told the police you saw one of the golf course maintenance people about the same time you discovered the body."

"Yes. Mowing the 14th green. Then, after I leashed Siggy and climbed out of the dry wash, the flag guy came along in his cart."

"The flag guy?"

She explained.

"And these were course employees you had seen before?"

"Yes. I knew them both." Pause. "By sight, that is. I don't know their names."

"Any of the neighbors' lights still on?"

"I can't say. As I told you, I'm in a semi-trance, mostly staring straight ahead."

"Was the sun up? Or was there only pre-dawn light?"

"I guess the sun was up. Again, I can't really say for sure. All I care about when I start jogging is that there is enough light for me to see. So I don't trip on something and twist or break an ankle."

"How long are you up before you begin your morning jogs?"

"Not long. I brush my teeth, put on my jogging suit, eat some yogurt, then I'm off."

"I take it your husband isn't a jogger."

"Boyd's not a morning person. He shaves, showers, dresses, eats breakfast, and drives to work all in his sleep."

"He's not around today, I take it."

"Nope. He left Friday night. Flew to Las Vegas to a convention. He owns Boyd's Used Cars in Sahuarita. There's a used-car dealers' convention at the Tropicana this weekend."

That made sense. Used cars and the Tropicana went to together. Lots of mileage on both. The Tropicana could use an oil change and a new set of shocks.

"Mind if I ask why you didn't go with him?" I said.

With a smirk, she said, "He told me I'd cramp his style."

"And would you?"

The smirk remained. "I have my own style and it doesn't require me to be anywhere near Boyd, let alone cramp him."

She toyed with the top button of her blouse. Whether consciously or not, I wasn't sure. I wasn't about to ask what her style was — at least just yet. But I was certain she would feel obliged to treat me to an exhibition of the techniques involved and I wasn't in the mood for that kind of show-and-tell. I might lose my train of thought — among other things.

"You feel comfortable staying here alone." I said it as a declaration. Turning it into a question seemed a bit off, as though I might be challenging her abilities to cope.

"I'm not alone. I've got Siggy." As if on cue, the dog hopped into her lap. Master protector and detective intimidator.

"What sticks out in your mind most about the murder scene? If you don't mind focusing your memory hard on what you saw."

"Jesus, that's easy. All the cigarette burns on his back and legs. I mean, what kind of cruel monster would do such a thing to another human being? I'll never be able to flush that picture out of my mind."

None of the TV or newspaper reports mentioned burns to the body. But then that would be among the cops' primary holdbacks to help them sort the wheat from the chaff when phony confessions and sham witnesses began showing up.

As far as who would do such a thing? Sadism may be unique to the human species, but it is hardly unique within it. Maybe it's even genetic. Just watch any small gathering of four-year-olds for a few minutes and you'll see how almost instinctive cruelty is, both verbal and physical.

I stood, thanked Mrs. Dupree for her time, and handed her my card with my cell phone number on it.

At the door she asked me, "What's in this for you, Mister Detective? Is someone paying you to hunt down Bobby's killers?"

"You said killers. Plural."

She shrugged. "I'm no detective, but I've been thinking. Christ! How can I not think about it? As I said, I can't get the image out of my mind. But just think about all those cuts and burns on his back. Do you think one person, acting alone, could have done that to him? Wouldn't he have struggled? Fought back? I mean, that many marks on his back and legs would have taken some time, right?"

"You're absolutely right. Thanks for pointing that out." I turned to leave, thinking that this woman is not as dumb as I might have initially thought.

"You didn't answer my question," she said.

"What's in this for me? I'm just a nosy kind of guy. I'm like Sigmund, only with a duller sense of smell."

"Well, good luck sniffing out the killers."

7

Gwen Dupree could easily have been right about multiple killers. I was driving back to my sister's house when my cell phone rang. The caller was Jack Stonecipher, a fellow Las Vegas gumshoe, sometime competitor, sometime collaborator.

"How they hanging, Wiley?" he said when I recognized his number and decided to pull over and answer.

"Upside down, Jack. And yours?"

"Out the window. Flapping in the cool, cool breeze."

"And what brings you to my virtual door?"

"I need a favor, buddy. You are in Tucson, right?"

"Sort of."

"I need you to check out an address for me and see if there is a body living in it," he said.

"Call and see who answers."

"The place won't have a land line, I'm sure. Besides, I want eyeball confirmation."

"You want me to knock on the door and count the numbers of bullets that exit in my direction. Is that what you're asking?"

"It's a woman I'm hoping is there."

"So I should look for red nail polish on the bullet tips as they whiz by me."

"I don't think she's carryin'. And, even if she is, she probably won't shoot from the hip."

"Meaning she takes careful aim."

"No, no, no. She's harmless."

"Harmless women don't need guys like us tracking them down. Now what's the real scoop?"

He laid it out for me. An Anglo embezzler with a Latino boyfriend. The victim was a high-tech software company in Henderson. The lady was one of their accountants. Accounts payable. She'd dummy invoices to a vendor that turned out to be an account she had set up for the purpose. She'd begun immediately after the previous audit by an outside firm. By the time auditors came around again, she had skimmed a couple hundred thousand dollars and left town the day before the auditors arrived.

I said to Jack, "You're sending me to the boyfriend's house, right?"

"The boyfriend's mother. He was living with my quarry and working at the Venetian."

"As a what?"

"A cook."

"So he's probably carrying," I said.

"A stolen French knife maybe."

"Funny. Okay, I'm on it. Give me the address."

I wrote down an address that I knew to be in South Tucson, which is a nearly-all-Hispanic tattoo on the south edge of Tucson's ass. Lots of nice hole-in-the-wall Mexican restaurants, mostly small, dumpy houses protected by rusting chain-link fences, and full of lots of mean dudes you don't want to fuck with.

Lucky me. I was going to get to fuck with one. Or at least try.

Jack Stonecipher and I had been helping each other out for several years now. No formal agreement; just a handshake. No money ever changed hands. Mostly it was the kind of exercise Jack had just asked me to help him with. We kept tabs on who owed how many favors to whom. The unspoken limit was twice a year each of us had a favor coming from the other. This was Jack's first call to me in ten months. I hadn't called him in over a year.

However –

"Jack, I would like some immediate reciprocation, if you don't mind."

"Reciprocation? Does that come in pints or fifths?"

"Pounds and ounces."

"How many pounds' worth you want?"

"You weigh it when you're done. And keep your thumb off the scale."

"Let me have it."

I lied and told Jack I needed some information about a case I had been working on and had hit a dead end with before I left to come to southern Arizona. Why I lied, I wasn't sure. Maybe because I like to keep my competition off-guard, even when he's friendly competition.

What I wanted Jack to check on was Gwen Dupree's story that her husband was away in Las Vegas. I had no reason to doubt her, other than my general uneasiness about women who drink bourbon before lunchtime. The spiking of my sister's coffee didn't push Adelle into that category, of course. Then there was the fact that her husband was a hawker of used cars. I've never walked onto a used car lot without thinking to myself: If only these aged clunkers could talk. What would they confess to? Tampered-with odometers were always the first piece of cosmetic surgery that popped into my head. And I didn't suppose entrepreneurial con men married entirely honest women.

I figured verifying Mr. Dupree's whereabouts wouldn't take Jack long and I could then satisfy myself about that piece of minor, admittedly prejudiced, tidbit of curiosity, cross it off my list, and forge ahead with serious inquiries. Besides, Jack would feel better for having paid me back for my helping him out.

"We're going to Tucson, Adelle. You've been cooking for me almost every night and now you're distraught over this Bobby Shane killing. A trip to Tucson and a good Mexican meal will help distract you and reward you," I told my sister when I got back to her house.

"We could eat somewhere closer. Tucson's a bit of a drive," she argued.

"Mischa's."

"Oh, well. That sounds great."

Of course, it did. There wasn't anything comparable in Arroyo Arenoso or Sahuarita that I knew about. Elaine's, in Tubac, was good, but it was also probably closed on Sunday night. Misha's is one of the hole-in-the-wall Mexican places in South Tucson. *Gringos* eat there without getting kneecapped between their cars and the front door. And even if there were a gauntlet to run, the food is worth the risk.

8

Micha's was packed, with a birthday party filling the rear banquet room. But the owner found a table for us and we feasted. The noise was a bit much for carrying on conversation, so Adelle and I simply held hands and gazed meaningfully into each other's eyes, as though we were a pair of newlyweds on our honeymoon. My sister was pleased that I was staying on for a while longer, even if the occasional cause for my remaining was an unpleasant one.

I have no idea why Adelle never married. She had a few boyfriends in her college days. She is bright, charming, and not a bad looker. She was always the one who did the breaking off. She may even have received a proposal or two. She still won't talk about her old boyfriends. I'm pretty sure she's not a virgin, but she hasn't been in bed with a man – or woman – for at least ten years. Well, that I know of. I try hard not to pry.

When I offered to drop her off at a public library or a mall while I went about my business for Jack, she declined. Nor was she interested in a movie or anything else that would part her from my company. I finally gave up trying to place her out of potential harm's way.

"I'll sit quietly in the car and listen to your satellite radio," she said.

I only hoped that would be safe enough for her. I didn't think telling her I keep a shotgun wrapped in a blanket in the rear of the Jeep would add to her peace of mind. Probably just the opposite, even though it's a double-barreled Krieghoff Classic with a manual cocking device on top of the tang in place of a safety so there is no way it can discharge accidentally.

A concealed shotgun in Arizona ain't no big thing. Hell, in Arizona I could probably toodle down the interstate with a 75mm Howitzer trailer-hitched to my Jeep and receive 2nd Amendment salutes from the locals. I wouldn't even have to carry proof there wasn't a shell in the breech.

Besides the Krieg, I carry a S&W 386, which is a .357 with a two-inch barrel and fires seven shots. With my nearsighted inaccuracy, I need the extra pops. Also, tucked into a steel holster, affixed under my dashboard out of sight on the right side of the steering column, is a Taurus 941, an eight-shot .22 caliber, also with a two-inch barrel. I keep the Taurus there in case someone with road rage pulls up beside me and threatens me with something more dangerous than a middle finger.

Overkill? No, no. It's happened. On a busy interstate. I flattened the poor bastard's right front tire and sent him careening into the median, where, at 75 mph, he hit the concrete support holding up a busy overpass. A week later the Nevada Department of Transportation decided the support column needed protecting with a couple rows of rubber barrels. I agreed.

The deceased turned out to be the husband of a woman I had been spying on. He mistakenly thought I was screwing her, a fatal non-sequitur based on two nosy neighbors' telling him of seeing my car parked across from his house on evenings when he was out of town. He was a salesman with a large territory.

But the guy she was actually screwing was the CEO of the life insurance company she worked for. The company's board of directors had hired me to gather evidence that the CEO and the guy's wife were indeed coupling so that the board could fire the CEO for violating company policy.

I wasn't even sure what the company's policy was. I hadn't asked for a copy of the company's policies or even of its mission statement. I assumed the policy in question was the standard one forbidding company executives from dipping into the hired help. But, for all I knew, it forbade him from having more than five mistresses at a time and she was number six. Corporate morality ain't what it used to be. Probably never has been.

The Goody Two-Shoes world of Ozzie and Harriet was also the world of HUAC and above-ground nuclear testing. The latter, of course, is a recent legacy of my adopted state of Nevada, along with mob-controlled gambling and pussy for rent sanctioned by the state. Where else in the universe, besides Nevada, can a guy stand in one spot and simultaneously feed quarters into a one-armed bandit with his right hand, get a legalized blowjob, and hold a Geiger Counter in his left hand that's going clickety-clack faster than an Amtrak diesel racing across Montana? "Only in Nevada" might even beat "Only in America" as the ultimate satirical punch line.

In any case, I showed the insurance company's board of directors glossy-colored photos of the CEO and the wife humping away like a pair of crazed weasels. The CEO departed the company with a silver parachute, the wife departed the company with the clothes on her back, and her husband departed this world in a cheap casket.

The board was pleased with my work. I had mixed feelings about it. Sure, I had accomplished what I had been asked to do. But an innocent man had died from my efforts and I had been directly responsible for his death. I know. He tried to shoot me and, instead of shooting back at him, I shot at his car. Even so, I felt shitty about the whole squalid episode. Still do.

We found the house bearing the address Jack Stonecipher had given me. The chain-link fence was as rusty as a '49 Ford and the house hadn't known a brush full of paint since the Coolidge Administration. Grass was considered an unaffordable luxury in the neighborhood. So were weed whackers. Gophers came standard. I hoped the occupants hadn't sprung for an optional Rottweiler.

I parked my Grand Cherokee on the far side of the street a couple doors down and left my sister in the car to wring her hands and fill her ears with noise from the Grateful Dead Concert channel. She promised me she'd keep the doors locked.

With a flashlight in one hand, Messers Smith and Wesson in the other, I crossed the street. The street was empty as far as I could see in both directions, which wasn't very far. South Tucson didn't deem street lights to be one of the public services it was obliged to provide to that part of town.

The curtains were drawn and I saw no lights glowing inside. As I slowly approached the front door I noticed neither a porch light nor a doorbell was visible. I began to wonder if electricity was also optional, although there are battery-operated wireless doorbell systems these days. But I didn't see a button of any kind to press.

So the boyfriend's mom was living in what was basically a small cave with windows, while Miss Embezzler – her name was Susan Jennings – had probably already booked tickets on a cruise ship bound for Santorini and Mykonos for herself and her boyfriend, whose name was Eduardo Ruiz. Maybe they planned to take the mother along, but I doubted it. Cruise liners charge a supplement for singles and I couldn't imagine a chick with a Latino gigolo booking a suite for three, with mama sleeping on a pullout sofa.

Knocking in a situation like this is an invitation to all kinds of repulsive weirdness. I know cops do it on TV and then shout "Police". But the parameters TV script-writers operate by are not the same as mine. If they were, I'd have been meat in a morgue long ago. I eased my way around to the side of the house. There were no shrubs to hinder me. I hoped there wasn't any dog shit either.

Cheap but effective blinds blocked my view into the one window on the west side of the house. The back door had a window. And there was a screen door with rips in the screening. I turned on my flashlight and, after reminding myself curiosity could kill more than a cat, shone my light through the screen, through the back door window.

No dog growled, no guns spewed bullets at me. I let out a sigh and peered in. The kitchen had a Formica table and two chairs with upholstery showing more rips than the screen door. The table top was bare. Atop a small stove sat a pair of pots. Next to the stove was a counter stacked with dirty dishes. Same with the sink. Maybe Mama Ruiz didn't live here any more.

I saw a doorway leading into the next room, probably the living room. But I couldn't see what that room held. The screen door squeaked when I pulled on its handle. I should have figured, but my heart leapt anyway at the sound. I found a small rock nearby and propped the screen door open. Then, I turned off the flashlight and tucked it into my belt. Pressing my back against the wall, I reached with my right hand to try the door knob, while readying the S&W with my left.

The knob turned. And turned some more. I gave a slight push and… voila! The door had not been locked. It opened an inch or so without a sound. Okay, I thought. Again no evidence of a dog crouching in wait; no gunshots shattered the window or splintered the door. But something hit me. A familiar smell.

It wasn't the smell of grease or burnt frijoles or stale beer or moldy cheese. Nor was it roses, carnations, or lilies, although it was the smell of something that helps florists flourish. It was the strong scent of what funerals are all about, what fills a casket piled high with flowers. Death was in the air and it nearly made me puke.

I pulled the door shut, took several deep breaths of air that was as fresh as it ever gets in South Tucson, and considered my options. How big a debt did I owe to Jack Stonecipher? If I didn't enter the house, would the cops tell me anything if I called them and then hung around? I didn't really want to explain my presence to them.

I finally decided I owed it to Jack to find out for myself who or what was putrefying. But that conclusion didn't come to me immediately or obviously.

I pushed the door open fully and stood back, letting the tsunami of stench roll into the backyard. Whatever shuffled-off mortal coils were rotting away had been doing so for a while or two. At least only stench emerged from the house. No ghosts, bats, vampires, or other hellish imps came wafting out.

Courage doesn't come in little packets, like aspirin tablets. If it did, I'd carry several in my pants pocket. Booze helps, but I didn't think I wanted to find a liquor store and tank up, then return to face whatever horror was waiting inside. With my luck, I'd get pulled over for a DUI a block before I got back. Even allowing that Adelle could drive, I knew it was a bad idea.

What's the Brit motto? Keep calm and carry on? I decided I'd give that maxim a try. So, covering my face with a pocket kerchief, I stalked in. Why I thought a kerchief mask would help, I can't fathom. I'd be breathing the same damned air, with or without the nose covering. Did I suppose stink-molecules are the size of salmon roe?

No bodies on the kitchen floor or in the living room. The bathroom was unsightly, but not from gory flesh. That left the bedrooms. Two of them, separated by a tiny hallway. I mentally flipped a coin and entered the front bedroom first. And there she was, sprawled on a twin bed with, I was pretty certain, a pair of bullet holes in her forehead.

In that neighborhood the sound of two gunshots would not have been any more remarkable than the sound of yard dogs barking. If any neighbors or passersby had heard gunfire, they would more than likely have attributed it to a loud TV, where the rat-a-tat music of weaponry garners more accumulated air time than commercials for beer, fast food, and car insurance combined. Real guns discharging would have merely been subliminal background noise, like drumbeats at a Clapton concert.

The dead woman was too young to be the mother of a Latino stud, so I figured the bloody corpse was Susan Jennings. When

I saw the flies and maggots, I wondered how flies had gotten in, The screen door was ripped, but the back door itself was closed. I figured the flies had been in the house already. That's why they're called house flies. Duh.

Such thoughts were meant to distract me from thinking about what I was seeing. I thought of Gwen Dupree. When telling me her story of finding Bobby Shane, she didn't mention puking or being dizzy or even feeling slightly ill. But she had been determined to get a leash back on Sigmund. Diversion behavior. That's the mode she went into. Me, too. Keep yourself busy and think about anything but the ghastly reality in front of you. Then I remembered I still had another bedroom to examine.

Thankfully, no bodies there. So I forced myself to return to the front bedroom. The sooner I ID'd the body and searched for anything relevant, the sooner I could get the hell out. I found the dead woman's purse. The photo on her Nevada driver's license confirmed she was Sue Jennings. Sadly, the crummy DL photo was an improvement on the face Miss Embezzler was going to take to her grave.

Nothing else of consequence in her purse. No cruise line tickets. Maybe Eduardo had pilfered them. Or one of them. If his name was on one of the tickets I suppose that one counted as what was rightfully his. The rest of the contents consisted of the usual crap. I guess. I've never been one to rummage through women's handbags unsolicited. Well, no. Not never. But I don't make a habit of it. By rumor, most women's purses are miniature versions of Fibber McGee's closet.

The money. Wow! I needed to get my priorities in order. Jack had told me Sue had foolishly converted her winnings – what else would you call it when you walk out the door carrying the house's money? – to cash. And Jack was certain she had not taken out insurance on the cash. So where was it?

I didn't look very hard. Even the most *macho*, mean-spirited Latino male doesn't kill his girlfriend because she gave him a less than stellar blowjob. Ergo: He killed her for her cash and was lolling on the beach in Playa los Corchos by now, telling mama to fetch him another cold bottle of Pacifico. The room was even too small to have a closet. I opened both doors to an armoire made of cheap plywood. Empty. I looked under the bed but didn't count the dust bunnies breeding there. Nothing else. A cross hung on one wall; a stylized painting of Hay-soos on another. I quickly checked behind the painting, but only because that's what any good TV detective would have done. No two-hundred-thousand-dollar bill featuring an engraving of Warren Buffet was taped to the back of the frame.

I suppose a more thorough searcher would have lifted the dead lady's skirt to see what might have been taped to one of her thighs. Not me. Even the dead are entitled to some respect. So, having left my fingerprints and DNA all over the house with nothing to show for my effort but a dead woman I could now be easily connected to, I skedaddled.

Outside, no cops, thugs, or ghosts from Christmas past were waiting to harass me. I walked back to my car as if I were merely out for a casual evening stroll, although anyone with an IQ above room temperature knew that was not a neighborhood where an Anglo would meander alone after dark for the purpose of improving his health.

At my car I had to shine my flashlight on my face before Adelle would unlock the doors. She had clearly been experiencing her own nightmares. Nothing or no one real had appeared to scare her, just the usual ghoulies and ghosties and things that go bump in the night. Music by the Grateful Dead apparently hadn't helped either.

"I didn't see any lights come on, Wiley."

"Heavy curtains."

"Was the person there you are looking for?"

"Yes. She's there."

"Was she of any help?"

"Some."

"Is everything okay?" Adelle's becoming suspicious stemmed from the fact I am not usually given to such clipped answers, à la Gary Cooper.

"I can now call Jack and tell him I fulfilled his request."

"Good. Let's get out of here."

Amen to that.

Pay phones have gone the way of buggy whips, eight-track tapes, and typewriters. Everybody and his three-year-old daughter owns a cell phone these days. Except for… barrio Hispanics. They shove quarters into pay phones and wire their dollars to Grandma Rosa in Zacatecas via Western Union.

Adelle thought I was calling Jack, but I wanted to phone the police instead. I told my sister I had stupidly forgotten to charge my cell, which was why I was looking for a pay phone. Thankfully, she didn't ask why I couldn't wait until we returned to Arroyo Arenoso before I made my call to Jack.

My cell phone was actually fully charged, but I had put it on silence. Otherwise, if it rang Adelle would have caught me in a lie. I knew cops could trace my cell phone and I obviously didn't want to have to explain to authorities what I had been doing entering Mrs. Ruiz's not-so-homey little house unbidden.

I found a pay phone on the outside wall of a *carniceria* a few blocks away from the house where I had left Sue Jennings' body. The phone was being used by a *macho*-looking dude with two arms full of tats bulging from a muscle shirt. He perched astride a Harley and gave a cauliflower ear to whoever was on the receiving end of his conversation. I waited. He talked. On and on and on, flapping his free arm in wild gestures. Twenty minutes later he was still gabbing. I had seen guitar strings snap from less stress than he was putting on his vocal chords.

Finally, Adelle whispered that she had to pee. Somehow that thought triggered her memory of seeing a pay phone just outside the front door at Micha's. So I drove back there and called the police while Adelle went inside and used the lady's restroom.

I waited until I heard sirens in the near distance. Then I couldn't drive away fast enough to suit either one of us, until fifteen minutes later, when we both saw the spotlights in the distance off to the right as we neared the freeway exit leading to Mission San Xavier Del Bac, also known as The White Dove of the Desert. The small church glowed an eerie blue white color in the glare of the spotlights. But seeing the mission, I eased off the gas pedal a tad, assured at last that God was still in His Heaven and all was right with the world. Adelle said nothing, but breathed an audible sigh of relief. More likely because she hates how fast I drive, rather than because she had been overcome with some kind of eye-opening religious epiphany.

9

I waited until Adelle was in the shower before I called Jack on my cell. He answered on the seventh ring.

"I found your lady embezzler."

"Was her boyfriend with her?"

"Nope."

"Does she have the money?"

"Nope."

"Could you get her to talk?"

"Nope."

"Can I get you to talk?"

"Yes. I found her with two bullet holes in her forehead. They'd been there a while. I looked for the money, but if I were her boyfriend, do you think I'd shoot her and then take off, leaving the cash behind to pay for her funeral?"

"You might, but I doubt if Eduardo Ruiz would."

"Thanks. I called the cops from a pay phone, doing my best imitation of you."

"Thanks back atcha. No hints of where Ruiz might have gone?"

"No, but how many guesses do you want?"

"He has family in Cuernavaca. What about his mother?"

"What about her?"

"Oh hell, of course she would have gone with him."

"Somebody left behind a lot of dirty dishes. But no 'for sale' sign in the front yard. What about my stuff?"

"I'm working on finding your guy. FYI: The used-car dealers' convention took place five weeks ago. So that's a no-go. You might ask the missus why she lied to you. Or did you give me the wrong dates? It won't be the first instance where you operated on Egyptian calendar time."

"That's the Hittite system, Jack, and their first month was the Month of the Fruits."

"I'm not touching that one, Wiles."

I said, "You know, perhaps it wasn't the lady who lied. Mayhap hubby was on a clandestine assignment to check out Area 51 for the western branch of the Roswell Clan."

"If so, you need to ask the feds for help. However, if he came to Sin City for nefarious purposes better left unexplained to his spouse, I'll find him. Even if he is registered under Demetri Dzhindischakvilli."

"I appreciate it."

"I'll call you when I know something. And thanks again for finding the corpse. She won't get you in any trouble, will she?"

"Left my DNA scattered like pearls from a broken necklace, but no prints. I don't think my DNA is on file anywhere. Just my swirls and whorls."

I hung up wondering about Gwen's Dupree's veracity. I decided not to mention Jack's finding to her. There could be an innocent explanation for her telling me Boyd's declared purpose for not being home. I doubted it, but my cynicism has gotten me into deep shit before. Best let her explanation lie dormant and see how well it fit in or deviated from whatever other information lurked in the near future for me to pick up and examine.

Philosophers, prosecutors, and crime investigators are aware there are two theories of Truth. One is known as the Correspondence Theory. Tales people tell, yarns they spin, explanations they give either do or don't correspond to The Facts. But sometimes facts are difficult to collect.

So the second theory, known as the Coherence Theory of Truth does not rely on facts. Instead, the truth of any given proposition depends on whether or not other propositions fit with it neatly, like pieces of a jigsaw puzzle. Criminal cases based on circumstantial evidence are an example of a prosecutor's relying on the Coherence Theory. If all the pieces don't fall into place, chances are the case is weak.

So I intended to wait for other pieces to fall into place neatly before passing judgment on either of the Duprees. That called for patience on my part. As Adelle will tell you, patience is not a formidable part of my character. So I was going to have to bite my tongue, to use a painful image.

I hoped Adelle was going to sleep better than I was. No reason she shouldn't, except she had dipped a lot of tortilla chips into Micha's salsa bowls. So had I, but that was not going to be the reason for my insomnia. Contemporary Mexican art is rife with images of violence and gore. Human violence; human gore. Sue Jennings' corpse was a case of life imitating art. Now the nightmare I witnessed on the bed would convert to a nightmare in my head. I doubted that even a couple fingers' worth of my sister's Wild Turkey and a handful of IB's would spare me from a tortured several hours.

10

Monday

I followed Adelle to her high school and she introduced me first to Jane Wheeler, Arroyo Arsenoso High's choral instructor. She was young and attractive and made me wish my own high school's singing teacher had looked so delicious. Maybe I would have learned to carry a tune. In Las Vegas guys who will never hold a candle to Sinatra or Tony Bennett still haul in bigger bucks than gumshoes. And don't have to press their own pants.

"So you're Adelle's little brother. I'm pleased to meet you at last," Miss Wheeler said and I shook her hand. I noted the absence of a wedding ring on the hand I didn't shake. "I've been wanting to meet you."

Lucky me. I normally don't fall in lust so quickly, but with Jane Wheeler I allowed myself to make a momentous exception. Not that I held out hope that granting her immunity from that scruple would get me much of anything. But you never know. Well, no. Often you do know. And the certainty provides scant comfort.

"You know about Bobby Shane Hollsworth, don't you?" I began.

She lowered her head and bit her lipsticked lip. "I can hardly believe it. So much talent. So much vitality. And packed into such a decent person. Why do the good die young, Mr. Poynter?"

"Same reason the bad do. Something or somebody gets in the way."

"Adelle told me you hope to find that somebody."

"Help look at least."

"We're all so grateful. Thank you." She reached out and touched my arm.

I felt goose bumps and hoped I wasn't blushing. "What can you tell me about Bobby?"

"Oh, I can tell you so much. But I assume you want me to stick to what might be relevant to his murder."

I nodded and tried to smile my yes-please smile and not my god-you're-gorgeous smile.

We were in her classroom and she gestured for me to take a chair. It was one of those half-desks, the kind schools buy by the hundreds for right-handed pupils. Being left-handed, I emerged from primary school resentful that all four of the desks for left-handers were always broken and stuffed atop one another in a janitor's closet, seemingly placed there waiting for Jesus to heal them as an oh-by-the-way miracle during The Second Coming, before He paid off the national debt and after He cured cancer. The immediate result was that I had to angle my writing paper in the same direction right-handed kids turned theirs. Then I had to hook my left wrist and forearm like a reverse question mark to minimize smudging soft pencil lead atop my freshly scrawled script. My success at neatness in penmanship was nil. Doomed. And, by the end of each school day, the outer edge of my lower left palm was black as Spongy Simmons' face.

Terrell "Spongy" Simmons, as an aside, is a Las Vegas welterweight boxer and a friend of mine. He does imitations of black celebrities very well and occasionally gets hired to do a weekday stand-up routine in some of the city's lesser lounges. Otherwise, he is a man of little note. He's a shitty boxer, even though, as his nickname strongly suggests, he's capable of absorbing a lot of punches. If only he knew how to throw them as well as he delivers one-liners.

Miss Wheeler reverse-straddled the desk in front of me, making her below-the-knee skirt ride up. But I was good and didn't try to determine the color or contour of her panties.

"Bobby had so much musical talent. A strong voice with a wide range. I'm sorry he wasted so much of it on infantile lyrics. I was hoping he would develop a wider appreciation. As far as his instrumental talent, I thought he had a remarkable scope. Mr. Sechrest will confirm that, I'm sure. He's our band director."

I told her I intended to interview him next.

"If Bobby had any enemies, I was not aware of them. He was immensely popular – among both sexes. I think he knew he was a budding rock star, and the local scene was going to serve only as a warm-up stage for him."

"What did his fellow band members think of him?" I said.

"You'd do better to ask them," she said. But, from the look on her face, I sensed there were issues I needed to discover. I already knew Bobby was a homophobe.

"Bobby's musical appreciation showed a maturity many young men his age lack."

"How is that?"

"He had a sincere reverence for gifted musicians from prior generations. Not many young men his age show the proper respect for their musical elders. Most of his contemporaries, including the other three members of his garage band, deem veneration of the old gods sissified. So many of these budding talents are not even aware to whom they owe their techniques and the state of their instrumentation. That is so sad."

I could have told this young woman that teenagers who behave as though they were born yesterday because they somehow believe the world began yesterday are not limited to nascent musicians. On one of my previous visits, a year or so earlier, Adelle had told me, with an air of incredulity, that a sizeable majority of students in her civics classes thought the Vietnam War, one of the defining events of our parents' generation, had been fought between Sparta and Athens and had occurred during some vague period between when dinosaurs flourished and when Christopher Columbus set sail in search of Disney World. Perhaps my sister had spared Miss Wheeler that observation, not wanting to rattle the Pollyanna perspective of one so young and still free of cynicism. More than once Adelle has reminded me, quoting Ambrose Bierce, that cynicism consists of seeing the world as it is and not as it ought to be. Let Jane Wheeler acquire such an outlook at her own pace, if she was going to.

The choral director continued. "Did you know Bobby's nickname for himself was Rhubarb Red Junior? One of his heroes was Les Paul and one of that man's early stage names was Rhubarb Red."

"It sounds like a character Red Skelton would have invented," I said.

"Les Paul was –."

"I was only joking. I know who Les Paul is and was. Half of the Leo and Les show. If I'm not mistaken, there is hardly a rock guitarist in the last thousand years who hasn't owned and played either a Leo Fender or a Gibson Les Paul instrument."

"Les Paul was also one of the ten best guitarists ever, too," Ms. Wheeler said.

"I've heard he's on most knowledgeable people's list."

"Yes, and Bobby Shane worshiped the man. He was familiar with Les Paul's biography as well as any music historian. And he owned one of Gibson's classic Les Paul models. Bobby's father paid a fortune for it to give to his son on Bobby's thirteenth's birthday."

"So who would want to kill this prodigy, Miss Wheeler?"

"I can't conceive that Bobby had any enemies. Could he have been murdered by mistake?" she said.

I hadn't considered that. And refused to consider it now. Bobby was pretty distinctive looking. Even those who might think *gringos* all look alike would have a difficult time confusing Bobby Hollsworth with anyone else, I thought. Accidental death? Maybe, if he had died of a gunshot wound. But knives rarely stab someone inadvertently. I've never heard the Andrew Sisters or anyone else sing a version of the once-popular tune that had the repetitive line, *"I didn't know the gun was loaded and I'm sooooo sorry, my friend,"* substitute 'knife' for 'gun' – even as a parody.

Adelle and I found Sebastian Sechrest in the band room using one finger to plink out Gershwin's "I Got Rhythm" on an aging Steinway. Trying her best not to appear to be the bald-faced liar she surely felt herself to be, my sister gamely told the band director that she had asked me to look into the murder of Bobby Holls-worth by way of helping out Chief Morton.

He shook my hand. "I'll be glad to help any way I can. What a sickening end to such an outstanding young man."

Sechrest was a pale, mousy-looking man. Wire-framed glasses. Thin mustache, sandy hair that was receding quickly. Slouch-shoul-dered. He looked like he'd been born wearing the crooked bow tie that sprouted from his collar and hung like a wind-snapped iris. I guessed forty-ish. Raspy voice, though I didn't detect the stale-tobacco cloud that engulfs nearly all smokers. Maybe his mother had jammed a broom handle down his throat when he was a kid.

Adelle took her leave quietly, slinking away like a cat burglar. Before we left her house she *just knew* her fibbing to her colleague about her role in my probe would come back to haunt her. I assured her ghosts had better things to do than pick on ladies with virtu-ous characters and good intentions.

"You know what they say the road to hell is paved with, Brother," was her comeback.

"Fool's gold?" I said, trying to make her smile.

"Good intentions. That's what."

"All that means is that your intentions will burn in hell, not the rest of you.'

"I hope you're right."

I sat on a folding chair in Mr. Sechrest's office and he eased him-self into a chair behind his desk. "Bobby Shane and I had our differences, but I respected that boy a lot. I cannot imagine who would want to stick a knife in his back," he began.

"What differences did you have with him?" I said.

"Musical differences."

"Of what sort?"

"I pleaded with him to take up an additional instrument. He refused."

"Why the plea?"

He laughed a low laugh. "I have no quarrel with garage bands, but that's all Prickly Pear Jam would ever be. Such bands have their place, but they're a nickel a trainload. I tried to get Bobby to see that, talented as he was, he was not the next Jimi Hendrix; that his group was never going to be front and center at the next Altamont or Woodstock. They likely would never even become an opening band for some more famous group. At best they could become a tribute band, touring backwater towns and playing in bars smelling of stale beer and blue-collar sweat."

"Stuck in Lodi," I said.

"Exactly."

"What did you suggest?'

"The clarinet. It's a versatile instrument. Marching band, symphony orchestra, jazz quartet. I assured Bobby he was talented enough to become a good musician. Good enough that I thought I could get him a musical scholarship to one or more of the big schools. U of A for sure. But maybe better, despite his grades."

"No interest?"

"None. Not even when I reminded him Mozart, Strauss, Sousa – no one – scored a symphony, a waltz, or a march for the electric guitar. I told him no school was going to fund his efforts to play 'She Shook Me All Night Long'."

"Music aside, how well did you know him?" I said.

"Scarcely at all. We always talked music."

"Always here?"

Sechrest's eyes narrowed. "We went for coffee a couple of times. Arroyo Arenoso has no Starbucks, but Jesse's Café brews a decent cup of coffee."

"Bobby was into caffeine?'

He nodded. "Pepsi and Red Bull."

"Ever invite him over to your house?"

Sechrest bristled, as I thought he might.

"Sorry. I've got to ask. Nothing personal."

He made clear he thought my question had been intensely personal. "I wouldn't have a job right now if that had happened."

Leaving open the possibility that the thought had crossed his mind, but that he had deemed the risk of inviting Bobby to have been too steep. "Did Bobby have a girlfriend?" I knew the answer. The point of my asking was to see if I could spot a hint of jealousy. Maybe even more than a hint.

"Bobby has been dating Kristy Serling, another one of our seniors," he said. Indeed! His answer didn't overtly drip jealousy but it was there, semi-frozen like sap on a tree when spring weather turns cold again after a warm spell. But how libidinous was the jealousy I sensed? I wasn't sure.

Sechrest didn't wear a wedding ring. I had already pumped Adelle for background information early that morning. She didn't know a whole lot. All part of her determination to remain clueless on as many topics as possible. So whether the man had ever been married or had ever even shown any interest in seeking female companionship – I deliberately substituted *skirt-chasing* when I asked Adelle about it – my sister did not know. She had no idea if the man was asexual, bisexual, or homosexual.

"I just assumed he is heterosexual," she had said, giving me a born-yesterday look when she said it over breakfast. "Isn't that reasonable?"

"Reason has nothing to do with one's sexual predilections, Dell."

"It's genetic, I think. Isn't that right?" she had said.

"Could be. Or maybe it's God's Will or maybe it's whatever is in the baby formula or in the Cherrios or –."

"Oh, stop it, Wiley. You're putting me on now. I know you are."

"Did you know that Cheerios used to be loaded with tri-sodium phosphate, Dell? The same stuff that comes in cleaning products? Like Boraxo."

"I didn't know that."

"Yep. General Mills has now substituted potassium for sodium but still, maybe that kind of shit is what determines folks' sexual orientation. What do you think?"

"I think you need to get your mind off sex."

"So you don't think good old Sebastian is a queer and that Bobby was his boy toy?"

She gave that more thought than I anticipated she would. She mulled it over the entire time she was donning her sweater and adjusting her hat. Finally, she passed judgment. "No. I definitely don't think Mr. Sechrest is one of those faggot people."

"Faggot people? Is that like pod people?"

"I have no idea what you are talking about now. Pod people? What are they?" Adelle said.

"Aliens who sap and impurify our precious bodily fluids. Then they steal our souls and replicate our bodies."

"What are you babbling about?"

"Come on, Dell. Surely *Dr. Strangelove Thwarts the Invasion of the Body-Snatchers* is mandatory viewing by every freshman at Arroyo Arenoso High. It's a drive-in classic. Joe Bob Briggs himself says so."

"Let's get out of here. I think you poured an ounce too much of Wild Turkey into your morning coffee. That's what I think."

Not so. I had poured precisely the right measure.

After Sebastian Sechrest decided I was fishing for an admission from him that he was gay and that he had either seduced or attempted to seduce Bobby Shane Hollsworth, the man ceased being forthcoming. In fact, he finally stood and announced that our interview was over, that he had pressing school duties to attend to.

'Tis a seriously flawed feature of the human condition that even dweeby gnomes like Sebastian Sechrest have longings for sex. Where Sebastian found gratification – beyond his right hand – was something I didn't care to speculate on. We know where priests go, whom they seek out, when they aren't buggering each other. I only hoped that horny, homely high school band directors did not pursue similarly accessible prey.

11

The other people at the top of my list to interview were all students at Arroyo Arenoso High: the girlfriend and the other band members. But I knew I didn't dare interrupt their school day. I had no doubt every student on campus would know Bobby was dead well ahead of the school's official announcement to them all. Although school district headquarters had already brought in what are known as grief counselors, I was certain the best consoling – as opposed to counseling – these kids were going to receive would come from each other. There's nothing wrong with, and much that is therapeutic about, a collective cry session. The students were officially too young to hold a good, old-fashioned wake, where everyone gets roaring drunk before breaking down and sobbing. I was, however, willing to bet a bottle of Kentucky's finest that some of Bobby's classmates would gather later in the evening to commemorate Bobby's passing with a similar rite – one that included beverages to aide in loosening both tongues and tears.

A man underneath a white Cattleman Stetson was standing by my Jeep when I emerged from the school. His blue uniform and the black-and-white car with blueberry flashers atop it parked nearby told me this might be Chief Morton or one of his minions.

"You must be Wiley Poynter," he said when I approached.

"Last time I looked in the mirror, I still was. And you must still be Chief Morton." I could see his name tag.

"Duly appointed."

We shook hands.

I don't keep a photo in my imagination file of what a generic small-town police chief looks like, but if I did, it wouldn't resemble Morton. The chief had let middle-age overwhelm him. Spider-veined cheeks, a paunch that hung over his belt, and a thin white mustache. He looked like the kind of guy a stand-up comedian picks on in his audience to get a cheap laugh.

"What can I do you out of, Chief?"

"Other way around, son. I'm here to remind you that you are not a homicide detective in my department. So you need to butt out of my case, stop pretending you are one of my deputies."

"I'm merely engaged in a bit of citizen's curiosity, Chief Morton."

"Some folks think what you're doing constitutes harassment," he said.

"Do some of these folks have names?"

"Try Sebastian Sechrest."

"That was quick."

"I just happened to be in the neighborhood."

I smiled. "Mr. Sechrest fully consented to allowing me to interview him. Invited me into his office for a chat, in fact."

"He tells a different story."

"Check with my sister. She introduced me to Sechrest and was there when he agreed to let me ask him a few questions."

"I think Sebastian's objections started when you got too personal, son."

"He didn't mention wanting to screen my questions ahead of time. And, besides, he may have jumped to some hasty conclusions about what I was really asking him."

"He tells me you called him a faggot. That's harassment."

"No. I gently put it to him as an inquiry."

"If you'd ask me that question, gently or harshly, I'd put you on your back, son."

"And the local judge would grant your plea of self-defense, right?"

"Damned right, she would. Now lay off. Your license is no good in this town. Or even this state. It's no better than a piece of toilet paper. And if you keep on keeping on, son, I'll rip it out of your wallet and wipe your ass with it."

"But you wouldn't harass me, would you?" I said, laughing.

"Of course, not. That's against the law, son."

"And even you are not above the majesty of the law, are you?"

"Not even on Monday mornings.'

"What about three a.m. on Saturdays?"

"Don't push me, Poynter. I'm serious. My department can handle this case. None of us were born yesterday."

"When was the last time you had a murder on your hands, Chief? Arroyo Arenoso isn't Phoenix. Or even Tucson. And definitely not Las Vegas."

"I worked a few when I was a shift commander in Tucson. I know what I'm doing."

"I'd like to think we are both on the same side, Chief Morton."

"You think I might cover something up, son?"

I sighed. "Must be something in your town's Kool Aid, Chief. A jump-to-conclusions parasite of some ilk. Better have the EPA check out Arroyo Arenoso's water-quality level."

"Just be warned. I don't want to trip over your gumshoes again. And, if your sister likes her job, she'll tell you the same thing and help you pack your bags for Las Vegas."

"You hit the wrong button there, Chief. I'm making due note that you've threatened Adelle. She teaches civics, in case you aren't aware of that. And before long you might just find her in your face, giving you a much needed lesson in history and government."

He clearly did not know what to think of that. He must have realized his last remark tiptoed along the boundary of impropriety, because he backed off.

"Just keep your butt off school grounds. We don't like strangers hanging around our campuses, much less stepping onto them. I'll bust you next time you cross over that line. Your sister's permission isn't good enough. Understand?"

"Fully."

"Good. And don't go trying to contact any of the high school staff at their homes. I mean it. Butt out of this case."

I looked at my watch. "I think you missed your last pop of Valium, Chief. By my watch, it's past time for you to take another happy pill. Why don't you go wash it down with some coffee and a donut."

He took off his Stetson and shook it at me. "You're heading for trouble, son, if you continue in that vein."

"Trouble pays my rent, Chief."

"I hope it also pays your hospital bills."

He had me there. My health insurance consisted of keeping my reflexes sharp enough to dodge bullets and sidestep sucker punches.

12

Tubac is an artsy-fartsy Potemkin village south of Arroyo Arenoso constructed for the sole purpose of luring in snowbirds then mugging them. Gwen Dupree owned a yard-art gallery, Arte de Casa-Delantara, near the main entrance to the maze of shops built to look like pueblos. Some of the art work filling the small courtyard glassy-eyed punters had to walk through to reach the cool interior of her shop struck me as rather adorable. However, when I stopped to examine the price of contemporary yard fashion, the charm receded like a dove taking wing at the sight of a coyote creeping toward it. All the furniture in my living room didn't cost as much as the belt-high mariachi player strumming a guitar, the whole of the works – right down to his sandaled feet and spindly toes – made from welded rebar. It beat the hell out of having a flock of pink plastic flamingos feeding in your front yard and drawing head shakes from the neighbors. But I imagined that a real mariachi band, maintained in the backyard guest house, would cost less than the cute little guys playing silently in the courtyard.

The buxom blonde swishing an ostrich-feather duster at the kitsch greeted me as though I were her favorite uncle. That form of warmth was a bonus. Her low-cut blouse, clearly meant to advertise her premium pair of non-verbal charms, had already raised my temperature faster than any of the feeble efforts at bio feedback I had ever tried.

"I'm looking for Gwen Dupree." I had decided that, rather than waste the rest of the morning and early afternoon waiting for school to let out, I would try popping a few more questions at the jogger who drank cheap bourbon.

"I'm terribly sorry, but she's gone for the day. She was only here for a few moments this morning," Blondie told me.

"That's too bad. Any idea where I can find her?"

The woman sized me up quickly – and thoroughly. I imagined she was used to sizing up men methodically, while the men she judged were fixated by her trophy rack. I apparently passed muster. "She went to see her doctor in Tucson. Are you aware that she is the poor soul who stumbled onto that young man's body in Arroyo Arenoso Saturday morning?"

"Yes, I know. That's what I want to see her about."

"You're a policeman?"

"A private detective."

"Ooooooo."

I wasn't quite sure what to make of that response. I didn't think I had flexed my biceps. Nor did I judge her clever enough to formulate a double-entendre, going from private detective to private dick and stare at my crotch, all in the time it took her to purse her lips and coo. But maybe I was being hasty in my estimate. Einstein flunked math as a kid, I've been told.

"Her doctor?" I managed.

A vigorous nod from Blondie set her chest in motion. I stared off into the middle distance, which put me in visual contact with a shelf full of ceramic hula girls. "She said something about getting a prescription for sedatives."

That figured. I could have used one myself at that moment. Just then I heard customers come in behind me. I stepped aside so Gwen Dupree's handsome kitsch-peddling assistant could give the newcomers her welcome smile.

The shoppers consisted of a middle-aged couple and a pair of toady-looking pre-teen brats, a freckled girl with red-white-and-blue plastic braces on her teeth and a lad wearing coke-bottle glasses. The boy reminded me a lot of Jerry Lewis' *Nutty Professor* role. A nerdy, stupid look.

When the wife saw Blondie, both her look and her demeanor changed faster than a speed-trap red light. She caught her husband in full ogle, poked him sharply in the ribs, and motioned toward the door through which they has just entered. It was now an exit. She made brushing motions at the kids and, as she took each of her offspring by an arm, she gave her husband a laser-look that would cut diamonds. The hapless schlemiel sighed, took a last look at the delights he would never know, hung his head, and followed her out.

Blondie looked at me. "Gee, what did I do?"

I reflected on the last lines from Yeats' "For Anne Gregory":

> *'I heard an old religious man*
> *But yesternight declare*
> *That he had found a text to prove*

That only God, my dear,
Could love you for yourself alone
And not your yellow hair.'

"You didn't do anything," I assured her. "Some people simply do not appreciate exquisite art when they see it. That's all."

She smiled. "You've got to admit there are some pretty lovely items in here."

Not all of them for sale. Or so I supposed. I left without pursuing that issue.

I headed north to Sahuarita to check out Boyd Dupree's used car lot. I figured I was mostly wasting my time, energy, and gas money, but I still had time to kill. What could Gwen Dupree's husband contribute? He was out of town, at least according to Boyd's wife, although, unless he was also a time traveler, he couldn't have been at the Las Vegas convention she placed him at.

Why had she told me that? I felt certain it wasn't a memory slip. She hadn't hesitated when she told me where he was. But perhaps she was speaking from certitude, rather than certainty. Maybe he was in San Diego, Chicago, or Timbuktu and had told her he was going to be a Sin City conventioneer. Maybe he's one of those "I've got a gal in every port" philanderers. But if so, it's unlikely he had gone to the real used-car-dealers' convention. His wife was not a dumb woman. He might as well have told her was going to his mother's funeral – twice, two months apart.

I put a call into Jack Stonecipher, got his *2001: A Space Odyssey* Hal-voiced answering machine, and left a message for him to see if he could check the roster of convention attendees. If Boyd had been there, I doubt if he would have used a pseudonym. My guess was he hadn't been anywhere near Las Vegas while his fellow used-car dealers partied. But that was just a guess, based on a hunch, which was based on my summary judgment of men who peddle pre-owned vehicles to pay their country club dues. My hunches have occasionally been known to take on the color and odor of baby shit.

Sahuarita is mostly a new town, one with new cracker-box houses sitting no more than arms' lengths apart, but with upper middle class pretensions. Otherwise, why would a chain convenience store put up an outdoor coin-operated dog wash between its car wash and its gas pumps?

Boyd's Pre-Owned Motors resided between a Super Wal-Mart and a national-brand hardware store. Make that *mostly upper middle class pretensions.* Clearly not everyone who had decamped Tucson for the quieter environs of Sahuarita was a doctor, lawyer, or Indian chief. And, given that the price of a gallon of gas now rivaled minimum wage, Wal-Mart employees were not going to be commuters. Low-end employees, who often have to choose between toilet paper for the bathroom and milk for the baby in those last few days before another paycheck, are far more sensitive about the price of a gallon of gas than they are about the price of a six-pack.

The salesman who approached me as I stood admiring a 1998 Mustang convertible the color of sun-dried tomatoes was as smarmy as a silent movie villain.

"You certainly have a discerning eye," he said as he held out his hand. He meant my judgment of fine auto flesh, I'm sure, but

I took him to mean my shrewd assessment of slimy car hustlers. Gentlemanly scholar that I am, I didn't say so. Miss Manners frowns on anything short of hypocrisy in such situations.

"Gene Elliott," he said, waiting for me to pump his paw.

"Wiley Poynter."

"My pleasure, Wiley. This baby is the finest machine in stock at the moment. Very low mileage; single owner, a librarian at Flowing Wells High School in Tucson. She never missed an oil change, kept it tuned and polished as if it was the only car she'd ever own. Real pride of ownership."

I waited to see if he was going to tell me she parked it in her second bedroom so she could hear it if it sneezed in the middle of the night.

"So then why did she turn it into a homeless orphan?" I said.

Without missing a beat, he said, "Her daddy bought her a brand new Beemer for her fortieth birthday."

This guy was smooth as crème brûlée. But he'd over-baked the sugar crust. I couldn't fathom a librarian driving hell-bent down the freeway in a topless Mustang. Or showing up for work in the Ultimate Driving Machine. Maybe I had a faulty imagination, but then a sharpie like him should have caught that flaw in my character right off and have fed me a less flossy tale of pre-ownership.

I had read recently that as much as four percent of the overall American population could be classified as sociopaths. That is, they lie, cheat, steal, and even murder without qualm or pang of conscience. Of those four percent, one quarter of them – one percent of the population – is where they belong: in prison. But what about the other three percent? The study determined that a vast number of those folks can be found in sales and marketing. That study gave me a new perspective on Gene Elliott.

"I'm looking for Boyd Dupree. Is he around?" I said.

"A friend of his?"

"No. A young man was murdered in his neighborhood Friday night and I'm simply questioning residents of the Country Club to see what they might have seen or heard Friday night."

"Ah! A police detective." His 'Ah!' may have suggested a thrill of discovery, but his shoulders sank like a soufflé. His body language said it all: No commission here.

I was out of Rollie Morton's jurisdiction, so I didn't offer to amend his conclusion.

With a tone of indifference he said, "I haven't seen boss man around since mid-day Friday. He was purportedly off to Las Vegas."

"Purportedly."

He gave a half-shrug. "Business of some sort. He goes there a lot."

"Convention maybe?"

"Naw. That was several weeks ago."

"What then?"

"You're asking the wrong guy. I just work here. Didn't you talk to his wife?"

"Not yet," I lied. "She wasn't at her gallery when I stopped by."

"Check with Jean Dexter inside." He thumbed toward the sales office. "Jean keeps his calendar. She's his secretary. Knows everything."

"Everything. That'll be handy."

"Don't tell her I said that. I'm on thin ice already. One bad word from her and I'm gone."

It's a rare office that runs smoothly, if at all, on those days when the chief administrative assistant phones in well and takes a soap opera holiday. I found Jean Dexter sorting out the day's mail when I tapped on her open office door.

"Excuse me, I'm looking for Boyd Dupree."

"And you are?"

"Name's Wiley Poynter. I'm investigating the murder of a young man in Arroyo Arenoso Saturday. The murder took place at the country club where Boyd lives."

"I read the newspaper." A smug glare.

"I'm sure you do." I glared back with my best no-nonsense-detective façade. "Boyd?"

"Las Vegas. He left Friday, which means he wouldn't know anything."

"And I can find him where?"

"Las Vegas."

"Big city. Please narrow it down."

"I'm not his travel agent."

"But I bet you've spoken with him since Friday."

"How would you know?"

"Would you like me to subpoena your telephone records? Your power game doesn't amuse me."

"He didn't say where he was staying."

"But when he's in Las Vegas he usually stays where?"

"He doesn't play favorites."

"Everybody who goes to Las Vegas plays favorites. That's how the casinos pay their rent."

She lowered her eyes. Game conceded to Wiley. Poynter 1, Dexter 0. "Sometimes he stays at the Luxor, sometimes at the Golden Nugget."

"Thank you, Mrs. Dexter." I turned to leave.

From behind me came, "It's Miss Dexter."

Pissy losers always want to get in a final dig at the winners. Na-na-na. I smiled and headed for my car. Outside, Gene Elliott stood with two young Hispanic males next to the reddish-brown Mustang. He was talking rapidly, they were kicking the tires. I assumed his apocryphal high school librarian had morphed into a Latina hospital nurse who knew all about, and dutifully respected, good health – both in humans and in automobiles. Having just shoveled some bullshit of my own, I didn't begrudge him a few shovels full of his own.

I phoned Jack Stonecipher and left a message for him to check out the Luxor and the Nugget. When I checked my watch I realized I had to hurry to get to my meeting with Adelle and two of Bobby Shane Hollsworth's fellow band members.

13

Perry Crisp and Jason Altheiser had agreed to meet with me at Two Girls Pizzeria on Duval Mine Road in Green Valley, the sprawling retirement community between Sahuarita and Arroyo Arenoso. Adelle had agreed to be there as well. According to my sister, the other member of the band, Richie Maldonado, the drummer, had after-school errands to run for his invalid mother and would meet us later that night at a restaurant where his brother worked.

Perry Crisp, whom Adelle had warned me went by the nickname of "Apple", was the Prickly Pear Jam band's rhythm guitarist. Jason Altheiser, called "Alzheimer's" by his closest friends, played bass. When I joined them they were munching on a thick-crust pepperoni-and-sausage pizza and had tall sodas sitting in front of them. Adelle introduced me.

"You really a private eye?" Perry said.

I showed him my license.

"So who killed Bobby?" Jason said.

I laughed. "My first question to the two of you was going to be, 'Which one of you killed him?' Your question, Jason, must be to throw me off. So that suggests to me that you did it? But you don't need to confess just yet. If you remember, confessions on TV shows only occur when the program is about to run out of its allotted schedule time. Our show is just beginning."

Perry said, "I don't think Jason killed Bobby."

"Tell me why you don't think so," I said.

"He doesn't have the balls."

"You bastard. Don't you start in on that," Jason said, grabbing Perry by a shirt sleeve.

I reached across the booth to separate them.

Adelle said to me, "Wiley, stop goading them. Just ask them civilized questions, please."

I dropped my grip and sat back. "You're right, Sis." To them, "Sorry, guys."

They stopped glaring at each other and both gave me a sour look.

"I take it there is, has been, some tension between the two of you."

Perry said, "Every band has its disagreements."

I said, "So I hear. From the Beatles and the Stones on down. Tell me about yours."

Jason looked at Perry and said, "You go first. But don't you dare bring up any –."

"Don't tell me what to talk about, Jason. You're the one with secrets," Perry said.

"Everybody has secrets, guys. But if they are relevant to Bobby's murder, then they've got to come out," I said.

Adelle, bless her, chimed in. "Anything that might help find the person or persons who killed Bobby needs to be brought out."

Both young men stared down glumly at their half-eaten slices of pizza.

If my memory served me right, being an eighteen-year-old American male was a mixed blessing. They had so much to learn, yet they thought they knew it all. Bubbling over the rims of the intellect like molten lava was a bottomless fissure vent of raging hormones that triggered acne, a calorie-needy metabolism, and prurient thoughts by the gazillions.

"So what were the issues, guys? Ego, money, drugs, or girls? All four? Three out of four? Two?"

Both young men looked up at me, then at each other.

"I couldn't find a bypass around being a teenager either. Been there, done that. Fun and fuck-ups in about equal measure. You can speak in front of my sister. She watched me live through it – and died several times in the middle of it all. There isn't much shit she hasn't seen, heard, or had to put up with. I was a royal pain in her ass."

The guys looked at her. Adelle nodded, trying not to blush.

Jason spoke. "No drugs. Honest. We weren't into that. None of us."

I looked at Perry. "True," he said. "We're clean. And that included Bobby."

"That leaves ego, money, and women," I said.

Perry said, "Bobby was an asshole. Full of himself. He wouldn't listen. He might have an ear for music, but he was tone-deaf otherwise, if you know what I mean."

So much for not speaking ill of the dead, but Perry was heading in the right direction, beginning to open up about things I needed to know. Or thought I did.

Jason said, "Bobby was a tyrant. A dictator. He insisted he knew what was best for all of us as far as the direction the band ought to take. He wouldn't listen to any of us. He wasn't even open to suggestions."

"We were on the verge of losing it," Perry said.

"Losing it?" I said.

"Breaking up. Calling it quits. Seeing how Bobby liked playing solo."

Jason nodded in agreement.

I asked, "Did this come to blows?"

Jason shook his head. "Just lots of shouting and screaming. Lots of 'Fuck you' and 'Fuck you back' kind of raging."

"Nothing physical?" I said.

"Throwing stuff. Tantrums," Perry said.

"Not at each other. Just throwing pencils, ripping up sheet music. Mostly Bobby did that."

"So he was the violent one?"

"Not the only one," Jason said.

"But mostly," Perry added.

"Any threats exchanged?"

"None," Jason said a bit too quickly.

Perry bit his lip. In a lower voice he said, "Bobby threatened Jason."

Jason snapped, 'I warned you. Button it."

I gave Jason a hard stare. The kid simultaneously looked scared and angry. "All right, damn you, Perry. Go ahead. Tell them."

Calmly, quietly, Perry said, "No, Jason. You tell them. It's gonna come out anyway. They're gonna dig deep. Better it comes from you and comes out sooner than later."

A single tear formed in Jason's left eye. "Okay. Okay." Pause. He looked at Adelle. "I'm gay. And Bobby Shane threatened to tell the world if I continued to get on his case about what direction the band was taking."

I looked at Adelle, who had told me Jason had come out of the closet already back in December.

She said, "Jason, I told my brother you came out just before Chrsitmas."

He looked at me , trying to suppress embarrassment. Or so it appeared to me.

"Only to a few people. Very few," Jason said. "People I trust, like you Miss Poynter."

"Are you still feeling shame, Jason?" Adelle said softly.

"Maybe not shame, but it makes me damned uncomfortable having to live and deal with a bunch of fucking homophobes all day every day."

"Who else knows about your orientation, Jason?" I said.

He paused to think. Then said, "Bobby knew. Perry and Richie know. Mr. Sechrest knows."

Sechrest. Well now. I said, "I've spoken with Mr. Sechrest. He was apparently close with Bobby."

Jason blurted out, "Mr. Sechrest has been trying to counsel Bobby, to get him to lighten up, to try to understand that I'm not some wicked monster, that I'm not going to try to sneak up on him in the PE locker room and try to kiss him or blow him. He was trying to help me out by helping Bobby."

"How did Mr. Sechrest know you are homosexual and that Bobby was a homophobe."

"We were in Mr. Sechrest's office one day after school. The three of us. We were discussing some of Dylan's music and what it meant. Somehow it all just came out. I don't remember anymore exactly how. But it did."

"And was Bobby responding positively to Mr. Sechrest's thera- peutic ministering?" I said.

A shrug. "Bobby stopped calling me a bitch, stopped making remarks. But I know he didn't mellow. Just kept his mouth shut about it. The looks he gave me still kept coming."

"Did you tell that to Mr. Sechrest?"

"No. he didn't need to be told. He could tell. I wish Mr. Sechrest hadn't poked his nose into my business in the first place. I'm sure he meant well, but his butting in only made Bobby act more snide. His verbal aggression was easier to take."

I made a mental note to take a deeper look at Mr. Sechrest and his dealings with Bobby, to see if the band director's failed effort at counseling Bobby Shane had led him try alternative ways to alter the young man's behavior.

I asked Jason, "How did Bobby learn that you are gay? When you came out?"

"He came over to my house a couple months ago. It was a weekend. My folks had gone to Phoenix. I had friend down from Tucson. Bobby walked into my house without so much as knock- ing. He found me and my friend –."

"Your friend's name?"

Jason ignored my question. "Bobby said he was there to remind me about band practice that night at his house. Then he just stared at me with a really nasty smile, shook his head, and left."

"Your friend. I'm sorry, but I'm going to need his name and address," I said.

"Andy has nothing to do with any of this."

Maybe. Maybe not.

Adelle talked Jason into providing Andy's full name and Tucson address.

"You're still in the band. Bobby's disgust obviously didn't provoke him to want to kick you out?" I said.

"I play a mean bass and Bobby knows it. Knew it."

Perry said, "Bobby brought up the subject of kicking Jason out, but Richie and I told him to forget it. We told him Jason stays or Richie and I walk, too."

"So let's turn to the subject of women, gentlemen. Any interpersonal conflicts there?" I said.

Jason eagerly chimed in. "Yeah. Plenty."

I looked to Perry, who looked at Jason.

"You tell him, Jason. I'll get too angry to get it right."

"You sure?" Jason said.

"I'm sure. You're an astute observer."

"I don't know about that? I wasn't always around."

"Just tell him. You know the basics."

"Okay." Jason cleared his throat. "Bobby had a girlfriend, her name is Kristy. She used to be Perry's girlfriend. Bobby kinda stole her from Perry."

"Kinda?" I said.

"She dumped me," Perry said glumly.

"And Bobby, the asshole, rubbed it in," Jason added.

"I guess I wasn't aware of that," Adelle said, sounding apologetic. "I'm sorry, Perry."

Although getting dumped is a common enough event in high school, that it's widespread doesn't mitigate the anguish – and often the bitterness. Misery may love company, but being in good company rarely softens the blow.

Perry started to say something, then apparently thought better of it. He mumbled a barely audible, "Rotten bastard!"

"You talking about Bobby?" I said.

"I asked Kristy why she was trading me in for Bobby. She wouldn't tell me. All she said was 'Ask Bobby Shane'. So I did."

"And?"

"He told me Kristy preferred him because he has a bigger cock." Perry blushed even as he said it.

Adelle looked up at a ceiling fan, maybe trying to pretend she was miles and miles away. I wasn't about to pursue that line of explanation.

Jason recognized when silence drags on seconds too long, to the point of becoming embarrassing, and finally interjected, "Women. Feh!" And then he realized his faux-pas. "I'm sorry, I didn't mean you, Miss Poynter."

"Does that mean you don't consider me a woman, Jason?" she said, raising an eyebrow.

"No, ma'am. I meant girls our age."

"Male lovers are less fickle?" Adelle said.

"I'm not an expert on that – yet. But, yeah. Andy can be a prick sometimes."

I shifted the direction of the conversation a few degrees. "Was Kristy still seeing Bobby?"

Jason chortled. "Now we open a new can of worms."

"Meaning?" I said.

Perry was quick to explain. "Rumor had it Bobby was seeing another chick behind Kristy's back."

I looked down at my notebook and saw that I had started drawing triangles unconsciously. "Does the chick have a name?"

The two boys looked at one another. Perry said, "Go on. You brought it up."

Jason said, "Her name is Juanita Bardella."

Out of the corner of an eye I saw Adelle look taken aback. "Sis, you have something to contribute to this rumor?"

She looked reluctant to speak, but went ahead anyway. "I thought Richie Maldonado and Juanita were an item."

Perry sneered. "Naw. That's Richie's wishful thinking."

More to the point, I asked, "Is Kristy Serling aware of this rumor."

Jason guffawed. "Damned right she is. And is she pissed."

"Does Richie know of the rumor?" I said.

"I guess he does," Perry said. "Neither Jason nor I have the balls to ask him, but he's done a lot of extra moping lately."

Jason said, "Again, Bobby sneaking off with Juanita is only a rumor. Both of them have been extreeeeeemely cagey about what's going on between them. And for good reason."

I said, "That reason being?"

Perry snorted. "Jesus! Kristy would cut Bobby's balls off if –. Ooops! That's not a cool thing to say, is it?"

"Just a metaphor, right?" I said.

"God, I hope so," Perry said.

"Kristy has a temper?"

"A bit," Perry conceded.

"Any sadistic tendencies?"

Jason piped up. "Just a typical female cockteaser."

Perry gave him a nasty look.

I turned to Adelle and said, "Could you arrange for me to interview Kristy?"

Before my sister could answer, Perry said, "She works at Graciela's. Dinner shift seating hostess." Adelle had already told me that. But Perry added, "Today is one of her days off."

I knew it was far too early to try to interview Bobby's parents. Doing so in their home would work best, but they lived in Chief Morton's territory. So that was an issue I had to think through. I thanked the two young men for their time and insights and left them to finish their pizza in peace. Adelle told me she would stay and leave with them. I assumed that was her way of letting me know she would try to convince them I wasn't as big a jerk as I might have come across to them. I told her I would be home after I had spoken with Richie Maldonado.

14

Skyler's Family Restaurant sat a block west of the interstate on Avienda Zapata in Arroyo Arenoso. The waitress who came to seat me pointed out Richie for me. He was sitting in a rear booth, sipping a soda.

After interviewing Perry and Jason, I asked myself how likely a teenager would be to commit murder. Kill one of its own. I reminded myself what I had thought near the end of my talk with Gwen Dupree about four-year-olds. Some parents did a better job of civilizing their young than others. By the time four-year-olds reached their mid-to-late teens, sadism among many, I was certain, had waxed, not waned, despite efforts, great or small, by parents, teachers, families, and others to repress anti-social tendencies in these budding adults. After all, if murder were limited only to hardcore sociopaths, there would be a lot fewer homicide detectives from Boston to L.A. drawing overtime pay.

I'd met a few drummers in my time and judged all of them to be minimally crazier than the sanest loon. A couple of them I was familiar with spent more time on distant planets than they spent on our local cinder in the void. My first impression of Riche Maldonado did not give me that same creepy feeling. For one thing, his eyes weren't glazed over from a drug stupor.

The kid was a tad overweight and the burger basket a waitress brought him as I introduced myself and sat down wasn't going to help his waistline or his arteries. But I wasn't his food sheriff. So I kept my eat-healthy opinions to myself.

"You know why I'm here, right?"

He nodded as he bit off a mouthful of bacon cheeseburger. "Talk about Bobby," he said while still chewing.

"Know who killed him?"

"If I did, you'd have heard about it by now, right? I got no idea."

"Who were his enemies?"

"Who wasn't? That'd be a lot shorter list."

"Not a loveable guy?"

"He tried, but not very hard."

"Kristy Serling."

"That *chucha*. What about her?"

"You tell me. You're the one with opinions about her."

"Perry's an idiot for wanting her back. Bobby stole her just to prove he could. And she let him. Fuckin' little *puta*."

"I understand she's been pissed with Bobby lately."

"You would be too if the person you're into cheats on you."

"Juanita Bardella."

"Don't go there," he said. He stopped shoveling food into his mouth, came up out of his eating crouch, and his eyes narrowed.

"I'm afraid I have to."

"Okay. She's maybe the reason Kristy is – was – pissed at Bobby Shane."

"Maybe?"

"Bobby can be a sly little fucker when he wants to be."

"I'm picking up a lot of Bobby hostility from your direction."

"I'm just the drummer. I don't play the melodies."

"Which makes you resentful?"

"I could have taken up the guitar. I didn't."

"Back to Bobby's enemies. Who, besides you, Perry, Jason, and Kristy had issues with Bobby?"

"Try his bookie."

"Bobby gambled."

"Big time. Well, not big money, but it added up. It was his addiction. He didn't smoke, didn't drink much. Chased pussy, but that's nothing. Point spreads became his drug of habit."

"Winner? Loser?"

"He wasn't as smart as he thought he was."

"Where did he bet?"

"Phone bets. Some grad students at U of A run a shop out of their house near campus. Baseball, football, golf, hockey, basketball. Bobby was mostly into college hoops, but not exclusively."

"How much would he bet?"

"A hundred here, a hundred there."

"And he was upside down?"

Richie nodded slowly. "Couple of grand, last I heard, which wasn't recently. I tuned out."

"Where did he get his gambling money?" I said.

A shrug. "Beats me. He wasn't robbin' Circle K's."

"How long had this been going on?"

"Couple of years. He met a guy at U of A. Guy in the marching band. He got Bobby hooked."

"Did he ever hit you up for money?"

Richie laughed. "He knew that would be a waste of time. I'm always broke."

"What was the problem with his bookie?"

"I don't know. He just said there was one. But maybe it got solved," Richie said.

The question was: *How* did it get solved?

Just then a cook emerged form the swing door that led to the kitchen and walked over to our table, wiping is hands on a messy apron before slapping Richie on the back. "Your burger okay, bro'?"

"Just right." He gestured toward me. "This dude is a detective. He's investigating Bobby's murder."

The cook held out a hand. "Fabian. I'm Richie's older, smarter brother."

I shook hands.

Richie poked his brother. "If you're so fuckin' smart, what are you doing flippin" burgers in a joint like this?"

"Hey, us rich guys gotta put on a humble front, right? So we don't get mugged going to or from the bank, depositing our millions."

"Millions. Right," Richie said. "That's my big brother. Always full of shit."

To Fabian I said, "How well did you know Bobby?"

"Well enough to keep my distance from the motherfucker. I'm not surprised someone got tired of Bobby's crap and shoved a dagger into one of his kidneys."

"What crap do you mean?" I said.

"Women and money. The same shit that eventually gets every guy's dick in a wringer. Man, don't you watch Humphrey Bogart movies?"

"Not everyone with female and/or money woes ends up face down in an arroyo wearing only his underwear," I said. "What made Bobby pay a higher price than the rest of us poor males?"

"Greed, man. He chased too many women and chased the wrong kind of money. That's a dangerous brew, dude, as I keep telling my little brother. Get a work ethic. Then keep it. Chase honest dollars and honest women." He paused. "I know, I know. Both are hard to find. But ya gotta keep lookin'."

"Fabian, the philosopher fry cook," Richie said. He looked at his brother and said, "Get back to the kitchen and earn your honest dollar. You ain't earnin' it standin' here."

"How angry has Perry been over losing his girl to Bobby?" I said, as Fabian returned to the kitchen.

Richie gave me a were-you-born-yesterday look. "You never had a chick dump you and take up with a dude you thought was a *pedazo de mierda*?"

A piece of shit. I shook my head. My laments weren't the issue here. "Is that what Perry thought of Bobby?"

"Pretty much."

"Why did he stick with the band?"

"To make music, man. I take it you don't play."

"No."

"Then you wouldn't get it."

Maybe I didn't *get it*, although most often I didn't let those who played the insider card, the "You had to be there" or "Unless you're one of us, you couldn't possibly understand what we're talking about", get away with it. In this case, maybe Richie had a small point I could concede.

My own experience with cuckolds – working as a PI in Las Vegas I had known plenty – the aggrieved party's instinct is to commit double assassination. Catch them together *in flagrante delicto* and off them both. But not always. Now and then an angry-but-forgiving schlep only kills the rival male, then hopes, sometimes even begs, the wayward female to return for one more try at living happily ever after.

But such cases are also crimes of rage and I knew of only one case where the cheated-on husband showed *sufficient restraint*, if that's what you could call it – the judge openly scoffed when the murderer's attorney used the phrase – to torture the man he caught in bed with his wife. Still, rare as such an instance is, that case shows it's possible.

I turned to the subject of the remaining band member. "Jason. How was he getting along with Bobby?"

Riche stared at a half-eaten pickle that had fallen off his burger. Finally he said, "They had some issues."

"Such as?"

"Bass players tend to be more intellectual than guitar players."

"Jason was pressing Bobby to play more switched-on Mozart?" I said, knowing better.

"Not exactly."

"What exactly then?"

He refocused on the pickle.

"That Jason is gay?"

"Yeah."

"And that Bobby was a homophobe?"

Richie looked up.

"A gay hater?"

A nod.

"How did you and Perry react to that tension?"

"I got nuthin' against queers."

Right.

"The issue I'm trying to resolve here is how intensely Jason might have felt about Bobby's constant putdowns."

Riche put down his sandwich and gave me a hard look. "All right. Jason was mad as hell. One time Jason broke his bow over his knee and went after Bobby with the broken pieces."

"How far did that go?"

"Jason pinned Bobby to the wall and told him that one of these days, if Bobby kept up that kind of fag-sneering talk, Bobby would find himself pulling broken slivers from a Bud bottle out of his ass."

As I let that sink in, Richie added, "Jason ain't a wuss. He may look like it, but that dude is hard as nails underneath his pasty face."

I said, "Back to Bobby's gambling."

"What about it?"

"Do you know if he drove into Tucson to place his bets, pick up his winnings – when he did win?"

"I don't know nuthin' about any of that," Richie said. But his look told me he might know something.

"In Las Vegas, where I live and work, bookies sometimes have runners, guys who pick up bettors' tickets and cash, drop off winning payoffs. And usually they also serve in the added role of enforcers when those who bet on the cuff don't pay up in a timely fashion for their misjudgments."

Richie scowled. "Their what?"

"Their losses. Their losing bets."

"I don't know anything about that stuff. All I know is that Bobby was a regular player. Told me so himself."

"He had a U of A bookie, you said."

"Yeah, that's what Bobby told me. But I don't know any details, man. All I know is that, whenever he had a big win, Bobby thought he was so cool his shit didn't stink."

"And when he suffered a big loss?"

"Then was the time to give the dude space, man. He was hell on a horse."

"What sports are you into?" I said.

He laughed. "Look at me, man. Do I look like an Olympic swimmer? I don't play nuthin'."

"A spectator?"

He looked around, but the nearby booths were empty. "I go to cock fights a lot," he said in a hushed tone. "I don't bet no money or anything like that. I leave that to Fabian."

"So Fabian's a betting man?"

"Sure. He knows his birds. He also has a pretty sharp eye for good boxers. Latino boxers, that is. He's got some change down on Friday night's Ramon Salazar-Pepe Fernandez bout."

"Yeah, the featured bout at Caesar's Palace," I said. I'd seen posters spread all over Las Vegas before I left town.

"You got tickets?" Richie said.

"No. I'm going to be stuck here," I said.

Most of the fisticuffs I had witnessed over the years had taken place in back alleys. No tuxedoed ring announcers, no referees, no towel-draped, scar-faced seconds, no buxom babes strutting placards to tell those at ringside what round was coming up. Besides, I'd never seen an alley brawl go more than one round anyway.

"Too bad. It's going to be a doozy," Richie said and finished off the remainder of his sandwich.

15

When I returned to my sister's house, Adelle had placed a computer printout from two of the newswire services on the kitchen table. The headlines on both were the same: *Las Vegas Embezzler Found Murdered in Tucson.* The police had apparently broken the news too late for the *Daily Star* to get it into newsprint.

"That is the address you were sneaking about Sunday night, was it not?" she said, as she mashed potatoes to go with the Swiss steak she had taken from her freezer.

"Yep. That's where we were."

"Where you were. Did your flashlight shine on any dead bodies while you were poking about the premises?"

"Just one."

"And that was the real reason for wanting to find a phone booth? To call the police?"

"It was."

"Thank you for sparing me the details at the time. I was edgy enough without finding out there was a corpse within screaming distance of where I was waiting," Adelle said.

"You are very welcome." I fetched a beer from the fridge.

"Do you or the police know who killed her?"

"Her boyfriend, I imagine."

"Are you going to be involved further?"

"No. All Jack asked of me was to check out the address to see if Miss Embezzler might be there or have been there."

"And the boyfriend?"

"He's in Mexico, if he knows what's good for him."

"And the money?"

"I would imagine it's sitting next to him."

"Might your friend Jack ask you to go to Mexico?" she said, finishing the potatoes and putting them into a serving bowl.

"I don't think so. And I wouldn't go if he asked."

"Are you sure?"

"I've lost my enthusiasm for Mexico, Dell. It's no longer user-friendly. Maybe Cabo is still safe enough, but this guy wasn't headed there. He has family inland, just north of Mexico City. If I were still twenty-five and dumb as I was at that age, I might accept a contract to hunt him down. But not now. Even Stonecipher won't go looking for him there and Jack's ballsier now than I ever was."

After leaving Perry, Jason, and Adelle at the pizzeria, I had phoned Adelle back and asked her to ask Jason for more information on his buddy, Andy. If Jason was willing to disclose Andy's phone number or address, I intend to check out in person how angry Jason's friend was at Bobby Shane. I thought Jason might be more agreeable to disclosing a contact point with Andy if I weren't present. I was right. He gave Adelle Andy's cell phone number. When I called Andy he reluctantly agreed to meet me at a deli near campus for lunch the next day. He dropped his defenses when I explained that my purpose was to clear his name as a possible murder suspect. That wasn't my goal at all, but as long as he thought so, I didn't mind misleading him.

Once I had provided my sister with the few added details she was up to listening to without being traumatized, I placed a call to Las Vegas. This time I phoned an entrepreneur friend of mine by the name of Calvin Denhart, known to everyone simply as Hex.

Hex owned and operated a betting parlor in the downtown area of Sin City, off Fremont, and called his establishment Teaser's Spread. More than one out-of-town male yahoo had wandered through his front door, having formed a conclusion from the place's title that Hex's bookie shop was either a strip joint or a whorehouse. Such gentlemen were invariably disappointed and quickly shown the door.

Once upon a time, Hex liked to tell his customers, two middle-aged women dressed as if they were toddler twins – pink pants, pink tennis shoes, and yellow blouses covered with cuddly bunnies and multi-colored tulips – walked in and asked how much the luncheon buffet cost. When Hex explained that there was no buffet, the ladies apologized, left, and then returned to explain their mistake. They had thought the flashing blue neon "T" in Gothic scroll on the outdoor sign was a "C" and concluded they were walking into Caesar's Spread, which they took to be branch buffet site of Caesar's Palace.

According to Hex, he never knew his father and got his nickname from his mother, who was a single parent trying to raise a hellion, while simultaneously attempting to conduct the rest of her business of living out of a tiny apartment. She worked graveyard shifts as a cocktail waitress to pay for daytime childcare. Her day-time job was dancing as a stripper. She started calling her freckled, red-headed, surprise child "my Hex" or simply "the Hex". The title caught on among the other children at the daycare lady's house. Before long, the definite article got dropped and "the Hex" came to be known by one and all as Hex Denhart. As Hex put it, "Now only my birth certificate calls me Calvin."

The bookie shop has been a silver mine for Hex. *A teaser spread* in betting parlance is a point spread greater or lesser than "the line", which is the point spread generally agreed to by bookies and published on the daily sports page, among other places. "The line" is created by teams of recognized handicappers, most of whom work out of Las Vegas. The bettor pays a premium to the bookie in order to be granted a teaser point spread.

When a bookmaker knows most of his customers or is in a position to choose some or all of them, as Hex is nowadays, then said bookie can entice those customers to wager larger sums by creating special terms, although such terms never represent a char-itable gesture on the part of the odds maker. They merely seem to be. Hex, like every one of his bookie competitors, is driven solely by the fools-and-their-money-are-soon-parted principle.

On the other hand, I was a guy for whom Hex would do almost anything and do it for free. When Hex was a teenager and working as a valet car parker at the old Aladdin, still living with his mom, and turning over most of his tip money to her to help out with rent and groceries, I saved Mrs. Denhart from what I learned was yet another cheat-'em-and-beat-'em boyfriend, after receiving a des-perate call from Hex one evening, begging me to find the guy who stole his mother's supposedly hidden stash of rent money.

I met the kid on a street corner, liked him instantly, listened to his story, and took the case on a percentage basis. When I caught up with the boyfriend and lifted his wallet from him, while he clutched his groin as part of my lesson to him in not paying close enough attention to my lecture on the perils of committing petty larceny, I discovered how few bucks he had actually filched. Talk about crime not paying. His risk-reward factor doubled when I kicked him a second time. But the upshot for me was that I ended up reducing my contract percentage to zero. That small gesture, however, was worth every penny I sacrificed. And pennies it was. Hex has been in my pocket every since.

"You're in Tucson? Shit, Wiley, you could have stayed here in your home town to get sand blown in your face."

"Ah, but this used to be Mexican sand, Hex. Ever hear of the Gadsden Purchase?"

"Sure. Hector Gadsden, right? A regular Speedy Gonzalez. Played shortstop for the Padres, who sold his contract to the Yankees for seven mil and some change."

"God, you've got a memory, Hex. That happened what? Almost a hundred and sixty years ago?"

"Give or take. Dates I'm not so sharp on. What's your pleasure, my man? Just name her. Blonde? Brunette? Half-and-half?"

"Half and half?"

"I can't always guarantee the carpet will match the drapes, my man."

"Since when have I needed a pimp?" I said.

"Hey! I saw those few flecks of gray the last time you stopped by. I bet you're starting to find out the young pretty chicks don't give it away as readily as they used to. Even the newbie amateurs, the ones who don't know your cock from your elbow, expect a little something to show your appreciation after they play starfish and moan like a lost calf." He made feeble moaning sounds.

"Remember what the old Texas Ranger said."

"About young pussy being overrated? Sure, I remember," he said.

"I'm calling because I need your sports-betting expertise, Hex, not your pimping talents," I said to try to put the conversation on track.

"You planning on tossing a fiver on U of A?"

"Not me, but someone else here has been dropping a hundred here and there. On U of A and others."

"With hoops, don't take points against them. With football and baseball you never know. In those two sports they're one of the harder teams to handicap."

"What I want to know is where a guy can place his bets down here without going online or to a casino? I'm hearing stories that there might be an underground parlor run by some grad students. You have any knowledge about something like that?" I said.

"I do. I like to have knowledge of my competition, even competitors that far away. You want a private-line phone number? Tell 'em Al Capone sent you? What do you need?"

"An address would be better."

"Can do. Gimme a sec."

It took Hex nearly two minutes, but he read one off to me. "I don't have directions, Wile. I've never been to Too-Sahn."

"I can Google map it. Thanks."

"Mind if I ask what this is about?"

"Murder."

"Oh my. In that case, will you do your damnedest to keep the name of Hex Denhart out of it?"

"Hex who?"

"Thanks."

16

I had no idea how long results of the forensic evidence collected by police Chief Morton would take to be processed. According to my sister's report, police interrogators at the high school appeared to focus on gathering information on possible drug connections. A deal gone wrong perhaps. Or someone cutting into someone else's territory. Southern Arizona was a battleground among competing Mexican and Columbian drug cartels. Of course, rock musicians and recreational drugs had been inseparably linked for decades. No one had much reason to suppose even garage bands were immune from that bonding. Start 'em early. So the cops were probably on the right track. Or at least pursuing the most likely one. Still, no one had tied Bobby Shane Hollsworth to drugs yet. As for his fellow band members, I saw nothing there either. Both Perry Crisp and Jason Altheiser swore none of them did drugs.

I was hardly an expert, but I had seen enough dopers in Las Vegas – in bars, in schools, on the streets at 3. a.m. – to imagine I had a keener eye for brains and blood systems fueled by whatever popular illicit street chemicals were *au currant* than the average citizen, or even the average cop. The search for runaway kids was a staple of my profession and the trails were routinely littered with needles, vials, and residue-lined baggies of various sizes. I was confident I could recognize a stoner when I met one. Perry, Jason, and Richie each got a pass from me. I rated them clean, except for maybe a backstage or under-the-bleachers Friday night swig or three of cheap beer.

With the address from Hex I could accomplish a Tuesday morning two-fer: Check out the off-campus betting parlor and have a talk with Jason's boyfriend, Andy, whose last name was Kudarski. He was two years older than Jason, Adelle told me. Jason had met him at a music summer camp in Michigan his sophomore year when Andy had been a senior at a high school in Scottsdale.

Over wine, cheese, and a Canlis salad, Adelle and I discussed my interviews with the three remaining boys of Prickly Pear Jam. My sister could not imagine any of them being involved with the death of their band leader. Adelle wasn't so naïve as to have a blind faith in the innocence of youth in general, but she did have rather strong feelings that none of these three young men was capable either of committing, or participating in the arrangement of, the murder of Bobby Shane Hollsworth.

"I simply don't see it in them, Wiley. None of them. Yes, there are some strong feelings of anger and bitterness in each of them. But their shared love of music and their devotion to being members of something where the whole is greater than the sum of the parts is very powerful. I can feel it."

"No question, Sis. But at least one of them believes – maybe all three believe—that the whole might be improved by removing and replacing one of those parts."

"But we're talking murder, Wiley, not replacing a cane-back chair with an upholstered one. Murder, not voting Bobby Shane out and voting Elvis Whoever in. I can't picture any one of those three boys putting a knife into Bobby's back, however much they may have disliked him. I simply can't see it. And please don't tell me I suffer a lack of imagination in that regard."

I wondered. But she went on.

"I have been teaching high school long enough to observe the level of civility among students – and between students and faculty, students and administrators – steadily decline to the point that I have both witnessed and experienced confrontations between students and adults where I have been genuinely frightened. Maybe not frightened for my life, but scared to the point that I expected the verbal violence being committed would surely escalate into physical violence. Serious physical violence. That never happened, but the tipping point was close enough in one instance that I was on the verge of running as fast as my granny shoes would let me for the nearest telephone to dial 911."

Even when she was getting worked up my sister has always had a way of maintaining as much of a sense of decorum as she could manage. Going ballistic was not her style. She would have made a good battlefield commander.

She went on. "I know you scoff at the notion of women's intuition, but I do consider myself a very good judge of character, even of those who do their very damnedest to mask their true nature. And, with each of these three boys, my sense is that not one of them is a murderer. I know I would be laughed off a witness stand, but that is my testimony to you."

On whole, my sister has always possessed excellent instincts. On the other hand, my own dismal experience reminded me that juvenal correction centers are full of clever little shits. The smile and smile and be a villain types. Paradigm examples of smirking sociopaths.

To Adelle I said, "I respect your judgment, Sister. I understand that you knows these guys far better than I do. Trust me, I know all too well that first impressions are hardly definitive. But I am reserving judgment. I'm not going to try to hang any one of them on a hunch. I may not quite always believe in the principle that better ten guilty men go free than one innocent man hang." I smiled. "Nine maybe. But I am committed to unearthing solid evidence as much or more than any cop. And certainly far more than a great many prosecutors."

We were sitting in the living room in a pair of wing-backed chairs, a lamp table between us. Adelle reached across the narrow table and patted my hand. Wine has always put my sister in a touchy-feely mood.

"I know you care about justice and truth with a capital 'J' and a capital 'T' as much or more than most people do, Brother."

The bottle of vintage Napa Valley merlot was two thirds of the way toward becoming a dead soldier.

"Me? Naw. I'm just out to make a buck. It's easier to have criminals as my adversaries than honest people. Criminals are usually dumber. So at least I'm not at a disadvantage."

"Always the cynic, Wiley. Even regarding your own merits. But underneath –."

"There is no underneath, Dell. I wear my simple thoughts on my sleeve, along with my–. See? Along with my spilled wine."

"False modesty."

"I think not."

She giggled. "Perhaps you and I should ring down the curtain on this cry-in-our-beer session. I'm feeling just a wee bit high and I'm probably acting like I'm at a fool-so-feelish stage. Am I?"

"Definitely not. You're doing just fine. And we're not sniveling into either beer or wine."

"Still, it's only Monday, meaning I have to teach in the morning. If this were Friday, I'd be glad to help you squeeze the last drop out of Mr. Merlot. And maybe even ask his wife to join us."

I helped her to her feet and gave her a goodnight peck on the cheek. "Sweet dreams."

She teetered as she walked slowly toward her bedroom, holding out her arms to balance herself, and I hustled to help balance her, lest she fall and have less than sweet dreams.

17

Before putting myself to bed, I made one last phone call to Las Vegas. This one went to a young woman whose contributions to my success were many – far more than Hex's. She was a Korean-American by the name of Hyun-Ok Park, but she went by Stacy. She had a master's degree in math and computer science from MIT and now lived in Las Vegas to be near her maternal grandmother. She owned and ran a security-consulting company. She was an expert at internet, as well as brick-and-mortar, security.

I met her through her grandmother. Stacy had hired me some years back to do a background check on a man who was pushing hard to get her grandma to sell a particular piece of real estate, a several-acre hunk of vacant land in an industrial park in nearby Henderson. The old woman had inherited money from her parents in Seoul and had invested much of it strategic plots of land in and around Las Vegas.

Because Stacy's grandmother had taken an instant dislike to the man who was making her a lucrative offer, she had asked Stacy to look into the man's background. When Stacy found nothing about the man or his company anywhere in cyberspace, she hired me to do a shoe-leather search for information.

The man, an Asian, and his company, both consisted of masks behind masks behind masks. Two Reno business fronts led to three others in Vancouver, B.C., which finally led back to Hong Kong. The man, Chou Lei Wu, and his brother, Ming Lei, had fled Hong Kong in 1997, along with thousands of other well-to-do HK residents when the Brits decamped, leaving the islands and their people to the robots wearing Mao uniforms.

Only half of the Wu brothers' businesses were legitimate. And those existed only to launder the money taken in by the shady ones. My discoveries had required me to spend a week in Vancouver, during which time I experienced what I will call – in deference to time, space, and modesty – multiple *harrowing moments*, spaced over four of those seven days. I had poked my nose into Chinese establishments that did not suffer gladly *laowai* devils snooping around. However, no RCMP divers had found me submerged beneath the pilings of Vancouver's waterfront; no dumpster divers had found me bleeding on their secondhand sub gum yuk. So, considering all the possibilities, I had achieved my goals with admirable aplomb. Meaning: without having my ass handed to me.

When I returned to Las Vegas, I recommended to Stacy that she urge her grandmother to tell Mr. Wu to go fly a kite, suck an egg, or whatever other, perhaps more delicate metaphor Koreans use when conveying the message to someone to shove a business proposition up his descending colon.

Stacy took my advice, paid me well for it, and we've been friends and more ever since. Grandma eventually sold her Henderson property to a reputable national chain at a grand profit and was happy. So now I was phoning Stacy at her home to ask for assistance.

"Tucson? You have anything to do with that dead embezzler woman?" she said by way of a start.

I filled her in on my belated and lamentable role.

"No shit? Yuk! Double yuk. You calling to ask me to trace the boyfriend in Margaritaville? You know Mexico still runs on Mañana Standard Time and communicates more via tin cans attached to waxed string that by cell phones."

"No, dear. I figure he'll get his the minute he starts carelessly waving the cash around a bit too conspicuously. If he hasn't already. Honor among thieves became unfashionable when Nixon's toadies started pointing fingers at each other and prime-time TV broadcast booths became the confessionals of choice."

"So why have you joined me here in my kitchen? I'm sipping at a Heineken and wearing a flimsy bathrobe, by the way," she said. "I was hoping this call was someone offering to come over and show me a good time."

"Sorry."

"You never even offer me telephone sex. Cheap bastard. Probably figure you'll eat up too many minutes working me up to a proper orgasm, right?"

"Which Heineken are you sipping at?" I said.

"Number Three. But I had a shitty day at work and my *Mal-mu* has gone to LA for the week." Her grandmother. "I'm lonely and sullen and –."

"Horny."

"Damned right. And all I get is a call from you. I've told you before how avid and talented I am in bed. And I know you're not gay. Am I too young? Too ugly. Too… Korean?"

"Too much a friend and business associate?"

"That combination doesn't stop other guys from wanting to –."

"I know. But I'm not other guys."

"Which is good – for the most part."

"Maybe some day."

"Yeah. Sure. So what's this call all about?"

I explained and she said my request should not prove difficult at all.

"That's it?"

"Yes."

"I suppose you want it yesterday."

"In the morning will do."

"Might as well start now. I don't have anything else to distract me. Do you hear? Poor me. Let me hear it from your end. Poor Stacy."

"Poor, poor Stacy. I'll make it up to you."

"Promise."

In faux-tenor she said, "This call is being recorded for your protection." Pause. "Oops. Backspace. Delete." Low voice again. "For my protection."

"Good night, Stace."

What I had asked Stacy to do was not illegal. For once. Well, most of it wasn't. I wanted the names and any background information available on the guys who ran the bookie site near the University of Arizona campus. Plus, I wanted any background details she could find on Sebastian Sechrest. The illegal part was my asking her to check on Boyd Dupree's recent credit card use, in particular for where he might have charged a room in Las Vegas. I added that, if she came up with a hit, to pass the information on to Jack Stonecipher.

I'm sure many of my requests to Stacy, even when they're not blatantly unlawful, require her to push the limits of legality. But then she once explained to me, "Everybody repeatedly claims that the bad guys are always one step ahead of the security geeks. Well, the way to overcome that is not only to think like a bad guy, but to act like a bad guy sometimes, too. Right?" I often provided her entrée into mimicking the bad guys.

Tuesday

When Stacy called me the next morning I made the mistake of asking her how she had slept.

"Are you kidding? Even my goddamned vibrator batteries died on me," she snapped.

But she had gathered the information I asked for.

"The Sechrest dude must be boring. Born in Williston, North Dakota. Hoo-ha! Got a bachelor of arts degree in music education in instrumental music from Dickinson State. That's also in North Dakota. He went on to get a master's degree in music at UCLA. That's El Ay, nor Arr Ay, thank you very much. Rots a ruck, eh?"

"Velly good," I said.

"Fork you, round-eyed devil. Anyway, this Sechrest bee-bopper got his first teaching job in Flagstaff, then moved down to Phoenix, and has been at his present location for three years. He took over when his predecessor died of a coronary at age forty-three."

Stacy then provided me with what she found about the sports-betting parlor. It was being run out of a three-bedroom house off 4th Avenue, just south of Speedway Boulevard. That put it just west of the U of A campus and slightly north of the still-limping-along hippie district.

Three former students lived in the two-story rental. The lease was in the name of Kirk McMullen, age 32, from Glendale, Arizona. The second member of bookie team was Randy Franklin, age 30, also from Glendale. And third was Colby Ambrose, age 29, from Peoria, Arizona.

After giving me the basic data she had gathered on the three men, Stacy said, "You going in armed and dangerous, Wiley?"

"Do I need to?"

"The third dude, Colby, has issues. His arrest record indicates he does not play well with others. Currently working part-time as a bouncer at a tavern called O'Banion's, he apparently is quick with both his temper and his fists.

"Several arrests, but only one conviction. All for assault. No jail time. He pleaded guilty and was sentenced to community service as a first-time offender. In the other instances, apparently sympathetic juries decided the folks he pummeled the shit out of all had it coming. Currently, however, there is a civil suit pending with Colby named as the sole defendant. It's been filed by one of those vics for violating the man's civil rights. Must be a black dude. The plaintiff's first name is Duwannashawn."

"Do I detect a hint of Asian superiority toward African-Americans?" I said.

"Who? Me? Just because they all look alike? Hell, so do you people," Stacy said, laughing.

"Now it's *you people*, is it?"

"To us bucket-heads, all *wehgukin* look alike, including you, *baeg-in*."

"Thanks."

"At least you all look alike *above* the waist." I heard her snicker.

"I won't go there."

"You got issues… there?"

"What else do you have?" I said.

"I'm looking at a photo of the Ambrose guy. He must buy sailboat spinnakers and turn them into muscle shirts. He is wide at the shoulders. And his face is one of those that tells you he sprinkles nails on his corn flakes. I bet he can crush a pony keg with one squeeze. So watch out, Wiley."

"Br'er Fox, he lay low."

"I'm guessing .22 bullets ricochet off this dude's abdomen. So, if you have to shoot him, aim for his nose. It looks like it's been broken a time or two."

"You play too many video games in your spare time, Stace."

"What else has a lonely girl got to do? Especially when she's got dead vibrator batteries. When you come back to Las Vegas bring me some new batteries, will you? Or, better yet, bring me some kimchi and we'll curl up together on my sofa and watch old Brando movies together."

Brando. *Streetcar? Waterfront? One-Eyed Jacks?* At least those all had Karl Malden in them, too. "Thanks for all your help, Stace. Send me a bill."

Stacy had also told me she could find no records indicating the house she had located for me was a business of any kind, let alone an illegal betting parlor. That figured. And none of the three occupants' bank accounts showed any large transactions. Apparently the online passwords each of the men used were as transparent as the ones I usually chose. Or else Stacy had penetrated the security of the banks themselves. I hadn't asked. Some things you don't want to know. The details of how Stacy operates rank among those.

Soon after I spoke with Stacy I headed to Tucson. Once there, I parked a couple blocks from the house and walked to the front door. Colby Ambrose answered shortly after I pressed the buzzer. No mistaking him. Shaved head, a fire-breathing dragon tat on each bicep, and a black muscle shirt fronted with a photo of a young white male clutching a svelte, redheaded young female whose ass was pressed into his crotch. The shirt's caption read: *Dirty Boogie Now.* Cody wore a pair of ragged cut-off jeans and was barefoot.

He also wore a black eye, a cut lip, and badly bruised knuckles. Being a bouncer clearly came with a few downside risks. Obviously not every rowdy drunk felt cowed by this dude's size. And, unlike professional boxers, bouncers didn't have ringside cut men to treat their cuts with a styptic pencil.

"Yeah?" Voice deep as a grizzly's growl.

I recoiled. But then I was sober. "You don't look so pretty good. Are you all right?"

"You should see the other guy."

"I'd rather not."

"Whadda ya want?"

"A friend of mine who used to work at O'Banion's told me you might be interested in sub-leasing this place for the summer." I thought it was a plausible lie.

"Who's your friend?"

"Jeremy Castleton."

"Never heard of him."

I shrugged. "He said he knew who you are. Colby Ambrose, right?"

"Yeah. But Kirk never mentioned to me anything about sub-leasing. Jerry who again?"

"Jeremy Castleton."

He shook his head. "Naw. Your friend got it wrong. We ain't going anywhere."

"Sorry. Thanks for your time."

"No problem." He waited until I reached the sidewalk before he closed the door.

I walked to end of the block, then turned around and knocked on the door of the neighbor on the west side of Colby's not-for-sublease house. I saw no buzzer. A lady I guessed to be sixty opened the door cautiously.

"Good morning, ma'am. My name is Harry Gates and I'm with the insurance company that issues the coverage for the house next door, the one here just to the east of yours. Before we issue a new policy to the owner, we are doing a routine check on how his tenants behave and I am hoping to get your opinion about them, if you are willing to share it with me." I talked fast and hoped she wouldn't close the door in my face.

Instead, she opened the door wider. She was dressed as though she was preparing to go out for tea and biscuits at the

Jockey Club. She wore a dainty yellow dress with a lace collar. And she had applied pancake makeup to her face thicker than the stucco on her house. Perfume rolled off her like a surf wave at Maui. At her feet a Westie terrier peered up at me suspiciously.

She smiled and said, "I'd be glad to tell you about those fine young men. They are such nice boys. Why just last week all three of them came over to help me move a daybed from my one of upstairs bedrooms down to my back parlor."

"Are they ever noisy? Do they throw wild parties? Anything like that?" I said.

"Oh, no. Never. Why I hardly even know they're there. And so polite. I just wish my neighbor on the other side, Mr. Claxingham, was half as considerate as those three young men. That man is rude and condescending."

I thought, shame on Mr. Claxingham, misbehaving to such a kind, gentle soul. "And your name, ma'am?" I made a show of holding up a pen and notepad.

"I'm Sarah Lee Housely and I've lived here for forty-two years."

"Thank you, Mrs. Housely."

"It's Miss Housely, thank you very much. Don't get me wrong, young man. I value men for what they are, but I never met one I considered worth the effort it would take me to domesticate him properly."

She had a point. I walked away and headed back to my car, hoping Miss Sarah's perfume had not clung to either the fibers of my clothes or to the fibers of my being. By the time I eased myself in behind my steering wheel I caught myself softly singing, "Everybody doesn't like something, but nobody doesn't like Sarah

Lee." I cursed, because I knew I'd have that damned ditty stuck in my head off and on for the next two days. And I was right.

Five minutes later I parked across the street from Bison Witches Bar & Deli, where I had agreed to meet Andy Kudarski. A cute waitress seated me at a booth when I told her I was meeting some-one. She returned with two menus.

I ordered ice tea and waited. I wasn't sure what I had hoped to learn by visiting the house which allegedly served as an illegal sport-betting site. Sometimes you just want to get the feel of who and what you might be dealing with. I got a serious feel for Colby Ambrose without even coming close to squeezing his biceps. His rap sheet told me he was far from being a gentle giant. But I had to ask myself: Could he stick a knife in a bet-welcher's back? The answer I arrived at, just as the waitress set my tea down in front of me was: maybe.

I re-thought Sarah Lee's cupcake description of Colby and his buddies. "They're such nice young men." Neighbor after neighbor of busted serial killers has said the same thing about a psychopath living next door. "So polite, so friendly, so helpful."

So what does being a nice young man mean? As long as you bury the bodies, leave no odor of decay, no whiff of impropriety, conduct your daily public business in a civilized manner, you're cool. Home free. A respected member of your community. Even if part of your other daily business consists of stabbing, garroting, or shooting other human beings.

The deli began filling up with other patrons. Andy had warned me to get there early. Seating was limited and the place was popu-lar. I decided to order and flagged the waitress. Thirty minutes and one giant pastrami on thick rye later, I paid and left. The crowd waiting for tables was getting more restless by the minute and I was taking up a four-seat booth by myself.

Outside, I tried calling Andy but got his voice mail. I disconnected without expressing to him my opinion of no-shows. I still wanted to meet with him. So why risk pissing him off?

18

By early afternoon I had returned to my sister's house. Jack Stonecipher still wasn't answering his cell phone. Stacy Park answered hers but had nothing new to report. She said she was still looking for a bank account for the Tucson bookie boys. I told her I pictured a basement vault full of cash.

"How does the dirty money get laundered?" she said.

"Maybe it doesn't," I told her.

"And if the house burns down?" she said, snickering.

"Then they have to explain to a Tucson fire chief what's inside the fireproof box."

She said, "I'm also looking for potential online backup of their records. Not likely, but possible. Depends on this guy Kirk's dumb factor."

"Disks into the safe or to an outside security deposit?"

"If it's outside, maybe I can trace it. Or do you care? You're not a fed looking for illegal gambling," she said.

"I know. But if it turns out they're into murder, it gives me information leverage."

"I'll keep at it."

"Thanks, Stace."

The doorbell rang. I knew it couldn't be Mrs. Fortunato. The gossipy neighbor would know Adelle would be at school. I guessed Jehovah's Witnesses. Door-to-door salesmen have gone the way of door-to-door milk deliveries. The wiry-looking man standing there when I opened the door had a brush haircut and what artists call piercing blue eyes. At that moment they were glaring at me.

"Sorry. Adelle's not here."

"I'm looking for you, if you're the detective who's been harassing my son's friends."

"Wrong detective. I haven't been harassing anyone."

"Like hell. I want you to stop and stop now."

"I'm pleased to meet you, too. Wiley Poynter. And you are –?" I held out my hand with little hope of exchanging a hand shake. I was right.

"Doug Hollsworth. Bobby Shane's father."

"My condolences on your son's murder."

"I don't want your condolences. I want you to stop poking your nose into what's not your business."

"Murder's everybody's business, Mr. Hollsworth. Your son was a pupil of my sister. She's as concerned as anyone about finding who killed him. I've offered my humble assistance. I'd like to think I am on your side."

"We don't need your help. That's what we pay the police department for. Now back off."

"I wish I shared your confidence in Chief Gordon and his minions. But I don't. Small-town police forces rarely confront homicide and when they do they are all too frequently not particularly talented at dealing with it. The case of JonBenét Ramsey in Colorado may be the most publicized and dramatic instance of homicide-solving failure, but, believe me, the country teems with similar events that are now cold-case files. Many of them very cold indeed."

The man paid no attention. "I want you to butt out. Do you understand?"

"I fully understand what you are asking, but I have no intention of doing as you ask. I am not harassing the people I speak to. In every case, I have had full cooperation and consent. Nor am I breaking any laws."

"Police interference is legal, is it?" he snarled.

"No. But I am in no way disrupting or hindering their inquiries. My examination is simply running parallel to theirs." Actually, it wasn't, but my spiel was intended to get the man off Adelle's doorstep more than to enlighten him.

He clenched his fists tightly, yet I didn't get the feeling he was on the verge of punching me. I was sure that, as a firefighter, he possessed a great deal of self-control under duress. I counted on that trait to hold in this instance.

"If I find out you've fucked this investigation up in any way, any way whatsoever, I'll be back here and, so help me God, I will see to it that –."

I pointed to his fists, then held up both of my hands, palms open. "If I muck this up, I will oblige you. I'll stick out my chin and give you a free swing. I will have earned that much. In the meantime, I suggest that you cease to –." I caught myself. "No. I'll not consider this harassment on your part. Let's just call it a not-entirely-friendly exchange of views. I also suggest you and your wife put your heads together and strive to think of everything about your son's nature and behavior – including all his activities that you know about – over the past few months so that you may present a comprehensive story to the police."

"Are you suggesting Bobby was involved in something shady or illegal. Because if you are –."

Another peace gesture from me. "No, no, no. What I am talking about is that you build a comprehensive picture of your son. Who he was; who his friends are; what he did on a daily basis. Paint yourself a detailed picture. It will surely be the small details that prove to be most important. A forgotten detail could prove crucial. Something unknown to you and your wife – or so I am fondly assuming – led to his murder. That unknown will only surface, if it does, by intense reflection on the minutiae of your son's life. You now owe it to him to get to know him like you've never known him before."

I let that thought hang in the air.

Some of the hostile air that had puffed him up drained out of him. He stared at me without speaking for several seconds, then turned abruptly and headed back to his car.

I called out to him. "Mr. Hollsworth."

He stopped and turned. His anger now blended with grief and disorientation.

"When you've given all of this a lot more thought, I would appreciate your help. I'd like you and your wife to share with me what you remember; allow me to prompt you both to see if you might be able to remember even more. I obviously didn't know your son, but I know he didn't deserve the fate some cruel bastard handed him. I want to help find that person. It's part of what I do."

Without answering, Douglas Hollsworth, firefighter and father, returned to his car and drove away. When my cell phone rang a few minutes later, Jack Stonecipher was on the other end of the call.

"I got your messages, Wile. And Stacy called. She said that, through Dupree's Visa card, she found him registered at Aliante Station. I'll check it out."

That took me aback. "I wonder what he's doing out there?" The far north end of town.

"Maybe he's trying to peddle some of his clunkers for use in one of the speedway's demolition derbys," Jack said.

Aliante Station is one of the newer casinos in the Station chain. It had been built near Las Vegas Motor Speedway and the hotel had quickly become popular with the NASCAR crowd. But the speedway promoted a year-round schedule, also hosting USAC events, such as midgets, and sundry NHRA hot rod shows, as well as NASCAR races. And Labor Day always featured a demolition derby.

"Let me know. I'm still trying to figure out if he lied to his wife or if she lied to me. Let me know if he's humping anyone besides the local hookers," I said.

"Will do. Oh, FYI, Eduardo Ruiz was dumber than we gave him credit for. He's been picked up in San Antonio. Apparently on his way to Fort Lauderdale. He has a cousin there who works on a cruise line. The cousin was going to get him some discount tickets on a cruise through the Panama Canal. The dumb fuck stays on this side of the border in order to save a few bucks on a boat ride, all the time he's carrying a suitcase full of enough cash to buy his own cruise ship. I'll never figure out some of these clowns."

I said, "Is the cousin male or female?"

Jack laughed. "You're right. I hadn't thought about that. Maybe the cousin is a better piece than money can buy."

"Was Mama with him?" I said.

"You kiddin'? He dropped his mother off in El Paso, gave her a fistful of greenbacks to exchange for pesos, then told her to cross over into Juarez and catch a bus for wherever."

"The Florida cousin is a female. Bet on it," I said.

"Right. I'll call you after I check out the Aliante."

"Don't forget to dress up like a Billy Bob and be sure to mention your cousin in Talladega. You might be eligible for a discount."

"Discount? Why, with a pinch of Skoal, a dab of Pennzoil aftershave, and a quick flash of my wad of Ulysses S. Grants, I'll charm some pretty desk clerk into comping me a top-floor suite. I'll tell her I'm the Whale from Sylacauga."

I said, "Just make sure you know the names of the coaches in Tuscaloosa and Auburn. With your luck the clerk will be a newbie, just off the boat from Birmingham."

"Gotcha, boss."

The accusation by Doug Hollsworth that I had been harassing the people I interviewed stuck in my craw. What put that bee in his fireman's bonnet? After not much thought, I decided the affront had to have been generated by Sebastian Sechrest. I made a mental note to revisit the band director soon and see if I could adjust his attitude – along with his bow tie.

19

Adelle was not going to be home for dinner. Tuesday nights were special getaway evenings for her. She belonged to a local literary circle, consisting mostly of retired librarians and schoolteachers, mostly from the Midwest. Once a week they gathered in a living room of one of the members and read favored passages to one another from beloved tomes, mostly Victorian and pre-Victorian-vintage novels. Titles Adelle had mentioned were Dickens, Jane Austen, and Arthur Conan Doyle, even though the latter had outlived Queen Vicky by some thirty years.

And, because most of the ladies in Adelle's book circle had spent their lives and careers in the Midwest, the event preceding their reading exchange was as cherished a tradition as the works of fiction themselves – a potluck supper. Most of the women, Adelle claimed, prided themselves on, and had earned kudos for, their casseroles. My sister, by contrast, was envied for her Southwest dishes and the smell of her Chicken Enchilada Santa Fe still hung in the air as I contemplated the need to feed myself. So I decided on Mexican and knew just where to go. I told myself that where I was headed would even permit me to snare two chickens with one throw of a gaucho's bola.

Cantina Graciela, where Kristy Serling worked as a hostess, was a gray adobe building with fake *vigas* across the roof front to make the building appear as if had been built a hundred years earlier. I knew better, because Arroyo Arenoso itself was less than sixty years old. I also knew there had been no previous pueblo village on the land the town now occupied.

The cantina resided in a prime downtown location, at the intersection of Avenida Casita Turquesa and Calle de Niza, the main street through town. I parked in the nearly empty lot in back and watched a cook with a net over his hair toss a pair of trash bags into a dumpster while shooing away a mongrel dog.

The cantina's interior walls were covered with large, glossy, acrylic murals depicting scenes from Aztec and Mayan legends. On one was a javalina-wielding warrior poised to hurl his spear at a jaguar ready to pounce on a hapless maiden lying on the ground. In another a feather-capped chieftain held an arrow aloft in one hand while pointing to a soaring eagle with his other hand. Most of the murals portrayed muscular bronzed males defending beautiful, vulnerable, lighter-skinned females who either lay prone on stony terrain or else huddled fearfully behind rocks too small to hide them.

Not a conquistador or Catholic priest anywhere on the walls. The overall theme reflected a proud and potent civilization which, though hardly paradise, had not yet been brought to its knees by emissaries from the Spanish crown.

A woman who turned out to be Graciela herself saw me staring at the art work, stopped wiping down a table, slung her bar towel onto her shoulder, and approached me. "What do you think, eh?"

I said, "It makes an interesting contrast when you consider this building perches on a street named for a loathsome priest."

She laughed. It was a pleasing laugh and echoed off the murals. "Ah! Marcos the Liar. You know his story then," she said.

"I know he was the man who conned Coronado into looking for the Seven Cities."

"And they found them! Zuni villages filled with ragged children. Full of blowing sand, but no gold." She laughed again. "So much for conquistadors, eh?"

"I notice a shortage of them, too, on your murals."

"De Niza was known as Marcos the Liar already when he whispered in Coronado's ear," she said. "And off Francisco went anyway. What's a fool!"

"The Zunis are great silversmiths. I've bought my sister several pairs of gorgeous earrings made by Zuni craftsmen."

"Silver, yes. But not gold. And the Spanish were too stupid to find even the silver."

"Am I too late to get lunch?" The cantina was empty except for a pair of barflies wearing baseballs caps and well-worn cowboy boots.

"Normally, yes. It's almost dinner time, Señor. But for you I will make an exception. You know what a scoundrel De Niza was. I'm impressed."

"Thank you. And, speaking of silver, do you stock Silver Patron?"

"I do. Of course. A margarita for you then."

"No. Straight liquor. No salt, but a slice a lime."

"Coming up. And here's the lunch menu."

When Graciela Bardella went off to pour my drink I seated myself in a booth where I could look out on the street named for the notorious Franciscan friar. When she returned I ordered spinach enchiladas and fish tacos.

"My murals are not too violent to suit you?"

I took a sip of tequila. "Compared with contemporary Mexican art, they are quite peaceful actually."

"Yes. Two young locals did them for me. I had to… how do you say? Contain their enthusiasm."

"You contained them very well."

"Indeed! You should see their other works."

"Violent. Lots of grotesque faces," I said.

She nodded. "When Dia de los Meuertos comes around you should see the town. They put their stuff everywhere and it makes *gringo* Halloween seem like–." She folded her hands together, prayer like, and posed a faux-beatific smile. "Like the Blessed Mary and Jesus." She pronounced Jesus as Hay-soos.

I finally got to the point of my being there. "Does Kristy Serling work tonight?"

Graciela gave me a look then glanced at her watch. "In an hour and a half. Six o'clock. The dinner rush doesn't begin until then." She paused, then said, "Now I recognize who you must be. You are the detective from Las Vegas, the one Rollie Morton wishes would keep his nose away from his murder investigation of the high school boy."

I thought her use of high school boy represented a deliberate distancing of herself from the young man. "Did you know Bobby Shane?"

She hesitated, then said, "*Por quito.*" A little bit.

"Did he come here often?"

"To eat?"

I gave her a come-off-it look. "To see Kristy."

"Once in a while."

"Meaning?"

She scowled. "Every night Kristy worked, I had to warn both of them about his interfering with her doing her job."

"Did he take the warning?'

"Not from me, but Kristy knew I was serious. Yes, she has a cute smile and a cute ass, but so do plenty of other girls who go to the high school. I like her and she is reliable. She doesn't drink; she doesn't smoke. But even so –."

I got the message. Kristy is easily replaceable. Apparently Kristy got the message, too.

"What's your name, Mister Detective? Rollie told me, but I have since forgotten."

"Wiley Poynter."

She giggled. "Wiley? As in the coyote?"

"Yes."

"What was your mother thinking to give you such a name?"

"I don't know. I never asked her."

"You should ask."

"She's dead."

"I'm sorry." A shrug. "Eh! We all make mistakes."

"What else did Chief Morton tell you about me, besides my name?"

"That you are meddling in his murder investigation."

"Meddling."

"*Si.*"

"No, I don't think so. I don't think Chief Morton has much experience in solving murder cases. So I am trying to help him by lending my experience."

"He calls it meddling." She turned and walked off to hand my order to the cook, who I hoped washed his hands after taking out the garbage. She returned quickly. "Tell me how you can help solve this murder, Señor Wiley Coyote."

"I poke my nose into people's business."

"Rollie is poking, too, of course."

"Yes, but I have a feeling he doesn't quite know where or how to poke to get the best results."

"And you do?" She looked skeptical.

"Tell me more about what you know of Bobby Shane."

"Ha! What makes you think I know anything?"

I gave her another stop-toying-with-me look. "Surely in this town everybody knows everybody else's business. And I'm sure Graciela Barella knows more than anyone else."

She sat down across from me. "No. it doesn't work quite that way. In this town we know everything about the *gringo,* but they know almost nothing about us… us *critura marrones pequeñas.*"

I smiled. "That's what you call yourselves? Little brown critters?"

"There may be more of us, but that does not mean we are big."

"But you know everything about the *gringos.*"

"*Nosotras no sabemos todo.*" When people feel stress, they tend to lapse back into their language of childhood.

"I don't expect you to know everything, but surely you've heard rumors."

"*Yo no soy un chisme.*"

"Señora, I am not accusing you of being a gossipmonger. But surely you've heard things."

A slow shrug that only Latinas can effect.

"You've heard something that might help me? A clue of some kind?"

She looked up at the Aztec warriors, but then crossed herself. "Bobby and Kristy, they fight."

"A serious quarrel?"

"When a woman threatens to cut off a man's *cojones*, that is serious, no?"

My knees instinctively edged closer to one another.

"What prompted such a threat?" I said.

Just then a pair of middle-aged snowbirds wearing sunglasses walked into the restaurant and looked about, their sunburned faces a mixture of awe and bewilderment. They removed their shades and continued to peer around cautiously, as if an Aztec god might suddenly loose a bolt of lightning at them.

Graciela stood. "I have new customers. You would do best to ask Kristy why she made such a threat. But do not question her here, on my time."

My cell phone rang. The call came from Adelle, who had stopped home to change clothes before heading to her literary group's gathering. She said that the school's principal, a Mrs. Haydenfurth, had scheduled a memorial service for Bobby in the school auditorium Friday morning. Mr. Sechrest would give a eulogy on behalf of the faculty; Juanita Bardella would speak for the students, given that Perry Crisp, Jason Altheiser, Richie Maldonado, and Kristy Serling had all declined the principal's offer to address the assembly.

"Don't you think that odd?" Adelle said, referring to the refusal by some of Bobby's closest friends to honor him.

"There is obviously a lot of collective anger there, Dell. The principle of speaking only good of the dead is itself dead. I hope Juanita chooses her words carefully."

"I think Mrs. Haydenfurth intends to provide her with lots of advice."

"Have fun at your meeting," I said.

"I intend to. Where do you intend to dine?"

I explained that I was already sitting at Graciela's.

"Enjoy," she said, and hung up.

My enchiladas and tacos arrived, delivered by the cook himself. His hands looked clean and I set about replacing the growl in my stomach with the burning sensation of jalapeno-laced salsa. By the time I finished eating, a younger waiter whose name tag identified him as Jose Luis brought my check. A young cashier with a face resembling Graciela's – perhaps another daughter – took my money and gave me change. Graciela herself had disappeared.

20

"So how was your discussion session?" I asked Adelle when she returned home. I was watching a Charlie Chan movie, *Meeting at Midnight,* from 1944, streaming from Netflix on Adelle's 40-inch Samsung when she returned home. I preferred Warner Oland to Sidney Toler in the Chan role. Oland had preceded Toler in the earlier '30's Chan flicks. But Netflix only had the Oland films available on DVD. When the studio released *Meeting at Midnight* the movie bore the title *Black Magic.* The plot involved a bizarre collection of spiritualists and occultists. It was far from my favorite, but I had decided it would do.

"We discussed *The Redheaded League* and read portions from it. It's not one of my favorite Holmes stories. The gimmick is too contrived," she said.

"And the food?"

"Many excellent dishes, as always. What did you manage to find to eat?"

I told her what I ate at Graciela's.

"Her chicken enchiladas are almost as good as mine."

"But her tacos aren't."

"I know," Adelle made a face. Then she took a look at what I was watching. "Oh, my God, who is that?" She was pointing at Mantan Moreland in his role of Birmingham Brown, Charlie Chan's chauffeur.

I explained.

"Sounds and looks mighty racist to me," she said.

"That was the '40's. Yes, Birmingham is a Step-and-Fetchit type buffoon role. But nobody calls him 'nigger' and Mantan, like Hatty Daniels, was thankful to have regular studio employment, even if it amounted to playing stereotypical clownish characters."

"Feets, don't fail me now?" Adelle said.

"That's from another '40's movie. Also the title of a Herbie Hancock album. But, yes, Mantan might as well have said it. That's the level of script dialogue he got."

Adelle put her hands on her hips. "And the reason you are watching this film?"

"Detective documentary?"

"Yeah, right."

I shrugged.

"I have almost as many satellite channels as there are stars in the sky, plus several thousand Netflix streaming options and this is what I come home to find you watching?"

I stood and put my hands on my hips, mocking her faux-indignation. "You have a public library full of classics, including the entire canon from Conan Doyle to choose from and you come home to tell me you and your friends spent an entire evening nattering at one another about *The Redheaded League?*"

She smiled. "*Touché*, Brother. I guess I should have seen that coming."

"Glass of wine? A beer? A finger of Turkey?" I offered.

"No, thanks. I don't wish to teach with a headache in the morning." She paused. "That reminds me. School scuttlebutt is that Chief Morton is abandoning his drug-deal-gone-wrong theory. Or at least backing off from it. I hear tell that the coroner has told him the burn marks on Bobby Shane's body were inflicted after he was dead."

"Oh, really? That's interesting. Someone wanted it to look like he had been tortured."

"Indeed! And did I forget to mention the police found Bobby Shane's truck? It was hiding almost in plain sight. Parked behind the bowling alley. Someone at the bowling alley reported its being there Sunday morning, after the news of the murder was spreading like wildfire."

"Any reason it was there?" I said.

"Well… Richie works at the bowling alley as a pin-setter. Bobby Shane, by the way, was very much opposed to Richie's working there. He kept telling Richie that Richie was going to end up with broken fingers, or a broken hand or wrist one of these days and then he might no longer have the necessary agility to manipulate his drumsticks."

"To which Richie replied?" I said.

"Richie continued to work there. So I can only imagine that conversation," Adelle said, giggling slightly.

"Speaking of Richie, Dell, do you think you could ask Richie to meet with me again? I'd also like to meet with Kristy and Juanita." I told my sister that one of the reasons I ate at Graciela's was in the hope of finding Kristy there.

"I'll see what I can do," she said.

"And try not to let Sebastian Sechrest know what you are up to." I explained the visit from Bobby Shane's father and who I suspected put the bug in his ear that I was harassing the students.

"Sometimes Sebastian can be worse than Mrs. Fortunato. He's a very bitter man. I'm not sure why. Sometimes I think that man goes out of his way to make trouble for people who don't deserve it."

I said, "By the way, Dell. Where is this scuttlebutt coming from?"

She gave me a sheepish grin. In a low voice, she said, "Pillow talk."

"Oh really? Whose pillow? Or is that a secret?"

"Not if you promise not to tell. I'm pretty sure I'm the only one she told."

"She. Does *she* have a name?"

"Swear on mother's grave not to tell?"

I reminded her, "Mother's grave is along way from here."

"You can be so literal-minded when you want to be."

I held up my hand oath-style. "I hereby solemnly –."

"Stop it. Her name is Chloe Logary. She teaches algebra, trigo-nometry, and pre-calculus. Her husband in on the Arroyo Arenoso police force."

"And he won't be for long if Chief Morton finds out state secrets have been dribbling out of his mouth and onto Mata Hari's thousand-thread-count pillow," I said.

"Exactly."

"My lips are sealed."

"I hope so. But then you've always been pretty good about keeping stuff confidential."

"Yes indeed. I lied to Mom and Dad many a time to cover your sneaky back side. Like Sergeant Schultz, I knew nothing."

"Anyway, Chloe knows my brother is snooping around. Besides, I'm not sure how much confidence she has in Chief Morton."

I said, "I hope she doesn't put that opinion in any e-mails. Or worse, on her Facebook page."

"Chloe is smarter than that."

I hoped so. Yet, here she was, blabbing restricted information to my sister. Everyone confides in one person he or she is sure won't pass on a deep secret. And, before long, the whole world knows. One innocent drop of gossip eventually produces a flood. And each drop holds itself harmless of contributing to the collective result.

I wished Adelle good night and headed back to the TV to see what was playing on HBO. At that moment my cell phone rang. The caller was Andy Kudarski.

"Sorry I didn't show up for lunch yesterday. I was in bed – passed out. And, no, I wasn't hung over. I was doped up – prescription stuff. Legit. I belong to a martial arts group here in Tucson and we held some no-holds-barred, free-for-all matches the night before. I sort of got the shit kicked out of me. Several of the members have been around a lot longer than I have and have their black belts."

"So let's arrange for another meeting. Okay," I said.

"I'm feeling well enough to meet with you, but not well enough to scarf down any Bison Witches grub. We can meet here at my place, if you like."

"Okay. When?"

"You name it. I'm the one who stood you up."

"Tomorrow? Lunchtime again?"

"Sure. But I don't have anything to feed you."

"How about I bring you some Jewish penicillin."

"Some what?"

"Chicken soup."

"Yeah. That'd be cool. I think my jaw is flexible enough to chew some soup."

I wrote down his address and directions how to get there. He lived in an apartment complex off Campbell, north of Speedway. Adelle appeared in her nightgown and I gave her a goodnight peck. Then I watched a couple of episodes of *Lie to Me* via Netflix. I liked Tim Roth's role as a cocky, in-your-face psychologist. He was the opposite of Charlie Chan. Nothing polite or humble about his Cal Lightman character. But, like Charlie, he got the job done. The villains all went to jail.

I finally went to bed, but I knew I wasn't going to sleep the sleep of the dead. I've never been convinced the dead sleep anyway. Sleep, to me, implies you eventually wake up and I didn't hold much faith in resurrections or Judgment Day.

21

Wednesday

I fixed myself an omelet stuffed with chorizo and green onions before setting out for Tucson. Adelle had already left for school, having left me a note that she had been unable to find the morning newspaper and assumed Mrs. Fortunato's boxer had escaped her neighbor's yard again and had stolen it. An infrequent but annoying occurrence, according to my sister. Ironically, the brindle beast's name was Fetch.

In Tucson I stopped on Fourth Avenue at the Antigone Bookstore to look for a hostess present for Adelle. The store is one of the few surviving independent bookstores in chain-addicted America and advertises itself as *"zany... with a feminist slant"*. My sister was one of its regular customers. After browsing briefly, I settled on books by a couple of local authors. One was a how-to book on desert landscaping. Adelle was a firm opponent of grass in the desert and especially the water requisite to keep it green. Her yards, front and back, were filled with sundry cacti and a couple of acacia trees, but I thought maybe she could find a new idea or two that would add some luster without adding much in time or expense. The second book was a novel, a thriller with a female Shakespearean-play director as protagonist. I knew nothing about the author, other than the jacket blurb touting her as a former award-winning teacher at Harvard.

My next stop was the Golden Dragon restaurant on Speedway Boulevard, just east of Campbell. There I asked for a double order of hot and sour soup and a single order of chicken chop suey to go. If Andy Kudarski was a beaten up as he claimed he was, he needed veggies to mend his hide and his soul. The Dragon's chop suey contained Chinese cabbage, bamboo shoots, mushrooms, carrots, celery, water chestnuts, broccoli, and bean sprouts. I also asked for an extra dash of white pepper in the soup.

The young face that answered the door when I rang the apartment door bell looked as if he had gone five rounds with Ali – without wearing gloves. The kid's left eye was swollen nearly shut. He held an ice pack to his face. I wondered if he had given thought to abandoning the jade earring in his right ear. His ear lobe looked as though his opponent, whoever he was, had tried to rip in out.

"Are you Poynter?" he said sullenly.

I nodded and held up the takeout containers. "Doctor Wiley Chan Poynter, acupuncture, chop suey, and murder investigation. Number One Son not available to assist. You are Andrew Kudarski?"

With what I took to be an affirmative grunt, he opened the door and beckoned me to enter his humble abode. It was not only humble but messy.

"Sorry. I've been too fucked up to clean the place. Hope you don't mind."

I thought, and what if I did mind? Would a pair of brown-skinned maids instantly appear and tidy everything up? I gave him an I-don't-mind shrug that I didn't entirely mean. I had the feeling that, if he had been in tip-top shape, the place would not look much different.

He plucked a couple of soiled sweatshirts from the end of a sofa and gestured for me to sit where they had been. He flopped into a brown beanbag chair on the far side of a glass-top coffee table.

I set the Chinese food on the table and tossed him a packet with a plastic fork and spoon. "Eat. Then we'll talk."

"Thanks. It's been a while since I've eaten. I hope I can manage the soup without a straw." He placed the ice pack on the coffee table, fiddled with the spoon pack, then slurped some of the hot and sour soup and found he could deal with it.

I spooned a few mouthfuls of soup and watched him pick out the mushrooms and set them aside before launching into the rest of the chop suey.

After a while he set down the food box and plastic fork. "So Jason's fearless bandleader backed into a knife, did he?"

Always good if my interviewee sets the tone of the conversation for me right off. "You've met Bobby, I take it?"

"Oh, yeah. I know all about Banjo Bobby."

I made a give-me-your-impressions-of-him gesture.

"I'd just as soon piss on him as look at him," he said, and screwed up his face.

"I'm afraid you've missed that opportunity."

"So I hear. Too bad."

"Would you care to enumerate the ways he rubbed you the wrong way?" I said.

Andy Kudarski tensed. "Rubbed me the wrong way?" he said, unsure how to take it. "Are you fucking with me?"

I gave him a poker face and said, "Words and phrases do often have a knife edge to them, don't they? Rubbing. Fucking. And it's obvious your ears are keenly attuned to hints of snide jabs and insults, right?"

"You know Jason and I are flaming faggots, don't you?"

"If that's how you choose to describe yourselves."

"No. That's how Bobby Shane Almighty Hollsworth chose to describe us."

"Jason has told me Bobby was disdainful of your sexual orientations."

"Disdainful. Right. Makes it sound as if he disapproved of my choice in neckties. 'Oooooh, Andy, that's a bit to bright, and maybe a tad too wide for current fashion. Why don't you try the darker, narrow one?'"

I said, "How about mocking, condescending, derisive, scornful, or sneering?"

"Sneering? Yeah. That comes closest. But even that doesn't capture the sense that Bobby thought we are vile, despicable monsters, scaly little ogres with red eyes, green skin, and purple tails that slither around in the dark, make howling sounds, and leave trails of oozing yellow slime. That's who and what we are, Mr. Chinese Take-out Man. Swamp creatures with vocal chords."

"So? Did you kill him?"

"The thought crossed my mind. More than once."

"That doesn't answer my question."

"So it doesn't." Pause. "No, I didn't kill him. But, even if I did, I'd still be telling you no."

"Did Jason?"

Andy cocked his head. "I honestly don't know if he did or not. Have you asked him?"

I nodded.

"Of course, he'd say no," Andy said, matter-of-factly. "Confessions are for the last three minutes of Perry Mason, aren't they?"

I smiled. "I didn't think you would be old enough to know who Perry Mason is."

"Reruns, my man. Syndication. Dibs and dabs of royalties forever. It's what keeps small-time character actors in lunch money when Hollywood shows them the door. Why, I even recognized your Charlie Chan impersonation."

"Really? You know who Charlie Chan is/was?"

"I took a course in 1930's & '40's film history," Andy said.

"He was an emperor in the Ping Pong Dynasty period, right?"

"Give me some credit, please."

I said, "Okay. And you're also right that confessions are the last refuge of feeble screen plays – plus every episode of Perry Mason."

"Short of a written and notarized confession, how may I really help you?" Andy said. "Sure, we all hated Bobby. But Bobby Shane Hollsworth haters, when formed up single-file, make for a mighty long line, Mr. Detective. It runs for miles and miles. Over hill, over dale. And I must tell you, there are plenty of nastier bastards than us in that lineup."

"Who is 'we'?" I said.

"Come on. I'll show you."

Andy's bedroom turned out to be much tidier than I had anticipated, given the messy living room. His bed was even made and free of bachelor-living-alone litter. One wall was papered with posters of martial arts photos, some portraits of Asian men, most of whom were wearing the traditional *gi*. The only face I recognized was that of Bruce Lee. Other posters showed young men in what I took to be traditional combat poses, mostly pairs engaged at close quarters.

On the opposite wall, above a dresser, hung martial arts weapons, knives, sticks of various lengths, throw-able, sharply pointed, star-shaped pieces, and a set of bamboo-and-chain weapons I knew were called *nunchakus*. A Jewish friend of mine at UNLV who had a black belt in karate owned a pair and had once demonstrated how they represented a vast improvement – his description – over police nightsticks.

Atop the dresser sat a group photo Andy picked up and handed to me. "These are my guys," he said proudly.

"And they are –?"

"We call ourselves the Chicken Wings. It's a play on the phrase Wing Chun, which is our style of martial art combat. The name comes from a Chinese woman named Yim Wing-chun. She was a disciple of Ng Mui, an abbess at a Shaolin Buddhist temple called Siu Lam during the early part of the Qing Dynasty. Around the year 1700. The government was convinced Ng was hiding revolutionary enemies of the state. According to the legend, when Ng fled, she saw a snake and a crane fighting. She later incorporated those creatures' movements into a style of boxing. Our discipline is named for the young female pupil, Yim Wing-chun, to whom Ng taught her new style of martial art."

"So you're now the Chicken Wings."

"Others call us the Chicken Wing Queers. All of us in the photo are gay, including our instructor – the guy in the black *gi* in the middle – Quan Chin Lee."

"Mr. Lee doesn't look any older than the rest of you," I said.

"He's isn't – by much. Twenty-nine maybe," Andy said.

"I don't see Jason."

"He's not a member of our group. At least not yet. We meet with Mr. Lee on Thursday afternoons. Not enough time for Jason to drive up from Arroyo Arenoso after school, then get back in time for band practice. But he says he intends to join as soon as he graduates. He's coming to U of A, you know. Right now I give him an informal lesson whenever he and I get together on our own. I'm not very good yet, as my face attests to. But I hope to earn my black belt eventually."

Well. So much for the stereotyped notion that all homosexual males are pansies. That false assumption could get a straight guy's ass kicked. And probably has.

"Do any of the other Chicken Wings know Jason?" I said.

"They all do. Jason's come to some of our parties."

"Are any of your comrades aware of Bobby Hollsworth's homophobia?"

"Yeah. It's common knowledge."

I stared at him.

"You think any of us believes the way to eradicate homophobia is to kill off assholes like Bobby? Jesus, man. It would take genocide on the scale of the Holocaust to wipe them all out. Bobby Shane Hollsworth is merely one snowflake in the avalanche, man. Time and patience is the only answer. That's what Quan Chin Lee keeps preaching to us."

I nodded. "But not everyone is equally up to the task of suffering fools gladly."

"I know that. We all know that. But we aren't killers."

"You can speak for everyone?"

"Well… I'd like to think so."

"But?"

A shrug.

I had to decide whether I wanted to interview each of the other members of the Chicken Wings. My decision was: Not yet. I had other toes to toast first.

22

I left Andrew Kudarski adding more ice to his facial pack. Clearly no punches got pulled at Mr. Lee's strip mall martial arts dojo. I wondered what that attitude did for the honorable instructor's turnover rate. Maybe Quan Chin Lee owned a trust fund and didn't worry about student tuition to pay his rent and utility bill. For the next couple of weeks Andy's face was not going to serve as a very good advertisement for lessons in successfully kicking ass.

As I walked back to my car I had flashes of an ad page from my Uncle Lloyd's collection of classic comic books. A dude named Mac, described as a ninety-pound weakling, lay on a beach minding his own business. A tough-guy jerk walks up and kicks sand in Mac's face. How does Mac respond? He signs up for Charles Atlas' Dynamic Tension program and eventually receives the Diploma for Physical Perfection from the Charles Atlas Physical Culture School. I forget how much such a diploma cost. Adjusted for inflation, it was probably more than Mr. Lee charged a dweeb like Andy to learn to pound sand up the asses of those who kicked sand in his face. Or called him a faggot.

After leaving Andy's apartment I drove west on Speedway, turned onto Fourth Avenue, and began looking for a place to park. I had decided to take another crack at talking to someone at the betting parlor about Bobby Shane's gambling habit.

As I crossed Fourth and headed east, I saw two black-and-whites belonging to the Tucson Police Department parked in front of the house and saw Miss Housely standing on her porch in her bathrobe gazing at events next door. Two uniformed cops emerged from the betting parlor; then one abruptly turned and reentered.

Miss Housely's Westie saw me and began yapping, causing the old lady to turn. When she saw me she gave me a little wave of recognition. I waved back and continued up her walkway to inquire if she knew what was happening.

"Didn't you read this morning's newspaper? Or watch the morning news on TV?" she said.

I silently damned Mrs. Fortunato's boxer again for absconding with Adelle's *Arizona Daily Star*. I professed ignorance to Miss Housely and apologized.

She filled me in. "One of the nice young men who lives there was murdered last night."

"Which one?" I said.

"The big fellow."

Although I had not met Colby's housemates, I assumed she meant him. "The one with the dragon tattoos on his arms?"

She nodded. "Such a kind, gentle soul. Poor man."

Gentle? I doubted that. Kind? Maybe now and then. Poor? In the sense of unfortunate, yes. Otherwise? Eh. "He was killed inside the house?"

"Oh, no. His body was found in an alley several blocks from here. Over toward campus. Some students discovered him around midnight."

"Do you know what killed him?"

"The newspaper describe his death as a result of multiple stab wounds to his back," Miss Housely said with a shudder.

Pending the coroner's verdict, no doubt. But I didn't suppose poor Colby slipped on a banana peel and fell backwards onto a medieval iron maiden.

"I hope you have a solid alibi, Miss Housely. Will your West Highland terrier vouch for your being at home all night last night?"

She smiled. "I'm sure he will, if called upon. And I assure you, Bagpipe is a trustworthy witness."

I looked down at Bagpipe and he gave me an I'll-say-what-ever-she-tells-me-to-say look. Unconditional loyalty. Too bad it's not contagious.

"Will this affect the landlord's insurance?" the old lady said.

I had nearly forgotten the subterfuge I had fed her on my first visit. "Uh, no, ma'am. I don't think so. Not unless we find out there is dangerous or illegal activity going on within the premises." I hoped that might prompt her to tell me if she had a clue about the bookmaking business the occupants were operating.

"Oh, I don't think anything like that is likely. They are such all such nice, sweet boys."

Lordy. Yet another instance of the serial-killer's-neighbor syndrome. *Sancta simplicitas!* I thanked Miss Housely for her information. She in turn apologized for my finding her still wearing her nightgown.

"Some days I simply don't feel like bothering with the formalities of putting on attire suitable for receiving. At my age I am entitled to such eccentricities. The world may take me or leave me as they find me."

Bagpipe added a damned-right bark of concurrence. I returned to my car and drove back toward Arroyo Arenoso, wondering if there was any connection between the murders of Bobby Hollsworth and Colby Ambrose. And, if so, what it might be.

I had no sooner exited the interstate, headed toward my sister's house when a city cruiser came up behind me with his flashing lights on. I dutifully pulled over. As I handed over my Nevada driver's license, I saw the policeman's badge read: Michael Logary.

"Just confirming that you are Mr. Poynter. Chief Morton wants a word with you. He even said to add 'please'. But he also said to tell you 'pronto'."

"And what reason did he give?" I said.

"I'm just the messenger, sir."

"Well, you may tell the chief that you have delivered the message."

"Have a nice day, Mr. Poynter."

The trick to having a nice day is to find one. Nice days don't grow as thickly on the tree as they did when I was a kid trying to figure out whether to spend a leisurely summer afternoon oiling my Reggie Jackson baseball mitt or polishing my Jack Nicklaus McGregor golf clubs. I can't remember the last time I strolled into the orchard and plucked a nice juicy day off a tree without even having to reach above my head. Nowadays, "Have a nice day" is as full of wishful thinking as, "Good luck finding cheap gas."

Finding out what the chief of police wanted could wait. If I was going to get my ass chewed on, I wanted to undergo that torment on a full stomach. Mid-afternoon and I hadn't eaten since breakfast. Adelle's refrigerator offered slim pickings. No one could accuse my sister of being a food hoarder. Instead, she had a French housewife penchant for shopping every day. Sufficient unto each day are the fresh veggies therein, could be her motto. Concomitant with that, she was not a fan of leftovers. I cut off a chunk of sharp cheddar cheese, sliced it into pieces, slapped the pieces between some lah-dee-dah crackers, washed each mini-sandwich down with a swig of Coors and called it lunch.

Arroyo Arenoso's municipal buildings took up a small corner of a wannabe industrial park on the western edge of town. Police headquarters faced the Fire Department. A common parking lot for cops and firefighters separated the two red brick buildings. Nearby I counted six buildings with identical architecture that housed other state and local government agencies, including City Hall. I guess governments counted as industries, too. The only non-governmental structure on the designated land so far was an auto parts warehouse.

Chief Roland Morton sat behind a large oak desk. This was the first time I had seen him without his hat on. In his case, male-pattern-baldness genes had nearly completed their evolutionary task – for whatever intelligent-free design purpose the powers of the universe had created them. I don't care what sex-starved, drooling old ladies claim. Bald is not beautiful. Hirsute trumps glabrous every time.

The chief had his feet propped up on his desk and didn't move when a tomboyish-looking female deputy ushered me into his office and closed the door behind her when she left. I declined his offer to help myself from the half pot of what smelled like burnt coffee sitting on a side counter. I did accept the visitor's chair across from him.

"I've been checking up on you," he said by, way of introduction.

"And what did you discover?"

"My counterparts in Las Vegas don't think much of you."

"Nor I of them."

"Yeah. They told me that, too. They said you aren't much good for anything other than finding a missing person every six months or so. And that, they assure me, is strictly an achievement based on the blind pigs and acorns principle."

"That principle, however, does produce more success than the –." I paused to clear my throat before singing, "'Leave them alone and they'll come home, wagging their tails behind them' principle, which is their first, second, and third lines of attack whenever someone files a missing-person's report with them."

"I imagine most folks who go missing in Sin City are of age and do so of their own volition," the chief said.

"Subtract those folks and there are still a lot left over," I replied.

"LV Metropolitan PD also tells me you can't seem to keep your nose out of murder cases."

I scratched my head. "Funny. They don't give a shit about a missing person until said missing person turns up dead. And then they suddenly take a proprietary interest in the said missing person. Butt out, they say. We'll handle it now. We're the professionals."

"And so they are."

"Tricking themselves up in uniforms may allow them to call themselves professionals. But it doesn't make them any more competent than the clowns in Cirque Soleil at solving how the missing person – whom they assume ran off of his or her own accord – is now dead, not of his or her own accord."

"But you are competent?"

I stood and, in a mock-bass voice, said, "Let the record show, Your Honor, that the defendant, Mr. Poynter, has demonstrated equal or better competence at solving the murders he has investigated than the Clarke County Homicide Unit. And that the defendant is fully prepared to swear to that competence under oath."

"You're here because I'm offering you a truce. Sit down and convince me you can solve Bobby Shane Hollsworth's murder faster than I can."

I sat. "All I can offer is my past record. I admit that is merely inductive evidence. No guarantee. But more than a hint that I can likely be of help."

"So what have you found so far?"

"No, no, no. So far I've unearthed *nada*, but even if I had –."

"You'd withhold evidence?"

"I'd withhold unsubstantiated speculations."

He sat and stared at me, mistrustful.

I said, "I hear a rumor you are working on a drug-deal-gone-sour angle."

He mimicked me. "No, no, no. So far –." He laughed at his own cleverness. He consulted some notes. "I spoke with a Lieutenant Adrian Lindstrom in Missing Persons on the LVMPD. He actually had a couple of kind things to say about you – amid all the crap he shoveled on you. Detective Captain Stan O'Rourke had nothing good to say about you. I believe the words *arrogant* and *asshole* came up several times each in his conversation with me."

"That's because the letter 'A' is as far as Stanley ever got when he tried to learn the alphabet. If his mother had taken the time to stand him in front of a mirror, *blatant bullshitting bastard* would have rolled right off his tongue, based on the self-image he was seeing."

Maybe Chief Morton had gotten that impression of Captain O'Rourke, too, because he changed the subject. "You've been driving into Tucson an awful lot. You like to drive? Or just like to burn gas?"

"Better restaurants."

"Can't your sister cook to suit you?"

"She's a great cook, but she's not my personal chef. She has a day job, if you recall. She definitely works harder than I do. Herding two or three dozen teenagers is tougher than herding a hundred cats."

"I know. I contribute one of my own to her colleagues' herds."

"So I can't expect her to come home from riding the range and turn into the chuck wagon cook. Besides, I'm fond of lunch. She's not even around at lunchtime."

"Try Maya Quetzal." He spelled it for me. "Guatemalan food. You'll like it. It's on Fourth Avenue."

"I think I've seen it."

"If you're not going to go away, all I can do is warn you not to get in my way."

I said, "You've already warned me not to tread on you. Got it. If it's works in California, then surely it will work in Arroyo Arenoso."

"What the hell are you talking about?"

"Never mind. I'll do my very best not to ruffle your feathers. Scout's honor."

"I doubt if you were ever a Boy Scout."

"No, but I shadowed them and copied their every move."

"Get out of here."

I stood, gave him a Boy Scout salute, and tried to count how many feathers Chief Roland Morton had left for me to risk ruffling. He was not amused by my salute. I saw him start to salute me with a middle finger, but he broke off the gesture before he got very far, no doubt deciding it was too unprofessional. Instead, he cocked his head back and looked down his nose toward me, a more dignified way of reminding me that he was the uniformed professional and I was but a pitiful street-clothed amateur.

23

Adelle had arranged for me to meet with Kristy Serling and later with Richie Maldonado at the town's public library, which occupied the old city hall. My sister had told me that, prior to the town's putting up a new city hall in the industrial park, the library has been in a house built by a local cattle baron and occupied by his family for five generations, until the *gringo grandee's* great-great grandson, an only child, failed in his duty to produce a male heir.

I recognized Kristy in spite of her bearing little resemblance to her junior-year photo that Adelle had shown me in the high school yearbook. Her hair was now shorter, her facial features a year closer to the finished look of an adult. The yearbook photo also reminded me that black and white photos fail to convey fully the artifice women intend when they apply makeup. Seeing Kristy in the flesh for the first time, I deemed she had overindulged herself masking her natural beauty. She looked as tarty as an on-stage teenage Miley Cyrus. The only trait that stood out as consistent between who I saw now and the teen in her yearbook photo was the sneer. Maybe she had been born with it. Some women are. Some men, too, for that matter.

My sister had arranged with the head librarian for me to use a small conference room that she told me used to be the city manager's office. When I introduced myself to Kristy and told her to follow me, her handshake and expression were both icy. But at least she complied, however reluctantly.

Kristy sat across from me and immediately folded her arms and scowled. But body language that screamed "Just try to get something out of me" was nothing new to me. I had also learned, however, not to challenge such a posture or even remark on it. Doing so would only increase the unspoken tension.

"I already told the police everything I know."

"Everything? That must have been an all-day interview. Congratulations on being so patient with them," I said.

A peevish shrug.

"You were very upset with Bobby just before he died. What did you tell the police about that?'

A sneer. "Nothing. They didn't ask about that."

"I wonder why not?"

"I dunno. They wanted to know if Bobby did drugs. Shit like that."

"Okay. So I'm asking. Why were you upset with him."

"He was seeing that bitch."

"Whose name is –?"

"Juanita Bardella," she said, trying to look bored.

"Did you ask him why he was seeing her?"

"He said he wasn't seeing her. Fucking liar. I saw him with my own eyes."

"Did you tell him that?"

"Of course. He still denied it."

The Lenny Bruce Defense. Deny everything. Even if they show you pictures.

"What then?"

"I asked him if I had to follow him around twenty-four seven with a camera."

Kristy was too young to have heard of Lenny Bruce.

"What did you see Bobby doing with Juanita?"

"I saw him with his tongue in her mouth."

"Anything else?"

Another shrug. "Bobby's too clever to let the bitch suck him off in public. He no doubt took her out to the county park or else home and into his bedroom."

That sounded to me as though it was the voice of experience speaking.

"Did you break off your relationship with him?"

"Hardly. I figured he'd tire of the spic bitch fast enough; find out she wasn't nearly as hot as he thought she was. Juanita's not the first."

"First what?"

"Not the first pussy to think she's the cat's meow. To give Bobby a taste, only to have Bobby find out she's nothing but baby food, boring mush."

In *Charlie Chan's Greatest Case*, the master detective claims, *"Cat who tries to catch two mice at same time goes without supper."* Could Charlie be wrong? "So you were content to remain patient, let him grow bored with Juanita," I said.

"I didn't like it. But what else was I going to do? Go back to Perry? When you get used to steak, you don't go back to hamburger.

And who else was there? Our high school isn't exactly brimming over with studs. I'd have to go all the way into to U of A to find somebody as hot as Bobby. But even there, a primo chick like me has to do a lot of shopping so she doesn't end up with some frat fuck who's all cock and no brains."

She paused for moment. As I started to ask a question, she started up again. "I went to a few parties at the U. My cousin Emily goes there and she invited me. Most of the parties were cool and a couple were really cool. But you've gotta be careful."

I remained silent, so she went on. "I mean, playing strip pool with guys is a thrill, but once a girl's naked, it can get pretty complicated. I found out it's better to play strip games with guys I already know."

"And trust?"

"Yeah."

I decided to hold off a bit asking about Perry. "What do you think of Jason and Richie?"

"Exact opposites."

"In what ways?"

"Jason's a self-pitying little shit. A born whiner. He's always feeling sorry for himself. Worse, he loves wallowing in martyrdom. It's always 'Poor me. I'm so abused."

"Abused?"

"Okay. Picked on. What does the wimp expect, being a gay *caballero* on a redneck ranch? Of course, everybody thinks he's icky."

"And Richie?"

"Richie's okay. Nothing wimpy about him. He's not exactly *macho*, but he's got Latino pride. He simply oozes a, 'Fuck you, *Gringo*. We were here first' attitude."

"Do you consider him a friend?"

"Not really. We get along, but we definitely don't socialize. The greaseballs stick to themselves, just like all the Mormons. Richie mingles more than most. I mean, he's in Bobby's band, isn't he? Still–."

"Still what?"

"I don't know." She paused. "Don't ask me what's going to happen there. About the band, I mean."

"Perry."

"What about him?" she said. Snippy.

"What did you mean saying he's hamburger?"

"Perry's boring. No sense of adventure. No imagination. There was… an edge to Bobby that I found exciting. Bobby was a risk taker. He liked to push things to the brink, you know? 'Peer into the abyss without falling in.' Those are his words."

"But earlier you said he was always cautious about where he took girls to make out," I said.

"He considered sex in public over the edge. But mooning people or streaking across the county park? Challenging me to join him in going skinny-dipping in a stranger's pool? That was all cool. Stuff like that."

"What do you know about Bobby's gambling habit?" I said.

"He liked to bet on sports teams. Sometimes, when he won big, he'd surprise me with a new pair of earrings. Or some kind of bling."

"Did he win big often?"

"Not often enough to suit me."

"Did he ever lose big?"

She gave a hesitant, "I don't remember."

"Think hard, Kristy. It may be important."

She didn't have to mull very long. "Okay. Yeah. He lost big a few times."

"Where did he get his money to place bets with?"

"Uh, I'm not sure. His own money, I guess. The band got paid for local gigs."

I took a chance, speculating on what I had not even the slightest evidence for yet. Serious gamblers call my bluff *betting on the come.* Betting on cards I didn't hold – yet. "I'm pretty sure he bet a lot more money than he earned, Kristy. And I'm pretty sure even you figured that out some time ago."

Bingo. She failed to maintain eye contact. The answer she was searching for apparently was somewhere high on the wall behind me.

"Maybe his dad gave it to him," was her first feeble stab at covering up something she knew.

Another blind bet on my part. "I'm pretty sure his dad was unaware of the extent to which Bobby placed sports bets. It's even very likely Doug Hollsworth didn't know anything at all about his wagers."

She continued looking off into the Middle Distance.

"Kristy, who loaned him the money?"

"I can't say."

"But you know, right?"

No reply. Rather than press the issue and risk losing her altogether, I changed the subject. "Who do you think killed Bobby?"

"Not me."

"Then give me another name."

A vigorous head shake. "I don't know and don't want to guess."

"That's fair. False accusations can be very damaging."

"Can I go now?" she said.

"You may. But I hope you will call me or come see me if any new information falls into your lap. Or if you think of anything you decide might be important. I'm sure you want to help find Bobby's killer or killers."

"You think more than one person murdered him?" she said.

"I don't know. But I'm keeping an open mind." I gave her my card, with my cell phone on it.

Just then Richie Maldonado peered into the room through the narrow pane of glass next to the door. Kristy stood, turned to go, and saw Richie's face. She turned back to me and said, "Richie knows more than I do."

"About what?" I said.

"About everything." She said it in a low voice, as if Richie might hear her through the thick door.

I opened the door for her and thanked her for seeing me. I then beckoned Richie Maldonado into the room.

24

"So what lies did she tell you?" Richie began, as he sat down where Kristy had been.

"Is Kristy a liar?"

"She's been known to fudge the truth big time now and then."

"Can you give me an example?"

He laughed. "Just one?"

"The stage is yours, Richie."

"I bet she told you what a whore Juanita is, right?"

I was non-committal.

"She dumps on every other good-looking chick in school. Make that every chick. If a chick isn't especially hot, Kristy tells everybody about that, too."

"Damned if you are; damned if you're not?"

"You got it. You know how people say about some folks: that you can tell when they're lying 'cause their lips are movin'. That's Kristy."

"And what about you?" I said. "How do I tell when you're lying to me?"

"I'm not, man. I got nuthin' to hide."

"You're just a drummer in a rock and roll band."

"That's me."

"You work at the bowling alley, I hear."

"A little bit. Sunday afternoons. After church. I'm the pin boy, but that gig ain't what it used to be."

"I thought everything was automated now," I said.

"It is. But somebody's gotta keep an eye on the robots. Sometimes they fuck up. Or take a coffee break, you know. Then I gotta reason with them. But mostly I sit and do my homework. Not bad, getting paid to do homework."

"You're aware Bobby's car was found behind the bowling alley Sunday morning, aren't you?" I said.

"Yeah, but it's there a lot. I didn't think nuthin' of it."

"Even though you knew Bobby was dead? Surely you knew on Sunday, before you went to work, that he was dead."

Richie stared at the wall for a minute, before saying, "Of course, I knew he was dead. But I didn't think much about his truck being at the alley. It's there lots of Sunday mornings."

"Why is that?'

"He likes to have Kristy or whoever meet him there. And they usually take her car – or whatever chick he's takin' out on Saturday night."

"Whatever chick."

Another time-out stare. Then, "Okay. Yeah, Bobby plays around. Cheats on Kristy."

"With Juanita?"

A reluctant, "Sometimes."

"The same goes for Friday nights?"

"Yeah."

"Any reason Bobby prefers not to use his truck?"

"Couple of reasons."

"And they are?" Like pulling teeth.

"If you take a look at the interior of Bobby's car, you'll see. He was a slob. And the upholstery was torn. No music. His system was broken and he didn't have the bucks to get it fixed. Plus –." A long pause.

"Go on."

"If you used a chick's car, he didn't have to worry about some chick finding a bra or panties or used rubber or some other... evidence, I guess you'd call it... that another chick had been there."

"Smart thinking."

"Even so, Bobby was juggling so many pussies at one time, he was just begging to get caught."

"And did he?"

"I don't know, man. I honestly don't know."

"Who, besides Juanita and Kristy, was he... seeing?"

"You trying to get me in trouble?"

"No. I am trying to find out who killed Bobby and the information you're holding onto just might help."

"And maybe it won't, in which case I'm going to get a ton of grief with nuthin' to show for it."

"That's the price you pay for being such an insider to Bobby's love-life circus."

"I ain't no insider, man. I'm not even a player in that game."

"Other girls' names?"

"Okay. Judy Mason, Tanya McCafferty, and Melody Tribbolett. Two of them are cheerleaders. Juniors. Judy plays clarinet in the band. She's a senior."

I wrote the names down. "Can you think of anybody else you think I ought to talk with?"

He thought for a moment and finally said, "Did you talk with them guys in Tucson he placed bets with all the time? Or to Jason's homo friends?"

"I have spoken with Jason's butt buddy, Andrew. But tell me why the bookie would be upset with Bobby, when Bobby was such a gold mine for him?"

A devious shrug. "I got the feeling the guys let Bobby start placing a few bets on the cuff. Is that what they call it? Letting him bet with money he didn't have. And I think Bobby got deeper and deeper in the hole."

"Why would a bookie allow Bobby to operate on a bet-now-pay-later plan? That's not a smart play."

"Maybe the guy figured Bobby was good for it. And found out afterwards Bobby couldn't come up with the cash."

"Are you guessing, Richie? Or is there something you know that you're not telling me?"

"I'm just telling' you stuff that Bobby told me. Well, he didn't tell me directly. Bobby was always beating around the bush. You know what I'm saying?"

Maybe I understood; maybe I didn't. A smart bookie had to have some kind of leverage over Bobby to allow Bobby to float his bets. And a dumb bookie doesn't remain a bookie for very long.

I told Richie he was free to take off and he didn't need hesitate to see if I really meant it. After he left I sat at the small table and made notes, trying to make sense of Bobby Shane's murder without imagining any of the people I had interviewed thus far as suspects. Instead, I asked myself about what Bobby's body and its location could tell me – if anything.

Multiple stab wounds are often the sign of heightened anger. The many cigarette burns to the body, inflicted after Bobby was dead, according to the coroner, signified to me cold calculation, an obvious effort to mislead. The fact that the forensic pathologist determined almost immediately that the burns came belatedly indicated the killer was what the Brits call too clever by half, meaning less cunning than he thought himself to be. Or herself.

Could someone simultaneously be both intensely angry and calmly scheming? I wasn't sure. Perhaps the idea of the burns occurred to him after he had regained his composure. That seemed possible.

As for the arroyo where Bobby's body was found, how did he get there? Neither police nor news coverage mentioned any suspicion, let alone assumption, that Bobby had been killed where he was found. No blood in the sand. But neither were there any abrasions to his body from his having been dragged to the scene. Nor was the posture in which he was found suggestive of his having been dumped dismissively. Rather, he had been placed. Carefully positioned even.

Could one person perform that task? Yes, depending on the person. A female? Unlikely. But not just any male could hoist Bobby, carry him to the stream bed, and lower him without further damage to his body. And then leave no trace of having hauled him there. I didn't have the coroner's report, so I had no idea where lividity had occurred – where blood settles immediately after death, leaving clear signs of accumulation.

A single, strong male could do it, I judged. A Colby Ambrose, for example. But I had my doubts about Colby's having the wits to cover his tracks so expertly. Was Colby part of a murder plot? And was he killed to silence him? If so, why would Colby *et al* want to kill a good customer? Or was Bobby becoming a problem customer? If he was, what kind of problem looms large enough to lead to murder as the way to eliminate such a problem?

And why place the body in the arroyo? Is there a significance to the arroyo? Some meaning to his having been laid out at that particular spot in that particular arroyo? If he was not killed where he was found, there were literally a gazillion much more convenient places to get rid of a corpse. Why inconvenience oneself? If the plan was that his body not be found for a while, for whatever reason, the Sonoran Desert is a very large place. On a regular basis bodies are found that had gone missing weeks, even months, previously. Circling buzzards are no sure giveaway. Many species of creatures provide carrion.

Why leave Bobby so close to civilization, if the point is to hide the body? Or was that the point? Maybe the point was to have him found, but found in a puzzling location. If so, the killer achieved that goal. But why was that his goal? What's his message? Why would leaving Bobby's corpse in a dumpster or a dark alley or in the middle of a parking lot or on the lawn of the high school not do?

I closed my notebook. I was thinking too hard. Maybe leaving him any one of six dozen places would have worked just as well and the killer simply selected the arroyo as more or less an oh-what-the-hell choice. I decided I was reading too much into the killer's choice of drop site. Time to move forward. See what I could learn about Colby Ambrose and then try to figure out if his murder had any connection to Bobby's.

25

Sex and booze have trumped book-learning as far back as Plato's Academy. So why was I surprised to find O'Banion's tavern packed with college students on a Wednesday night? Grade inflation maybe. Class enrollment guarantees an 'A'? Where were these profs when I went to college?

I flashed my shabby PI license to the doorman and asked to see the manager. The kid checking identification didn't look to be old enough to let himself in. He took a hard look at my credentials, then looked at me slantwise, tugged on his earring, and said, "Oh, what the fuck. All the way to the back, past the pissers. Knock first."

The banner over the bar announced the night was "2-4-1 Ladies' Night". I assumed that meant cheap drinks for coeds rather than an invitation to a ménage. Women appeared to outnumber guys by a substantial ratio. My best guess was that it was 6-4-1 Guys' Night in that respect. And my hasty appraisal, as I headed toward the rear of the huge, multi-room, warehouse drink emporium, was that plenty of prime female flesh had already shown up, along with a multitude of lesser beauties and a nearly equal number of wouldn't-look-appealing-till-closing-time chicks.

The manager was a fortyish-looking dude named Lance Beck. He was a dude in every sense of that unkind description. He sported thinning hair, a paunch, a mustache in need of a trim, and far too many gold chains for a man without an Italian last name.

"Colby Ambrose? Yeah. Really sad about Cole, eh?" He offered me the only chair in his office, while he sat on the edge of his cluttered desk. I failed to sense the sadness he expressed. When I nodded my agreement with his remark, he confirmed its lack of depth by saying, "But life goes on, right?"

I wanted to say, "Not for Colby", but neither sincerity nor sentimentality seemed to be in order with this "dude". "What can you tell me about him?" I said and mentally switched my bullshit sifter on to full power.

"Great guy, let me tell you. Truly a gentle giant. He got on really well with my entire staff. And did a great job, too. He had a way with my customers, you know?"

"What way was that?"

"Colby was a tough love kind of guy. But smooth. Oh, man, was he smooth. He knew exactly how to diffuse a situation. Know what I mean?"

"Go ahead and explain," I said.

"Naturally we get our share of rowdies in here. It goes with the territory, right? I mean, guys come to have a good time and occasionally some of them end up having too good a time. You know."

"Drunk and disorderly."

"Well… yes and no. The reason I hire guys like Colby is to prevent our good-time Charlies from reaching the disorderly state."

"He was persuasive that way, was he?"

"You got it. He has the look. Know what I mean? I like to say that Colby could stare the piss out of a guy. Get it? Stare the piss, not scare the piss."

I nodded that I had indeed 'got it". I then asked, "Did Colby work Monday night?"

"Hum. I can't remember. Let me check." He rummaged through some time cards. "Yeah. Matter of fact. Put in five hours. Nine to close."

"I saw Colby yesterday morning. Late. Close to noon. He looked like he'd gone several rounds with Tyson. Well, except that neither of his ears had been chewed on. But he had a swollen eye; cut lip. Pretty badly bruised."

"Oh man, he didn't get that here. I guarantee that. No problems Monday night. None at all. And I was here the whole night." The man looked shocked that I would even suspect there could any connection between A and B.

"Wasn't there a knife murder in here in the recent past?"

"Nope. That was at Maloney's and resulted from a fight between two patrons."

"Know anybody mad enough at him to want to kill Colby Ambrose?" I said.

"Like I told you, everybody here loved Colby."

"A gentle giant."

"Exactly."

"Are you aware if Colby had any connections to gambling?"

"You mean like… the Mob?"

"Not necessarily. But illegal."

"Oh hell. Colby got involved with our annual Super Bowl bets here at the tav. And, of course, with March Madness pools. I guess technically both of those are illegal, but who's going to enforce, eh? I mean, every barbershop and white-collar office in America runs those, right? You tellin' me somebody killed Colby because fuckin' Duke or North Carolina didn't win the NCAA championship again? Come on."

"No. I mean daily, weekly, monthly sports bets. All year 'round."

Lance's eyes gave him away. "No. I can't say as I know about anything like that going on around here. Certainly not in my tavern. You tellin' me Colby was involved in something like that?"

The filters on my sifter clogged up with that last set of claims. "No enemies here. No illegal activities of any note here. Thanks for your time, Mr. Beck. I have several other places to check out. I appreciate your time and cooperation."

"Any time, my man. What a tragedy! I want whoever did this brought to justice. Swift, stern punishment is in order, don't you think? I'm no soft-on-criminals kinda guy. Know what I mean?"

I knew what he meant. I'm sure he was a hang-'em-high kind of guy all right. So long as his neck was nowhere near the noose.

On my way out I stopped to take in a couple minutes of a Coyotes-Red Wings game on one of the many big screens in the Sports Fans' Room. No sooner had I stopped to watch than a fight broke out between a Coyotes' defender and the Red Wing's star left-wing man. The camera zoomed in to catch the fisticuffs up close and personal, as the sports saying goes. Maybe Colby Ambrose had gotten too close to the screen while watching a hockey game and, as the camera zoomed in on a jaw-to-jaw, skate-to-skate brawl, one of the on-screen pugilists threw a 3-D roundhouse that caught Colby square in the face. But that seemed unlikely, if only because, if that was the way Colby's face took on the look it bore when I saw him, Lance Beck would surely have been the first to confirm to me that's how it had happened.

I grew bored with the hockey fracas and turned to leave when a winsome brunette grabbed my arm with one hand, while waving an empty beer schooner with the other.

"Buy me drink, Handsome?" She batted her glittered-spangled eyelids like a battery-driven Barbie with the on-button stuck.

"Why should I do that?" I said in as even a voice as I could muster.

"Because it's buy-none-get-none-free night. That's why," she said and squeezed my arm harder. She had clearly found a previous mark to fill her glass. Her speech was slightly slurred, though she was far from drunk.

With my free hand I waved about the room. "Have the rest of these gentlemen exhausted their cash? Am I the only one left flashing dollar signs in my eyes?"

"The only one who looks like he'd be fun." Obviously well-practiced flattery was among what I suspected were numerous other well-practiced talents. "Come on. I bet you've had a hard day and could use a cold beer, too."

I couldn't argue that.

"This place has two dozen choices of beer. You can tell the bartender you're buying two for me and that I'll give you one of mine. How's that?"

"You're very generous."

She laughed. "You bet I am. In more ways than one, Mr. Handsome." Still holding onto me, she pointed with her schooner hand. "See that blonde over there? The one wearing the red scarf around her neck?"

"I see her."

"That's my roommate. As soon as she finds a guy she likes –. I've already found mine –" – another arm squeeze – "—we going to go back to our place and put on a show for you guys. You like to be entertained?" Before I could answer, she went on. "Of course, you do. Mindy and I are gonna treat you guys to some dazzling entertainment. Well, Mindy does the dazzling part. I do the sizzling part." She giggled. "Dazzle, sizzle, yeah, yeah, yeah." She gave me another round of eye-batting. "But first you've gotta have a beer with us. To loosen our in.. inhib…inhibitions, don't you know."

"I'm sorry, but –. What's your name again?" I said.

"I'm Tammy. That's Mindy over there."

"I'm afraid I'll have to take a rain check, Tammy. I have other business to finish tonight."

"It's not raining, Mr. Handsome. It never rains in Tucson. Your rain check would be a forgery."

"Even so, I'm sorry. I'm sure you're as sizzling as you say you are. But I simply don't have the time or energy for sizzle tonight."

"Don't try to tell me you've had a better offer."

"No way. It's simply not in the cards tonight."

She pulled me close and whispered, "Who said anything about cards? Mindy and I will skip the poker part and get right to stripping for you. Hell, we know we'd end up losing anyway."

"Sorry. Not tonight. Now I must be on my way."

"Shit." She finally let loose of my arm and walked away like a whipped puppy.

I made my way to the door, knowing Tammy – or whatever her real name was – would not suffer another five minutes without finding some lucky fool to fill her schooner and later help her fulfill her stripper fantasies. Maybe Mindy's too.

My car was parked on Ninth Street, three blocks east of the tavern. By the time I crossed Hoff, a block away from O'Banion's, both foot traffic and street lights had disappeared. When I stopped to retie a shoe I heard voices coming from the nearby alley. Stressed female voices.

"Please, you have our purses. Let us go. Please. Stop doing this," said one voice.

"Don't hurt us. Take our money or whatever you want. But stop," pleaded a second.

A male Hispanic voice said, "Shut up. What we want is to see you, baby. Don't move or my knife may slip and you wouldn't want that to happen."

A second male, also Hispanic, said, "We want to see your pretty skin, baby. All your skin, but just your skin. So don't force Juan to draw blood. Be still and he'll only pop your buttons, eh?"

Both women simpered but said nothing.

"There, my lovelies. Now off with the blouses. Let them fall to the ground."

Moments later the second male said, "Now hold very still, *mi chiquitas*, while Juan slips his knife between your gorgeous melons. He only wants to cut your bras, not your awesome bazoombas."

Juan said, "Look at those big mamas. They can hardly wait for me to set them free, eh?"

"No, please," both women begged in unison.

"There. You're bras are worthless. Now slip them off," Juan said.

Silence from the women. A low whistle from one of the Latino men.

Juan again. "Now unbutton your jeans."

The second male. "Do it, bitches. We don't have all night."

More silence.

Then Juan. "Okay. Good. Now slip your thumbs into both your jeans and your panties. Slide them down and off together, *Comprende?*"

Still in a crouch, I reached back and slowly removed my Smith & Wesson from its holster. My eyes had slowly adjusted to the darkness. Just then a train whistle blew a single toot and I nearly jumped out of my shoes. The Amtrak station was three blocks west of me. If that was the westbound Amtrak – I looked at the illuminated dial on my watch and figured it might be, then the train would blow its whistle again. And it did. Two long toots. As it did I stood and rushed toward the sound of the voices.

Neither Hispanic male heard or saw me coming until it was too late for them to react. I fired twice, aiming for the nearest man's legs. He let out a scream and fell, clutching a leg. His knife clunked onto the alley pavement and he began to curse loudly in Spanish, emitting a piercing wail.

I raised the S&W and pointed it at the second man, who had frozen, his knife extended toward me. "Drop the knife and run or you're next," I shouted. "Drop it! Run! Go! Now! Do it or you're dead!"

He dropped his weapon, turned, and ran. He was too scared, too stupid, or both even to bother running a zig-zag pattern as he retreated.

The two young women stood petrified, their arms pulled in against their bare breasts. One managed to choke out, 'Don't hurt us."

I told them, 'Quick. Gather your clothes and come with me. We have to get out of here. Now!" They didn't need to be told twice.

"My shoes," one cried. "I can't find my shoes."

The only light came from a small, overhead fluorescent lamp over the steel-barred back door to a shop. The second woman got down on her knees and finally said, "Here, Sheila. I found your shoes."

I waited for both women to put on their shoes and fumble into their buttonless blouses. Each clutched a ripped bra in her hands. "I want each of you to hug me close. I'm going to hold you tight. Bury your faces in my chest and walk fast. We've got to move and keep moving. I'll guide you." I put my gun back into its holster and we headed out of the alley and back toward the tavern.

You can always count on some fools to adhere to the where-angels-fear-to-tread principle. Sure enough, we had no sooner turned the corner onto Ninth when several young males came rushing toward us.

"What's happening? We thought we heard gunfire," one of them called to us as he came running toward us.

Clutching the women's heads tightly to my chest, I shouted back, "Shots from the alley. Two, I think. Then I heard footsteps. Someone running. I'm moving these women to safety. Check it out, but be careful."

More men came, along with a couple of women. I kept my two charges moving, the three of us walking as fast as we could with-out stumbling over each other's feet. When we reached O'Banion's a large crowd had gathered outside. The smell of stale beer and cigarette smoke drifted out from the open door, along with the ear-pounded opening chords from Deep Purple's "Smoke on the Water". We stepped into the street to skirt past the throng. After every few steps, I would whisper to the women, "It's going to be all right. You're gong to be safe." I hoped I was right.

26

One block north of the tavern I stopped in the recessed opening to a bead shop and loosened my grip on the women. "You
may breathe now, ladies. Take some deep breaths, but don't say
anything. We should be safe here at least for a few minutes." I
looked behind us and no one was coming. The only sound was
the siren of a Tucson PD black-and-white echoing off the buildings. It sounded as thought it was still in the distance, but getting closer.

"Close call, ladies. But those two men can't hurt you now."

"Thank you, thank you, thank you," one of the women said, and
began sobbing.

I put an index finger under each woman's chin and raised
their heads until we made eye contact. "Now listen to me. Both
of you. First, you have to get away from here. Did you come in
a car?"

Both nodded.

"Where is it?"

"A block from where –." Her eyes teared up.

"Okay. I'm going to take you there. But we'll take the long way around to get there. When we get to your car I want you to go straight home. Do you live together?"

Two more nods.

"Good. Next, and this is very important, you must speak to no one about this. No one. Not even your closest friends. The reason is: Those guys surely have lots of *amigos*. Right? And sooner than later, no matter who you trust to tell about what just happened, word will eventually get back to those *amigos*. At that point you both will find yourselves in very deep trouble – again. Understood?"

Vigorous nods.

"I hope so."

We walked slowly down Eighth Street. The two women hunched their shoulders and held their blouse fronts together. I followed behind them, looking or my shoulder every few seconds, but no one was following us. I didn't know which one was Sheila. It didn't matter. One was blonde, one brunette. Both were attractive, even ragged-looking as they were. We continued all the way down to first Avenue, turned right, until they stopped at a white Toyota Corolla.

"Get in, make a u-turn, and go straight to your apartment or wherever you live," I told them.

"Thank you so much. You've been more than kind."

"I'm sorry this happened to you both," I said. "I know you'll want to talk about it. When your adrenalin panic wears off, you'll both feel like chattering to someone about what happened. It's natural. A way to let loose your pent up fear and anger. But don't. You may come to regret it."

Both nodded, but I had no doubt one or both would tell someone – in complete confidence. As if such promised intimacy was ever trustworthy, let alone sincere, outside a confessional.

As the Corolla swung out of its space and made a wide turn, I noted the license plate number. Then I headed toward my own car. I was reaching for my car keys when I heard a voice behind me call, "Sir? Stop for a moment please."

I turned slowly and saw it was a uniformed policeman. I allowed my right hand, which was edging underneath my sports coat and toward my S&W, to drop to my side. "Yes, officer?"

"Where are you coming from?" he said.

"I dropped my sister off at the Amtrak station. Then I walked up Fourth Avenue to see what hours Antigone Books kept. To avoid the crowd in front of O'Banion's, I walked down Eighth to First. What's all the commotion down on the corner?" By then several black-and-whites had gathered, their blueberries flashing. And I heard what I assumed, from the sound of its siren, to be a Fire Department aid car or an ambulance.

"There's been a shooting. Did you see anyone running anywhere on your walk here?" the cop said.

"No. I'm sorry. I didn't. Was anyone hurt?"

"Yeah. There's a guy down. Mexican."

"Mind if I get out of here then? I don't care to be part of that kind of action."

"This your car?"

I pressed my key and the parking lights came on. "Yep."

"Mind showing me some ID?"

"No. I'm going to reach for my wallet, okay?"

He stepped closer and held his nightstick in a way that he could handily thwack me if he thought I was reaching for anything other than my wallet. I showed him my driver's license.

"Las Vegas, eh?"

"Somebody has to sweep the streets and wash all those hotel windows."

"You don't strike me as either a street sweeper or a window washer."

"I'm a supervisor. I *habla español*."

"Maybe I should take you down to help translate for the greasy brown fucker who got himself shot. He's howling like a banshee. All in Spanish, of course."

"I'd rather not. My knowledge of Spanish profanity is somewhat limited," I lied.

The officer gave me an I-understand look.

"How badly is the guy hurt?"

"He may be ridin' a donkey the rest of his life. He sure as hell won't be walking. The piece of shit had a knee blown out."

"Was he carrying?" I said.

"Only a knife. Not exactly a fair fight, eh? But who cares? I'm sure the greaser got what was comin' to him."

"Hey, wasn't a guy knifed in an alley right near here last night?" I said.

"Matter of fact –."

"Not a very welcoming neighborhood."

"Seems not."

"May I go?"

The cop nodded. "Make a u-turn and take First. Everything's closed down toward O'Banion's. And have a safe trip back to Las Vegas."

"Good luck finding whoever you're looking for," I said and left before he asked any more questions.

On my drive back to Arroyo Arenoso I gave some thought to the possibility that Juan and his buddy might have knifed Colby Ambrose. But the chances of Juan's sticking a knife into Bobby Shane seemed remote. And I was convinced Bobby's and Colby's murders were somehow connected. Too much of a coincidence not to be. Or so I fondly imagined. If Juan knifed Bobby, why drive his corpse all the way to Arroyo Arenoso? That made no sense.

The hour was late and I realized I hadn't eaten since lunchtime. I pulled off the interstate at Sahuarita, filled the Jeep's tank, and went into the McDonald's next door for a double quarter-pounder. The drive-through was open, but I was weary of sitting in the Jeep. I was the only indoor customer and the young staff made clear by their hostile glares that they resented my interfering with their closing procedures.

I sat at a booth near the restrooms so the staff had to go out of their ways to make their collective displeasure known. The fries were cold and hard, but I didn't complain. In my mind I replayed the shooting incident and wondered what I might have done if Juan and his male companion had been joined by others in watching Juan force the two women to disrobe.

My course of action, I decided, would have depended on how many hostile Latinos I would have had to confront. The Smith & Wesson 386 held seven rounds. I mused about my estimate of 6-4-1 when I was in O'Banion's and gave the notion a new twist. Six Latino males; one Wiley Poynter. Hmmm. I definitely would have limited myself to one shot at Juan. Beyond that? I had no idea how the remainder of the men I was facing would react. Sometimes you don't know what you will do in such circumstances until you actually have begun the engagement. The infamous fog-of-war principle on a miniscule scale. I reminded myself I would never make a very good general. So many variables; so little time to decided.

Supposing Adelle was asleep when I opened her front door, I took off my shoes and skulked in as if I were a wayward husband sneaking home from an assignation. As happened with most such errant men, I supposed, I got caught.

"Is that you, Wiley Poynter?"

"No, Dell. This is your local cat burglar, come to filch all your turquoise and silver jewelry."

"Why so late?"

"Like all such intruders, I was hoping you would be sound asleep."

"Well, I'm not. So you can turn on some lights, before you trip and break something I value more than your leg."

"Yes, ma'am." I found the switch on an end table lamp and turned it.

My sister appeared in her housecoat. "Where have you been?"

"In Tucson," I said to keep matters simple. And foggy.

"Are you all right? You're not in any trouble, are you? You didn't go back to that awful South Tucson house, did you?"

"No, Dell. I was on Fourth Avenue."

"The only places open this late on Fourth are the taverns. You didn't drink and then drive all this way, did you?"

"I'm as sober as a Mormon bishop."

"Well, let me tell you. I've known a couple Mormon bishops who –. Never mind. Have you had anything to eat?"

"Yes." Besides the double burger, I had actually eaten all the cold fries. Starvation does strange things to men.

The philosopher Bertrand Russell, when once asked his views on mysticism, pondered for a moment, then said, "*Some people drink too much and see snakes; others eat too little and see God.*" After leaving the Sahuarita McDonald's, I had no desire to see God hovering over the moonlit Santa Ritas. I told myself that was why I had finished the gawdawful fries.

"Would you like to tell me what you were doing in Fourth Avenue taverns so late, if you weren't drinking?" my sister said, easing herself onto the sofa.

"Turning down propositions from winsome young strumpets and interviewing the manager."

"That's believable. I don't see you as the sugar-daddy type."

"You don't?"

"No. Shagging coeds is not your style."

"Excuse me? Such language from the abbess will not be countenanced."

"I wasn't born yesterday, brother dear."

"If you were, I'd scarcely be a glint in our sainted mother's eye."

"What did you talk to a tavern manager about?"

"About one of his former bouncers."

"I see. Would that bouncer happen to be the one who was found murdered in an alley near Fourth Avenue Tuesday night?"

God bless the six o'clock news. "It would so happen."

"And why do you care about the murder of this bouncer? Is his murder connected to Bobby Shane's?"

"I don't know, but it might be. How perceptive of you."

"As I just said –."

"You weren't born yesterday. I know. That was Judy Holiday."

"I'm surprised you remember that movie."

"William Holden. Broderick Crawford."

"You're just a retro kind of guy."

"That's why I'm such a Charlie Chan fan. But not the sugar-daddy type. Alas."

"Alas, my ass."

"There you go again."

"I suggest we both march ourselves to bed. But first, I'm going to have some milk and cookies. Would you care to join me?"

And so Adelle and I sat at her kitchen table, munching ginger snaps and 'nilla wafers, just like we used to do when we were kids. The only difference was we drank one-percent milk instead of whole milk. And the cookies had no trans fats. Self-appointed food sheriffs were everywhere – more numerous, more vigilant, and more aggressive than elected sheriffs.

27

Thursday

I waited until my sister left for school before I took my Smith & Wesson out to clean it. I also brought in the Taurus and the Krieghoff. Keeping one's metal buddies well-oiled and dirt-free was a ritual I learned as a nineteen-year-old. My drill instructor at Fort Benning – a nasty piece of work named Bruce Franklin Traylemann, Butt-Fuck for short – instilled in me the tenet that a clean weapon was a happy weapon. And Good Ol' B-F assured us shit-for-brains recruits that a happy weapon would some day save our miserable, worthless lives, whereas an unhappy weapon was guaranteed to earn us a flight to Delaware's Dover Air Force Base, home of the military mortuary, in a body bag.

In the middle of my gun-cleaning rites I placed a call to Stacy Park and asked her to find the address attached to the license plate I had memorized the night before.

"Bad guys?" she asked.

"Nice girls."

"How nice?"

"The kind who don't like to be forced at knife-point to strip in dark alleys."

"I know girls like that," she said. "Did you drop your Superman cape off at the dry-cleaners yet?"

"No, but I'm sitting here cleaning my S&W."

"Oh, my. I bet your Wyatt Earp hat needs re-blocking, too."

"No, but Ike Clanton is likely going to need an artificial knee."

"You're one cool dude, Wiley Poynter. You're going to have to show me your six-shooter one of these days. Maybe you can make my day. Or better yet, make my night."

"The barrel on my S&W is only two inches long, Stace. Same with the Taurus."

"Ah shit!"

"Sorry."

"Don't tell me that's so they don't get caught in your zipper when you've got to whip them out fast."

"Something like that."

"You own a shotgun, too, right?"

"Double-barreled. And very long."

"Then you can show me that. I got no issues with my boss playing footsy with the hired help," she said. "I'll ride shotgun for you anytime."

"Footsy?"

"You got to start somewhere."

"*Pies a cabeza.*"

"Oh yes. I like that idea."

"Fantasize all you want, but don't forget to trace the plate, please."

"Yowsuh, Massah Wiley. I be gittin' right on dat."

"*Todos abrazos*, Stace."

"Yeah. Sure. Promises, promises."

No sooner had I closed down my cell phone than it rang. Kristy Serling was calling.

"I know who was giving Bobby the money to bet on sports teams."

"Who?"

"Not over the phone. I'll meet you at the public library again during school lunch hour. We have a closed campus, but I'll figure out a way to be there." Click.

When I finished cleaning my arsenal I phoned Jack Stonecipher, but got no answer. I left a message for him to update me when he found it least inconvenient to do so. I then placed a call to Boyd's Used Cars, telling the pleasant woman who answered that I was a columnist for the *Tucson Business Weekly* and wanted to speak to Boyd Dupree about setting up an interview for an article we would be running in a few weeks on successful businessmen operating on the fringes of Tucson. The phone receptionist told me that Boyd had only been in for a few minutes that morning and now was gone for the day. I told her I would try again later.

When I hung up my phone rang again. Popular me.

"Got a pencil?" Stacy apparently already had the info I asked her to track down.

"Ready."

"Mr. and Mrs. George Bausch, with a Scottsdale address. You want their street name, number, and zip code?"

"Do they have a daughter?" I said.

She laughed. "Yep. Sheila Bausch." And she read me the daughter's address.

"Thank you."

"I hope she's a hot piece of ass, because I'm jealous."

"You needn't be, Stacy. I only plan to send flowers."

After a pause, "I'm sort of disappointed in that answer, Poynter."

"Why is that?"

"She owes you, dude. And you don't intend to collect. Is she a skag?"

"Not at all."

"Then I guess I don't understand. Is she underage?"

"I doubt it. I'm pretty sure she and her friend were headed toward a tavern."

"That doesn't mean she isn't jailbait."

"Let's just say she's gorgeous, she's of age, and I don't plan to try to screw her. Or her equally attractive girlfriend."

"Now I'm seriously disappointed in you," Stacy said.

"Don't be. I simply have a lot of other things on my mind right now."

"You're telling me sex takes a low priority, right? I call bullshit. You're a man for chrissakes. So man up, dude. What's the real issue here?"

To get her to hang up I lied. "Okay. Flowers are just to butter her up. To make sure she doesn't forget me."

"That's better. Good luck. And I expect photos when you nail her. A video would be better. That's my price for breaking the law to track her down. Okay?"

"Glossy or matte?"

"On that I ain't choicy. Just so they're clear and show lots of naked action."

"I didn't realize you were such a voyeur, Stace."

"Damned right I am. But I want to see people I know. There are a gazillion porn sites on the web these days, but do you think I sit here all day ogling buck-naked strangers? Hell no. What a bore that would be. Even BDSM sites are a drag. But seeing you plunking gorgeous coeds would be a turn on, especially if they are damsels you rescued from serious danger. At knife-point! Wow!"

"I'll keep you posted, Stace."

"You'd better."

Lordy. The average male had nothing on oversexed Stacy. That woman needed to buy a treadmill and put in some serious miles on it. Work off some of that libidinous energy. That, or make sure she always has plenty of batteries available to keep her hand-held toys humming.

With slightly more than an hour to spare before meeting Kristy, I drove to the flower shop in Green Valley that I remembered seeing. I selected a vase of orange chrysanthemums for delivery from the display book the clerk showed me. I gave her the address where I wanted them delivered.

"Name of the recipient, sir?"

"Sheila and friend."

The clerk, a chunky, middle-aged woman with an infectious smile gave me a puzzled look.

"I didn't get her girlfriend's name."

The clerk shrugged. "A message to be included?"

"Mum's the word," I said.

I watched the woman struggle to refrain from rolling her eyes. "Inside joke."

"And how would you like it signed, sir?"

"Pistol Pete."

The woman's hand froze for a moment before dutifully writing down what I had told her. "Anything else for you, sir?"

I said not and paid in cash, having stopped on the way at a local branch of the bank I used in Las Vegas to tap a cash machine.

"Will delivery tomorrow be satisfactory, sir? Or would you prefer another day?"

"Tomorrow will be fine."

I wasn't sure why I was sending these two women flowers. The more I thought about it, the less sense it made. Unless –. No. But then –. I don't know. Was it Freud who said that the most interesting secrets are the ones we keep from ourselves?

28

I waited forty-five minutes in the library for Kristy to appear. Then I left and waited another twenty minutes in my car, parked where I could see the library entrance. No Kristy. Nor did she call to explain her absence. I tried calling her cell phone number, which my own cell had logged. I got her voice mail. But I didn't leave a message because I didn't want her to detect how irritated I was. She might decide to cut me off if she sensed even the slightest hostility from me. With no other immediate plans, I drove to see if Chief Morton was in his office and available to see me. He was and he was.

"You've come to provide me with the solution to Bobby Shane's murder, right?" he said, waving for me to shut the door behind me and take a seat.

"Sorry. Not even close."

He stared at me for several seconds, sizing me up, then sighed, and said, "Neither am I."

I jumped right in with what I wanted to cover with him. "Did Bobby Shane own a cell phone? Sure he did."

The chief said he did. "Let me explain where we stand on that, just to prove to you we're not quite as big a bunch of bumpkins as you suppose we are."

I gave him a who-me? look.

He said, "We've done two things. From his iPhone carrier we've asked for – and received – records of all his calls. Nothing dramatic turned up. His last call was from school to Perry Crisp, who then told us Bobby had phoned him reminding Perry to bring some extra guitar gadgets to Saturday's scheduled band practice at Bobby's house. His last text messages were a message from Juanita Bardella asking him if he could give her a lift home. He responded in the affirmative."

"Boring," I muttered.

"I agree," the chief said. "The second thing we've done is to ask the county prosecutor to ask Apple for the ongoing data they sort of admit to collecting about their ability to track iPhone locations." The sheriff held up his hands, palms open. "Privacy issues about that are still being debated and rattling around in the courts. I just decided to ask the DA if we could try to jump in and see what was available. Are you familiar with any of Apple's data-collecting?"

I nodded. "Apple argues that, for its users' benefit, they have programmed iPhones to provide GPS positioning via Wi-Fi hot spots and cell towers, because doing so is a lot faster than relying on satellites. Why they deem such tracking necessary is not crystal clear to me."

The chief seemed impressed. "I suppose it will do no harm to tell you that we have not recovered Bobby's iPhone. It's not in his house, not in his truck, not anywhere else we've searched. That's one reason we want Apple's data. To find the phone and to see where it's been lately."

"Ah! So that's the clarity I've missed. You hope it's at the bottom of the killer's underwear drawer," I said.

"That would be nice."

I changed the subject. "Did you hear about the knife murder in Tucson that happened Tuesday night?"

"Of course, I did. What about it?"

"Do you think there may be any connection?"

"It's possible, but –."

"But—."

"Knifings are not exactly rare events in this part of the world. Among Hispanics knives are the preferred method of settling differences. Guns are expensive, unless you steal one. But knives? Every Hispanic male gets a switchblade for his first birthday."

"And murderous intent is more prevalent than larcenous intent, you're saying?"

The chief shook his head. "A great many Hispanic knife killings are acts of passion. Or spur-of-the-moment rage. After a couple of beers or shots of tequila, Señor Gomez hints to Señor Garcia that perhaps Señorita Garcia, his daughter, has been offering her sexual favors for a fistful of pesos. Next thing you know, Señor Gomez is lying on his back, several pints of his blood spreading quickly across the cantina floor."

"This victim was a *gringo*," I said.

Morton smiled. "No white guy has ever pissed off a member of our esteemed Hispanic community."

"*Touché.*"

The chief opened his desk drawer. "Let me show you something – in strict confidence. The public, meaning the frigging media, doesn't know about this yet. And I don't want them to know just yet. Got it?"

"Mum's the word," I said and smiled.

"What's so funny?"

"A personal joke – on myself."

"Take a look at these."

He pushed several photos across his desk. They were close-up shots of Bobby Shane's backside, each with the coroner's label affixed to it. "The knot on Bobby's head looks nasty, but the coroner said the blow that caused it wasn't what killed him. And ignore the cig burns. They're irrelevant. But look at the cut wounds. What do you see?"

"Pretty ugly," I said.

"Have you seen many knife wounds?" he said.

"No."

"These are uglier than most. And the pathologist finally figured out why."

He pushed another piece of paper toward me. "He thinks this is the style of weapon used to make those cuts. The pathologist, by the way, has seen plenty of knife wounds. He's worked in Los Angeles, El Paso, San Antonio, and New York City. Ever seen one of those?"

I lied when I shook my head. I had seen one recently. What I was now looking at was a photo taken from an internet website on martial arts weapons.

Chief Morton said, "That object goes by several names: push dirk, fist knife, push dagger."

The knife I was looking at bore a similarity to a simple wine-bottle-opening corkscrew. It was T-shaped, with a short blade. And at the top of the blade, near the tip, a projection came out toward the handle – making the knife appear to be a large fish-hook. "I see now why Bobby's cuts were so jagged."

"Mean-looking device, isn't it?" the police chief said.

"Very wicked."

"The holes in the back of the dead bouncer up in Tucson don't show any sign of this kind of weapon being used on him. His cuts were clean. In and out. Whereas this nasty piece of work –."

I said, "Popular among those in the martial arts, is it?"

The chief nodded.

I decided I couldn't hold back as much as I would have liked to sit on. "You aware that Jason Altheiser is gay, are you not?"

"I've heard rumors."

"Well, the rumors are true. And Jason has a boyfriend, a student at U of A named Andy Kudarski. Andy and a group of other gays at the university belong to a martial arts club. They take lessons from an Asian gay man who is an expert in a form of martial arts called Wing Chun. You might want to look into it."

"Obviously you already have."

"But, without a badge and a uniform, I couldn't get very far."

"Uh-huh."

"Bobby Hollsworth was a rather virulent homophobe, Chief. You shouldn't have to prod Jason very hard to find out Bobby taunted the hell out of him about his sexual orientation."

"Is that right? You clearly have a talent for speaking with these young guys that I lack. I wasn't able to get much of anything out of Jason. Or Perry or Richie."

"Maybe next time you should deputize my sister and invite her along," I said. "Her presence puts the boys more at ease than your beady eyes and Stetson do."

"Beady eyes?"

"Check 'em out. You have a pair of tiny blue laser beams that seem to look directly into people's souls. Maybe folks suppose they don't need to open up to you, because you can unearth their secrets just by glaring at them."

"Now that would be a talent I'd almost sell my own soul for," Chief Morton said, smiling.

"But that would take all the challenge out of your job, Chief."

"Fine. There are too many challenges sitting in this chair."

"Counting the days until your retirement, are you?"

"With this economy, I can no longer count that high. The way things are going, my retirement home will be a casket."

"Well, give Jason your piercing stare and asking him about gay martial arts friends. Maybe something will shake loose."

"And what is your next step, Mister Private Detective?"

"I haven't talked with Juanita Bardella yet." Then I added, coyly, "I may have another conversation with Kristy Serling."

"Don't you go too hard on the Bardella girl or you're have her mother to answer to."

"I know. I've met Señora Graciela. She's definitely no wallflower."

The chief laughed. "Hell, there isn't any room on her walls for so much as one more flower. Have you been in her cantina?"

"I have."

"Nothing like a little mayhem and cruelty to go with your dinner, eh? Jesus, those Mayans and Aztecs thought no more of letting blood flow than you or I would think of turning on a water faucet."

"Civilization remains a mighty thin crust, Chief. Scratch it at your peril."

"Well, damn it, somebody is always scratching it. That's why I have a job."

I stood to take my leave.

"Nice talking with you, Poynter. Keep in touch, if you don't mind my beady eyes trying to read your mind once in a while."

"Not at all, Chief. It will be my challenge to try to keep the curtain drawn."

"The Wizard of Oz didn't have much luck doing that."

"Then maybe neither will I."

Back at my car I tried calling Kristy again, but she didn't answer. I thought about whether I should have mentioned seeing a push dagger on Andy Kudarksi's bedroom wall, but decided the police would find it for themselves soon enough. Chief Morton would discover that I had visited Andy, but he would have no reason to suppose I had been in Andy's bedroom, unless he mis-imagined I was swishy. And, if Andy happened to mention to cops that he had taken me into his bedroom to show me photos, I could simply deny I had seen the dagger on his wall. After all, unlike Roland Morton, I lack beady, blue eyes with keen vision.

29

I parked across from the entrance to the students' parking lot at Arroyo Arenoso High, trying my best not to look like a child-kidnapper there to offer candy to unsuspecting young girls. Three more attempts to call Kristy Serling only produced three requests to leave a voice message.

I would have tried to call Adelle to ask her to try to track Kristy down on campus, but my sister, as part of her reverse snobbish-ness, refuses to participate in the cell-phone revolution. She was a decade behind in succumbing to the purchase of a microwave oven. I bought her flat-screen television for her. And she owned a desktop computer only because typewriters have gone the way of the Dodo bird. Her use of the internet has been minimal – Netflix streaming mostly. And the six o'clock news.

Any detective, public or private, will tell you that surveillance work is both ass-numbing and mind-numbing. I'm still in search of a palliative for the former. Clever minds have come up with sev-eral sops to avoid boredom. But the trouble with crossword puz-zles and sodoku is that they require the puzzle-solver, for lengthy periods of time, to take his eyes off that which he is supposed to be surveying.

My solution is to keep on hand in my car one or more of the logic-puzzle books of Raymond M. Smullyan. After reading one of his witty anecdotal puzzles, I can then stare off into the Middle Distance – which often encompasses the front door of a cheating housewife – and ponder a solution to a conundrum posed by Professor Smullyan while I survey. The volume I held while waiting for Kristy to appear – or not – was titled *King Arthur in Search of His Dog & Other Curious Puzzles.* By the time I figured out who, among Annabelle, Betsy, and Cynthia, owns a nameless cat, only ten cars remained in the lot.

Along with mulling over Smullyan's riddles, I thought about Chief Morton's dismissal of a connection between the murders of Bobby Hollsworth and Colby Ambrose. I deemed his discounting any tie to be off the mark. For one, fuzzy as my memory was about the full slate of weapons on Andy Kudarski's bedroom wall, I was reasonably confident I had seen more than one knife, more than one style of knife. For two, I myself drive around with a varied arsenal in my Jeep and on my person. Were I the type, I could handily murder three different people in a very short time, using a different firearm in each instance. So different knives clearly was not proof of different murderers. Perhaps someone only wanted it to look as though a pair of unrelated villains was involved.

Police, to my mind, too often possessed an all-too-narrow vision of what they call the MO: method of operation. Think of chairs. What does a Windsor chair have in common with a bean-bag chair? Not much. Yet we call them both chairs – without abusing the general notion of *chair.*

Putting mind over matter doesn't always succeed. Finally, ass-numbness trumped boredom. I gave up waiting for Kristy to appear and headed toward Graciela's cantina. For no compelling reason, I didn't put much store in Juanita's poking Bobby Shane repeatedly with a fist knife, yet she was the one principal involved with Bobby I hadn't spoken with yet. Yes, there were the other bimbos Bobby had been fooling around with, but no one yet had placed any of them in a context of having murderous intent for any reason. Maybe, like Chief Morton's dismissing a Colby-Bobby connection, I was missing something there. If so, I could always pick up on it soon enough.

"She ain't here," Graciela herself told me when I entered her colorful cantina and inquired about her daughter. "But she usually drops by between school and home. So, if you want to wait around, I'll buy you a beer."

"Thanks. I'll wait, but I'd prefer a rain check on the beer. A soda would be good. Heavy on the caffeine," I said and headed toward *el baño*. When I returned Graciela has parked a can of Mountain Dew on the bar and she was leaning next to it.

She handed me the soda and said, "Juanita called while you were in the can. She's not coming by. She's going to a girlfriend's house to practice the speech she's giving at assembly. The school is holding a memorial service for Bobby Hollsworth and Juanita was chosen to speak on behalf of the students."

"So I heard. You must be proud of her," I said.

"Very."

"Do you know if she was dating Bobby?"

I got a whoa-what-are-you-suggesting look from her. "No. I don't think so. Bobby was a nice kid, but I try to discourage my girls from dating *gringos*. Nothing good can come from it, I tell them."

"Nothing good."

She laughed. "I got nothing against good-looking white guys. But… but Bobby's family isn't Catholic, for one thing."

"And for another?" I said.

"He's just not right for my Juanita."

"In what ways?"

"Bobby's a musician. I mean, I like music. And, hell, my brother plays the *vihuela* in a mariachi band. Oh, you should see him. He looks so very handsome in his silver-studded *charro* suit. Maybe you have seen him. Do you like mariachi?"

"I do."

"Benito's group, *Los Caballos Rapida*, competes every year at the mariachi festival in Las Vegas. Have you attended?"

"I went once, but not recently."

"Too bad. Me? I go every year. For our family it is a grand event, almost a pilgrimage."

"A very wholesome family outing," I said.

"Eh! While there, my husband, Frank, and I, we send the kids to a movie so we can pull the slots and play a little blackjack. I don't let my Frank go to the strip clubs though."

"As long as you don't lose big, slots and blackjack can be thought of as just another vacation expense."

Graciela nudged me. "Hey! Sometimes I even win a few bucks."

"And declare it on your income tax return, I'm sure."

"Are you kidding? I never win that much."

"So when might be a good time for me to have a few words with Juanita?" I said.

Graciela turned and looked at a calendar taped to the mirror behind the bartender's station. "Today's Thursday? The memorial service is tomorrow. Come tomorrow night after the dinner rush has come and gone. I'll see that Juanita is here to speak with you."

"Thank you. I'll be here."

She added, "I'll even treat you to dinner. But you must pay for your own liquor, if you order some. State law, you know. No free booze for customers."

"Not ten minutes ago you offered to buy me a beer," I reminded her.

"I would have put money in the till for it. Then it's not free, eh? Now I gotta go. Tomorrow night after dinner hour for Juanita."

"Thank you again." She never did get around to telling me the other reasons she didn't care to have Bobby Shane fooling around with her daughter.

I picked Adelle up for dinner and took her to Solaris in Green Valley. She had been there before and judged it above average, especially compared with other choices in the area. For a drink I chose a glass of Woodford Reserve. Neat. Double.

"My, my, Brother. I take it you want me to drive home. What's with the double?"

"Some days are like that, Dell. At the end of a day like today, the best thing to do is pickle it."

"What went wrong?" she said.

"Not much. Days when things go wrong are not necessarily bad days. It's the boring, no-real-accomplishments days that sometimes weigh the heaviest."

"I see." But I knew she was just saying that to be agreeable.

For her entrée my sister ordered cranberry-marmalade chicken, despite my mumbling about the dish's description on the menu: *Tastes like a crisp autumn evening*. Harumph. That's the first I was aware that evenings tasted like anything, let alone chicken soused in cranberry marmalade.

As I recalled, such a description is what philosophers call a *category mistake*. The putting of a description to an object when the description doesn't really apply – in any context. For examples, a *schizophrenic triangle* or a *melancholy spoon*. Now such wise men could add *tasty evening*.

I ordered salmon and had my choice of having it delivered mesquite style or smothered in fresh mango salsa. Well, I certainly didn't want stale mango salsa. In fact, I didn't want mango at all. Trendiness in America almost inevitably takes on an avalanche effect anymore. Kiwi, pomegranate, and mango had all become über-chic these days – to the point that it was now easier to buy a box of kiwi-mango-pomegranate corn flakes that it was to find a box of plain old retro, fu-fu-free corn flakes.

For dinner conversation Adelle and I discussed the Constitution and the economy. I didn't mind. After all, she taught both government and economics at the high school. We skipped discussing the Second Amendment, because we both had concluded some months back that the Supremes' latest ruling on that was poppycock on stilts. Dell's students' current assignment was to write an essay about the merits and demerits of the Electoral College. In her economics class her latest assignment for her students was to research whether private enterprise was always more efficient at any task than any government agency. She wanted the students to come up with more than mere anecdotal evidence to argue whether such a theory was factual or merely a fiercely held ideological myth.

I liked having such discussions with my sister. She was a bright woman, articulate, and witty. A bit unshakeable in some of her own beliefs. But who isn't? And that evening's dinner dialogue kept both our minds off murder. I was beginning to feel a need for such a breather. So I welcomed discussing matters where I knew Adelle had the upper hand in her grasps of both facts and the theories we discussed. I rarely mind engaging in conversation with people who know more than I do about a subject. I learn a lot that way. Often I find out things I didn't even know I didn't know.

For dessert we swung by Kelly's Ice Cream and Yogurt. Then Adelle drove us back to her place, wondering more than once along the way why I chose to drive a Jeep. I told her it was because I couldn't afford a Rolls, and, even if I could, searching for missing persons in Nevada often took me places a Rolls Royce would find annoyingly déclassé. I told her she had to trust me on that. An *annoyed Rolls Royce* was not a category mistake. Merely a mistake.

Good citizen that I am, I had turned off my cell phone while in the restaurant. Alas, others hadn't, but I deem it equally rude to go about playing phone-sheriff. I was brushing my teeth when, apparently from holding my brush, I pictured my phone in my hand and realized I hadn't turned it back on. When I did I saw a missed call from Kristy Serling. As a kid I always thought the game of tag to be great sport. Phone tag, however, is not.

I called Kristy and she answered on the first ring.

"You've got to stop him, Mr. Poynter. Please, stop that man. Tell me you'll stop him."

"Please calm yourself, Kristy, and tell me what man you are speaking about."

"Mr. Sechcrest," she practically bawled into the phone. "You've got to stop him!"

"Stop him from doing what?"

"No! Not over the phone. Not over the phone."

"Then tell me where and when we should meet."

"In the morning. In front of school. I promise I'll be there. I promise, I promise."

"Very well. Is seven-thirty okay?"

"Yes. Please tell me you'll stop him."

"I'll do what I can. I promise."

She hung up and I sat down on the edge of the bed, staring at my phone. Sechrest. From my first impression of the man there was something about him that had put me on edge. I now was fairly certain that, in the morning. I was going to find out what it was.

30

Friday

I didn't tell Adelle about my phone conversation with Kristy Serling. She would surely be giving the band director suspicious stares soon enough. But first I wanted to find out why the man was going to deserve my sister's scorn. I parked my Jeep where I had parked it a day earlier and I waited again, this time with better success, I hoped.

As it turned out, Kristy showed up a mere five minutes late, meaning I hadn't even begun to panic yet. She had approached from the rear on the passenger side of the car. So I didn't even know if she had driven, walked to school, or had been given a ride. When she climbed into the front seat beside me I could see that she had already been crying.

"Tell me how Mr. Sechrest has upset you." I said.

"First, you must promise not to tell anyone. God, I'd be so embarrassed. And my parents will kill me if they find out."

"Let's not talk so casually of murder, please, Kristy."

"I'm not. If they find out, I'll never be able to face them again."

"Okay. Just start at the beginning."

She took a few seconds to compose herself and to organize her thoughts. "Mr. Sechrest called me into his office yesterday afternoon after school. He said he had a job for me, a job he would pay me to do for him."

"What kind of job?" I said.

"He called it modeling, but what he meant was that he wanted me to pose naked for him." She swallowed hard, then continued. "He said he already had photos of me in the nude and he wanted to take more."

"You've posed for him already?"

"No! I haven't. But I believed him when he said he had photographs."

"Bobby," I guessed.

She nodded. "Mr. Sechrest said he had downloaded photos of me naked from Bobby's cell phone."

"With Bobby's permission?"

"I don't know. What does it matter? Mr. Sechrest has them."

"I suppose it doesn't. So what did you say to Mr. Sechrest in response?"

"I told me there was no way I was going to model for him."

"And then he threatened to blackmail you, I'm guessing."

She nodded and wiped away several tears. "He threatened to put the photos of me on the internet, as well as send copies to my family and friends."

"Anything else?" I said.

"Yes. He said it might put my mind at ease to know that Bobby had posed for him, that Bobby had come to his house several times and posed nude. That he, Mr. Sechrest, had lots and lots of photos of Bobby naked. He added that I obviously already had experience modeling with my clothes off, because he said the photos Bobby took of me naked were clearly not photos he had taken of me unawares."

"How did you respond to Mr. Sechrest?" I realized I had phrased that badly when Kristy game me a look of righteous indignation.

"I told him no way!"

"But he wouldn't take no for an answer, am I right? He repeated and emphasized the internet threat."

She let out a deep sigh. "He gave me a deadline to change my mind. Eight o'clock tonight. Unless I phone him and agree, he said I could count on the photos being posted, both to the internet and in the mail, by noon tomorrow."

She grabbed my right arm. "Mr. Poynter, what can I do? Will you stop him? Please tell me you will."

"You don't want to go to the police with this?"

"No! I don't want this to become public. Don't you understand?" she said.

"I understand."

"And one more thing about Mr. Sechrest. He was the man who supplied Bobby with the money for Bobby's gambling habit."

"In exchange for –."

A shrug. "Bobby never told me he was modeling nude. I learned that from Mr. Sechrest. But I suppose –. No, I don't know. He only said Mr. Sechrest was giving him gambling money. When I asked Bobby why, he just said he was doing work on the side for Mr. Sechrest. I asked him what kind of work and he was vague. Music work. But now, I guess –. God, I wish now I'd never agreed to let Bobby photograph me with my clothes off."

"If Bobby took the photos with is cell phone, do you know if he sent them to anyone else?"

"He claimed not. And no one else has ever told me they've seen the photos. That was really stupid of me anyway. I know that now. Stupid, stupid, stupid."

"Does much sexting – isn't that what it's called? – go on among students here?" I said.

"Some, but not much. A couple girls I know have taken phone pictures of themselves and sent them to their boyfriends or to guys they were hot for."

"I'll have a very private talk with Mr. Sechrest. I'll explain the potential consequences of continuing to harass you."

"Can you get the pictures back?" Kristy said, giving me a pleading look.

"I don't know. By the way, no one has mentioned Bobby's cell phone. I don't think the police found it. Nor have they found his clothes, for that matter."

"Mr. Sechrest claims to have hard copies of the photos. He said he's printed some off and scanned them into his computer."

I said, "When did Bobby take the photos of you?"

"Just after school started, I think. Yeah, we went to his house after the first football game, instead of going to the post-game dance. His parents had gone to Phoenix for the weekend."

"When is your birthday?" I said.

"June second."

"So you are still seventeen."

"Yes."

"That will give me some added leverage with Mr. Sechrest. You're technically still a minor. I can remind him how the police and the DA might view that fact."

Kristy shouted, "I told you I don't want you to go to the police."

"I won't, if I can avoid it. But there is no point letting dear Sebastian know that. Let him mull over the consequences of possessing, let alone distributing, child pornography."

"I'm not a child."

"In the eyes of the law you still are."

"Unless I murder someone. Then they'd want to try me as an adult. So they could hang me," she said with a sneer.

"True enough. I'm not supporting courts' attitudes. I'm merely repeating what they are," I said.

"Damn the courts! Damn Mr. Sechrest!"

"Any other secrets you want to share with me? Any other surprises that might prove relevant?"

"Isn't that enough?"

"I think you've given me plenty of ammunition. But the forewarned-is-forearmed rule has a lot of merit."

"You're not going to tell your sister, are you? Please, please don't."

"No, there is nothing to be gained by Adelle's knowing about the photos of you and those of Bobby."

"Thank you."

I watched her walk across the street, trying mightily to dab away the last of her tears. Being a teenager is a ghastly limbo, a gray, chilling pit between a soon-forgotten childhood paradise and the persistent hells of adulthood. It's a marvel any of us survive it.

31

I was deciding when and where best to confront Sebastian Sechrest when I received a call from Bobby Hollsworth's mother.

"Doug and I would like to meet with you," was all she said.

"You tell me when and where. I'll be there."

"Is now convenient? At our house?" she said.

"That will be excellent," I said.

Mrs. Hollsworth gave me directions.

I had decided not to try to confront Sechrest on campus. Instead, I would return later and follow him home. Ten minutes later I parked across the street from the Hollsworths' middle-class tract home in a tidy neighborhood about a mile from where Bobby had been found. The house was a Southwest cookie-cutter home of sandstone-colored stucco with a red-tiled roof, two-car garage; desert landscaping with several barrel cacti and single one-armed saguaro in the middle of the front yard; a rail porch fence and Mexican birds of paradise for hedge across the front of the house. Mrs. Hollsworth met me at the door.

"Thank you for coming. Please come in. I'm Lydia." She held out a well-tanned hand for me to shake. She wore a white sheer blouse and jeans. She was an attractive woman. Tall and lissome; blonde, brown-eyed and judicious in her use of makeup and perfume. A slightly discolored front tooth was the only mark I noticed. She obviously wasn't vain enough to pay her dentist to mask the flaw. I took that to count as an indication of character strength – to wear a minor but visible blemish so comfortably.

I declined her offer of coffee and scones. Her husband emerged from the back of the house. This time he shook my hand, and then we all sat together in the living room. I gestured broadly that they had the floor; I had come to listen.

Mrs. Hollsworth began. "Our Bobby has been dead almost a week now and the police seem to be getting nowhere. Because of that Doug and I welcome any help you can lend to finding his killer, Mr. Poynter."

"I'm working hard on it, Mrs. Hollsworth, but so far I'm afraid I may be no closer to a solution than Chief Morton is. But I intend to keep at it. Things continue to turn up that may or may not lead somewhere."

Lydia Hollsworth excitedly jumped in. "What sort of things?"

"I'm afraid I'd rather not say. In case they are dead ends or false leads, I want to protect the people in whose directions they point. That standard TV caveat I'm sure you've seen and heard: *Names withheld to protect the innocent.*"

"Are any of them strong leads?" Doug Hollsworth said.

I lied and said, "I simply don't know yet. I'll only know by continuing to pursue them."

"How can we help?" Mrs. Hollsworth said. "We feel so help-less. Anything we can do to help you out, please tell us."

Her husband nodded. "We knew Bobby better than anyone, obviously."

I wondered. How well do the parents of any teens know their children? Two generations are almost always divided by language. And these days, at the rate cultural change accelerates, they hardly speak the same language at all. The younger generation under-stands that such is the case, but my unfortunately extensive experi-ence in dealing with runaway teens convinced me that few parents grasp that critical fact. Even teens who never – or rarely – contem-plate decamping for some mystical parent-free paradise, recognize the difficulties in communicating with mom and dad. Or, all-too-often these days, step-mom, step-dad, or a single parent.

"Bobby obviously didn't come home the night before he was found. This didn't alarm you in any way? From what I can tell, you didn't call the police," I said.

Lydia spoke. "No. It was the police who came by to tell us. Well, me. Bobby often came home very, very late on Fridays and Saturdays. Doug was working one of his long overnight shifts and wasn't even here. I had taken a sleeping pill, as I often do, and most likely wouldn't have heard Bobby if he had come home. I sel-dom heard him come in when he was quite late. And on Saturday morning his bedroom door was still closed. So I –."

She began to choke up. I waited silently.

She wiped away a tear and continued. "I assumed he was sleeping late. Then Chief Morton came to tell me Bobby was dead."

I said, "Tell me about Bobby; then tell me about his friends."

Doug and Lydia looked at one another, silently deciding which would speak first. Bobby's father finally took the initiative.

"Bobby was a pretty typical teenager, we think. He took a keen interest in music and sports. And, of course, his real talent was with music. Though he loved sports, he was not very athletic, certainly not talented enough to play, other than in intramural activities. But he was gifted at playing the guitar. Academically? Lydia and I encouraged him to hit the books, but I'm afraid he wasn't as studious as we would have liked. He earned B's and C's. He was too passionate, I think, about his music. And for some reason he preferred to study batting averages and shooting percentages far more often and more readily than he buckled down to algebra or history or English. As I say, he had little athletic talent. But he did watch sports on TV a lot."

His mother jumped in. "Poetry was his favorite part of English. That's probably why he was such a successful songwriter. Well, I mean in so far as he wrote most of the original songs the band used."

"The band," I said. "Tell me about the other members."

Mr. Hollsworth took a turn. "The other three guys are all likeable. And Bobby got along well with all three of them. In fact, from what I could tell, they all got along just fine."

From what he could tell. That clearly wasn't very much.

"Were there ever any blowups?" I said.

"I can't think of any," Bobby's father said.

His wife appeared to want to contradict him, edging forward in her seat as if poised to spring. But then she seemed to reconsider. Finally she said, "They only quarreled about small things, as any group like that surely does. How much time to practice and when was the best time to do it. What their stage outfits should look like. Those kinds of little issues."

"Never any big issues? Money? Women?"

Doug Hollsworth said, "They're just a garage band. It's not as though there was millions of dollars to quarrel over. Or even thousands. And, as far as women go, they all had girlfriends they were happy with." He looked at his wife quickly and she didn't meet his gaze. "Well, I'm pretty sure three of them had girlfriends."

I said, "I know about Jason. And, from what I'm hearing, Bobby was far from thrilled with Jason's sexual orientation."

Doug Hollsworth snapped, "Well, why should he be? I don't see why anyone and everyone has to agree with, or even accept, someone's sexual orientation any more than he should be forced to agree with some else's politics."

"Now, dear. Calm down," Lydia Hollsworth said.

"Well, it irks me that gays think the rest of the world is obliged to kiss their asses," Doug Hollsworth said.

Lydia said, "Now, Doug. No one is asking you to do that. All they want is for you to show a little more tolerance."

The firefighter merely snorted.

"Was Bobby acquainted with any of Jason's Tucson friends?" I said.

"Certainly not," Mr. Hollsworth said.

Lydia shook her head in agreement. "Bobby might have met some of them once, but it was strictly by accident."

I said, "Kristy Serling."

"She's a wonderful girl," Lydia said, smiling.

"She comes from a good family. We know the Serlings," Doug Hollsworth added.

I said, "And she was a serious source of friction between Bobby and Perry Crisp."

"Bobby couldn't help that," Lydia Hollsworth said.

"Perry is under the impression Bobby stole Kristy from him," I said.

"Perry's full of shit," Bobby's father said. "Kristy made perfectly clear to Perry that she preferred our son to him. Perry simply couldn't deal with that."

"Richie Maldonado," I said.

"Richie's okay," Lydia said.

I thought to myself, if ever damnation by faint praise applied, her summary of Richie was a paradigm example.

"Just okay?" I said.

Doug Hollsworth said, "He's a pretty fair drummer, according to Bobby, but we really don't know much else about him."

Or try to find out, I imagined.

"Those people tend to stick together, you know. They treat us like outsiders, for chrissake," Doug said.

"And are we?" I said.

"White people made this country what it is," he said.

I wanted to say, "Xenophobe Nation?" But I refrained. He had used *Those people*. Them and us.

Lydia said, "Richie is a very friendly young man. And polite. There is nothing personal to dislike about him."

But the undertone was that, if Mrs. Hollsworth had a daughter, she wouldn't want the daughter to marry Richie.

"Polite, maybe, but he had an attitude," Doug Hollsworth said.

"What sort of attitude?" I said.

"I can't quite put my finger on it. Not exactly contemptuous, but close. Like he could take or leave all of us."

"Maybe he could," I said.

"Drummers are all a bit flakey, Bobby used to say," the man said.

"I wouldn't call Richie flakey, Doug. Just quiet," Lydia said.

"A quiet drummer," I said.

"Stand-offish. That's what the kid is," Doug said.

"Do both of you still want to stick with your 'They all got along fine' line?" I asked puckishly.

"As I said, it was nothing serious," Bobby's father said.

"Nothing that would lead to murderous intent, right?" I said.

"Definitely not," he said.

"No. None of those other boys would want to kill Bobby," Lydia said confidently.

"Would you mind showing me his room?" I said. "I'm not looking for anything in particular. I would simply like to get a better feel for your son. I know that sounds very amorphous, but I find that it helps me. I spend a lot of my time looking for missing teenagers and I've picked up useful…well, vibes, for lack of a better term, more than once. Quite often in fact."

Bobby's bedroom was scrubby-Dutch tidy, no doubt neater than when he was alive. The single bed with its matching Arizona Cardinals bedspread and pillow cases was made. On one wall I noted an Arizona Wildcats pennant, Diamondbacks and Phoenix Suns wall logos. His posters of stars were of Randy Johnson, Kurt Warner, and Steve Nash. Three white guys, I noted.

The opposite wall paid homage to guitar legends: Jimi Hendrix, Eric Clapton, Carlos Santana, and a pair of oldies, Les Paul and Hank Williams. The latter poster was not of Junior or the Third, but the original Hank Williams. No racial exclusion in Bobby's guitar heroes.

Hanging beneath the posters was an electric guitar with a white body and a black neck and headstock. When I stepped close to admire it, Doug Hollsworth said, "That's a Gibson Les Paul Custom SG Sidebar Classic. I gave that to Bobby for his thirteenth birthday."

"We gave it to him," his mother corrected.

"Paid over three thousand dollars for it," the proud father said.

"Very impressive," I said, meaning the guitar itself, the birthday gesture, and the price.

I then walked over to the sports wall. "Bobby didn't play on any teams, other than intramural?"

"No. Despite his incredible hand coordination playing guitar, he was a bit of a klutz on the field and on a court," his father said with a touch of melancholy. "Lord knows, I tried to work with him. But he couldn't field, couldn't hit, couldn't put a ball through the hoop. And at golf he had an incurable slice."

I said, "Did he play any online fantasy sports games? Have a football, baseball, or basketball team in one of the online leagues?"

"Not that I know of," Doug said. He looked at his wife, who shook her head.

"I don't see a computer."

"We have a desktop in the bedroom we use as a sort of office," Lydia said. "But Bobby rarely used that. He had his own laptop, but the police took that to check it out."

I wondered if the cops would find any nude photos of Kristy, Bobby, or perhaps someone else. I hoped not.

"What about his cell phone?" I said.

Doug Hollsworth said, "It hasn't turned up. We have no idea what happened to it. Bobby never mentioned losing it."

Lydia added, "And he took it with him everywhere. For all I know he slept with it under his pillow." At that thought she began to choke up.

A framed photo on his dresser showed Bobby standing on the deck of a boat. He is beaming as he shows off a large greenish-yellow, bulbous-headed fish. His father said, "That was taken a couple years ago right after school was out. We spent a week in La Paz on the Sea of Cortez side of Baja Sur and went out on a charter boat a couple times. That's a Dorado Bobby caught. As I recall it weighed just over forty pounds."

Lydia said, "La Paz is more affordable than Cabo and the charter boat captains speak pretty good English."

Perhaps she got the notion I was planning a fishing trip to Baja. I wasn't. And if I were, my Spanish is sufficient for me not to worry about whether any of the locals *habla inglais*.

"Does Bobby own a camera?" I said.

"Not a real camera. He prefers to buy those cheap throwaways. He'd never shown any interest in photography," his mother assured me.

Except for Kristy modeling her birthday suit.

"Are you a sports betting man, Mr. Hollsworth?" I said.

"Not really. I usually put a few bucks into our Super Bowl and March Madness bracket pools at the firehouse. Why do you ask?"

"Just curious. I live in Las Vegas. I feel I have to promote the local economy. You don't ever head up there for a weekend to drop a roll of nickels in the slots?"

He shrugged. "God, I can't remember the last time we were in Las Vegas. Do you, hon?"

"Years ago," Lydia said. "I doubt if we'd even recognize the place now. I hear it's changed a lot."

I said, "It has. Even I'm surprised sometimes after I haven't been on The Strip for a few days. Where I remembered a vacant lot, a mile-high hotel has sprung up, seemingly overnight."

Mrs. Hollsworth said, "It must be fun to live in such a lively city."

I inferred she was telling me Arroyo Arenoso was not a thrill-a-minute town, as if I had yet to discover that for myself. "In my line of work I experience more grim days than entertaining ones. Las Vegas nights are even worse."

"Why do you stay there, if it's so awful?" she said.

"Because I never lack work there."

They both just stared at me. It was time to hit them between the eyes.

"What can you tell me about your son's compulsive gambling habit?" I said.

"His what?" they said in chorus.

"Bobby was constantly betting on sports events. Not just the Super Bowl and March Madness, but on baseball, basketball, and football. Both professional and college football and basketball. And by constantly I mean weekly throughout those sports' entire seasons."

"Who told you this?" Lydia said angrily.

"Several people who had direct knowledge."

"Who?"

I shook my head. "Several of his schoolmates. I don't intend to name names—just yet."

"My god!" Lydia said. "Doug, did you know anything about this?"

Her husband said, "Hell no! Where did he get the money, for chrissakes?"

"Good question," I said deceptively.

The two parents looked suspiciously at each other. "Not from me, I swear," Lydia said.

Bobby's dad said, "How much money are we talking about?"

"Apparently several hundred dollars a week," I said, not really knowing exactly.

"Bobby didn't have that kind of money," Doug Hollsworth said.

"Where did he come up with it?" Lydia said.

I said, "I'm looking into that."

"Did he win usually?" the father said.

"According to those he told about his gambling, his losses far exceeded his winnings."

"Oh, Jesus!" Doug thought for a second, then said, "Who was he placing his bets with?"

"A bookie joint in Tucson."

"That's not even legal," he said.

"No."

Lydia said, "I had no idea he was driving to Tucson every week. How did he manage that?"

"He may not have. There may have been a bookie runner here." My friend Hex Denhart used several runners in Las Vegas.

"Do you think Bobby was killed because of his gambling?" Mrs. Hollsworth said.

"It's one possibility, although the question arises: Why kill a golden goose?" I said. If Sebastian Sechrest was fronting Bobby money in exchange for Bobby's modeling nude, the answer may have been far more complex.

"I simply can't believe any of this. How could I not have known?" Lydia said.

Doug Hollsworth expanded that to, "How could we both not have known?"

I hated to leave the two of them with more questions than answers, but I was in the same state, as I pointed out to them. I left them with both of them giving me assurances they would contact me if they uncovered, or thought of, anything new that might help.

Regarding Bobby's gambling, I considered the possibility that one or the other of them either knew, or at least suspected, their son was participating in sports betting well above and beyond the two or three annual big events that everybody and his brother pony up five bucks for. But, if one or both of them had suspicions, he, she, or they immediately went into denial. "Not my Bobby. He can't possibly really be doing that. Ergo: He's not." Everybody knows how easy it is not to believe what one doesn't want to believe.

32

After leaving the Hollsworth house I still had more than three hours on my hands until Sebastian Sechrest left school for home. No school events were scheduled for Friday evening. I had checked with Adelle regarding that. There was no Friday night football game or basketball game for him to attend to conduct the marching band or pep band. Sechrest could head home, kick his shoes off, prop his feet up, and sip a cold one. Or so he fondly imagined.

Adelle had discreetly inquired – via Jane Wheeler, so as to keep a distance between the query and me – whether Sechrest had any plans for the weekend. He didn't. So I was hoping he would go directly home, even if he had dinner or movie plans in Tucson for later in the evening. If he headed somewhere else, I would have to improvise a Plan B.

I picked up a sandwich, chips, and soda at Subway and drove to the city park. Several mothers, some pushing strollers, were entertaining their pre-school children there. And a young, ebullient teacher – probably from the nearby elementary school – led her class in playing several children's games on the browned out

Bermuda grass in one corner of the park. The late April temperature was in the mid-eighties, which was comfortable, especially knowing triple-digit temps were not far off. The park was big and I found a shady spot beneath a mulberry tree to sit, eat, and contemplate. The laughs and squeals of happy children were distant and only mildly bothersome.

Bobby Hollsworth's parents seemed straightforward enough, but I had been deceived by parental behavior before. Faux-sincerity and counterfeit grief came as easily to some parents as genuine anguish and heartfelt authenticity came to others. Perhaps my not being a parent myself contributed to my cluelessness, although I am rarely a backer of you-had-to-be-there-to-understand claims.

I also had to ask myself why might one of Bobby's parents be driven to kill him. A discovery of something unbearably shameful was all I could think of. But what would that be? The kid's gambling addiction? Unlikely. They would be disappointed, probably even dismayed. Angry? Maybe. But enough to murder him? Very doubtful.

Nude photos of their son, taken by someone else, was a different matter. Knowledge of those might well represent a tipping point. I had no idea how religious the Hollsworths were. Most people are sensitive to some degree. That's why we have laws against child pornography. Emotional enough to toast their son? Possibly. Often a tipping point cannot be predicted. What takes one person to the brink, sends another one over the edge. I had to admit that, if one or both of them had killed or had knowledge of who killed their son, each of them did a grand job masking the knowledge.

I was still convinced a connection existed between the deaths of Bobby Hollsworth and Colby Ambrose. Mrs. Hollsworth was right. If Bobby made his bets directly – in Tucson – he would have had to drive to the big city often enough for his absences to be noticed. Yet, no one noticed. So, he had to have used a runner. My friend Hex used runners, sending them to make pickups and deliveries all over greater Las Vegas. None of Hex's runners were especially bright guys, but every one of them was impeccably honest. They had to be. Otherwise, they would have found themselves taking a one-way trip down a very deep hole.

Colby Ambrose had to be Bobby's runner. I was sure of that. Colby was part of the betting parlor operation, but he wasn't smart enough to perform any tasks requiring brainpower. He was a leg man. And why does a leg man end up dead? For the reason I gave why Hex's leg men kept their jobs or lost them. Honesty and dishonesty.

When I claimed all of Hex's runners were honest, I mean all his current runners. Hex possesses almost psychic powers with regard to who his clients are and how much they bet. Twice in the past trusted runners tried to skim money from amounts they had picked up from bettors. Both of those runners – one was a young woman – went missing soon after Hex suspected he had been cheated. In neither case did Hex hire me to look for the missing runner. Nor did I volunteer.

So maybe Colby was skimming; maybe Bobby knew about it. Maybe he was in on it. That was a black hole worth sticking my head into. But first, I needed to find out more about Kirk McMullen and Randy Franklin, who had to be the brains in the trio. I called Stacy Park and fed her the two men's names.

"You want everything, including their shoe sizes, right?" she said.

"Pretend they're both potential boyfriends for you," I said.

"You mean you want photos of them naked?"

"Only if they have meaningful scars or tattoos. X-rays of broken bones would be better."

"You gonna pay me weekend rates? After all, I may have to forego several wild parties tonight and tomorrow night."

"Do I ever question your invoices?" I said.

"Come to think of it, you did once."

"But that was when we first started working together," I said.

"I decided to test you. See if you pay attention."

"An inattentive detective doesn't remain a detective very long, Stace."

"Okay."

I added, "If I had not mentioned the phony invoice charge you slipped in, would you have brought it to my attention?"

"You'll never know. But you trust that I would have, right?" she said.

"Have I ever mentioned to you what Hex does to co-workers he no longer trusts?"

"Do you dare tell me?"

"No, but I could feed you some pretty strong hints."

"He does more than just fires them, right?" she said.

"A lot more."

"But you're different from Hex."

"Not in every way."

"Which ways aren't you?"

"You don't ever want to find out," I said.

"I guess I don't. Okay. I'm on these two clowns like flies on –."

"On a screen door."

"Yeah."

"Have a fun-filled weekend, Stacy."

"And you watch your backside."

"As soon as I learn the trick."

"Speaking of tricks, how was Miss Sheila? Did she send you a thank-you note? Or deliver her thanks in person?"

"Focus on McMullen and Franklin."

"It's the age of multi-tasking, Poynter. Unlike you, I can pat my head and rub my belly simultaneously."

"Then do it. Talk atcha later." I pressed 'end' on my cell phone.

What a relief it always is when people do what you hope they will do. Sebastian Sechrest left school when I hoped he would. And then he drove straight home. I pulled behind him in his driveway just as he was exiting his whale-sized sedan and was in his face before he could shut his car door.

"Sebastian, old bean. How good of you to invite me over for a chat. I was hoping you would."

He was so startled he dropped his car keys. "What are you doing here? Get off my property before I call the police."

"Not so hasty, my man. If the police show up, they'll want to search your house. And that includes your computer files. How welcome a search would that be?" I said, crowding him.

"I don't know what you're talking about. Now go away."

"No, no, no. We're going inside and have our little chat."

"We're going to do no such thing."

"You're out-voted three to one." I showed him my handgun. "Smith, Wesson, and Poynter vote we go inside. Now pick up your keys very slowly and walk toward the door."

When he hesitated, I pushed the tip of the gun barrel up hard under his nose. "Care for a nosebleed?"

He gritted his teeth and stammered, "You wouldn't dare."

"Oh, I definitely would dare. And no jury in the land would convict me for shooting a vile and slimy pedophile like you. A few good looks at all the teen porno photos you own and I do believe that twelve men tried and true, and that includes women, would wish I had saved them the bother of having to listen to your pitiful defense before they convicted you."

"I'm no such thing."

"Oh, the DA will love hearing you proclaim your innocence on the witness stand. The more you deny, the more years behind bars he'll ask for. Not that you'll last very long in prison anyway. Do you know what prison inmates do to convicted pedophiles?"

Sechrest's eyes widened.

"Rather than tell you, Sebastian, I'll let your imagination soar. But let me fuel your fantasy. Imagine a dozen of the biggest, blackest, meanest dudes you've ever seen forming a circle around you. Are you getting the picture?"

Sechrest bit his lower lip.

"Inside. Let's see if we can spare you some of the horror that could befall you."

I spun him and pointed him toward his front door; then shoved the S&W hard into his back. Once we in his house, I locked the door behind us and motioned for him to take a seat on his sofa.

"This is an outrage," he said and glared at me.

"Not compared with what you've done."

"I've done nothing."

"Make it easy on yourself. Tell me where the photos are, both hard copies and the names of the computer files," I said.

"And if I don't? You're going to shoot me?"

"Oh, no. No shooting. I'm going to pistol-whip you. It's quieter and just as effective. But you can spare yourself. The choice is yours."

"You're disgusting."

"Don't try to turn the tables and make yourself the victim here, Sebastian. That's a loser's game. Just man up and tell me now what you'll end up telling me eventually anyway."

"There's nothing to tell. I don't know where you got the story that I am in possession of teen pornography, but your source is mistaken."

I took a deep breath before saying, "I guess I should have brought Kristy along and about now I would hand her a sharp knife. I'm sure she could get you to repeat the blackmail lines you've been feeding her."

"I have no idea what you are saying. Kristy Serling? I barely know the young woman."

"Barely. I like that. How do you manage to maintain your clever sense of humor, Sebastian? I hope you still have it after you've lost a few of your teeth."

"I have nothing more to say."

"Sebastian, Will Rogers once claimed there are three kinds of men. A very few who learn by reading. A few more who learn by observation. And the rest who insist on peeing on the electric fence for themselves. Now are you insisting on doing the equivalent of peeing on the fence regarding finding out what pistol-whipping is all about?" I tapped the butt of my S&W.

He simply stared at me. I raised my gun and he instinctively covered his face with both hands. I knew he would. So I landed the first blow on his left knee. Knees are ultra-sensitive to pain, as he discovered. And, when he clutched at his knee, while yelping, I landed a second blow to his right elbow. Elbows are even more sensitive to pain. Yelping turned to screeching. I could have called him a sissy, but tougher men than he was react the same way. Jolted nerves are no respecters of courage. Rambos howl as loudly as wimps when struck on crucial – and very vulnerable – spots. I didn't require a black belt in martial arts to learn that.

I watched Sebastian's eyes tear up and waited for him to stop yelping. Then I said, "Round one. How many are you good for?" I'm not sure he even heard me. Badly hammered nerves create a buzzing in the ears, as well as hurt like hell. I repeated myself.

"You'll go to jail for this. I'll sue your ass."

"Idle threats are always part of Round One, Sebastian. Spit them all out and then decide if you are up to Round Two. I'm patient. Well, up to a point."

He whimpered incoherently and began to tremble.

"Look, Sebastian. Tell me where the photos are before I end up tying you to my rear bumper and dragging your bloody carcass down to police headquarters with your computer sitting comfortably in my front seat. Once other people see those photos – and they will, if you don't show them to me first – the whole town will show up to watch Chief Morton feed you to a pack of starving Dobermans."

He dropped onto the sofa, curling himself into a fetal position.

"It's over, Sebastian. You're outed. As soon as Mrs. Haydenfurth finds out what you are, you won't find a teaching job this side of hell. Your school district won't play Vatican and shuffle you off to some other venue to start over. Hand over the photos; then you can lock yourself in your bathroom and slit your wrist veins, blow your brains out, drown yourself. Exit laughing for all I care. But I'll give you an opportunity to spare yourself enduring – facing – a public humiliation. You'll get to be in the next world by the time your shit hits the fan. But without the photos in my possession, you are going to get to face the music. How's that for an apt cliché?"

For the next twenty minutes Sebastian Sechrest showed me where he kept the nude photos of Bobby Hollsworth and Kristy Serling. He only spoke when spoken to, and then only in mumbled monosyllables. He handed over his hard-copy prints. I confiscated his desktop computer and his laptop. After searching his cell phone, I returned it to him. It contained no photos of naked teens.

I asked him, "Do you have Bobby Shane's cell phone?"

He shook his head.

"Then how did you get the photos of Kristy?"

In a low, slow voice, he told me, "Copied them from his cell when he was in the bathroom getting dressed."

"But you don't have his cell phone now?" I said.

A weak "No."

I never intended to allow him to take an easy way out. I used a pair of extension cords I found on a hallway closet shelf to tie him to a kitchen chair. I didn't want to search his house for a gun. I also didn't want him getting it and shooting me before I could exit his driveway.

"I'll send someone to untie you in a while," I assured him. He looked doubtful.

I was parking my Grand Cherokee in front of police head-quarters when Chief Morton emerged, looking to be in a hurry. I slowed him down. "I have some things I'd like you to take a look at, Chief."

"It will have to wait. I have three cars converging on Sebastian Sechrest's house right now. I have to run along."

Before I could decide how to play my hand, the chief took off.

33

I had no idea what combination of truth and lies Sebastian Sechrest would tell Chief Morton and his minions. I tried to tell myself I didn't much care. But I knew I had exaggerated the view that I would be handed a hero's medal for hammering the whereabouts of the porno files out of the band director. I could easily find myself facing assault charges, although a clever lawyer could surely sweet-talk a jury into voting me a get-out-of-jail-free pass. Or so I fondly imagined.

I put Sechrest's computers in the back of the Jeep next to the Krieghoff shotgun and covered them up with my emergency blanket. What to do with them remained up in the air. That might depend on Sechrest's story to the cops.

Adelle was in the kitchen grating cheese when I returned to her house. Taco mix was simmering on the stove top. "What have you been up to this day, Brother?"

I made a long story very short. "Not much. I had a picnic in the park, trying to meditate over the sounds of squeaking children."

"And what did you meditate on?"

"Oh, the nature of infinity. That kind of stuff."

"Infinity, you say."

"Yes. Did you realize there is more than one infinity? Several actually. And they're not all the same size."

"Adelle put down her hunk of cheddar and looked up at me. "You've been reading that man again."

"I have." *That man* was what Adelle called Raymond Smullyan, the mathematician whose puzzle books I read and adored.

"Anything else?" she said suspiciously.

"I made a few phone calls. I stopped by to see Chief Morton. He didn't have time for me. Something about going to see Sebastian Sechrest."

That got my sister's full attention. She gave the taco mix a stir and said, "Now why would the chief of police go to see Sebastian Sechrest, I wonder?"

"Maybe he wants advice on buying his daughter a new saxophone, "I said, playing dumb.

"Ellie already plays the violin," she said.

"Maybe he wants Sebastian to run for city council."

Adelle harrumphed. "I very much doubt that."

"Well, we'll just have to hide and watch, I guess."

My sister smiled. "You're better at that than I am."

"I've had more practice."

"Wash up, although dinner will be a while."

I took the cheese out of her hand. "I forgot to tell you, I've been invited out for dinner. Can you finish up your food prep and then refrigerate it for tomorrow might? I'll take you along and feed you."

"That's an offer I can't refuse. Where are we going? Or shouldn't I look a gift meal in the mouth?"

"Graciela's. The downside is that I'm interviewing her daughter, Juanita, in place of eating dessert."

"I don't mind. Do you want me to sit in on the interview?" she said.

"Good idea. It will surely help put Juanita at ease."

I helped Adelle finish her taco preparations. I wanted to be on our way to the cantina before Rollie Morton showed up on Adelle's doorstep to arrest me for assaulting Sebastian Sechrest.

Adelle and I were midway into our meal – *carnitas* for me, a *chili relleno* for her, and a beer each – when Roland Morton walked in the restaurant and looked around. A condemned man/last meal feeling hit me. And, sure enough, the chief walked directly toward us.

After talking off his Stetson, the chief nodded to Adelle. "Miss Poynter, good evening. How are you?"

Caught off-guard, Adelle forced a smile and said, "I'm fine, Chief. Would you care to join us?"

"No, thank you. It's your brother I came to see."

I swallowed and probably blushed. I figured Adelle was about to find out what a ruffian I can be at times. I'm sure I gave off a deer-in-the-headlights look. With a very dry throat, "What can I do for you, Chief?" barely escaped my mouth.

"I came to apologize to you, son. It was rude of me to dash off without finding out what it was you came to see me about," he said.

"Oh, it was nothing much. I...I just wanted to see if you had any more news to share. About either Bobby Shane or the kid in Tucson."

"As a matter of fact, I've just arrested Sebastian Sechrest for Bobby Shane's murder."

Adelle gasped aloud. "You've what?"

The chief nodded. "We received an anonymous phone tip that Mr. Sechrest had something vital to our investigation buried in his backyard. When we started digging we found Bobby Shane's cell phone and a plain brown envelope that contained photos of Bobby Shane and another under-age person I am not permitted to name. The photos showed these two people buck-ass naked. Not together, mind you. Separate photos of each."

Adelle's shoulders slumped. "My God. And I thought that man was relatively harmless."

"No, ma'am. Far from it," Chief Morton said. 'My dispatcher, by the way, says the caller was a female. The voice was very muffled but she's sure it was a female who placed the call. In any case, we've got it recorded. And we've already traced the call to a phone booth at the Tucson airport."

"Did Sechrest confess to murdering Bobby?" I said.

"No. But I'm sure he will." The chief chuckled. "Funny thing. When we arrived at his house we found the man tied up in his own kitchen."

"Tied up?" Adelle repeated.

"Yes, ma'am."

Here it comes, I thought. Ye olde handcuffs are about to be slapped on Wiley Poynter.

Instead, the chief said, "Mr. Sechrest said he had been the victim of a burglary. He said two young Hispanic males were waiting inside his house when he arrived home. According to him, they tied him up and stole both of his computers, a desktop and a laptop."

"He told us all of this before we told him we were there to dig up his back yard. I showed him the search warrant Judge Friedman had signed. Sechrest didn't even look at it. He just broke down and started bawling."

"So he buried Bobby's cell phone, eh?" I said.

"Sechrest denies it. Says he's been framed," the chief said.

"Did you check the contents of the cell phone?" I said.

"Nope. That poor hunk of plastic and chips is beyond salvation. Before he buried it, he baked it in his oven or something like that. The phone is fried. The plastic is partially melted and the thing won't work. But even broken it's solid evidence. And I intend to be there when the state gives that rotten bastard his lethal cocktail."

After the chief apologized for the interruption, excused himself, and left, Adelle said to me, "Wiley, you look kind of pale. Are you all right?"

"I'm just fine, Sis. The shock of Sechrest's being the murderer must have drained me for a moment."

"I know what you mean. The idea of that man's being a murderer leaves me feeling a tad woozy also. Whodda thunk?"

I was sure even a half-assed prosecutor could come up with a motive and plenty of opportunities for Sebastian to do Bobby in. Maybe Bobby asked for, or demanded, a bit too much money to support his gambling habit. Maybe he threatened to expose Sebastian for the dirty old man that he is. Nasty pieces of work like Sechrest never take kindly to being blackmailed themselves.

As for the weapon? Apparently Sechrest hadn't buried it next to Bobby's cell phone. So where was it? And why, for chrissake, bury an envelope full of nude photos? Well, criminals are almost never entirely rational and certainly not brilliantly so. Still, I had to wonder.

Juanita Bardella showed up on time, as her mother had promised. I almost wanted to excuse her, telling her I no longer needed to speak with her. But, because she had made time for me, I decided I had better go through the motions. Besides, maybe she could say something that would pile more evidence onto the case that Sebastian Sechrest was guilty of Bobby's murder. Or... point me in another, more convincing direction. I was far from sold yet on Sechrest's guilt – as Bobby Shane's murderer, that is.

Graciela introduced her daughter to me, then tactfully departed. Juanita was a stunningly attractive Latina with long, coal-black hair and skin every pimple-faced girl in America would sell her soul for. She wore a half-blouse, tied at the front, and low-rider, spray-on jeans over the edge of which the elastic band of her lavender panties showed. At the small of her back, just above the panty band, she had a tramp stamp. She saw me shamelessly stretching to get a better looking at the small red, blue, and yellow butterfly and turned to give me a better look.

She then slid into the booth across from me and said, "To the Aztecs butterflies are a symbol of the souls of deceased warriors and of women who died giving birth."

All I could manage was a dumb, "That's interesting."

"I guess you want to know what I know about Bobby," she began.

I nodded. "Are you aware that the police have arrested Mr. Sechrest for Bobby's murder?"

She blinked and said, mocking me, "That's interesting."

I said, "Why do you suppose Mr. Sechrest did it?"

"Mr, Sechrest and Bobby had a big fight, I know that. Bobby told me."

"A fight over what?"

She hesitated. "Money."

"Bobby wanted more?"

"Yes."

"And Mr. Sechrest refused?"

"Sort of."

"What does that mean?"

Juanita looked at Adelle and squirmed. "I don't want to talk about that."

"That? Do you mean the photos? We know about the photos."

She seemed surprised. "The photos of Bobby." A statement.

A long silence followed. I had played this game often enough to know that he who keeps his mouth shut the longest wins.

She finally said, "I guess you know about Kristy's photos, too."

I nodded.

"Mr. Sechrest was willing to pay Bobby more money, but only if Bobby could get Kristy to pose for him. And –." She dropped her gaze.

"And?"

"And me."

"Bobby refused?" I said.

"I refused," she snapped.

"Then what?"

"Bobby said that Mr. Sechrest told him, 'Convince them or else'."

"Them, meaning you and Kristy."

A tiny nod.

"What did Mr. Sechrest mean by 'Or else'?"

A shrug. "No more gambling money, I guess."

"What was Bobby's reaction when Mr. Sechrest gave him the ultimatum?"

"Bobby claims he blew up at Mr. Sechrest. But he also came back and pleaded with me to do it. He even offered to pay me from some of the money Mr. Sechrest would give him."

"You still refused," I said.

"Yes. Of course."

"Did Bobby say anything about Kristy's reaction?"

"He said she didn't want to do it either. Not for Mr. Sechrest."

"Are you, were you, aware that Bobby had photos of Kristy on his cell phone?"

She paused, but finally muttered a soft, "Yeah."

"Are you aware that Mr. Sechrest downloaded Bobby's photos of Kristy when Bobby had his back turned?"

"No." She seemed genuinely surprised.

"As far as you know, was anyone else aware of the photos Mr. Sechrest was taking of Bobby? Or aware of the photos of Bobby and of Kristy on Bobby's cell phone?"

She started to deny it, but her eyes gave her away and she knew I saw it in her panicky look. "Yeah," she muttered glumly.

"Who?"

"Perry."

"How did he find out?" As if I couldn't guess.

Juanita's lower lip trembled slightly. "I told him." Paused. Then she blurted out, "I thought he should know."

I am constantly amazed at how people attempt to justify their dubious behavior by trying to turn their actions into moral imperatives. Duty called, they claim.

"And what was Perry's reaction?"

"He was pissed."

"At Kristy?"

"More so at Bobby."

"How pissed?"

"Really, really pissed to the max."

"Did this surprise you?" Strictly rhetorical.

"That he was so angry at Bobby, yes. I wanted him to be angry with Kristy, not Bobby." The cat shows her claws and hisses.

"Did you ever hear Bobby speak of a Colby Ambrose?" I said.

"No. Who is he?"

"Bobby's sports parlor courier, the man who picked up Bobby's bets and delivered his winnings, if he had any."

Juanita gave me an odd look. "You got that wrong. Didn't Richie tell you?"

"Tell me what?"

She shook her head in dismay or disgust. I assumed her disappointment was with Richie, not with me. "Bobby's courier, or whatever you call it, was Richie's brother, Fabian. He collected Bobby's bets and took them to Tucson."

Now it was my turn to be disappointed with Richie. And I was glad I hadn't shooed Juanita away without questioning her. More fool me, if I had.

Juanita smiled impishly and said, "You know, I didn't turn Bobby down because I'm a prude. I'm not. Bobby's seen me naked lots of times and knows what a great body I have. Do you think so, too, Señor Poynter?"

I cleared my throat and was wondering how to respond when I felt Adelle kick my ankle. "Yes, I do. Definitely. You're very shapely."

"Thank you." She then jerked her thumb toward the cash register, where Graciela was standing, ringing up a customer. "The reason I said no to Bobby is because my mother would skin me alive if she ever found out. And she would find out. Believe me, she would."

She pointed up toward the wall next to us, festooned with colorful art depicting the Mayan and Aztec periods of Mexico's history. "She'd nail my hide to one of these walls and, for a week afterward, the luncheon special every day would be Juanita fajitas."

She grinned and said, "Someday maybe I will model my pretty flesh for *Playboy* or *Penthouse*. But not as long as I live under the roof of *mi madre aguila*."

Mother eagle indeed. I looked again at Graciela and saw a female Aztec warrior costumed in long white feathers and a great bronze beak. I thanked Señorita Bardella for her time and information and told her she was free to leave. As she walked away, her narrow hips moved as rhythmically as though they were a pair of percussion maracas. Cha, cha, cha; cha, cha, cha. Adelle kicked me again. I assumed this time for ogling too candidly.

34

Throughout my talk with Juanita, Adelle had said nothing, expressing herself only with the toe of her shoe. On the drive back to her house I apologized for inviting her sit in on what turned out to be a discussion of a rather touchy issue.

"Will you please stop it, Wiley? I resent your treating me as though I were some witless twitbrain. I deal with these on-the-verge-of-adulthood young people every day. I have more than a faint notion about what they think, what they do, what they talk about. My shock point has risen considerably from the days when I was just out of graduate school. Nothing that was said this evening came as any surprise to me."

"I'm sorry, Sis. I don't mean to treat you like a nun."

She scoffed. "Nuns, my dear brother, are no more naïve about the world than the priests who go about buggering young boys. A nun's habit has always been misunderstood to represent innocence and ignorance. It is a symbol of neither. A nun's habit is little more than a convenient mask."

"You've become cynical in your dotage, Sister."

"My view does not represent cynicism. I am merely separating myth from reality."

"There are those, Adelle, who claim a cynic is merely one who sees the world as it is, rather than as it is thought to be," I said.

"Ambrose Bierce. I know. I'm the one who told you he said that." She changed the subject. "Do you really think Sebastian murdered Bobby?"

"He might have, but I'm not convinced."

"What makes you think not?"

"I don't think he had sufficient motivation – unless Bobby threatened to expose his photographic predilections. I'm not sure Bobby did threaten him. Sebastian was Bobby's golden goose after all."

"People have committed murder for far more trivial reasons," Adelle reminded me.

"Indeed, they have. But killing Bobby was not a trivial matter. Killing someone over something inconsequential is almost always a spur-of-the-moment action. Done hastily and sometimes even unintentionally. Second degree stuff. Or manslaughter. But one doesn't plunge a push dagger into someone's back either acciden-tally or as part of a petty quarrel."

"Drunken perhaps?" Adelle said.

"That's possible. Does Sebastian drink?"

"He's not a teetotaler, I know that. But I don't think he's an alcoholic either."

"He wouldn't have to be to end up in a drunken rage, though it helps," I said. "But what bothers me most at this point is the cops' finding photos buried in the backyard, along with Bobby's phone. And an anonymous caller telling the police where to look for the phone. If Sechrest had the phone in his possession and buried it, who else would know he had it and also that he had buried it? And why would someone else know?"

"You're saying it would be unlikely for Sebastian to tell anyone else?" she said.

"Yes. Closet porn photographers are, by nature and necessity, highly secretive. And I'm guessing Sechrest is a loner in most other respects as well. Am I right?"

Adelle said, "I don't know the man all that well, but yes. He's not married. He currently doesn't have a girlfriend. Hasn't had one since I've known him." Pause. "Or boyfriend either. You asked me all this already once before, Wiley."

"You're right. I did. I forgot. Any social life at all?"

"Not much. Oh, he attends faculty and staff functions. But he rarely stays very long and never volunteers to help out in the planning or putting on of any event. Mostly, I believe, he keeps to himself and enjoys his music. He plays several instruments, though mostly the cello, and has a vast collection of CD's. In fact, he is the only person I know who still owns a turntable. In working order even. He has a large collection of vinyl albums, mostly classical stuff, operas and the like. He explained to me once that he is of the opinion that many of the great works of music still sound best when played on vinyl, that even the finest remastered works on CD's don't measure up to the quality on his vinyl albums. I wouldn't know. I have neither the training nor the natural ear to notice nuanced differences he claims to be able to distinguish."

I said, "So who was the anonymous caller? And how did the caller come to know where Bobby's phone was hidden?"

"A nosy neighbor?" Adelle said. She smiled and pointed to Mrs. Fortunato's house as I pulled into my sister's driveway and shut off the Jeep's engine.

"Maybe? Has Sechrest even mentioned having a neighbor from hell?"

"I can't say that he's ever mentioned his neighbors at all."

We went inside and I was still mulling the anonymous caller. Sechrest had tried to get Kristy to model for him. Where had that discussion taken place? At school or at Sechrest's house? I couldn't quite imagine Sechrest broaching the subject at school, for fear someone else might overhear him. Yet, I couldn't imagine Kristy going to Sechrest's home to be propositioned. I convinced myself she considered him a dirty old man well before he invited her to take off her clothes as a prelude to smiling for his candid camera.

Even so, she made the most sense to me in a backhanded way. She feared anyone else's finding out Sechrest had compromising photos of her. But by phoning the police she would practically guarantee such photos would be brought to public light. But if she had little faith I could stop Sechrest from uploading her photos to the internet or sending them to her friends and family, if she judged that she was doomed no matter what, she could have decided to make sure Sechrest would suffer exposure as a pornographer and a blackmailer as much as she surely was going to suffer literal exposure.

The question remained, however: How did she know the camera was buried in Sebastian's backyard? Had she been in possession of the phone all along and buried it herself to entrap Sechrest, knowing that he had hard copies of her photos that would be found and earn him an indictment? Or did she know someone else had planted the phone? I needed to talk to her to see if she would tell me.

Because I try hard not to be a cell-phone asshole, I had turned my phone off while I was inside Graciela's. Not until my sister and I returned to her place did I realized I had not turned it back on. I had missed two calls. One from Kristy; one from Las Vegas.

I called Kristy first.

"Damn you, damn you, damn you. I hate you," she screamed at me and then hung up. My repeated efforts to call her again got me nothing but a busy signal.

Interesting. Was she genuinely angry with me? Or was her screaming an attempt to introduce a red herring, make me think – eventually the police think, too – that she had not been the anonymous caller? That she was upset because photos of her had been found and that she thought I had let her down by failing to get the photos and files from Sechrest? I had no way of knowing whether she was sincerely outraged or merely being devious. So I put that dilemma aside and returned Dante Foster's call from Las Vegas.

Dante owns and operates an indoor shooting range on the east side of town, next to a gym where local prizefighters train. After getting an engineering degree at Purdue, Dante became an MP in the Marine Corps in the Gulf War. Then he refused to reenlist, despite the handsome bonus dangled under his nose. He reputedly told the Marines the government couldn't print enough money to entice him to sign up for another tour. Having lost interest in engineering, he tried being a cop in Reno, but he discovered he didn't like taking orders from police commanders any more than he had liked taking orders from Marine Corps officers. Then an uncle died and left him more than enough money to open the shooting range.

He kept just enough of a police instinct to agree to help Jack Stonecipher and me out now and then, as long as no traveling outside of Las Vegas was involved. Mostly, he didn't even have to leave his range. People and information walked through his front door. He did a lot of target-shooting himself and could often be seen walking around his establishment with his earplugs stuffed into his head. But, with or without earplugs, Dante Foster's hearing was keen. So was his sense of smell.

He could smell out guys and sometimes women, too, who had criminal records as effectively as Stacy Park could unmask them using her computer wizardry. Dante understood most of his clientele better than they understood themselves. Better yet, Dante was soft-spoken and discreet. Everybody knew and loved the man's smile and charm. What few people knew was the cobra lurking behind the charm.

"Bad news, Wile," he said when he answered. "Jack's in an ICU unit at North Vista Hospital. In a coma. Couple of guys worked him over very hard. I was going to let you know in any case, but, as I understand it, Jack was doing some digging for you lately."

"I'll be there as quickly as I can. Any word on the guys who did it?" I said.

"I'm working on that. Sluggo gave me the call. He knew you were out of town," Dante said.

Sluggo was the code name Dante, Jack, and I used for a lieutenant of the LVMPD. The three of us had rescued his younger sister some years back from a lunatic boyfriend who had essentially kidnapped her. When we returned her alive – and the boyfriend became permanently missing – the lieutenant pledged eternal fealty to the guys he dubbed the Three Amigo-teers. Eh! He's a cop, which means he has a limited imagination. But, in any case, finding the abductor and his abductee hadn't been all that difficult, but we didn't tell the lieutenant what a piece of cake it had been.

Dante passed on to me the details of the ambush on Jack, as the lieutenant had provided them to him. "The attack came as Jack was walking from his car to his office. You know how dark that back lot is at night. Anyway, a bus boy and cook who work at the restaurant next door were out back having a smoke when they saw two guys pop up from between cars, rush Jack, and beat him to a pulp. They wouldn't go to Jack's defense, of course, but after the attackers vamoosed they did dial 911. They told the cops the two thugs drove off in a piece-of-shit pickup truck. Red, no 'caps, badly damaged rear window. And, no, the restaurant guys didn't get a license number. They think it was an oversized Chevy, but we both know that makes it one among thousands in this town. The color, caps, and window will help though."

"Talk to any doctors?" I said.

"Yeah, but they say it's early times. I hate to tell you this, Wile, but in the Gulf I saw Iraqis and Kuwaitis in Jack's current shape. None of them lived happily ever after. Or for very long."

"Probably so. But keep this in mind, DF. Jack has always eaten his veggies. Takes vitamins, too."

"There's that. I just don't want you to get your hopes up."

"When are my hopes ever up? About anything?"

"I know: Better to be pleasantly surprised than to be bitterly disappointed."

"You got it."

"Want me to pick you up at McCarran?" he said.

"Sure. But I'll call you when I'm on the ground so I don't waste your time. What hospital did you say he's in?"

"North Vista."

I looked at my watch. "Friday night. I may not get a flight out tonight. All the nickel-slot ladies will have booked by now. But there's probably a six a.m. I can catch, even if it's booked solid. Some slug-a-bed always oversleeps or says 'Fuck it' and pulls the covers back over his head."

"I'll see you when I see you. Sorry."

"Dante."

"I know. Never apologize for what ain't my fault."

"*Mañana, amigo.*"

35

Using Adelle's computer I bought a ticket on Southwest Airlines' 6 a.m. non-stop flight from Tucson to Las Vegas. But, instead of going to bed as I should have, I kissed my sister goodnight and headed out to Skyler's Family Restaurant, hoping to catch Fabian Maldonado before the kitchen closed down. Because it was Friday night, I assumed the restaurant would keep later hours and that Fabian would be working. I was correct on both assumptions.

I arrived shortly after 10:30 p.m. and saw that Skyler's was open until 11:00 on Fridays and Saturdays. The manager told me Fabian was working until close. He explained the kitchen crew's closing clean-up chores usually kept them there until 11:30, sometimes a little later. When I told the manager what I wanted, he said I could sit in a booth and nurse free coffee and pie until Fabian was finished and had punched out.

I ordered a piece of coconut cream pie to go with the coffee and sat back to wait. Neither the pie nor the coffee was especially good, but free is free.

At 11:45 Fabian emerged through the double swinging doors of the kitchen. "Boss said you want to talk to me."

"Do you mind?"

A shrug. "Not here. Buy me a beer?"

"Sure. Where to?" I said.

"Follow me."

Fabian drove a custom low-rider mini-pickup. I guessed it might once have been a Mazda. He headed north on I-19 toward Tucson. I followed and kept watching for sparks to fly from the low-rider's fenders as they scraped asphalt, but none did. He took the Sahuarita exit, worked his way over to Pima Mine Road, and the next thing I knew we were pulling into the sprawling parking lot of one of the Desert Diamond casinos. How apropos for the conversation I intended to strike up with Fabian!

With Easter behind them, most of the snowbirds had already packed up their lawn chairs and golf clubs and were arriving back in Kansas or Manitoba, ready to thumb through slick brochures promising more fun in the sun via cruises through the Caribbean or sundry Greek isles. A few monster RV's were still camped along the fringes of the lot, but they represented only a fraction of those that would have been there in February and March.

From the number of cowboy hats and cowboy boots I saw inside the packed casino, most of the patrons were either locals or wannabe locals. The smell of cigarette smoke and stale beer was thick enough to make me almost wish they all were Mormons, but I soldiered on through the haze and finally took a seat next to Fabian at the bar.

The bartender looked like a female cage wrestler. She had a long scar across her left cheek and rough-hewn hands that made me suppose she might have been a blacksmith in her former life. She wore punk pink hair, sky-blue eye shadow, and a nose stud. I figured her for a diesel-dyke, but as long she gave our beers decent heads I didn't care who or what else she gave head to.

Fabian ordered two Coors, then turned to ask me what I wanted to drink. I asked for an Amstel from the tap and then plunked a twenty on the countertop, guessing how little change I would get.

"So whatcha wanna know, Mr. Detective?" Fabian said, after downing one of his beers in one steady gulp.

"Colby Ambrose."

"Beats me who killed him."

"How much contact did you have with him?"

"As little as possible."

"Which amounted to –?"

"He was usually around the house when I made my deliveries and pickups."

"What was Colby's job?"

Fabian laughed. "To stay the fuck out of everybody else's way."

"He obviously failed to stay out of somebody's way," I said.

"That's why I don't live in Tucson. Too rough for me."

I doubted that, but didn't say so. "Colby was a partner in the betting parlor though, right?"

"A silent partner. He put up some initial money. His old man is some kind of big cigar up in Phoenix. Heads up a fancy law firm, I think. Colby has – well, had – a trust fund."

"But no particular role in the day-to-day operations of the parlor?" I said.

"None that I know of. He was a nice guy, but one brick short in the head."

"If he had a trust fund, why did he work as a bouncer at O'Banion's?"

"You kiddin' me? So he could meet chicks and flex his muscles for them. His biceps, that is. I don't think he got to do much flexin' of the one that counts."

"Did he have any enemies?"

A slow shrug. "I didn't know him that well. Or want to. But you gotta figure a bouncer is gonna piss somebody off now and then, right?"

"Did Colby know Bobby?"

Fabian's pause to finish off half the second Coors told me he did. "Kind of."

"What makes you say that?"

A hard-thinking pause. Then, "I saw 'em together one time."

"In Tucson?"

"Here. The casino. Well, the parking lot." A laugh. "Bobby wasn't old enough to throw away his money here inside."

"What were they doing?"

"Just talkin'." He gave me a funny look. "Neither Bobby nor Colby was a queer, if that's what you're thinkin'."

I wasn't, but let it slide.

"Did they see you?"

"Naw. I was with my buddy Domingo. He drives a silver Dodge Ram. His beast don't attract attention like mine does."

"Did Bobby ever mention Colby to you?"

"Nope. Like I said, I only seen 'em together that once. And I wasn't about to ask Bobby what he was doing talking with Colby. None of my business. The less I know, man, the less time I gotta sit on a barstool answering some guy's questions, you know?"

"Yeah. I understand. Can I buy you another beer?" I said, finishing my own.

"No thanks. I've got to work lunch tomorrow. But first I gotta drive home. My truck's a cop magnet. So, even with these two beers, I'm gonna have to sit a while before I head out. Last thing I need is a DUI."

"You have always been Bobby's courier, correct?"

"Always."

"For how long?"

"Couple of years, I guess. Yeah. About the time the band became a regular thing. When they started getting' gigs and takin' in some cash."

"Does Bobby place bets with anyone else?"

A grin and a shake of the head. "There ain't no one else, man. The Tucson guys got no competition. Nice, eh?"

"Were you aware where Bobby's gambling money came from?" I said.

"At first it was his own money. Later it came from that band director guy. Mr. Sechrest is his name, Richie told me."

"Why do you suppose Mr. Sechrest fronted Bobby the cash to gamble with?"

Fabian thought about that, finally saying, "Beats me. Like I told you, Bobby ain't no queer."

"Why are you so sure about that?"

"Easy. 'Cause Richie tells me Bobby's been fuckin' the brains out of Juanita Bardella."

"Is Richie sure about that?"

"Sure, he's sure. He's got cell phone photos of them doing it. He showed me."

"How did he come to have those?"

Another shrug. "You'll have to ask Richie."

"You've seen the photos. Do they look like Bobby and Juanita are posing for Richie?"

"I don't think so. Bobby's got Juanita pinned. They're going at it so hot and heavy, I doubt if they even knew Richie was takin' their pictures. My poor little brother."

"Why do you say that?' I asked.

Fabian snickered. "Richie's had the hots for Juanita since junior high, man. Drooling like...like a St. Bernard. And along comes Bobby Shane, a sweet-talkin' *gringo*, and he's the one who gets to put his Chiquita banana into Richie's heartthrob. Makes me wanna cry."

Fabian was obviously mocking his little brother. I knew how Richie would feel if he knew. Adelle had spent a lifetime mocking my ways. But I still loved her dearly. I hoped Richie felt the same way about Fabian.

So Juanita had been humping Bobby while taunting Perry about Kristy's posing nude for Bobby. Not nice. And both Perry and Richie were angry as wasps whose nest had been stirred that Bobby was getting all the action. I was convinced that, for all her protestations, Adelle didn't know half as much about what was going on among the seniors in her classes as she imagined she did. But, for all the – no, *backstabbing* won't do – jealousy, spite, and carnal intrigue thick as molasses, I still had to question whether any of it triggered murder. I thought not. Otherwise, prom night at every high school from Boston to San Diego would end up running knee-deep in blood. Teenage spirits run high for sure, but even with hormone levels at mountain-high peaks, these kids were not mad as hatters. They assuredly understood "Get even", but nearly all of them had been sufficiently repressed by age seventeen to limit their payback to less-than-fatal conduct. Or so I fondly imagined. I hoped I was not as cluelessly gullible as I judged my sister to be.

By the time I returned to Adelle's house, I barely had time to pack a bag and head back to Tucson International Airport. I removed Sebastian Sechrest's computers from the Jeep and shoved them under the bed in the bedroom I used whenever I stayed with Adelle. I also placed the shotgun and my two handguns under the bed. I had no idea how long I would be away. I figured if I was gone very long, Adelle, obsessive about cleaning as she was, would start to dust under the bed, find the guns and computers, wince, shake her head in bewilderment, then try to keep calm and carry on.

I felt naked leaving all three of my weapons behind. But I had no choice. I would tell Dante to bring a handgun for me when he picked me up at the airport. I knew there was something desperate and childish about feeling vulnerable without a gun holstered at the small of my back, but there it was. Recognizing an obsession for the stupidity it is doesn't mean you can make it vanish with a wave of your hand. Philosophers from Plato to Kant to Freud have pointed out that the human mind is not a singularity, but rather closely akin to a quarrelsome committee. And they all agree, as well, that Reason is the most feckless member at the table.

36

Saturday

Looking down, I saw that the airplane I was on was over the Grand Canyon. Looking up, I lamented again that Southwest Airlines was the only airline with non-stop flights between Tucson and Las Vegas.

"Sir? Is everything all right?"

The middle-aged female flight attendant doling out peanuts and soda in my section of the plane was bending over speaking to me, I belatedly realized.

"What?"

"You've been looking up for some time, sir. Are you feeling ill?" she said.

"Not yet. But if I spot any sub-surface cracks along any lap joints in the roof, I might be."

"Sir, those problems have been taken care of with all our planes. This flight is perfectly safe, I assure you."

"An aeronautical engineer, are you?" I said.

"No, sir. Are you?" She gave me a smug look.

"No, but then I'm not the one issuing blithe assurances here, am I?"

"Just sit back and relax, sir. All will be well."

"With me, yes. But I have a fastened seatbelt. If the roof pops, you'll be the one who'll get a close-up look at the bottom of the Canyon."

"Sir, that is not going to happen."

"How long until we reach McCarran?" I said.

She looked at her watch. "I'd say another twenty minutes."

"Thank you."

I had an aisle seat. The guy across the aisle looked at me scornfully. I pointed to the ceiling of the plane and said to him, "I'm tired of watching. It's your turn."

The lady crammed into the middle seat to my left nudged me. When I looked at her, she whispered, "Are you seriously worried or were you just putting her on?"

I whispered back, "What do you think?"

"I think this airline has no sense of humor about the safety of its planes."

I laughed. "We'll see when we land. Perhaps I will be escorted off."

"You think?" she said.

"No. But you're right. They clearly don't like passengers to remind them of their recent problem. I might add that they apparently do have a sense of humor about their maintenance practices."

She said, "Close your eyes and think of something pleasant."

"Are you going to close your eyes and think of England?"

She said, "There you go. Sexual fantasies are great distractions."

"Are you speaking as an expert?"

She smiled broadly. "You found me out. Yes. I am a Dr. Ruth type. A sex therapist. I'm giving a speech on overcoming male inadequacies at the MGM Grand this afternoon. Would you care to attend?"

"Do I look like a man in need of your therapeutic techniques?"

"I can't judge by first impressions. I'd have to evaluate you more fully. In private, of course. So as not to embarrass you."

"You have no idea how easily I embarrass."

"Precisely my point. I would need to interview you and examine you thoroughly."

"Why does this happen to me?" I said.

"What is happening to you?"

"I get propositioned and I don't have time to submit.'

"I'll be in Las Vegas all weekend."

"May I have your business card and your room number at the MGM?"

"I don't know yet what room I'll be staying in. But once I check in, I'm sure the hotel will gladly provide you my room number."

"No. They're quite touchy about that. But with your card I can give them your name and ask them to ring your room."

Her card read: Alicia Braden, Ph.D., with an address in Tucson.

"Miss or Missus Braden?" I said.

"Miss. I don't care to get any closer than that to my work."

"Nor I."

"And you are?" she said.

I handed her my card.

"Oh my. Did you solve a crime in Tucson and are now returning home?"

"Not quite. I'm working on a murder in Arroyo Arenoso and I'm taking a break from that to see a colleague who is presently in a coma, having been beaten within an inch of his life. Another crime to solve."

"You live dangerously."

"Too dangerously at times, I'm afraid."

"How exciting!"

She shuddered ever so slightly. Whether from trepidation or from a tingle of exhilaration, I wasn't sure. Both, I imagined.

"Do make time to come see me. A bedside watch over a man in a coma is therapeutic, I agree. But after so long –. Well, your butt gets numb, your mind begins to wander, and your friend still doesn't know you're there. At that point, you should take a break. Get some exercise."

"Exercise."

"Yes, I recommend a lengthy workout."

"Any particular kind of workout?"

"Jogging is such a bore," she said.

Just then the forward-section attendant began his spiel about a last trip through the cabin, turning all electronic devices off, seats and trays into their upright positions, et cetera.

When the attendant had completed his pre-landing blather, Miss Braden leaned close and said, "I'm so taken with the phrase 'upright position'. What about you?"

"I'm downright thrilled by it."

"Oh, you're so witty." She squeezed my left bicep and held on.

We didn't speak again until we were exiting the passageway and entering the packed seating area. Miss Sex Therapist walked ahead of me. She turned so abruptly and unexpectedly I ran into her. Instead of stepping back, she pressed forward into me. "See you tonight at the Braden private gym?"

I nodded. Not because I necessarily meant it, but to give me some breathing space. I maintained a deliberate distance while she stood at the luggage carousel. She finally found her mauve suitcase and went off to hail a taxi. After fetching my luggage, I phoned Dante and he warned me he might be as long as half an hour cutting through rush-hour traffic. I told him to take his time, to drive safely, that Jack was unlikely to jump out of bed and run away.

My next call went to the MGM Grand. Feigning confusion, I inquired if I was correct that the sex therapists were meeting at that particular hotel. And if so, when and where they were meeting.

"That would be the Trans-Mississippi Association of Professional Sex Therapists, sir. They are meeting from 10 a.m. until 5 p.m. on level three of our conference center. Rooms 314 and 315."

"And is there a speaker named Braden by chance?" I said.

After a moment, the young voice said, "A Dr. Alicia Braden is listed as giving the main address. Her speech begins at 2 p.m., sir."

Ah! Suspicions allayed. She was not a fraud. In my career I had come across a sizeable number of people, mostly men, who carried with them fake business cards, touting themselves as CEO or Chairman of the Board of some lofty-sounding, but non-existent corporation. The point, of course, was to charm the bras and panties off gorgeous, naïve young females by the pretense of possessing power and wealth. Nearly all such men who resorted to such a ploy could never get to first base by relying solely on their real status.

Alicia Braden had puzzled me because she was only moder-
ately attractive and sliding into middle age. That combination,
I knew, induced horrific insecurities in some women. My initial
impression of her was that she could handily be one such female.
By the time I ended my call to the MGM Grand, I decided I had
been wrong.

Waiting for Dante to pick me up, I began thinking of Jack lying
prone and nearly lifeless in the hospital. That made me reflect that
a week had passed since Bobby Hollsworth's body had been found.
Quite often this was the time when families of murder victims
begin to dwell on the images they've put together in their heads of
how their loved one must look following the dreaded and unavoid-
able autopsy. Their near and dear, they know, will never look life-
like again. An open-casket calling will be inappropriate. As they
picture Y-incisions and cranial sawings, their frustration and anger
begin to grow exponentially. And those, like me, who are looking
for the perpetrator of the murder begin to be badgered, harassed,
screamed at and cursed. Blame for the crime begins to spread like
blood from a heinous wound until the victim's kin often can barely
distinguish the hunters from the hunted.

For that reason, I was glad, or at least relieved, I was no longer in southern Arizona. Doug and Lydia Hollsworth would be
reaching that condition soon, if they hadn't already. I couldn't
blame them. On the other hand, I didn't want them blaming me
for not having the murderer in hand. Maybe the arrest of Sebastian Sechrest would assuage them. Unfortunately, his being jailed
failed to allay my own growing apprehension that the murderer
remained at large.

37

Dante phoned to say he was stuck in traffic. Rather than stand out on the curb inhaling car exhaust, I remained in the terminal, but where I could see the curb. While waiting, I phoned and left Adelle a message to let her know my plane had landed, *sans* unexpected holes in its frame.

After I hung up, I looked around and saw a sixty-ish man wearing a John Deere cap competing with a woman I took to be his dowdy wife. They seem to be in a race to see who could feed silver dollars into side-by-side slot machines faster. It was easy for me to determine that Pops was losing, both to his wife and to the Clark County Airport System, owner of the slots.

When the machine had ingested the last of his coins he looked at his watch, looked again, then said, "Come on, Ida Mae. We don't want to miss our flight. We still got to go through that damned security line."

Just then Ida Mae hit three cherries and her machine belched out a couple pounds' worth of change. She clapped and squealed as if she had just guessed the exact value of the washer-dryer combo behind Door Number Three.

"Ida Mae!"

"Just you wait, Elmer. I ain't finished here yet."

"Okay. Go ahead. But I warn you. We're going to miss our plane."

Ida Mae gave Elmer Fudd a look that said she didn't give a shit if she missed the next hundred flights back to Ottumwa, Oskaloosa, Cedar Falls or whatever other pissant corn-field community they had decamped from to wallow in the bliss of Glitter Gulch. When I saw Dante Foster's Hummer 3 pull up at the curb, I felt a momentary twinge of melancholy that I would never get to know the final denouement of the *American Gothic Meets Las Vegas* show.

Dante was in surly mode when I hoisted myself up into the Hummer's shotgun seat. Even the City That Never Sleeps experiences a morning rush hour and Dante had been trapped in it. His lead-foot driving style was legend and he had once opined the only place a Hummer should be obliged to creep along at a cautious pace was the on streets of Baghdad.

I said, "With this beast you could have driven right over the top of anyone who slowed you down."

"Fucking old farts from Kansas. I wish to holy hell they'd leave their goddamned Cadillac Sevilles and Lincoln Town Cars parked in their barns. Why don't they just fly out and then take taxis?" he grumbled as he pulled out into heavy traffic.

"Economics, Dante. Economics. To frugal, hard-working farmers a Seville or a Town Car is not an extravagance, a taxi ride is."

He looked at me as though I had just told him two pair beat four of a kind.

I said, "Besides, do you really want to double the number of taxis in this town? That will mean doubling the number of lunatic, camel-jockey cab drivers."

"Can't fuckin' win, can I?" he muttered.

I said, "You know what snow blindness is, right?"

"Yeah. So?"

"There's an equivalent condition in the Midwest known as corn blindness. It comes from seeing nothing but green for a protracted period of time. That's what these old-fart farmers suffer from when they come to Las Vegas. It takes days and days of staring at flashing neon before they can see again. Corn blindness is what makes them drive so slow. They can't help it."

"Wiley, you spew more bullshit than Mauna Loa spews lava. Glad to have you back."

"I wish I was returning under more cheerful circumstances."

"Me, too. Oh, by the way, your new toy is on the seat behind you."

I reached back and brought up a shiny new handgun. "And this is–?"

"Read the grip. Sig Sauer. A P250. It's the nine millimeter model. Fifteen round mag clip. It's loaded. Plus I brought you two extra clips and a paddle holster. That one has a normal trigger length. Sig makes a short trigger model, but I figure you need all the lever you can pull."

"Thank you very kindly, sir. I'll love it dearly."

As Alicia Braden had pointed out to me, Jack Stonecipher wasn't going anywhere soon. So, instead of going straight to the hospital, Dante drove us to Jack's office, parking in the back, two spaces away from Jack's aging green and white Land Rover. We peered into the Rover but couldn't get in. Dante said he forgot to ask for Jack's car keys at the hospital, but that he would when we returned.

I figured we'd poke around to see what Jack might have left on his desk or in a file to suggest where he had been and who the goons who worked him over might be. Jack and I each had a key to the other's office. Dante had a key to both as well.

Jack was tidier than most bachelors. He kept his notes the same way he played poker, in the clichéd close-to-the-vest style. A half hour of rummaging around produced only what I knew already. Boyd Dupree had stayed at the Aliante Hotel.

Mostly Dante and I found copious notes relating to a case Jack was working on for a client of his own. Las Vegas has more than its share of lad-dee-dah people living in fancy digs, wearing elegant togs, and adorning themselves with lavish jewelry. Or rather *bling*, as the hip folks these days refer to gold chains, diamonds, pearls, and silver trinkets, both cheap and dear. And where there are upmarket ornaments lying about, thieves abound.

Jack's client had been a victim of a burglary ring specializing in unburdening rich folks of their blingy treasures. The socialite in question was especially interested in recovering a pair of diamond earrings which she claimed bore more sentimental value to her than dollar value. The lady's sentiment obviously ran deep, because the sparkly baubles were insured for six figures.

Jack wisely left hunting the thieves to the local gendarmerie. His approach had been to seek only the objects of the heist, paying weekly visits to every pawn shop in metro Las Vegas, both reputable and disreputable. The cops, too, made periodic stops at those same establishments, armed with lists of stolen loot. But many pawn shops were in possession of offerings that never made it out onto public display. There were goods and there were goods.

Jack combined the perfect blend of charm, wisdom, and cunning to tease out those treasures hidden from those not in the know – the back-door market. He figured his client's diamonds would be offered at auction in such a bazaar. Or else they would be whisked away, to be peddled *sub rosa* in Hollywood, Miami, Acapulco, Monte Carlo or some similar venue where Pretty People bought such luxury knick-knacks with no questions asked – and paid for them out of petty cash.

From Jack's office we went to North Vista Hospital. I hate hospitals, but who doesn't? The eerie, muted, ubiquitous blue-white light that hospital corridors emit gives me the creeps. Any second I expect a team of nurses and doctors to come flashing past me, answering a Code Black, or whatever color it is they respond to in a nano-second when alarms begin to blare from a semi-darkened room with its door half-shut. I am always poised to press myself against the corridor wall to let the emergency players pass and to pray for whoever's soul is teetering on the edge, primed to take a tumble – irretrievably perhaps – into The Abyss. And I'm not even a praying man.

I didn't recognize Jack, even when I stood next to him. He was wrapped like a mummy out of a Boris Karloff flick. During an interminable hour, his only other visitors were a pair of nurses, one an overly cheerful young thing, the other a scowling, just-dare-to-ask-what-I'm-doing Nurse Ratched stereotype. Plus the hospital chaplain, a round-faced, middle-aged woman wearing a for-God-so-loved-the-world expression on her face. I wickedly wanted to slap her into the next world. When she handed me her card, I shooed her out before she could spout any pious platitudes. She reminded me of Ambrose Bierce's ditty on piety:

The pig is taught by sermons and epistles
To think the God of Swine has snout and bristles.

My picturing Her Holiness with a pug nose made me feel better.

I had been sitting too long in an uncomfortable chair while watching numbers flash and squiggly lines peak and plunge in some sort of quasi-rhythmic patterns on the bedside monitor. Jack hadn't twitched any portion of his plaster-cast body by as much as a millimeter since Dante and I arrived. Finally, I decided I had seen enough. I signaled to Dante that I wanted to vamoose. He didn't argue.

With Dante's consent, I phoned Stacy Park and invited her to join us for lunch at Cajun Crawfish in Chinatown. Only now Chinatown is called the Asian District, lest politics-wise we incorrectly slight Laotians, Thais, Malaysians, Burmese, Mongol hordes, Khmer Rouge, the sons and daughters of Victor Charles and his Uncle Ho, and, of course, Koreans. Stacy happily agreed to meet us there and showed up wearing a low-cut blouse that emphasized the deep cleavage between her fulsome casabas.

Although I spoke with Stacy often, I rarely got to see her. She reminded me we hadn't faced off in nearly four months. My loss for sure. She was one handsome babe. Curvaceous. And exceptionally tall for a Korean, suggesting there was perhaps a redheaded, green-eyed brute hiding somewhere in the leafy branches of her family tree.

After we were seated and had ordered, Stacy told us that, although Jack used her search services occasionally, too, he had not contacted her lately other than to call about the task I had assigned him. So she had no idea what other activities of his might have turned him into a dead-Pharaoh look-alike. Midway through lunch the three of us were trading banalities, when Stacy asked, "Is she a dynamite fellatrix, Wiley?"

I dropped my crab pick and said, "Excuse me?"

"Sheila Bausch. Does she give great head?"

Dante dropped the cute, pink wild Gulf shrimp he had raised halfway to his mouth and gave me a wide-eyed look. "Yeah, Wile. Does she?"

"Sorry, Stace. You've mistaken me for someone who knows what you're talking about," I said.

Stace poked me in the ribs. "Come on. Out with it."

I raised up my hands, palms out. "I plead innocent, Your Honor. I never touched the lady in question."

Stacy slumped back in her chair. "I can't begin to express my disappointment in you, Wiley Poynter. Jesus H. Tree-Climbing Christ. You mean to tell us you send a chick flowers and then blow her off?"

"That I will confess to."

Dante shook his head in disbelief. "Maybe you belong in the hospital in a room next to Jack, Wiley. I am shocked. Truly shocked."

"I hardly know the girl."

"Okay. Let's hear it," Dante said. "From the beginning."

Given the BP fiasco, I had passed on the wild Gulf shrimp and instead ordered snow crab. Besides, I figured the poor schleps on "The Deadliest Catch" deserved as much of my custom as I could throw their way. But I had lost my appetite. Whether from embarrassment over my non-performance with Sheila or from watching Stacy scarf down enough oysters to gag a goat, I wasn't sure. Anyway, I pushed my plate aside and told Dante and Stacy the story of my late-night Wild West shootout in a back alley of Tucson.

When I finished, Dante gave a low whistle and said, "I'm impressed."

Stacy reached over, put a hand on my thigh, and whispered loudly enough for Dante to hear, "Will you show me your gun sometime soon, Cowboy?"

"If you don't mind waiting in line, Stace," I said.

"Who's ahead of me?"

"You mean besides Sheila? Well, now there's Alicia."

"Who's she?" Stacy said, looking semi-faux indignant.

So I also told her and Dante about my flight-to-Las-Vegas teté-a-teté with a female sex therapist.

When I finished Stacy said, "Shit! Now how long am I going to have to wait?"

"Depends," I said and gave her an impish look.

"On what?"

Dante spoke up. "You know, Stacy. On how dynamite a fellatrix she turns out to be. Right, Wile?"

I pointed a finger at Dante and lowered my thumb in a "Bang! You-got-it!" gesture.

Stacy pointed an index finger at me. "You owe me, dude. Big time!"

"Just send me an invoice," I said.

"I'll send you an invoice. I'll send you a photo of one Miss Stacy Park, wearing nothing but lipstick, perfume, and eye shadow."

"Okay." Then added, "That reminds me –." And I filled Dante and Stacy in on the latest developments of the murder case in Arroyo Arenoso.

38

I picked up the lunch tab and we decided to move our discussion to the Rojo Lounge, a dark, quiet bar in the Palms Place Hotel on West Flamingo. The hotel has no casino. So there would be fewer assholes available to stumble into our table, spill their drinks, apologize, and then tell us – in slurred New Jersey accents – that we all reminded them of their cousins back in West Orange.

We ordered a round of drinks. After that we sat and mulled over the best way to try to find out who had beaten Jack up. Once we knew that, we could decide how to deal with them. When I again lamented that I felt horrible getting Jack beaten to the proverbial pulp over what was nothing more than a minor discrepancy in a witness's story, a wild goose chase gone horribly wrong, Dante told me to ease up on myself.

"The way I'm seeing this, Wile, is that Jack got too close either to the jewel thieves or the fencers and that's what got him hammered. I'm sure all your sleazy used-car salesman was up to was getting a piece on the side. Guys rarely, if ever, hire muscle to beat the shit out of the PI who catches them with their pants around their ankles."

"Unless, of course, the pantless guy is mobbed up," Stacy added.

Dante jerked a thumb toward Stacy. "Listen to her. You think she's maybe an undercover Untouchable, Wile?"

I shook my head. "Stacy's way too smart to be FBI."

Dante smiled. "Young pussy, Mack trucks, and Hoover's gray suits."

Stacy said, "Come on, guys. That Texas Ranger line is apocryphal."

"A pockra who?" Dante said.

"Don't play dumb," Stacy said.

I said, "Playing dumb gets Dante lots of useful info."

Dante nodded solemnly.

"I wish I knew where Jack has been these last few days. I mean, besides making the pawn-shop rounds," I said.

Stacy asked, "Does Jack have a GPS? Or is he too proud for that?"

Dante and I both brightened.

Dante said, "Yes. He's careful to take it off his sun visor whenever he leaves his car. He stores it in the glove box."

Stacy said, "Bring it to me. Better yet, let's meet at Jack's office. You got his car keys, right?"

Dante moaned. "Damn. I forgot to get them from the hospital. But that's easy enough. Anything else you need?"

Stacy said, "Huh-uh. You guys go fetch his keys. I need to go back to my office to get my black magic box. Meet you at Jack's in, say, an hour?"

Officious hospital administrators refused to release Jack's keys to Dante and me. Jack's sister, we learned from them, was planning to fly in from Denver and they would gladly turn over Jack's keys to her. But they had no details regarding when she might arrive. Dante was friends with a locksmith who was willing to open Jack's Land Rover, provided we gave him a hold-harmless letter signed by both of us. Neither the locksmith, Dante, not I had any idea how legally sound such a document might prove to be. But with fond hopes, I typed up the letter on Jack's word processor. Then Dante and I signed it, and the locksmith was satisfied, even if the cops might not be as impressed, should they drop by and charge us all with B&E.

On a lark, while the locksmith was shoving one of his tools down between the driver's side window and the door frame, I called the MGM Grand and asked to speak with Dr. Braden. The operator rang her room, but she didn't answer. I opted to leave no message, deciding to try again later.

By the time Dante and I had dealt with the locksmith, Stacy showed up. She had traded the plunging-neckline blouse for a UNLV sweatshirt. Maybe she had judged that would improve my focus on the real task at hand. She had also brought along a black box with a handle. It looked for all the world like an old-fashioned portable typewriter case.

Dante pointed to the case. "Going bowling later?"

Stacy said, "Maybe. But not with this. Show me Jack's GPS."

Dante handed it over to her.

"Feeling chilly, were you?" I said to Stacy.

"Not especially. But you know as well as I do that when advertisements run for too long they tend to get stale."

"So you were running a teaser ad?"

"Did I make a sale?" she said, giving me a coquettish smile. Stacy placed her black box on Jack's desk and opened it. The box was full of cables and gadgets. That's my best tech-clueless description. Dante and I stood quietly and stared.

"This concatenation of wires, circuits, and plastic, gentlemen, is what is known as a DED – data extraction device. It's made by an Israeli company. With a wave of my magic wand, a softly whispered abracadabra, a puff of smoke, and an 'Open Sesame' I will now proceed to suck the memory out of Jack's little satellite triangulation toy. She held up what appeared to be a miniature cell phone, only it was half the size and a third as thick as my phone.

Dante and I sat down, then watched in awe as Stacy fiddled and diddled, plugged and unplugged, peered and hissed, poked and stroked her equipment and Jack's palm-sized GPS contraption.

"It's not a lengthy process, guys, but if Jack has some decent coffee tucked away in the cupboard underneath his pot over there, I would like a cup," She said, without looking up or pausing in her work.

I said, "You don't want to drink Jack's java. Starbuck's it ain't."

"Tea?"

"Afraid not, Stace. Tea is unmanly, you know. Jack would be embarrassed."

She came back, "It kept the Royal Navy going for a century or more."

Dante said, "That was rum, limes, sodomy, and the lash, Sweety."

"Next time tell me when it's BYO," she said. Followed by, "Voila! Jack has a computer and printer, right?"

"Old, but serviceable," I said.

"How old?"

"I'm not sure." I pointed toward a far corner.

Stacy examined Jack's investment in the age of computers. "Shit! This isn't old, it's ancient. Pre-Cambrian." She looked at me. "Before dinosaurs even."

"Before the Big Bang?" I said.

"Quite possibly. Anyway, this won't work." She then examined Jack's printer. "A dot fucking matrix? Holy crap."

I said, "It's newer than dots and dashes."

"Not by much," she said. "What a fossil! I'm sorry, but I'm going to have to go back to my office to find out what we've got here." She paused. "Or we could go to my place. Any one of my home computers will give me what we need. Damn! Had I known, I would have brought my laptop."

I felt a dainty trap had just been set. I countered, "Stace, I think Dante and I are distractions to you. Dante has offered to let me use his Jeep Wrangler while I'm here. It's parked behind his gun range. So, why don't you take your machinery and go figure out what the GPS holds, we'll go get the Wrangler, and meet back here?"

"How about meeting at my office. It's a lot closer to Dante's than this place is," she said.

"Okay."

We parted ways, with me agreeing to meet Stacy at her office as soon as I picked up the Jeep. Dante begged off, saying he had payroll taxes to complete and file. Month's end was closing in on him and the government had no sense of humor about late filings. Frugal Dante Foster was his own accountant.

Dante weaved in and out of afternoon traffic and I dialed the MGM Grand, asking the switchboard voice to please ring Alicia

Braden's room. On the third ring a male voice answered. I held my phone at arm's length and pressed 'End'. Five minutes and a dozen sharp tacks to starboard later, I dialed again, thinking the operator had given me the wrong room. Different switchboard operator's voice this time; same male voice answering again, this time after the first ring and churlish.

Oh well. I was disappointed Alicia herself had failed to answer. But then I remembered how other women had assured me of the difficulties attendant with trying simultaneous to answer a telephone and perform certain other oral tasks. Coinciding with the regret of not hearing Alicia's voice, I felt disillusioned at having gone, in a period of only twelve hours, from having my bicep squeezed with lustful intent to being discarded into that hackneyed trash barrel known as the dustbin of history. Oh well.

"Problem, Wile?" Dante asked as he casually sped through a yellow light gone red.

"Not any more. I've been deeply anguished for the last several hours, unable to decide which of two fine women to invite to become my bedroom playmate for the night. Now one of them has made other arrangements."

Dante gave me a quick glance before leaning on his horn and cursing the moronic chauffeur of the red Buick just in front of us. When the sounds of horn and profanity died, he said, to me calmly, "Why were you going to have to choose?"

Taken aback, I said, "For one thing, these ladies don't even know each other."

"All the better. And for two?"

To try to end this line of harassment, I simply said, "It's been a long day. I got zero sleep last night. I wouldn't have the stamina."

"That makes more sense," he said.

Minutes later he parked behind his indoor gun-range emporium, next to his black Wrangler, and we went inside. While Dante went behind the counter to fish out the keys to his Wrangler, I watched a shaved-head dude with a stud through his lower lip forking over bills to one of Dante's assistants. The guy's pate was not exactly bald. His entire head, face included, along with the rest of his visible hide, served as canvas for more skin art than any illustrated man in a Ringling Brothers' side show. I became curious what the covered parts of his body looked like – but not curious enough to ask for a peek. Not from this weirdo.

It worried me to think all the peace-loving folks at NRA headquarters deemed it a reasonable notion that this guy should be entitled to sleep with an Abrams tank under his pillow. However, if the world was going to end with a bang instead of Eliot's predicted whimper, every freak on the planet was going to want to participate in the fun, including this wacko. And he obviously wanted to show up for the Last Big Bang, not only with a pure heart, but with an accurate shooting eye as well.

I once asked a Las Vegas psychiatrist working on a teen-runaway case with me to explain the difference between a psychopath and a sociopath. Judging me incapable of comprehending his professional jargon, he put it to me this way. "A psychopath firmly believes that two plus two equals five. A sociopath, on the other hand, knows two plus two equals four, but he hates it." Mr. Wacko struck me as one of the latter.

"Tank's full, oil's been changed, windshield's washed," Dante said when he handed over his keys. "If you park in the dark with Stacy, warn her to take care. She wouldn't be the first chick to mistake the gear shift knob for something else. I don't want you to return my Jeep with teeth marks where the 'R' for 'Reverse' used to be." He winked, turned, saw the tattooed warrior, and, I'm sure, began to ponder the wisdom of granting men of such insalubrious appearance access into his establishment.

I was just switching on the Wrangler's ignition when my phone jingled. I hesitated answering, wondering if it might be Alicia's paramour calling to gloat. Curiosity finally overwhelmed me.

"Mr. Poynter?"

"Yes." I wasn't sure I recognized the female voice. I only knew it didn't belong to Alicia Braden.

"This is Jane Wheeler, your sister's colleague."

"Oh, hello Ms. Wheeler. What's up?"

"Bad news, I'm afraid. Adelle has been in a car accident. She hasn't been hurt badly, or so it appears. But an ambulance has taken her to a Tucson hospital to be checked over thoroughly. I thought you would want to know."

"Indeed! Thank you." I stalled, trying to decide what to do. Finally, I said, "I'll try to arrange to fly back as quickly as I can. What can you tell me about her injuries?"

"She was rear-ended by a retiree who surely shouldn't be allowed to drive. She was just returning from the Safeway in Green Valley. She may have a broken left foot, ankle, or both. And she has a nasty bump on her forehead. I happened to be returning home from a hair appointment when I saw all the flashing lights and recognized Adelle's car, its backside crumpled in the middle of a busy intersection. So I stopped just as EMT's were lifting her out of her car. We spoke for a moment before the ambulance whisked her away. She was coherent and no sign of blood anywhere."

"I'll try to catch a flight out this evening. I very much appreciate your calling me," I said.

"If you like, I can pick you up at the airport," she said.

I thought about that and told her, "My car is parked at the Tucson airport. But, yes. It would be very kind of you to meet me and I'll follow you to the hospital. Are you calling from your cell phone?"

"Yes. Do you want my number?"

"I'll have it in memory from this call. I'll phone you back when I have a confirmed flight and let you know when it's scheduled to land."

"I'll await your call."

I went back into Dante's shooting gallery, found him, handed him back his keys, explained what was happening, and asked him for a lift back to McCarran.

"Sorry about your sister, old bean. She's a gem," he said. He told his assistant he was taking off and away we went.

With Dante at the wheel, I just made Southwest's 7:20 p.m. flight, which, lucky for me, was the airline's final non-stop to Tucson for the day. After passing through TSA's wretched screenings, I phoned Jane Wheeler to let her know my expected arrival time. Then I called Stacy Park.

"Are you making this up just to screw me? Or rather not screw me?"

I assured her I wasn't. "Call Dante."

"Ha! He'd be in on your ruse, if you're conning me."

I offered to give her Jane Wheeler's number.

"Who's she? The bimbo you're going to boff instead of me? Of course, she'd tell me whatever you wanted her to tell me."

The hell-hath-no-fury principle needs to be expanded to include women who only imagine they have been scorned.

"I don't know what I can tell you to make you believe me, Stace."

"Nothing you can say. Instead, I want glossy colored photos of your sister writhing in agony, blood everywhere."

I thought for a moment. "Hack into the hospital's admissions records. You'll see she's there."

"What hospital?"

Oh, shit. Jane Wheeler didn't say. "I don't know. You'll have to try every hospital in Tucson, I guess."

"Hells bells. It will be easier just to buy new batteries for my vibrator. But I'm adding this to what you owe me, Buster. And it ain't gonna be cheap."

"That's fine, Stace. And I'm truly sorry."

"Yeah. Sure. Give your sister a kiss for me. But no tonguing her. Okay?"

Jeezus. "Okay."

I ran down the concourse and barely made my flight, getting stuck with a middle seat near the rear of the plane, stuck between a teenage kid constantly adjusted his iPod earplugs and reeking of anchovies and onions, as he chewed on a slab of pizza that included the kitchen sink for a topping, and an eighty-some-year-old lady in the aisle seat who must have bathed in a vat of cheap perfume just before arriving at the airport. I opened my book of logic puzzles and began reading about who stole a monkey from a zoo. I hoped there were going to be lots of suspects because the flight appeared to me as though it was going to be very long and bumpy. And I hoped to hell the old lady didn't take a notion to try to squeeze my bicep. If she did try, I swore to myself it would the last bicep she ever squeezed. I was in no mood for casual flirtations, even from eighty-year-old ladies.

39

Jane Wheeler met me when I emerged from the passengers-only secured area into the public waiting area. I was pleased to see her, glad to be on the ground again, thrilled to be free from the packed confines of the airplane.

"How was your flight?" she said, after gently embracing me with the now-customary European-style hug-to-the-right/huge-to-the-left physical greeting that has replaced more formal handshakes when women meet women and women meet men.

"I've had better. But here I am." I saw no point in serving up an explanation of how, for seventy-five minutes, I had been a human boundary line between two powerful, marshalled armies: the forces of Onion Breath on my left; the forces of Rank Perfume on my right. Such a clarification would only make me appear to be tiresome, when in fact I was merely tired.

"Your poor sister was taken to Kino Community Hospital. It's only a few minutes from here," Ms. Wheeler said as we walked toward the baggage carousel. "Have you had anything to eat? I mean besides those pathetic little bags of peanuts the airline serves?"

I was starving, but I was also eager to see Adelle. "I'm all right for now," I lied. "Perhaps after the hospital visit you'll allow me to buy you dinner, by way of thanking you for your being so helpful."

"All right," she said.

It was only when we arrived at the luggage-delivery area that I realized I had none. My suitcase remained in rear end of Dante Foster's Hummer, where I put it at McCarran Airport when I had arrived in Las Vegas. By now that seemed like days ago, although it had only been approximately fourteen hours. Dante and I never did swing by my condo in Henderson. Doing so was much too far out of the way from both Jack's office and North View Hospital, where Jack was being treated, if you could call lying in a coma being treated. When Dante brought me back to McCarran, I was in too much of a rush to think about extra clothes or to remember my bag in the Hummer's storage space. Thankfully, I had left most of my clothes at Adelle's, knowing I had to return to get my car eventually anyway. I had packed lightly for the flight up to Las Vegas, because I had closets full of clothes at my condo.

Although I forgot my bag in Dante's SUV, I did remember to ask three things of Dante. To call me if Jack's condition changed, for better or worse; to call me when Jack's sister – I didn't even know her name –arrived from Denver; to ask Stacy to please call me if and when she unlocked anything significant from Jack's GPS unit. I wasn't sure whether Stacy, given her current frustrations with me, would choose to call me without being prompted to do so by Dante.

A desk nurse in the emergency room at Kino Community Hospital informed me that Adelle had already been released and had left. That puzzled me.

"How could she just leave? She had no way to get home," I told the nurse.

Another nurse stepped up. "Miss Poynter left with a handsome man driving a pink Cadillac convertible." She smirked as she told me.

"Pink Cadillac convertible? You've got to be kidding," I said.

"Oh no, sir. It's hard to forget a car like that," the second nurse said. "I was the one who wheeled her out to it."

Jane Wheeler provided the rational explanation to what I was beginning to suppose was an emergency-room nursing staff high on hallucinatory drugs.

"Mr. Truesdell." she said, grinning as though she had made up the man and his name.

"Who is he?" I said.

"Oscar Truesdell teaches world history at our school. His hobby is tinkering with vintage automobiles. He buys them, works away on them until they are in mint condition, then sells them every January at the Barrett-Jackson auto auction in Scottsdale. One of his current projects is a pink Cadillac convertible," Jane said.

I was familiar with the Barrett-Jackson people because they also hold a similar classic-car auction in Las Vegas every September. "How did he know to come pick Adelle up?"

Jane Wheeler shrugged.

I said, "They're not an item. Can't be. Adelle's never mentioned the man."

Jane said, "Do you really suppose she tells you everything?"

"I'm her brother."

Jane made a face that said, "So?"

I dialed Adelle's landline and got her answering machine after seven rings. "They must be crossing the border at Nogo about now," I said to Jane.

"Sorry. I don't have Oscar's phone numbers."

"I hope my sister doesn't either."

"Oh, come now, Mr. Poynter. Oscar is a splendid fellow."

"Serial killers' friends and neighbors always say that about them, too."

Jane scowled. "I know Oscar pretty well. He wouldn't harm a –. Well, maybe a flea, but not your sister. They probably stopped for a bite to eat somewhere."

"Speaking of which, I lied to you at the airport. I was starved then and now I'm ready to eat furniture." I looked at the beds and chairs in the emergency room. "Not this furniture, but –. Never mind. Let's go join Oscar and Adelle."

"Are you saying you know where they might have gone to eat?" Jane said.

"No. I simply mean, let's do what you imagine they are doing."

Ms. Jane Wheeler gave me a look I wasn't quite ready to interpret. "You mean eat dinner?"

"What else?"

She repeated the look.

"Let's go. Meet me at the parking lot exit. Follow me and I'll pay."

I led Jane to the Silver Saddle Steakhouse on East Benson Highway, not too far north of the airport. I was as hungry as I had told her I was. And I meant for food, not for her. I had already decided not to play footsy with Jane Wheeler. I had two reasons for deciding to behave myself. One, I wasn't sure how my sister would react to my trying to seduce, or to letting myself be seduced by, one of her colleagues. And two, I really didn't want to give myself either an excuse or a good reason to want not to return permanently to Las Vegas. The difference, as I saw it, between Jane on the one hand, Sheila and her roommate on the other, was that Jane was an *objet d'art,* whereas the coeds were merely baubles. The latter, after being admired and toyed with, could be handed off. Fine art could not be.

So, Jane and I had a splendid dinner, made even better by splendid small talk. I ordered the twenty-four-ounce Porterhouse; she had a ten-ounce piece of prime rib. Over dessert I asked Jane if she was aware of any updates in the Bobby Shane Hollsworth case.

"Sebastian Sechrest has hired a top-of-the-food-chain defense lawyer."

"He's entitled."

Grinning, she said, "His attorney is from the firm of Crooks, Wiggins, and Leggett. The best criminal defense firm a million dollars can buy."

"Crooks. How apt," I said.

"Actually his lawyer is Lawrence Wiggins. He has a reputation for winning unwinnable cases. Joshua Crooks died a couple years ago, but the firm obvious continues to keep his name nailed to the masthead."

I leaned across the booth and whispered, "I'm not convinced Mr. Sechrest did it."

Jane looked surprised. "You're not? Then who do you think did?"

"That I don't know yet. But I hope to keep working on it. Provided no more of my closest friends and loved ones end up injured and being treated in hospitals."

"I'm sorry. You must think me rude for not asking earlier, but how is your friend who was injured in Las Vegas? Adelle said it was quite serious."

I gave her a quick rundown on Jack's condition, what little I understood about it.

"He was working on something for you when this happened to him?" she said.

"Yes. But he was also working on a case of his own which is far more likely to have triggered the beating. High-end jewelry thieves. He may have been getting close to identifying them."

"If so, why didn't they simply kill him?"

Good question. They would have felt safer surely. "Maybe they thought they did."

By the time we got back to Arroyo Arenoso it was late. With Jane close behind, I turned onto Adelle's street and, from afar, I could see a 1950's model pink Cadillac parked in her driveway. I was going to get to meet my sister's chariot driver-rescuer.

Adelle was on her sofa in her pajamas and housecoat, with her left leg propped up on a pillow when Jane and I walked in. Beside her stood a walker with yellow tennis balls for rear feet. She was sipping tea. I hoped she had had the good sense to gin it up a bit.

"Wiley! What a nice surprise! Is this your doing, Jane?"

Jane acknowledged responsibility.

"Wiley, I would like you to meet my good friend, Oscar Truesdell."

"Pleased to meet you, Wiley," he said, clamping a huge right hand onto mine.

The man was enormous. Tall with broad shoulders. And his neatly trimmed red beard matched his brushy eyebrows. Add chain-and-leather armor, put a sword in one hand and a flagon of mead in the other, stand him at the bow of a Viking warship, and he could be a piece of history, as well as teach it.

"My pleasure, as well," I said. "Thank you for bringing Dell home."

"No trouble at all. I was in Tucson already when she called and asked."

I gave my sister a sly sideways look. She flashed a smile back at me. "Interesting chariot your horses are pulling out there," I said.

"Took me a while to find that baby. It was gathering dust in some little old lady's garage in San Angelo, Texas. When she died, her son blew off the dust, took some photos of it, and posted it for sale on the internet. I snatched it right up."

"I hope she was tall enough to see over the steering wheel," I said.

"Didn't matter. Her son said she always had some local *paisano* chauffeur her about. She'd dress up in her finest clothes and have the Mex toodle her about town like the Queen of England out for a carriage ride. She was old Texas money and obviously had more than a touch of class. You should have seen her house. A plantation mansion overlooking the Concho River."

I said, "You fix classic cars up and sell them, Ms. Wheeler tells me."

"I do," he said and proceeded to tell me more about his hobby than I really cared to find out at midnight on a Saturday night.

Jane, too, listened politely to a tale I was certain she had heard before, until at last she stood and excused herself, invoking the lateness of the hour. Thankfully Oscar took the hint and wrapped up his narrative.

"I'd best be going, too. Anything else you need or want, Miss Adelle, you just let Oscar know," he said.

I tend to cringe when people refer to themselves in the third person. But what could I do? I saw Jane and Oscar to the door and thank them both profusely for their kindnesses to my sister.

When I returned to the living room, Dell said, "How is your friend, Jack?"

I told her, then passed along what Jane had said about Sebastian Sechrest's lawyering himself up with a defender sporting an impressive resume.

"What's you opinion about Mr. Sechrest, Wiley?" Dell asked as I helped her to her bedroom.

"He's an asshole and a manipulator-exploiter of young people for sure. Whether he's also a murderer, I don't know. Probably not, but I've decided I'd better either wait for Rollie Morton to come up with more damning evidence or else go out and find some myself."

"You will be careful, won't you?" she said.

I pulled back her covers, eased her into bed, gave her a peck on the cheek and said, "Aren't I always?" before turning out her light and closing her door.

40

Sunday

Adelle was still asleep, blissfully doped, when I awoke and began puttering around. The emergency-room doctor had written her a prescription for Percoset and Oscar Truesdell had stopped at a Walgreens to get it filled for her on their way out of Tucson. At McCarran I had remembered to hand back Dante's Sig Sauer, even if I had left my suitcase in his car. So now, feeling gun-naked again, I retrieved my weaponry from underneath my bed, put the Krieghoff and Taurus both back in their customary places in the Jeep, and re-hitched my holster to the back of my pants. I then shoved the S&W into it, first spinning the cylinder the way Clayton Moore, as the Lone Ranger, used to do with his single-action Army Colt .45 when I watched him on television reruns as a kid. Cue up the William Tell Overture.

My sister slept until almost noon. I fixed a modest brunch for us and she asked about her car. I had no idea where it had been hauled away to, but I assured her I would check into locating it.

"Wiley, my groceries are probably still in the trunk. Milk, eggs, sour cream, cottage cheese, butter. I was running low on dairy stuff. Good lord, all that stuff has surely gone sour by now. Yuk! Just imagine what a runny mess. And the smell!"

As we were gobbling the last of the bacon, I said, "Rather than get your clunker fixed, maybe you should think about getting a new car. Maybe something with a bit more pizzazz than a Honda Civic."

"I like my car. And it's not a clunker. Pizzazz I can do without."

"You bought it new when? As I recall, as soon as you bought it, you slapped a Kerry-for-President bumper sticker on it. That makes it what? A two thousand four?"

"Oscar said he would fix it for me. And you needn't bother finding where it's being stored. Oscar said he would find it and have it towed to his house."

"You want me to call your insurance company? Check out the name of the old fart who hit you and contact his insurance company?"

"I have the man's name and the name of who insures him. I'm not in a coma like your friend. I am perfectly capable of picking up the telephone and making my own calls."

"Suit yourself. Phone calls remind me. I have a favor to ask," I said.

"Go ahead."

"I'd like you to call the three remaining band members – Perry, Jason, and Richie—and invite them over for pizza and soda tonight. Tell them you are in serious need of some TLC and, oh by the way, my brother would like to speak with you again briefly."

"Am I really in need of TLC?"

"Definitely. And only they can provide it."

"I'm not sure I like the way you're using me," she said, making a sour face.

"Sorry, Sis, but you have a far better chance of getting them to show up here than I would. And it's for a good cause. I need to try to tie up some loose ends."

"Does that mean you now think Sebastian is guilty?" she said.

"I'll know better after I speak with the boys again."

An hour later Adelle had secured promises from each of the band members to appear at her house around dinner time. Meanwhile, I had been busy catching up on my notes. Just as I was finishing Dante called.

"Jack's being moved out of Intensive Care into a regular room. Private. And his sister has arrived. Her name is Helen. Helen Otley. Thirty-five-ish, divorced, not bad looking. She looks like she's easy to dance to; I'd give her about a seven and a half."

"Thank you very much, Dick Clark. Have you spoken with Stacy?"

"I have. She's agreed to call you. I take it she's has not done so yet."

"You take it correctly."

"Maybe she's still out looking for the right-sized batteries for her you-know-what," Dante said.

"She's not the play-before-work type, Dant."

"Maybe she went to the gym to work off some of her frustrations, trying to get back into the proper zen mode to deal with you."

"I'll zen mode her," I said.

"You'd better do something before the poor gal's a basket case."

"Don't you have any friends or associates who can torch her pants? You must know lots of super studs. Surely at least one of them is at loose ends at the moment."

"I don't like to think of myself as a pimp, Wile."

"How about that customer of yours with the *pies a cabeza* tats? I bet he'd be up for some hot Asian action."

"I wouldn't wish him on my worst female enemy."

"I'm not going to call Stacy and grovel," I said.

"I wouldn't expect you to."

"I mean, I'm hiring her to do a job for me."

"I understand completely." I could almost hear Dante laughing up his sleeve.

"I'll give her until tomorrow noon."

"Deadlines are good. And noon tomorrow is generous of you."

"Thanks."

"What if she fails to meet it?"

"I'll be forced to extend it, I guess."

"You sure you're not a Republican, Wile? You keep drawing lines in the sand and before long a whole century will have passed and you'll have lost count of the number of lines you've drawn."

"One line at a time, Dante."

"Wise plan. By the way, Sister Helen is worried about Jack's hospital expenses. Do you know if he has medical insurance?"

"He does. It's the same as mine. It's called a personal checking account. It doesn't cover much. And there's a huge deductible."

"That's sort of what I figured. What shall I tell her?"

I said, "Tell her what all the televangelists in all their million-dollar cathedrals would tell her: Prayer is the answer. Tell her to get down on her knees in front the hospital administrator and start beseeching. Or alternatively –."

"I think I'll settle for telling her I'm looking into it. Talk with you later."

No sooner had I finished speaking with Dante than Stacy called. "You're early," I said to her.

"What is that supposed to mean?" she said.

"You had until noon tomorrow."

"To do what?"

"Never mind. What have you found?"

"You mean besides my twenty-four pack of dildo batteries? Plenty. I found a physical site Jack visited three days in a row, two or more times each of those days."

"Bingo!"

"Better than bingo. I checked out the address. It's a small retail pad in the middle of a brand new warehouse district out on Aliante Parkway. Yeah, I know, but it's actually quite a ways from the hotel. And get this: It's a jewelry outlet. Or at least the storefront claims it is. Beckheimer's Gem Depot. Small letters on the window read: By appointment only. Except... there is no phone number, no e-mail address. Nothing to provide a way to contact the place. Interesting also, is I can't find a damned thing about any Beckheimer's Gem Depot on the internet. Zero, zilch, nada."

"Most interesting. Good work, Stace."

"Do we have a bad connection? Did I hear 'Great work' or something else?"

"Great work!"

"*De nada.* So you think this is may be the jewel-thief guys?"

"Highly likely."

"You want me to tip off the PD Pawn Squad?" she said eagerly.

"No. Definitely not. These guys' *cojones* are mine."

"So you're coming back?"

"ASAP, which isn't going to be until tomorrow. I got something going tonight." I knew that was the wrong way to phrase what I meant even as the words were emerging from my stupid mouth.

"Something going, eh?" she said with a definite edge to her voice.

"Interviews."

"Better not be pillow-talk interviews."

"Teenage boys."

"Whew! I know you don't wear a priest's collar. You're not even Catholic. Well, I'm going to check this place out further."

"Just be careful, Stacy. Remember what they did to Jack. As Charlie Chan say, '*Precaution much safer than daring.*' Okay?"

"I prefer Jackie Chan. To me Charlie Chan is little more than an Asian Uncle Tom."

I decided to let that pass. "Just don't do anything stupid."

"Leave that for you, right?"

"*Touché.* See you tomorrow."

41

Just before six o'clock each of the three musicians showed up and right at six the pizza delivery guy arrived with three large pepperoni pizzas and four orders of garlic cheese bread. I had already gone to the nearby convenience store to buy three twelve-packs of soda.

We ate and the guys dutifully commiserated with Adelle over her misfortune. I sat and listened. When the garlic bread had all been eaten and the three pizzas reduced to the unfinished outer edges of two slices, I explained to them that I wanted to interview each of them, one at a time, in private. I began by inviting Jason into Adelle's third bedroom, which served as her office and library. One wall was all bookshelves. She had an L-shaped desk, where she graded quizzes and exams and where her desktop sat. A wingback chair resided in one corner. I directed Jason to the wingback; I sat down in my sister's swiveling desk chair.

"Any further ideas about who killed Bobby?" I began.

"No. Andy told me you came up and talked with him."

"Bobby was killed with a push dagger. Were you aware of that?"
I said.

His eyes narrowed. "Andy has one of those."

"I know. I saw it. Lucky for him the police checked it out. It's
not the murder weapon."

"Andy didn't mention police."

"They came later. Do you know anyone else who owns a push
dagger?"

"Several of the guys in Chicken Wings have one. But none
of the other guys, aside from Andy, have met Bobby. Well, that I
know of."

"Did you know Colby Ambrose?" I said.

"Is he the guy in Tucson who got stabbed?"

"How did you know that?"

"I read the newspaper and watch TV news just like everybody
else."

"Have you ever met him?"

"Until I saw him in the news I never heard of him."

"Did you ever hear Bobby talk about him?"

"No. Why? Did Bobby know him?"

"They were seen together at the nearby Desert Diamond
Casino," I said.

"Bobby knows lots of people I don't know." Pause. "Knew."

"Do you know Richie's brother?"

"I know him when I see him, but that's all."

"Do you know what he does?"

"He's a cook at Skyler's."

"What else does he do?"

"Gives Richie endless shit."

"About what?"

"Just big-brother teasing crap. He and Richie get along real well, as far as I can tell."

"He was Bobby's betting courier. Colby was one of the owners of the betting parlor in Tucson where Bobby places all his bet."

"So?"

"So Bobby and Colby are both dead; Fabian was their go-between; You know Fabian through Richie. I thought you might have seen or heard something that would help tie Colby's and Bobby's murders together."

"Why ask me? Talk to Fabian."

"I have."

"I'm sorry. But I can't help you. I don't know anything."

"Okay. You may go. Thanks for coming. It means a lot to my sister."

"She was just your excuse."

"Partly. But she also got something good out of your coming."

"Whatever."

I nearly exploded. Of all the many ways to express not mere indifference, but contemptuous indifference, *whatever* has become the tiresome symbol of smug, ill-mannered aloofness. That a pimple-faced little prick would express such an attitude toward my sister, a woman who was trying her damnedest to teach this punk something useful and set a good example in doing so, angered me. However, with admirable self-restraint, I said only, "That remark, Jason, is not only simple, but simple-minded, and seriously out of line."

Startled, he stood and gave me a impudent stare.

I glowered back at him and he backed out of the room, then turned and made a hasty exit, without so much as saying good-night to Adelle.

My sister looked at me as if I might have pulled a knife on the young man. "Wiley, what happened?"

"He said something he shouldn't have and I merely told him he was out of line."

Adelle brought a hand to her face. "Oh, dear. Do I need to speak with him tomorrow?"

"I'm hoping he comes to you."

"I see."

I said, "I'll explain later." Both Richie and Perry were staring at me warily. To them I said, "Jason needs to learn some manners. I have no quarrel with either of you – yet. Richie, come along."

Richie Maldonado trudged ahead of me into Adelle's office as though he had been sentenced to a death march.

After seating him in the wingback and lowering myself into the desk chair, I said to him, "What reasons have you had for holding out on me about the fact your brother was Bobby Shane's sports-betting courier?"

I expected a slow, deep shrug and got it. "I'm disappointed in you, Richie. I misjudged you. I told myself you had nothing to hide. So you wouldn't. More fool me, eh?"

"I didn't want to be the one who might get my big brother in trouble."

"He's not in trouble. At least yet. At least not from me. I'm not a gambling sheriff. I'm not out to bust up the sports betting parlor or to get anybody who works for it busted. I'm from Las Vegas, where gambling is life itself. What Bobby and your big brother have been involved in is *patatas pequeñas*." Tiny potatoes.

"Yeah, well –. Fabian had regular dealings with Bobby. So I figured he would be at the top of your shit list if you found out. And then that dude in Tucson got killed the same way as Bobby –."

"Did you know Colby Ambrose?" I said.

"No, but Fabian did. He told me he knew him."

"And?"

"Bobby's not a queer."

"That's not what I meant. Did Fabian tell you saw them together in the parking lot at Desert Diamond Casino?" I said.

"No. Why should he?"

"Because he thought you might be interested?"

"I saw Bobby at school. I played in his band. Beyond that? We had separate lives."

"Do you have your cell phone with you?" I said.

"What if I do?"

"Rumor has it you have some interesting photos stored on it. Photos of Bobby and Juanita maybe?"

Richie's hands and teeth clenched.

"Well?"

"Maybe."

"Stop stonewalling me, Richie. You have photos of Juanita and Bobby having sex, am I right?"

He nodded guiltily. "After a basketball game. Everybody was headed toward the dance in the school cafeteria. I saw Bobby and Juanita sneak off toward the parking lot. I followed them. Jesus! He screwed her on the hood of his truck. And she let him."

Tears formed at the corners of his eyes. He wiped them away and then his look turned mean. "Goddamn him anyway."

"Frosted you pretty badly, did he?"

"I didn't kill him. But I'm not all busted up because someone else did."

"How's your brother taking Bobby's death?"

A shrug. "It'll cost him a few bucks. Bobby was one of his best customers down this way."

"Do you know who any of his other customers are?"

"No. That ain't none of my business. And Fabian's not one to shoot his mouth off. Even to me."

I waited.

"Okay. There's something else."

I waited some more.

"Don't tell Fabian I told you this," Richie said. "Swear you won't."

I swore.

"Fabian got in trouble once with one of the other guys at the betting place."

"Kirk? Randy?"

"I don't know. Kirk maybe. I've never met those guys. Just heard Fabian talk about them."

"What was the trouble?"

"Colby told Fabian that he, Colby, was going to log in a few bets now and then for Bobby without Bobby having to come up with any money right away. Fabian didn't like it, but Colby was one of the owners. Fabian was convinced Colby's partners didn't know. And, sure enough, the whole thing blew up. Kirk, or whoever, warned Colby and Fabian never to allow that to happen again."

"When was this? Do you recall?" I said.

"Not too long ago. Maybe three or four weeks before Bobby and Colby died," Richie said.

"Anything else belatedly pop into your memory about Colby and Bobby?"

"That's it."

I thought about asking him what nice words Juanita had said about Bobby at the school's memorial service on Friday, but decided that was salting the wounds of love. I told Richie he was free to leave and he left quickly.

So far Perry Crisp had been the minimally connected, almost invisible man in my investigation. He had no gambling ties to Bobby, no grudge against Bobby's homophobia. I knew from the beginning that Kristy Serling was the wedge between Perry and Bobby. What I hadn't known, until Juanita Bardella boasted of it, was that Perry was aware Bobby had taken, been permitted to take, photos of Kristy modeling herself *au naturel*. That had changed Perry's internal temperature considerably. Juanita herself had said so.

Seated uncomfortably in the winged chair, Perry took in everything in my sister's office – except me. No eye contact whatsoever.

"So, Perry, are you still trying to figure out what Kristy really looks like naked?" is how I began.

Eye contact at last. An icy stare. "I've seen her in the buff. We went skinny-dipping once."

"But you lack photos to remind you how delightful her private treasures look, right?"

"That's sick."

"That's not what Juanita told me. She said you are steamed as hell that Bobby was in possession of Kristy photos and you aren't."

"That slut will tell anybody anything just to get under their skin. If you didn't figure that out, you're a moron."

"Oh, I pegged Juanita early on. So why would she lie to me about something like that?"

"To get me in trouble. Juanita loves to fuck with people's minds."

"Richie supposedly has glossy-colored proof that, in Bobby's case, she was fucking with more than just his mind."

Perry came out of his chair. "Richie's a liar, too."

"You're telling me Richie and Juanita are both out to get you by telling vicious lies that they know will infuriate and exasperate you?"

He remained standing, but the tension in his body eased. "You got it."

"Anyone else spreading falsehoods about you?"

"Probably everybody."

"Can you spell *paranoid*?"

"Okay. Richie and Juanita for sure. I don't know about anybody else."

"Why are they out to hurt you?" I said.

"Beats me. I thought Richie was my friend. But that greasy little shit will do anything, say anything to please Juanita. She's got him wrapped around her pinky."

"Why is Juanita so vindictive toward you?"

"She's a natural-born little cockteaser. That's why."

"But why is she picking on you in particular?"

"I don't know. Maybe Bobby put her up to it."

"Bobby? Why would he do that?"

"Because one of Bobby Shane Hollsworth's foremost principles was: When you get 'em down, kick 'em."

"And he had you down."

"Oh, half the pleasure – maybe more than half – of stealing Kristy away from me was watching me squirm. He's as sadistic as Juanita. Those two were made for one another."

"And you were content just to roll over and let him kick you?" I said.

He sat back down. "Whoa! You're not going to trap me into saying I plotted some kind of revenge on him."

"No trap. Did you?"

"I didn't kill Bobby."

"But you would have liked to, right?"

"Who wouldn't in my position? Thinking vicious thoughts isn't same as doing them."

"You're not Catholic, are you?"

"Hell, no. Why do you ask me that?"

"The Catholic Church has this bizarre notion that it's as much a mortal sin to think of doing something evil as to go ahead and do it. So, if you contemplate killing someone, you might as well go ahead and kill him, because you've already punched your ticket to hell."

"Jesus! That's crazy."

"I'll see if I can get you an audience with the Pope. You can set him straight. In the meantime, you have a strong motive for killing Bobby Shane. And I'm sure you had plenty of opportunities."

"That doesn't mean I did it. Hey! Besides, the cops have already arrested Mr. Sechrest."

"And cops never make mistakes. Right?"

"They found Bobby's cell phone buried in Mr. Sechrest's back-yard."

"They did. But answer this theoretical question for me: If you had killed Bobby and took his cell phone when you killed him – the cell phone with photos of Kristy in the nude in that phone's memory bank – what would you do with the phone afterwards?"

He answered with a whiney, "I don't know."

"You'd want to set someone else up, wouldn't you? Who would you frame?"

"Why would I frame Mr. Sechrest?"

"He was Bobby's friend, but not your friend. Why is that?"

"I don't buddy up to teachers. I'm not a kiss-ass like Bobby was."

"Did you know Bobby was posing nude for Mr. Sechrest?"

No response.

"Did Mr. Sechrest perhaps invite you to model for him?"

Perry Crisp went pale.

"Did he?"

"I told the dirty old fart he could shove that idea up his perverted ass."

Doing my best Perry imitation, I repeated, "Why would I frame Mr. Sechrest?"

His lower lip quivered. "I didn't do it."

"Kill Bobby? Or frame Sebastian Sechrest?"

"I didn't do either one."

"Do you know who called the police to tell them where to look for Bobby's cell phone?"

"No."

"Any ideas?"

"Juanita? I hear it was a female voice. Muffled and disguised, but definitely female."

"How would Juanita know it was there?"

"I don't know, but it's just the kind of thing she would do."

"Did Juanita kill Bobby?" I was throwing a dart blindfolded.

"How the hell would I know?"

"She seems to confide deep, dark secrets to you."

"Well, she didn't confess Bobby's murder to me."

I stood. "No further questions of this witness, Your Honor."

"I can go?" Perry said, not quite believing his time before the Grand Inquisitor was over.

"You may go."

I've seen high-velocity bullets move more slowly than Perry Crisp moved.

Unlike the other two boys, however, he did stop briefly to wish my sister a speedy recovery and to say goodbye.

When I emerged from her office, Adelle was sitting on her sofa, scratching futilely at her foot-and-ankle cast.

"You look depressed, Brother."

"Demoralized is more accurate. I feel I'm no closer to pegging Bobby's killer than when I started."

"Do any of your suspects strike you as more likely than others?" she said.

I shrugged. "For all I know now, you might have done it."

"Well, thank you very much for your vote of confidence in my righteous character."

"You're such a nice woman, Sis. I'm sure all your friends and neighbors will give enthusiastic testimony to that. However, I must warn you. Such solid praise from such people is invariably a sure sign you are, underneath all the smiles and politeness, a vicious serial killer."

"Oh, come now, Wiley. You don't have any better Superman vision than Mr. McGoo."

"That's the dismal conclusion I've finally arrived at on my own. As I told you last weekend, I have no talents."

"Well, don't start developing a talent for self-pity. I won't have it."

"Maybe I'll go outside and snivel at the moon. The man in the moon will lend me an empathetic ear."

"Go right ahead, but no sniveling in my house."

"How about a nightcap, Sis?"

"Tomorrow's Monday. I have to rise with a clear head. So, no thank you. But help yourself, if you imagine a drink will ease your pain. I'm going to bed."

"Poor Wiley. Has to get drunk alone. Woe is Wiley," I moaned in exaggerated fashion.

"Oh, stop it. You've never made for a very compelling drama queen."

"And now, ladies and gentlemen, this nice sweet little old lady has decided to rub in my total lack of talent. Isn't she sweet? Isn't she lovely? Let's have a round of applause for the sweet little old lady in the ankle cast."

Adelle shook her head. "You don't need to get drunk. Your head's spinning already." She insisted on putting herself to bed. Rather, she wheeled herself off, leaning on the walker she had also had Oscar Truesdell purchase for her at Walgreen's.

42

Monday

After sipping away for an hour at a three-finger tumbler of Wild Turkey while playing Hearts on Adelle's office computer, I had gone to bed and slept the sleep of a useless fool. I had also purchased a one-way online ticket on a Southwest afternoon flight to Las Vegas. I figured Dante, Stacy, and I wouldn't begin trying to perform unlawful acts in the vicinity of the gem depot until near dark or later. And I didn't want to sit around with my thumb up my ass in some quiet bar in Sin City contemplating what criminal acts I might be capable of committing. Instead, I would busy myself in Tucson.

Adelle was gone by the time I rolled out bed with only a mild hangover. She had left me a note asking me please to let her know of my day's plans, if any. She had refused my previous night's advice to deliver a note from her doctor to the principal, Mrs. Haydenfurth, and take the few days off from teaching. She spewed some falderal about how tight the school district's budget was and how there were no quality econ-and-government substitute teachers available.

I scribbled a reply, microwaved some coffee dregs, hid my guns under my bed again, and then headed for Tucson, stopping in Sahuarita for fancy coffee and what McDonald's chooses to label 'Big Breakfast'." It wasn't, but it would keep my body and weary soul from going their separate ways for a short while.

Randy Franklin came to the door when I knocked this time at the sports-betting house. Fabian Maldonado had provided me with the descriptions of Colby's two business partners. Randy looked like one of the mannequins modeling the summer collection in Macy's window. He wore a polo shirt beneath a face that looked as if he sanded and polished it every morning the instant he got up. He had teeth that gave new meaning to the old whiter-than-whiter laundry detergent ads. Maybe he brushed his teeth with soap flakes. When I explained who I was and why I was there, he invited me inside, holding the door open wide in an I've-got-nothing-to-hide gesture.

I saw no signs of the gambling activities that went on there. Maybe the machinery for those was upstairs. We sat in a cozy parlor and he offered me a beer, reminding me the sun was over the yardarm somewhere in the world and that was good enough for him. When I declined, he excused himself for a moment and returned with an opened can of Keystone, suggesting to me he and his remaining partner, Kirk, may have had to cover some heavy losses lately. Keystone is only one cut better than cat pee.

"Bobby Shane Hollsworth?" he repeated when I asked him if was familiar with the name. "Sure. The kid who died down in –. Wherever. He was a good customer of ours."

"Did you ever see him with Colby?" I said.

"Not that I remember. The kid didn't come by to place his bets. We have couriers."

"Ever hear Colby talk about him?"

"Can't say I ever did."

I wondered how good or bad his memory naturally was. And whether he might be suffering from a convenient, momentary, highly selective blackout.

"Would you mind asking your partner when you see him?" I said.

"Sure. I'll do that. So you think there might be some connection then between this kid Bobby's murder and Colby's?"

"I'm hoping so."

He said, "The cops still think Colby pissed off some Mexican, maybe at O'Banion's."

"Except O'Banion's isn't exactly a gathering place for Latinos, is it?" I said.

"Naw. Like attracts like and O'Banion's isn't exactly a greaseball magnet."

On the other hand, Sheila and her girlfriend were attacked by two Hispanics within two blocks of the bar that was popular with the college crowd. So the cops were right not to rule out a similar attack on Colby. Possibly right in making that the main focus of their investigation.

"You know about what we do here then, right?" Randy said.

"I do, but obviously the cops don't. At least yet."

His handsome face went pale. "You going to report us?"

"Should I?"

He took a quick glance at the ceiling to buy some thinking time. "Kirk and I could make it worthwhile for you not to."

"You mean a bribe? I'm shocked," I said and smiled to let him know I was kidding.

"I'd have to check with Kirk, but –."

"I don't want your money. And you needn't worry. I'm not going to report you. I live and work in Las Vegas. If you don't take the local suckers' money, somebody else will come along to do it. Vice, too, abhors a vacuum." I stood. "Talk to your partner. See if he knows anything. Have him call me if he does." I handed the young man my card.

"Will do."

I hoped so as I thanked him and let him show me out.

Sarah Lee Housely was sitting on her porch in a straight-backed chair when I emerged and headed back to my car.

"Good morning, young man," she said and gave me a dainty wave.

"Good morning to you, ma'am. How are you?"

"I'm just fine, And you?"

"Peachy as ever," I said.

"How nice."

Bagpipe sat on the porch beside her. "And how is Bagpipe?" I said.

A low grumble rattled in the Westie's throat, as if to warn me, "Come any closer and you'll end up a half-eaten peach, cowboy."

"Oh, Bagpipe is just as jolly as ever," Sarah said, ignoring the evidence at her feet.

"That's nice," I said, for lack of any other drivel to spew. Just keep the little fucker on a short leash, lady, I thought as I continued on.

I stopped in again at the nearby Antigone Bookstore on Fourth Avenue to choose a handful of books for Adelle to read while she was mending. Because I was flying to Las Vegas before returning to Arroyo Arenoso, I asked to have them shipped. I didn't explain my reason why to the clerk and she gave me an odd look when I gave her Adelle's address. Rather than explain my reason to her, I thought it would make her day go faster if I left her to ponder my apparent eccentricity.

I was walking down the sidewalk to my car, which I had to leave a block away because that was the only parking space I could find, when I heard repeated honking from a car somewhere behind me. When I finally turned to see who was acting so rudely, I saw a white Corolla creeping along slowly with Sheila Bausch at the wheel and her girlfriend waving frantically at me out the window on the passenger's side. I stepped between parked cars and Sheila stopped beside me.

"Hey, Pistol Pete. How ya doin'?" Sheila shouted at me.

"Hello, ladies. I'm doing well, thank you. And how are you two doing?"

The girlfriend said, "We're great. Thanks for the fabulous flowers. My name, by the way, is Vicki. Vicki Robinson."

I shook Vicki's tan hand with its decoratively manicured nails, and said, "Wiley Poynter," to complete the formality.

"Thanks again for saving our bacon, Mr. Pistol Pete Poynter," Sheila said.

"My pleasure, ladies. I'm rather fond of bacon. I don't like to see it burnt."

Sheila said, "We figure we still owe you big time for what you did. You obviously found our address. Why don't you drop by some time and we'll treat you to a breakfast of bacon and eggs, along with some very succulent melons on the side."

Vicki added, "Sometime soon would be great."

"I'd be delighted. I'm off to Las Vegas this afternoon, but I hope to return in a day or two." I handed Vicki a business card.

"Wow! He's a private detective, Sheil. He actually lives in Las Vegas."

"Cool!" Sheila cooed. To Vicki, "Maybe he'll invite us up to Las Vegas for breakfast some time."

"Yeah, Mr. Wiley Poynter. Will you do that?" Vicki said.

"That could be arranged."

Sheila fumbled in her purse, found a pen and notepad, scribbled on it, and passed in across to me. "Our number at the apartment. Give us a call."

"Soon," Vicki said. "Although later is better than never," she added with a Marilyn Monroe style whispery giggle.

"In the meantime, ladies, stay out of alleys after dark."

"We promise," Vicki said.

"See you again soon, Wiley Pete," Sheila said and slowly drove away.

No question the private-eye racket pays poorly in terms of recurrent fat collectible fees, but now and then the side benefits make stress from a modest cash flow seem worth the deprivation.

43

On this flight home I had no sex therapist to make the flight seem less dull. I did manage not to scan the fuselage ceiling for nano-cracks. Both flight attendants were male and their imagined clever patter grew tiresome well before they wheeled the drink cart down the narrow aisle.

Again I had secured an aisle seat, this time near the rear of the aircraft. And, because the flight was only three-quarters full, the middle seat to my left remained empty at takeoff. Lucky me. A middle-aged man wearing a crumpled brown suit sat across the aisle from me and read *The Wall Street Journal* assiduously, alter-nately frowning and nodding as he turned the pages.

Once in an economic class my professor spent half a lecture period trying to clarify the differences between gambling and investing. His point was lost on me, maybe because I was too busy rescanning my notes for a sociology quiz the next hour. Perhaps the guy across the aisle was sufficiently learned to enlighten me. After all, he was on his way to Las Vegas, where perhaps he intended to plunk down his Google, Apple, and Exxon Mobile winnings on twenty-two red in hopes of doubling his fortune with one spin of the wheel.

At McCarran I hailed a cab, which drove me to my modest condo in Henderson. When I landed I had phoned Dante to pick me up at my place at noon. He told me he had offered his Wrangler to Jack's sister and she had accepted. So I was stuck hitching rides with him and Stacy or else taking my chances betting my life on the whims of cabbies whose skills driving autos had been honed on the dared-devil streets of Cairo, Damascus, and Baghdad.

My humble abode perched on Ramrod Avenue, west of Mountain Vista, only fifteen minutes from McCarran. I had bought the twelve-hundred square-foot conversion in 2004, three years before real estate began its skid down the slippery slope. Adelle had loaned me the down payment and I was lucky enough to have paid her three-year low-interest loan back to her early.

With three bedrooms, I slept in one, used one for an office away from my office, and kept one bedroom well-groomed for those rare occasions when Adelle paid me a visit.

Except for a handful of cheerless neighbors, most of whose names whose names I didn't even know or care to learn, I was now mostly surrounded by the ghosts of owners past. The exception was Myrtle Atchison, my nearest and nosiest neighbor. She was simultaneously a nuisance and a blessing. If a cockroach in my kitchen were to sneeze, she'd let me know about.

Las Vegas sat trapped in a time warp, a present-day setting out of a post-apocalypse horror movie. Those few real neighbors I had, including Myrtle, looked like characters out of a Harlan Ellison story. Or, to take a more historically mundane perspective, Las Vegas was well on it's way to becoming just another among the many dozens of mining ghost towns in Nevada.

The current crisis stemmed from the same roots as the one that created ghost towns past – grab-and-run greed. The avaricious mine operators this time around were better known as mortgage bankers. Some nights I fall asleep picturing mortgage bankers dangling by their necks from colorful ropes, all of them kicking futility as they swing like hundreds of Christmas-tree icicles from high-rise, neon-lit hotels along The Strip. The result of such a fantasy invariably is a deep REM slumber.

I showered for the second time that day, changed clothes, and sat down to sip on a beer while I waited for Dante. My cell phone rang and the caller was Kirk McMullen.

"Randy said you were asking about a possible connection between Colby and the dead kid down south, Bobby Hollsworth," he said.

"That's correct."

"I've got nothing definitive, but try this on for size. The Hollsworth kid called me one day a month or so ago. He'd been placing bets with us for over a year, but I had never met him or spoken with him. Fabian Maldonado, as you discovered, is my pickup-and-delivery man in that area."

"Yes. I know that much," I said.

"Well, Bobby told me he had a business proposition for me. He said that, in exchange for better spreads on games he bet on, he would cut me in on a deal he had cooked up to control the sale of a certain drug in his part of the world."

"A certain drug?"

"He wouldn't say what it was right then, but he talked enough to strongly suggest he was talking about some kind of pills, rather than something you smoke, inject, shove up your nose or rub on your knees. Painkillers maybe. I'm only guessing, but I think that may be a pretty good guess."

"And your response to him was –?"

"I respectfully declined. I've got a lucrative business going here in the house. I told him I was not interested in diversification. I feel I have to add that I'm scared shitless of Columbians, Mexicans, and whatever other brand of cigar-smoking brown fuckers I might find myself competing against. No thanks. Life's too short as it is."

"How did Bobby react to your disinterest?"

"He told me to grow some *cojones*. I politely told him I didn't need business advice from a guy who only had to shave once a week."

"And?"

"He hung up. But –."

"But?"

"After I put down the phone I noticed Colby had been hanging around in the next room, just beyond the door to my office. I have no doubt Colby overheard every word of my end of that conversation."

"Very interesting," I said.

"I thought that might tweak your ear buds."

"Thank you very much, Mr. McMullen. Now please explain to me why you didn't call me before about this? Or the police? You knew Bobby was dead. He no longer was a betting customer. I'm sure Fabian told you why. You had suspicions about a Colby-Bobby connection. So when Colby was killed, why didn't lights and sirens go off in your head then? Surely you knew I had come to your place to talk to Colby about Bobby."

"No. Actually I didn't. Colby never mentioned you to me. The first I knew about that was when I came home the other day. Our sweet-but-nosy next door neighbor, Miss Housely, told me, quote, 'that man' showed up at our house again today. When I asked Randy about who 'that man' was, it turned out to be you."

He had a point. I hadn't actually spoken to Colby about Bobby. I had pulled my sub-lease ruse with Colby and had never gotten far enough to work Bobby into the conversation before Colby had shut the door in my face.

Even so, what Kirk was telling me revealed a bagful of denial on his part. The instant he was told Colby was dead, he surely supposed Colby's and Bobby's murders could only remotely be coincidental. I imagined he simply wanted to keep his business from getting dragged into the picture, as in exposed for the illegal operation it was. So he kept quiet about a likely Colby-Bobby connection.

"By the way, did you ever allow Bobby to place bets on the cuff?" I said.

Silence.

"Hello?"

"I heard your question. Okay. I didn't, but Colby did without my knowledge. I put a stop to it as soon as I found out."

"How did you put a stop to it?" I said.

"Now wait a minute. No, no, no. A word to Colby was all it took. Got that? A verbal reprimand. Colby apologized."

"Did Colby say why he was doing it? Letting Bobby run up a tab, so to speak?"

"Colby said Bobby had done him a couple favors and he simply wanted to return the favors."

"What kind of favors?"

"I didn't ask because it didn't make any difference. I told Colby business is business and the kind of favor he granted has no place in our business. None."

"And Colby said?"

"Like I said. He apologized and assured me it wouldn't happen again," Kirk said.

"Did Bobby's bets turn out to be winners?" I said.

Pause. Finally, "No, they did not."

"Did you collect?"

"Damned right I did."

"But not with a pound of flesh," I said.

"I repeat. I did not kill Bobby Hollsworth; I did not kill Colby Ambrose."

"I hope not."

Kirk said, "Is Randy right? You don't intend to let the uniforms know what we're up to here? Or am I going to have to move my operation somewhere across town?" Kirk said, while I was thinking.

I responded, "I meant what I said. As long as you give the suckers an even break, they can bet the ranch on the '62 Mets to win the Series on a replay for all I care."

"Good luck finding the kid's killer. Do you really think the same person did Colby in?" Kirk said.

"I don't know, but I have to believe so. Tucson PD thinks otherwise. I have no connection between them other than Fabian's seeing the two of them together in a casino parking lot, plus what you've now told me. That's not much to go on, but it beats random coincidence."

Kirk said, "Obviously in my business I don't put much faith in randomness or coincidence, although every so often Random Coincidence somehow manages to cross the finish line a nose ahead of Tight Connections. Then I take it up the ass. But give me the favored horse every time and I'll come out ahead by bunches over the long haul."

"Provided you survive the short haul."

"There is that. So far, so good. Knock on plastic. Anyway, I hope I've been of some help. I must run. The Kentucky Derby is coming up and I need to reevaluate a couple horses. I think I may have set my opening teaser odds too high."

I said, "Maybe the horses will scratch and your mistake will be moot. You'll be off the hook."

"You have too much faith in good fortune, Mr. Poynter."

"I'm not a gambler, Mr. McMullen. Are you telling me I should become one?"

He laughed. "I'm afraid that would be like a coyote telling a rabbit to jump into his mouth. I'll call you again if I think of something else."

I thanked Kirk for the courtesy call. He had been helpful. Maybe.

Dante showed up on time, brought in my bag that had languished in the rear of his Hummer for days, handed me back his Sig Sauer again, and we headed for the hospital to check up on Jack and for me to meet his sister.

Helen Otley stood five-feet four, brown eyes, brown hair. She had a tiny mole at the right corner of her mouth. She said she was a hospital case worker in Denver so she was fluent in the arcane lingo of those who wore white and dangled stethoscopes from their necks. Maybe that would permit her to fend off, even put an end to, much of what I considered condescending bullshit shoveled at Dante and me by the hospital staff. I had no doubt these people cared and that most of them were competent care-givers, but I disliked being treated as though I were one of the virulent diseases they were paid to combat.

After putting in a respectful few minutes sitting bedside, Dante and I took Helen to lunch at El Cazador, where she alternately thanked us for our help and quietly bemoaned the growing size of Jack's hospital bill. Ever optimistic, Dante tried to console her with what amounted to a promise to host a fund-raiser or three. Dante was not Jerry Lewis. So I remained less sanguine than he about the prospects of coming up with more than a small percentage of the growing debt Jack was incurring.

"I can quit my job and nurse him myself at his place, once he is released. But, God, that could be weeks or months from now," she said.

I refrained from mumbling any blood-from-a-turnip bromides, even though I was convinced the hospital would end up pissing up a rope when it was all over. I felt sorry for the hospital, but it wasn't my fault Hippocrates had it by its blue-white neon balls. Maybe God should have made this best-of-all-possible worlds a less dangerous place to live in.

We dropped Helen back at the hospital. Dante had arranged for one of his minions to deliver his Wrangler to the North Vista visitors' parking lot and have the keys handed to her. Then he and I drove to Jack's office once again to meet with Stacy and have her detail what she had discovered about the gem depot and people who owned it.

On the way, I jabbed Dante lightly as he performed his usual traffic-snaking maneuvers. "Seven. Maybe six-and-a half."

Dante glanced at me briefly and shook his head. "That's cruel."

"You're going soft and your eyes are getting weak," I said.

"Some detective you are. You missed catching all her natural charms, Wiles."

"*Magnifying female charms very ancient optical illusion,*" I said, quoting my favorite movie detective.

"Charlie says that, does he?"

"*Charlie Chan at the Circus,* 1936."

"You dishonor Mr. Chan by misapplying him."

"Okay. I could be wrong."

"Glad you admit it," Dante said, smiling.

"I only said 'could be'. Charlie also said, '*Every Maybe has wife called Maybe-Not.*'"

"One of your loveable virtues, Wiley, is your occasional self-doubt."

Stacy sat glowering at a computer monitor when Dante and I walked into Jack's office.

"Pull up a chair, guys. I have a lot to show you," Stacy began.

When we were seated on either side of Stacy, she brought up a face on the monitor.

"Guys, meet Brent Michael Karsgaard, the majority owner of Beckheimer's Gem Depot. He lives out in the Belle Fiore section of Lake Las Vegas. Age thirty-one, from Chaska, Minnesota, a suburb of the Twin Cities. He has a degree in Chemical Engineering and Materials Science from the University of Minnesota, and from college he went to work for 3M until two years ago, when he moved to our fair city."

I said, "Materials science would give him insight into gold, silver, and diamonds."

Stacy said, "Yeah, but there's more. I found evidence he probably has an elaborate photography studio, maybe even a small film studio, set up in his home out at the Lake. I think he specializes in making... guess what?"

"Disney films?" I said, jokingly.

"Yeah. Right," Stacy said. She banged on the keyboard for a minute or so and brought up a different website. "Wiley, did you have Jack looking into anything related to Sebastian Sechrest?"

"No."

"Interesting. His name turned up in one of Jack's online searches. But wait. You asked me early on to do a background check on Sechrest. I think I may have mentioned that to Jack during one of his calls to me to check into what I was doing for you. I must have brought up Sechrest's name to Jack."

"So what did Jack find related to Sechrest?" Dante said.

"This is an ad that was posted very recently. It is a call for like-minded, discreet photographers and film-makers to call an 888 number to get an address to send their photos and films to have them converted onto DVDs. I've traced the phone. The number rings two places: Beckheimer's Gem Depot and Karsgaard's home. I also succeeded in accessing a list of people who have logged onto the site. One name that popped up is Sebastian Sechrest."

I said, "And Jack's GPS history shows he returned from Beckheimer's to his office the night he was beaten?"

"Correct," Stacy said.

"What about Boyd Dupree? Does his name turn up in anything connected to Karsgaard?"

"No. Only Sechrest."

Now it looked like Boyd Dupree's only crimes consisted of screwing a NASCAR bimbo or two, while lying to his wife about what he was up to. These days, that brand of cheating and spouse-deception not only weren't major crimes, they were not looked upon by many as even moral failings. Rather, on the subject of marital infidelity at least, many now agreed with Steinbeck's preacher in *The Grapes of Wrath* when he proclaimed, regarding morality in general, *"There ain't no right, there ain't no wrong. There's just stuff people do."*

Maybe, too, I'd been wrong in trying to find evidence absolving Sebastian. Instead, the play looked like Sechrest to Karsgaard to Stonecipher. Jack's beating appeared to be the work of goons hired by Karsgaard. If they could reduce Jack to a bleeding pulp for whatever reasons, they could just as easily have killed Bobby Shane. If Sebastian didn't plunge the knife into Bobby's back himself, there was an excellent chance he knew who did. *Femmes fatale*s make better film *noir* because of all the libidinous overtones, but *entrepreneur fatal*s are just as lethal and there are surely more of them. It was beginning to look as though Brent Karsgaard and Sebastian Sechrest were two of them.

"What about the gem depot pad? Can we get inside?" I said. I was eager to find more evidence connecting Sebastian Sechrest with Brent Karsgaard and whoever worked for him.

"No problem," Stacy said. "I've checked it out already. The place has an expensive state-of-the-art alarm system. However –." She leaned back in her chair and grinned.

"However –." I said.

"It's beatable."

"You can get into the gem depot then," I said.

"I already have. Sort of. Tonight will just be a matter of duplicating last night's effort," she said.

"What do you mean by 'sort of'?" Dante said.

"First, there are half a dozen video cameras inside. But, unlike the alarm system, the camera system is not state-of-the-art. Mainly, it's not self-contained inside, which is really dumb. There's not only a power feed on the roof, the whole control unit is in a box up there. A box that is both cooled and protected from the sun. And the reason it's up there is that it's solar-powered, although really all that needs to be outside is the solar panels. And the box is locked. But still, it's accessible – by me. Most burglars, of course, won't figure out that it's even up there. But for Super-Ninja Stacy… no problem."

She paused, apparently waiting for applause she didn't get.

"When I said I went inside I mean I opened the back door a crack to make sure there's no junkyard dog ready to bite our heads off. That was after I closed down the alarm and dinked with the cameras for a short while. No dog. And the key to our getting inside and staying there is to trick the cameras into appearing as though they are still on and functioning as they should. Both the alarm and camera feeds go directly to Karsgaard – to his home and to his phone and computers. I've got it set up so that what he will see tonight, in case he looks, is what he would have seen last night. I'm hoping nothing much has changed. Or, if it has, he won't notice."

"Isn't that dicey?" I said.

"Yes, but the alternatives are: one, shutting the cameras down, which he will definitely notice; two, letting the cameras stay on and hope he fails to notice three nosy people creeping around his premises. Sorry. That's the best I can do."

"It will have to do then," I said. "Good job."

44

The industrial park Bechheimer's Gem Depot resided in was served by a rent-a-cop patrol. A guy in a white mini-pickup with a yellow spinning light atop the cab drove by the rear door of the Gem Depot on an average of every fifty-four minutes, according to Stacy, who had taken the precaution of timing the security man over a three-hour period. On his third pass-by Stacy followed him and discovered he covered three other nearby warehouse complexes as well. At two of those he exited the truck and checked the door locks, front and back, of four businesses. Thankfully for us, Brent Karsgaard hadn't paid for that add-on feature.

All three of us slipped on latex gloves and paper booties. Stacy put her ear to the back door, gave a thumbs up, and in we went. The minute we were inside we all knew Karsgaard's business had nothing to do with gems, although lovers of porn DVDs would surely judge some of his inventory to be of gem quality no doubt. The owner's stint with 3M, along with his engineering degree, stood him in good stead for what he was really up to: converting homemade, amateur porn videotapes into high-quality DVDs.

He bought video tapes from a multitude of people eager to display themselves, friends, neighbors, and maybe even strangers acting out the pages of the Kama Sutra. However, from the still shots on the cases of many of the DVDs awaiting shipment to locations all over the globe, the carnal artistry Karsgaard had collected to sell made the Kama Sutra appear rather staid, if not downright dull.

The machinery the porn vendor had at hand was first-class, according to Stacy. I didn't ask how she knew that to be true. A sizeable portion of the interior of Karsgaard's business was devoted to packaging, labeling, pre-shipping storage. While Dante examined Karsgaard's office, Stacy and I randomly examined the cellophane-wrapped products.

The front cover of each DVD case bore the same style design. Four equal-sized still shots hinted at the delights contained on the disk inside. The cover photos left little or nothing to one's imagination. Now and then one or all of the participants' faces were shielded, usually by some inventive mask, and occasionally by a blur-out.

After almost fifteen minutes of "shopping" the goods, I hit a jackpot. There, in four glossy shots, stood a naked Bobby Shane Hollsworth, in each photo being ministered to by a shapely, equally unclothed female. In each shot, however, the woman on her knees wore a fanciful Mardi-Gras-type facemask. But nothing else. Well, perfume perhaps. And maybe facial makeup. The two blondes and two brunettes were all buxom. I had the feeling the women's hair in each instance was an ornamental wig, but I could have been wrong. As for the ladies' ample breasts, I had a long history of being pathetic when it came to distinguishing genuine from silicon.

Before pocketing the disk, I showed it to Stacy, who moved her flashlight up and down, to get views of the photos in different lights. Why, I don't know. Again, I didn't ask.

She whispered, "So that is the late, lamented Bobby Shane. He clearly didn't die a virgin."

Just then Dante appeared, took a look, and said, "Busy kid. By now he's surely discovered that Heaven's nothing like that."

Stacy said, "Unless maybe he was a suicide bomber on the side."

I reminded her, "Haven't you heard that you're not supposed to speak ill of the dead, Stace?"

"Yeah, but I get so tired of speaking ill of only the living. Know what I mean?"

Dante changed the subject. "Look what I found." It was a scratchpad with Jack's name, along with his office phone number and office address."

"Bingo! Game's on," I said.

Then Dante said, "Back in the office this guy's got a safe the size of a gun cabinet."

"Can you open it?" I said.

Dante shook his head. "I'd have to bring in ST." The initials stood for "Soft Touch", the nickname for one of Dante's in-and-out-of-prison acquaintances whose real name was Billy Meadows.

"How about you?" I said to Stacy.

She gave me a pouty lip and said, "I didn't bring my stethoscope. And, I have to admit – reluctantly, mind you – that Billy M. is faster than I am."

I shrugged. "Another time, perhaps."

Dante then said, "I found a ledger that appears to be people he buys from. But it's all in some elaborate code. Unless Stacy has an Enigma machine in the trunk of her car, we're SOL."

Dante added, "What I found that is helpful is a sheet showing Karsgaard has three minority-share partners. They appear to be salaried. I also have their addresses. Plus, he seems to have two hourly employees, each with a Hispanic surname. I'm betting those are the guys who worked Jack over. I have their addresses, too."

"Thanks, Dante. Anything else?"

"Nope."

I said, "I've got what I want. It appears that Sebastian was busier than I had imagined. None of the women on the disk I found are teenagers. I'm sure of that. I wonder what bait he used to lure them into camera range."

Stacy snickered. "Bobby appears to me to be pretty attractive bait."

I said, "Yeah, but everybody knows you'll bite on anything. So that's no help."

She punched me hard on my bicep.

"Let's vamoose. Make sure everything is back in order. And I have a suggestion."

Both looked at me.

"Let's pay Brent Karsgaard a visit."

Stacy blinked. "Now?"

"Why not? The notion that revenge is a dish best served cold isn't always true," I said.

Finding what the owner of the Beckheimer's Gem Depot had really been up to was satisfying. I now had additional material to hand over to Roland Morton. But payback for what Karsgaard had ordered done to Jack Stonecipher remained an unfinished item of business.

Tuesday – just after midnight

We first drove to Dante's gun range and picked up a white van he owned. The logo and lettering on the sides of the van could be altered to suit Dante's whims and purposes. In minutes he and one of his associates had turned the van into a plumber's vehicle advertising twenty-four emergency service in large block letters. As a prop Dante hoisted a large sewer-pipe snake coiled onto a mechanical roller into the back end of the van. But he removed the ladder atop the van, lest it give a nosy neighbor or passerby the wrong impression. Before leaving, we listened to Dante give instructions to a group of associates he trusted. He provided these men with the names and addresses of Brent Karsgaard's junior partners and wage employees.

Then we drove east to Lake Las Vegas, a fancy-schmancy planned community of hotels, high-end homes, and lush golf courses, all focused around a large, private, man-made lake. That Brent Karsgaard lived in a gated community amid sprawling luxury didn't slow Stacy and Dante down. Stacy had already determined no manned gatehouse fronted the section of homes where Karsgaard lived. Hoodwinking the electronic box requiring either homeowner identification or homeowner permission for guests turned out to be a one-minute exercise in hocus pocus.

Dante parked directly in front of Karsgaard's sandstone mansion, got out, and placed the sewer-pipe prop on the street immediately behind the van. All three of us were dressed in navy blue coveralls and wore matching brimmed hats pulled down low onto our foreheads. Stacy had her hair curled up underneath her cap. While Dante and I stood next to the van watching, pretending to be busy with equipment inside the open right-side sliding door, Stacy took off around the back of the house to check for an alarm system and to disarm it, if she found one. What seemed like an eternity passed, though it turned out to be fourteen minutes, before Stacy returned.

"Another overpriced alarm system disarmed; no dogs inside," she said.

Dante grinned. "Let's party."

I pulled out Dante's Sig, but he shook his head.

"Don't risk ruining the neighbor's beauty sleep, Wile."

"What neighbors?" Karsgaard's estate appeared to have its own private zip code.

"The desert air at night, Wiley. Why do you think, when you stand at the corner of Tropicana and The Boulevard, you can hear the coyotes howling on the south rim of the Grand Canyon?" Dante said.

Stacy whispered, "Yeah, Wiley. How come?"

From deep inside the van Dante pulled out three Walther PPK's, each with a silencer attached. "For things that go bump in the night."

The combination handgun and noise suppressor felt awkward to me, but I didn't argue. Stacy smiled as though she'd just been handed a pair of new designer shoes.

Using an illegal lock pick, Stacy opened the front door, then stood aside for Dante to go in. I followed and Stacy came in after me, closing the door quietly behind her. I was fearful the hinges would squeak. They always do in Charlie Chan movies. But these didn't. I judged squeak-free hinges to be one of the bonuses included when purchasing a multi-million-dollar house.

I made my watch dial glow and discovered the time was 1:51 a.m. No lights remained on downstairs. So we headed for the wide, curving staircase. Somewhere outside a dog barked and we all frozen momentarily. I backed up against the wall at the foot of the stairs, reminding myself how much I had dreaded night maneuvers at Fort Benning. I had been even more edgy later at Fort Lewis, where we often had to remain on training patrols for several days – and nights. Normally, I was no more afraid of the dark than any other nyctophobe.

When Dante directed his flashlight into my face I'm sure he saw the frozen stare. "You okay, Trooper?"

I nodded tentatively. He motioned that he was going up. This time Stacy followed and I took up guarding our rear.

No lights upstairs either and from the looks of the second floor we had our choice of five, maybe six, bedrooms. The hallway was wide and carpeted. From the glow of Dante's light, which he held low and kept pointed toward the floor, no lines of tin cans had been strung wall-to-wall, ankle high, as warnings of last resort.

How Dante determined which door led to the master bedroom, I never figured out. Maybe it was his Marine Corps training. At Fort Lewis our Army unit had spent many an hour learning build-to-building assault techniques, but never bedroom to bedroom. First, he checked to see that the lesser bedrooms were unoccupied.

Three people lay asleep in the king bed when we rushed into the master bedroom, flicked on the overhead light, and held our guns leveled. Our charge covered more ground than any of us expected. The bedroom was large enough to hold a high school prom in. But its sleeping occupants reacted slowly, each roused from what surely were blissful slumbers. Or maybe drunken ones.

"What the –," the only male in the bed started to curse as he sat up hastily and shielded his eyes from the sudden burst of lights. The two photogenic females, one on either side of him, propped themselves up on their elbows and muttered words I couldn't understand, other than "Brent".

However, the ladies' pupils adjusted faster than Karsgaard's. When they saw the muzzled pistols pointing at them, they shrieked in unison. And kept on shrieking until Dante told them to shut up.

Brent Karsgaard finally said, "Jesus Christ! How did you get in?" Leave it to an engineer to ask a technical question when faced with uncertainty and likely harm.

I said, "The sign on your open front door said, 'Come on in'."

"Who the fuck are you?" he said.

Dante ripped backed the covers and the sheets, making the two women squeal and hasten to draw in their arms to cover their breasts. "Toss your pillows on the floor." The women complied; Karsgaard didn't. Dante said, "Yours, too, Bucko." He took a step toward the bed and held his gun at arm's length, pointing it at Brent. The man gave in and did as he was told.

Dante then told him, "I knew a guy in Mississippi once. The very first time we were introduced the first words out of his mouth were, 'What kinda gun y'all carryin'?' At the time I wasn't carrying and told him so. He replied, 'Here in Lamar County everybody sleeps with a gun under his pillow and, by God, there ain't no crime in Lamar County, Mississippi.' I just want to be sure you weren't raised in Lamar County, Mr. Karsgaard."

"How do you know my name?" Tension made his voice quaver.

Stacy spoke. "Oh, we know all about you, you piece of shit."

The two women beside Karsgaard shuddered at the sound of Stacy's voice. One, a sinuous blonde with a mild sunburn, whimpered, "Please, don't shoot us. We don't know anything."

Karsgaard, perhaps trying to show he still held some sway in the room, snapped at her, "Shut the fuck up, bitch."

Dante pointed to a camera mounted high on the wall. Then he turned and pointed to another. He said, "In case those are light-activated, smash them, will you, Stacy?"

"My pleasure," she said and did so, with great showmanship.

I said, "We already know what kind of voyeur you are, Karsgaard. We don't need to see film of these two fine ladies in action to confirm that."

Brent Karsgaard slowly repeated, "What do you want?"

I walked closer to him. "We want you, my man. We're going to take you for a little ride."

Dante cleared his throat. "No use lying to you, Brent, old buddy. We're actually planning on sending you on a long ride."

I like to think there is a touch of the vigilante in most people. Repressed, for sure, but there. And usually only when a sense of serious injustice -- or the potential thereof -- occurs does the urge to take retribution into one's own hands well up. Brent Skarsgaard's dodgy activities potentially going unpunished, especially after what he ordered done to Jack -- gave Dante and me the impulse to make certain that he did not skate. We would not give him the opportunity to call upon a phalanx of high-priced lawyers -- coupled with potentially stupid or corrupt judges and shoddy police work -- to get him off.

45

Handcuffs are anachronisms. Oh, the police still use them and the latest styles feature less metal, and even that is made of lighter, strong material. As an engineer Brent Karsgaard would have understood all that. I'm sure he also would have preferred handcuffs to the nylon bands Dante had brought along to bind Brent's and the bimbos' wrists behind their backs. Nylon tends to gouge skin, especially when pulled as snug as Dante pulled the ties he used.

I'm sure the ladies would have chosen bracelets lined with soft, pink fur, had they been allowed to select their own wrist-restraints. All three of our hostage/prisoner guests flinched when Dante brought out the ball gags.

Rather than recoil, Stacy swooned. "Wow! As seen on TV!"

"What TV have you been watching?" I said.

"Pay-per-view bondage flicks," she said.

Even Dante looked up in surprise at that remark.

With the gags inserted, Dante went off to back his van up to one of the garage doors. Herding Brent and his ladies out to the street might allow some insomniac neighbor to spot us and dial 911. We then opened the garage door and loaded our guests into the back of the van, on their knees. Dante used more nylon bindings to tie their ankles together, finally connecting the wrist nylon to the ankle nylon with nylon rope, preventing our grumpy guests from being able to lie on their backs and kick out at us.

The downside to ball gags, Dante warned us, is that they tend to restrict air flow, potentially causing a problem for those with breathing issues. Hence, Stacy and I were obliged to monitor our prisoners, while Dante drove. He didn't say what the alternative was, should one of them begin to gasp or faint. Remove the obstruction and risk listening to screams for help, I supposed. Stacy chose to keep an eye on Karsgaard, leaving me the pleasant task of watching over the two women. Because all three of our guests were still stark naked, neither Stacy nor I felt discommoded by our observational duties.

From where we were Stacy and I were unable to see out to know where Dante was driving. I could tell he was driving more slowly and cautiously than he normally would. By my watch thirty-five minutes passed before Dante stopped and called back, "Time to free the ladies now. I'll come around and open up the back."

When the rear doors opened, I saw that we had stopped at Tropicana and Las Vegas Boulevard, that special place where Dante had assured me earlier I could hear coyotes from the Grand Canyon howling on a clear night. I listened, but all I heard were the sounds of traffic.

Dante and Stacy pulled the two bare naked ladies from the van, undid their bindings, gave them both shoves toward the sidewalks, and climbed back into the van. In seconds we were in motion again. I supposed the two women, standing on The Strip, wee confronted with the dilemma of whether to use their now-freed hands to cover their nakedness or remove their gags and cry for help.

For the brief time the van doors were open, I could see that few pedestrians walked the streets. Mostly taxis drove along The Strip. At the hour of 3:00 a.m., when the night creatures have emerged from the woodwork and are on the prowl, such fiends usually elect to remain inside the casinos, where no one with a *corazón puro* – a pure heart – is likely to be lurking.

Still, I was sure the bare-assed bimbos would draw at least a small crowd. And the ever-resourceful Dante Foster, to avert our own exposure to a wandering eye noting the license plate of our van, had the van rigged with a revolving set of license plates. The number any observer would record, when referenced by the LVMPD, would reveal that the registered owner of a white van with said number belonged to one Arthur M. Pettigrew, residing in Carson City. Further checking would unmask two facts: Arthur was non-existent and his address was a vacant piece of property on the outskirts of Nevada's capital.

From The Strip Dante drove to a building he owned in one of Henderson's warehouse districts near the small Henderson airport. Shortly after we arrived two more vans joined us and we took all our "guests" inside. Dante's associates introduced me to Brent's junior partners: Warren Phelps, David Lang, Eric Sizemore. Next, I met the two thugs who had put Jack Stonechipher into a coma, Jesus Ortiz and Armando Fuentes, who had been hauled in from a heavily Hispanic neighborhood in North Las Vegas by a pair of

Dante's trusted Latino associates known as the "No-No Brothers", Narcisso and Orlando Anaya. Like Karsgaard and his partners, Ortiz and Fuentes were bound and gagged.

The six prisoners were lined up against a wall, not to be shot but in order for Dante to explain their fate to them. When Dante, Jack, and I had first used this method of exiling vermin to the outer darkness, we had provided no pre-trip highlight account. Even now Dante's lecture would be *sans* photos or videos or even a travel brochure.

Their journey would be long and arduous. No three-legged-camel adventure over the Hindustan Range; no waste-deep trek through snake-infested bayous; no abandonment atop an Andes peak; no Siberian gulag. Rather, we sentenced them to a not-so-luxurious cruise to Singapore, locked in a sealed, containerized cargo box, the kind you see piggybacking along on Union Pacific flatbed cars. The freighter would leave from Long Beach and they would arrive there from Las Vegas locked in the back of an eighteen-wheeler.

To lessen their chances of escape, Dante and his minions would semi-embalm them in plaster casts. Their legs would be encased from the knees down; their arms pinned to their torsos similarly. Their bare waists would be free so that they could perform waste-elimination functions, although, after a while they would find themselves covered with their own excrement. Lest they starve or dehydrate, liquid sugar and water bottles would be hung from the walls of the semi's trailer and inside the cargo box for them to suck on like caged birds.

When they arrived in Singpore after many days at sea, the container would be opened by surprised recipients of the steel box, whose manifest clearly misrepresented the container's contents.

Once the dismayed beneficiaries of the box recovered from both the shock and stench of their discovery, they would, for their self-protection, call in the local police.

In Singapore punishment for the crime for smuggling pornography into the country is severe. And the police would indeed find pornography in the cargo box. Lots of it. All courtesy of Beckheimer's Gem Depot.

When Dante, Jack, and I had first arranged for someone to go missing from Las Vegas, sent off to Singapore in a similar manner, I had proposed including packets of heroin or cannabis borrowed from the LVMPD's evidence room, courtesy of Dante's covert contacts there. I withdrew my proposal after Dante had explained to me that any person caught possessing an amount in excess of two grams of heroin or fifteen grams of marijuana was subject to capital punishment in Singapore.

Caught with several open cases of pornographic DVDs would earn Brent Karsgaard and his fellow offenders only corporal punishment, a good caning each. That they were incapacitated when found would not eradicate, or even lessen, their punishment, according to Dante.

"Singapore officials are a humorless lot. They'd flog a corpse if they found an obscene picture in its vicinity or even suspected it of having jaywalked just before it died," he once told me.

The post-punishment fate of those we had previously sentenced to a trip to Singapore remained indeterminate. We were quite sure none had ever returned to Las Vegas and that was sufficient knowledge for us. Bereft of means, we assumed Brent Karsgaard, his partners, and his henchmen would struggle to survive in a city such as Singapore.

Still, Dante, Jack, and I have always considered ourselves charitable in our method of ridding our city of undesirables. The local wise guys employed a quicker, cheaper manner of cleansing the streets of filth: a bullet to the back of the head, followed by burial in a shallow sand pit somewhere halfway between Las Vegas and Tonopah. By comparison, we deemed ourselves humane.

Leaving the messy details to Dante and his proficient crew, I left with Stacy, who drove me back to my condo, where I hoped to get some sleep before catching a mid-day flight back to Tucson.

"Want me to fluff your pillow for you, Wiley?" Stacy asked, when she stopped in front of my humble abode.

"No thanks. The way I feel right now I'll be sound asleep before my head even touches it."

"No sex then, right?"

"Sorry, dear."

"Don't tell me that you're finally going to tell me I'm not your type."

"*Au contrere*, sweet Stacy. You're just my type."

"Well, then?"

"Truth is, I intended to invite you over tonight for a bit of snuggling. But that was before I knew my sister had been injured. Now it's going to have to be another time; maybe even another place."

"You mean someday we'll always have Paris?"

"Someday."

"Liar."

"Do I keep my promises?"

"Sure. To everyone else but me."

"Give me time to prove you wrong."

"How about 6:23 a.m. today?"

"No. But soon perhaps."

"*Perhaps* is a weasel word."

"Then definitely."

"Definitely, but not now."

"Exactly."

"You're worse than a weasel. You a wolverine."

"Not so. I'm from Stanford, not Michigan. I am a Cardinal."

"You're a turkey vulture. Vulture, vulture, vulture, picking at the bones of a poor Korean girl dying of a broken heart."

"You missed your calling, Stace. You should have an opera star. You could pull this dying-of-heartbreak every night in front of a huge audience."

"Oh. So now I'm a fat lady."

"No, no, no. The fat lady never falls to her knees and clutches at her bosom. She holds a sword high and bellows."

"What's the point of holding a sword over your impotent... neck?"

"Good night. Stacy. And good morning as well. I promise we'll party when all of this is over."

She laughed a cheerless laugh. "Your way of saying it's never going to be over."

"No, no. Soon. When I get back from Tucson."

"I know you. You'll drive back to Las Vegas from Tucson by way of Patagonia."

"Wrong. Patagonia is south of Tucson."

"That's what I mean. Argentina."

"The town of Patagonia is a bit northeast of Nogales."

"Fuck you. Get out. I need to drive to Double Your Pleasure to buy a bigger, better vibrator. Goodbye. Thanks for lots of nothing."

"See you later, Stace." I opened the car door.

"How about a front-seat blowjob? Right here. Right now. That won't take long. Will it?"

I got out of her car, then leaned down and said, "Don't despair."

"Easy for you to say. You got that Sheila person waiting in Tucson."

I was beginning to regret having had Stacy track down Sheila's address. Sort of. I closed the door and, as I watched Stacy drive away, I thought I saw the middle finger of her right hand salute me. But the light from the street lamp was feint. I could have been wrong. After all, she wasn't used to holding a handgun with a silencer attached to its muzzle. Maybe her hand ached and she was performing some sort of Oriental wrist-and-finger exercise.

46

I managed two loads of laundry, a half-hour nap, and a quick lunch of peanut butter on saltines before calling a cab to take me to McCarran. While waiting for the taxi, I realized I had been wearing the same sports coat for ten consecutive days. Feh. But I had only taken one jacket to Arizona and had not expected to wear it at all, unless Adelle and I went out to a chi-chi restaurant where the expectation for diners was business attire. Nor had I planned on the need to conceal my Smith & Wesson day after day. Technically I was on vacation.

I slept for most of the flight to Tucson, oblivious of my fellow members of the flying cattle club. Neither excess perfume nor rank body odor nor breath reeking of onions and garlic prevented me from dozing soundly. Not even the occasional squeal of an infant as yet unable to tell its mother, "Mommy Dearest, an imbalance in the equilibrium between cabin pressure and the pressure in my middle ear has reached the point that my fucking ears hurt."

In the Tucson airport parking lot I marveled for a second time in a week that I could still count four hubcaps on my Jeep. My tires had not been slashed nor my windshield smashed. Either my stars were blissfully aligned or else the parking lot had held a steady supply of vehicles more appealing to thieves and vandals. I saw no evidence that outlandish parking fees had led to enhanced security measures to deter delinquents and thugs hell-bent on destruction. I could only assume the city council's privileged parking spots had benefited from the revenue enhancement. New striping for them perhaps. Or bigger signs to warn away potential usurpers. In any case, I paid my fee and exited the lot, heading toward Arroyo Arenoso and Adelle's house. Sleep deprived, I wanted only to crash on the bed in my sister's guest bedroom. I only hoped I didn't crash before I got there. I didn't.

Adelle had only recently arrived home and hadn't expected me. Knowing she would be at school, I had seen no need even to try to phone ahead from Las Vegas. After landing in Tucson, I simply forgot.

"Wiley! What a nice surprise," she said when I walked in. "But, my God. You look like you haven't slept in a week."

"Not quite that long," I said as I gave her a hug and a peck on the cheek. "Sorry I didn't give you warning I was coming back. I didn't know myself until this morning."

"Have you eaten?" she said.

"Airport food. Airline peanuts."

"Let me fix us both a proper meal."

"Feed yourself, Sis. I just want to sleep."

"Perhaps that is a better idea. I wouldn't want you to fall face forward into a bowl of soup."

Wednesday

I woke up twelve hours later with no soup on my face. I had shaved, showered, and dressed by the time Adelle emerged from her room, dressed smartly, although the yellow tennis balls affixed to the rear legs of her walker detracted from the overall impression of élan.

"You look much better than you did yesterday afternoon, Brother," she said as she sat down to the coffee I had poured for her.

"Yesterday afternoon was it? Seems like a week ago, what little I remember of it," I said.

"*Sleep is pain's easiest salve, and doth fulfill all the offices of death, except to kill.*"

"Shakespeare? From what play? I don't recall that line. Not Lear; not Othello. Surely not Richard II, though it sounds like it might be. I could swear I know my Richards," I said.

"John Donne," Adelle said.

"No wonder I couldn't place it."

"But you're right, Wiley. The line does have a ring similar to Richard's hollow-crown soliloquy."

What is sleep? If it is a condition one puts oneself into in order to give one's mind and body a peaceful interlude, then I never sleep. In *The Feathered Serpent* Charlie Chan casually notes what to me is obvious: *Sleep sometime very difficult thing.* For me bodily thrashing is routine. And *to sleep, perchance to dream?* There is nothing chancy about it, Hamlet, old boy. But you got the *must give us pause* part right. On the other hand, I do some of my best detecting work just before, during, and immediately upon waking up from, an unsound sleep.

Those past twelve hours of riding the rails on Sleep's roller-coaster gave me a new – and perhaps useful – insight. After fixing eggs, bacon, and toast for the two of us, then doing up the dishes, I saw Adelle off to school, soothing her obsession with her flawless appearance by flicking several imaginary toast crumbs from her blouse collar. 'Tis a ploy I often use to appease her fretting. Once she was out of sight down the street, I loaded my weaponry into my Jeep and holster, and drove off toward Tubac.

I remembered the business-hours sign at Arte de Casa Delantara stated the gallery opened at 10:00 a.m. I would be early, so I stayed on the interstate and exited a few miles further south, where I visited Tumacacori National Historical Park.

The main attraction is the ruins of a not-ever-quite-finished, shabby-looking church known as Mission San José de Tumacácori. It is the last of several churches built in area by the Spanish. The first was begun by the Jesuits, under the ubiquitous Father Kino. Then, when the Spanish king expelled the Jesuits, Franciscan friars took over and continued the Church's work.

I walked about the hard, barren mission grounds, trying to imagine why the local natives, the tribes the Spanish called Pimas, acquiesced so readily to the entreaties and intimidations of a few tiresome priests. Unlike Pizarro and Cortez, these robed ersatz-fakirs came unarmed, except for their venomous prattle.

As I stood and looked up at the partially-built, and now crumbling, temple, I asked myself why people whose ancestors were content for generations with their pagan deities and plethora of mystifying, idiosyncratic spirits almost overnight succumbed to an alternative version of mumbo-jumbo that, if anything, made less sense. Was it because of the priests' snake-charming stories about a highly enigmatic, wilderness-wandering scold who, though he spoke primarily in hazy parables, promised not only eternal life, but one free from the hard-scrabble living the Pimas endured, generation after generation? Or was it because of the stories of this shaman's assurances of perpetual torture as the sole alternative to conversion, a certainty for those who refused to acknowledge in full a set of perplexing propositions about the nature of this über-priest? The carrot? Or the stick? False hope? Or genuine fear? Living in close proximity to the Apaches, the Pimas would have known what torture was all about.

I finally concluded I'd never know -- and moved on.

When I walked into Gwen Dupree's gallery of decorative outdoor ornaments, I was pleased to see the clerk I had previously dubbed Blondie was behind the counter again. Gwen, I was told, was not around. But that was fine. Blondie represented the centerpiece of the dreamy epiphany that had wakened me in the middle of the night. Somewhat akin to Saul's experience on his way to Damascus, when I awoke to this vision, I nearly fell out of bed, was nearly blinded by the light. And then I realized I had been so tired, I had tumbled into bed and fallen fast asleep with the overhead bedroom light still on.

"I remember you. Aren't you the detective guy who was here a week or so ago?" Blondie chirped. This day she wore a name tag that read: Carolyn Watson.

"I am indeed the very same."

"What may I do for you, Mr. Detective?'

I looked around to see if any other customers were in the gallery. I saw none. "You could begin by telling me what exactly your relationship with Sebastian Sechrest is?"

"Who?"

I repeated the name.

"I'm sorry. I don't know anyone by that name," she said.

"Maybe you know him some *nom de plume*. Or *nom de artiste*. The man you let videotape you having sex with teenage boys."

She blushed and looked around nervously to see if anyone else had heard me. "What do you want?"

From my coat pocket I pulled out the DVD case I had taken from Beckheimer's Gem Depot. My middle-of-the-night, literally eye-opening realization was that one of the blonde heads of hair in the disk-case-cover photo belonged to someone I had seen before – and had christened Blondie.

"I want to know the name of the man who captured this performance of you performing fellatio on a young man who was recently murdered. Is that asking too much? Perhaps you'd rather have Arroyo Arenoso's chief of police ask you."

"How much trouble am I in?" she said.

"Depends."

"On what?"

"The degree and timing of your cooperation. The clock is now running," I said.

She sighed deeply, and then said, "Boyd Dupree."

I felt light-headed for an instant. "Boyd Dupree."

"Yeah." She ran her orange-nailed index finger slowly across the disk cover. "The other blonde is Debbie Olson. She works here part-time, too. And that streaked brunette is my boss, Gwen Dupree,

Boyd's wife. I bet you didn't recognize her with that weird wig, did you? And the other brunette is Karen Crowder, a friend of Gwen's."

A second flash of recognition occurred to me. Something else in the set of cover photos – besides the blonde hair that I finally recognized as Carolyn's – had been rattling around in a poorly lit corner of my memory. I peered intently and only now I saw it for what it was. In the background, behind the image that Blondie had just identified as Gwen Dupree imitating a sword-swallower, was a portion of a dining room hutch, a small framed piece of cross-stitching above it, the edge of what I now remembered was an Infinity Classia stereo speaker. When staring repeatedly at the case-cover photos, my focus had always been on Bobby and the women kneeling before him. But the photo of Gwen and Bobby I now recognized as having been taken in Gwen Dupree's living room, with the camera aimed in the direction of the dining room that lay beyond it.

The air went out of me. How could I be so blind? Had I examined the disk-cover photos with the magnifying glass I keep in the glove box of my Jeep for map-reading, I would surely have recognized the background items earlier.

"Where did you get that photo?" Carolyn said. "And is that a DVD disk inside the case? Is that why you're asking about this... what did you say his name is? Sechrest?"

"No. I'm pretty sure Boyd is the one who ended up selling his video tapes to someone in Las Vegas, who then converted his tapes to DVD's."

"Boyd did that?"

"Most likely."

"Did he get paid a lot money for his tape?"

I said, "I have no idea."

Carolyn snorted. "He probably did it for the money. God, knows he needs a lot of it these days."

"Why is that?" I said.

Carolyn looked away, apparently embarrassed that she had hinted at some secret.

"Why?" I tapped my watch. "Look. I warned you. You're on the clock here."

She signed deeply. "Okay. Gwen has this little problem."

"What little problem?"

"A big problem actually. She's hooked on O.C.'s. Hooked pretty badly."

"O.C.'s."

"You know. OxyContin. Painkillers. Some people refer to it as hillbilly heroin 'cause it's got opium in it."

I thought, OxyContin. That's the stuff in the Percoset Adelle is taking for her busted foot.

Carolyn said, "Do you realize how much Oxy can cost these days? I've heard some black market dealers are charging a hundred bucks per pill. Can you imagine?"

I said, "How many a day does Gwen take?"

"I don't know exactly, but it's not like she's gulping a one-a-day vitamin. That's for sure. She pops 'em all day long. Sometimes even when Boyd's taping her in action."

So control of Gwen Dupree's painkiller supply very easily could have represented the leverage Bobby Shane was hoping to gain when he invited Kirk McMullen to go partners with him. And if Boyd found out about Bobby's plan –.

"Where is Gwen now?" I said.

"At home. I think she's waiting for Boyd to show up with… with a new supply of… well, you know what. I talked to her about half an hour ago. She called to say she wasn't coming in."

I grabbed Carolyn by a wrist.

"Hey. Let go of me."

I held on. "I'm leaving. Don't make any phone calls. To anyone."

She glared at me and twisted her arm, trying to get it free from my grip.

"You make so much as one phone call, I'll see you end up in Perryville for a long time as an accessory to a long list of sex crimes – for starters. You know about Perryville?"

She appeared to draw a blank. Or maybe she knew but didn't want to contemplate being on the inside of a state women's prison.

"The dykes in Perryville will line up two abreast, down the hall and across the exercise yard, to take a turn at having a handsome sweetie like you for a flesh-sandwich sex toy, Baby."

She cringed as if she had seen a pack of spiders crawling toward her.

"I'll know if you make a call. *Comprende?*"

She nodded and blinked away a nascent tear.

47

I hadn't driven two miles before I began to regret not leaving Blondie Watson hogtied and gagged in a backroom of the gallery. Supposing fear will freeze another person in a state of inaction can be a dangerous misplacement of faith. In this case, I realized reliance on the blonde's dread of going to jail might have been an imprudent bluff on my part. But too late now, I told myself. Woulda, coulda, shoulda. Into the Valley of Death rode the Dumb Gumshoe.

Stupid me. I didn't even know what distance half a league amounted to. I thought about dialing 911 and asking Rollie Morton to meet me at the Dupree house. But again, *Macho* Wiley opted for a one-man attack. What a fool! I had never even contemplated an epitaph and nothing clever came to mind as I barreled north on the interstate. I did trust Adelle to cobble together a short, tasteful, perhaps even memorable, obituary for me.

I didn't even have to ring the doorbell. I saw Gwen Dupree see me coming. She opened her front door as I was about to press the buzzer out of habit.

"Well, well. You're back. It's been a while, Mr. Poynter. What questions can I answer for you this time?" she said, oozing charm.

As I entered the house and stepped past the foyer, I glanced left quickly to confirm that the hutch, framed cross-stitch artwork, and stereo speaker corresponded with what was on the cover of the porno DVD case. They matched.

"I came to ask for your account of why your husband killed Bobby Hollsworth."

"He what?"

"Oh, knock it off. You're in this up to your carefully plucked eyebrows as his accomplice."

"You think Boyd killed Bobby?"

"I think, but you know, which is why you're going to tell me all about it."

"Have you been drinking?" she said.

"No. Have you?"

"After listening to your preposterous accusations, I definitely need a drink."

"Just numb yourself with OxyContin. About time for another pill, isn't it?"

Gwen Dupree edged toward her dining room liquor cabinet, backing away slowly and eyeing me warily.

"Who told you I require pain meds?"

"A little birdie told me. It's springtime, Mrs. Dupree. The birds are singing everywhere. And now it's your turn."

Boyd Dupree appeared from the hallway. "You don't know shit, Mr. Nosy Detective." In his right hand he held a push dagger.

"Ah, Mr. Dupree with the push dagger in the–. The what? The bedroom? The living room? The kitchen?" I said.

Dupree said nothing, standing there smirking. He looked different from his driver's license photo, which Stacy had sent to Jack. For one, his license declared him to be six-foot-three. I judged him to be barely six feet. Second, his hair was darker. Although license photos are notoriously unflattering, I was sure I was looking at a dye-job. A phony inside and out.

I added, "That rules out Colonel Mustard, Miss Scarlet, and Mr. Green. Or rather, Mr. Sechrest. I imagine it was you, Mrs. Dupree, who placed the anonymous phone call to the police, after you and your husband baked Bobby's phone, then buried behind Sebastian Sechrest's house. I'm sure Blabby Bobby told you all about what a dirty old man Mr. Sechrest is. And let me guess. One of you overheard Bobby talking on his cell phone to Colby Ambrose about hijacking your OxyContin deliveries, busting up your pipeline and holding your precious pills for ransom, eh?"

"Boyd?" Gwen said in an aren't-you-going-to-do-something tone.

"Let him talk, Baby. Let him talk."

"What else is there to say?" I gave a shrug.

My offhand shrug proved the tipping point for Boyd Dupree. He came at me, holding the push knife like a piston about to plunge into a cylinder, his arm retracted like a pushrod. But I was ready for him. Butt-Fuck Trayleman had taught us raw, obtuse recruits in basic training that practice, practice, practice is the key to not getting killed. I learned that lesson well enough to spend an hour now and then unholstering my Smith & Wesson from the small of my back while wearing sport coats I deliberately bought one size too big. It was Dante Foster who first explained to me how good tailoring might one day find me looking snazzily dressed while reposing prematurely in a casket.

I got off three rounds. That proved enough to down the charging murderer. Had he started his rush from further away, and had I been a better marksman, I would have attempted to aim my shots at non-vital points of his anatomy. But the range was close and my shooting skills are second-rate. I aimed all three bullets where even I was unlikely to miss – the center of his looming chest. Unlike my usual efforts at Dante's range, I scored three bullseyes. And even stepping backwards as I fired, Boyd fell at my feet, the tip of the push dagger's blade nicking the toe of my left shoe.

Gwen screamed and ran at me. Or so I supposed. I turned my gun toward her, but she fell to the floor, embracing her dead or dying husband and crying out his name. I took several deep breaths, lowered my gun, pulled out my cell phone, and – at last – dialed 911.

Soon sirens sounded in the distance and a long three minutes later I saw a familiar Cattleman Stetson appear from just beyond the dwarf-oleander hedgerow separating the lawn from the street. Behind Rollie Morton three of his deputies came up the walkway, followed by a pair of EMTs wheeling a gurney.

The chief congratulated me on my shooting, assuring me Boyd Dupree was dead before he hit the floor. Then Chief Morton gave me hell for pulling a stupid one-man cowboy act. He phrased his reprimand in terms of my having more balls than brains, immediately afterwards apologizing to a still-weeping Gwen Dupree for upbraiding me in such brassy terminology. I listened without remark, instead helping myself, unbidden, to half a tumbler full of the Duprees' third-rate bourbon and slumping down into a chair.

I didn't get very far into telling my story before the chief ordered Gwen to be taken away and held, pending formal charges, as an accessory to murder and likely other charges as well. Carolyn Watson and the other two "cover girls" were ordered brought in for questioning. The chief took down Kirk McMullen's name so that he could be interviewed later.

"I've got to hand it to you, Poynter. You don't sit still long enough to let any bamboo grow up your ass," the chief told me when I finished recapping my adventures.

"Were you in Vietnam?" I said.

"Do I look that old?"

I was loathe to tell him that, yes, he did. I was proud of myself that I mostly told the truth when questioned by Rollie Morton. I only fudged on a matter I was not likely to be caught out on later – how I had obtained the porno disk with Bobby and Gwen Dupree among the featured stars in one of the disk case's cover photos.

I told Chief Morton that Jack Stonecipher, at my behest, had been tracing Boyd Dupree's movements in Las Vegas. The reason for my asking Jack to do that stemmed from a minor inconsistency in the story Gwen Dupree had told me early on. That part was, of course, true. But then I said that Jack had gone to Brent Karsgaard's porno emporium and, while perusing the available offerings, had come across the disk with photos of Bobby on the case cover.

With Jack in a coma and Karsgaard in the middle of a trans-Pacific cruise, no one was available to contradict that falsehood, although I worried slightly that a really good defense attorney, should Gwen Dupree be lucky to find one, might well catch me out when one of his own investigators began backtracking the provenance of the lurid contents on the disk. But, even if the disk proved to be tainted, there was plenty of other evidence, I assumed, to put Gwen away for a very long time now that the police had legal access to the Dupree's house. Not until the following day would Dante Foster provide me with news that would cover my ass even better regarding the fib I had told of how I came into possession of the disk.

At police headquarters I put my narrative in writing, trying my best to keep a long story short without omitting any vital pieces. While I was seated in an interview cubbyhole composing my saga, I saw Sebastian Sechrest, still in handcuffs, in an outer office. I learned later that, although the murder charge was dropped, he was still being charged with being in possession of pornographic photos of a minor, Kristy Serling. He was on his way to be arraigned on that felony charge. He, too, saw me. I remained seated. Our eyes met, but no words were exchanged. He was on the far side of a large room full of cluttered desks.

I didn't expect him to thank me for finding an alternative suspect in the crime of murdering Bobby Shane Hollsworth. Nor was I about to display any relief that he was being freed from accusations against him that had now proven to be untrue. Each of us bore too much residual animosity toward the other for either us to rise above it. I had discovered and unmasked his dark secret and, for that, he could not forgive me. I could not forgive him for being an exploiter of the youths he was paid to mentor. I refused to believe that, Lear-like, Sechrest was more sinned against than sinning.

48

Finally permitted to leave, I left police headquarters and returned to my sister's house, hoping to kick back with a bit of privacy. But Adelle was already home.

She explained, "News spread quickly and a sort of campus-wide pandemonium ensued. So, wise woman that she is, Mrs. Haydenfurth, our principal, declared a half-day holiday, given that no one was going to accomplish anything useful anyway."

"Good for her," I said. "And...if it's officially a holiday, how about we celebrate? There's still some Wild Turkey going 'Gobble-gobble' in your cupboard." The effects of the cheap-shit stuff I had consoled myself with at the Duprees' house had long since worn off.

"Help yourself, Wiley. I'll pass and settle for a nice cup of tea, while you tell me what you've really been up to these past few days."

And so, with the bottle of bourbon close at hand, I spent the rest of the afternoon chronicling my bloody damned yarn all over again, judiciously tweaking it as best I could so as not to offend my sister's dainty and delicate Victorian sensibilities.

When I finished, Adelle said, "I hope Rollie Morton isn't upset that you, rather than he, uncovered the people and evidence that led to the Duprees."

"Maybe the chief will take comfort in knowing that, in a way, he was on the right track in the beginning. After all, the whole affair amounts to a sort of drug-deal-gone-bad kind of intrigue. Rollie simply misunderstood what kind of drugs were involved and what kind of people were involved."

"So Mrs. Dupree knew Bobby's body was in the arroyo before she ever began her morning jog?" Adelle said.

"Yep. And, because Bobby had been to her house so many times, she knew her dog would recognize Bobby's scent and likely go right to him. She and her husband figured that if she was the one who found the body, that would head off the police investigation from looking at them. That may be true. I don't think Rollie Morton and his staff ever considered them to be suspects at all – at any time. However, Gwen Dupree made a misstep when she told me her husband had been attending a convention in Las Vegas the weekend of Bobby's murder. When I discovered that convention had taken place weeks earlier, I asked my friend Jack to nose around to see if he could find out what Dupree had really been up to. Indirectly, that eventually led us to finding the video pornography operation with the photos of Bobby, Gwen, her friend, and two employees."

"Careless of her," Adelle said.

"She should have told me her husband was at a NASCAR event at Las Vegas Speedway. Or vaguer still, he was simply at the

Speedway. Had she told me that, I wouldn't have sent Jack on the hunt for what her husband was really doing. Now granted, Jack wouldn't have ended up in the hospital, but also Boyd and Gwen Dupree might very well have gotten away with the murders."

"But, at the point when you returned here with the bawdy disk, you still suspected Sebastian, correct?" Adelle said.

"Yeah. My questioning Carolyn Watson when I came back this last time was what made the Dupree angle pop up."

"Mrs. Dupree told you that her husband had gone to Las Vegas on Friday, did she not?"

"Yes. And I am kicking myself for not discovering that he didn't leave until Saturday. He had a reservation at a hotel in Las Vegas that began on Friday night. And he paid for Friday night. But he didn't fly up until Saturday. I should have found that out. Stacy could have dug that up, I'm sure. Hacked into Southwest Airlines' passenger check-in system or something. But at the time my only curiosity was what Boyd was up to in Las Vegas."

"You just assumed he was there?" Adelle said.

"Oh, for a moment I casually wondered if he had gone off somewhere else. San Diego, maybe, for a tryst. But later Jack discovered he did indeed have a weekend reservation at the Aliante Hotel in North Las Vegas. I should have somehow been able to find out if he was actually at the hotel the night Bobby was killed."

"Well, Wiley, you can't lose sleep over not thinking of something like that," Adelle said.

"Sure I can. In *Charlie Chan in London* my favorite detective points out, '*It is unasked question which prevent sleep.*'"

"Oh, you and your Charlie Chan movies." Adelle made her mother-hen clucking sound.

In my best sing-song voice, I said, "Man can learn lot by watching movies of honorable Hono-ruru detective."

"He never said that," Adelle said, giving me her evil-eye look.

"Maybe. Maybe not."

"What kind of man kills a boy, and then flits off to leave his wife to face the police by herself to tell them lies? I can't begin to imagine," Adelle said.

I said, "One confident in his wife's abilities as an actress, for sure. But otherwise, a very depraved man. Of course, his enabling his wife's drug abuse and his porn activities confirm that. Well, and cold-blooded murder."

Adelle said, "Boyd Dupree killed the young man in Tucson also?"

"Yes. Gwen Dupree told Rollie Morton he used a boning knife from the kitchen. How he surprised Colby or got him into the alley is unclear. Tucson police are looking into the details and trying to figure that out."

My sister said, "Why didn't anyone know Bobby was going to the Dupree house? I gather he was there fairly frequently."

"Gwen Dupree was smart on that point. Chief Morton told me the only female DNA found in Bobby's truck belonged to Kristy Serling and Juanita Bardella. Gwen would make Bobby park down at the bowling alley, where she would pick him up and drive him to her house."

"Ah ha!"

I laughed.

"So Mrs. Dupree is what is known these days as a cougar? Is that the right word, Wiley? A woman in her thirties, or maybe early forties, usually who enjoys –. Oh, what are they called? Boy-toys? Are those the correct terms, Brother?" She gave me a very sly look.

"Where did you learn such language, Adelle?"

"I'm not deaf, Wiley. I manage to hear a great deal of what my students talk about when they think this middle-aged frump isn't paying them the slightest attention. In addition, you used *boy-toy* yourself last week."

"So I did." My sister was proving to be not nearly as clueless as I supposed she was. "Those are the correct descriptions, Sis."

She nodded vigorously, a triumphant look on her face. "Obviously Mr. Dupree did not become outraged that his wife was having sex with Bobby. How odd."

"Any initial wrath quickly gave way to the idea that he could, in effect, hold Bobby hostage and make money from his wife's carnal antics. Later, probably when Brent Karsgaard demanded more variety in order to continue buying tapes from Dupree, Boyd talked his wife into drawing in her two attractive employees and her seductive-looking friend, Karen."

Adelle said, "By the way, what is going to happening to the Duprees' dog? Do you know?"

"The Duprees' next-door neighbor is looking after it temporarily, although Candy Rogers, a police woman on Chief Morton's staff, told me the neighbor wants to keep the dog permanently, should Mrs. Dupree be convicted."

Adelle let out a, "Ha! Fat chance she won't."

"Unlikely," I said.

"Wiley, didn't you tell me Mrs. Dupree poured herself a drink almost immediately after you showed up on her doorstep for the first time?"

"I did. That made me suppose she was a serious boozer, but now I think I may have been wrong. Combining alcohol and OxyContin can be lethal apparently. Even so, the apprehension of having to hide the fact she was an accessory to murder would rightly make her want to reach for the bourbon."

Adelle noted, "My Percoset prescription contains the warning that alcohol may intensify the effect of the drug."

"I'm sure she wanted to be in less pain all right," I said.

"Certainly less anguish. What about her addiction now? Will she just have to suffer cold turkey?" Adelle said.

"Rollie Morton mentioned having to get her some kind of treatment. I gather simply stopping taking, or getting cut off from, OxyContin is pretty brutal."

"Cruel and unusual?" Adelle said.

"I don't think it's that cruel. Unpleasant, for sure, but not dangerous to the point of being lethal, I don't think. I told him to let her suffer, but he said the DA didn't want her lawyers to have any sympathy angles to play in court later."

Adelle said, "Tell me about the knife Boyd was holding when he charged at you. Was he into marital arts, too?"

"No. Boyd Dupree came from several generations of Baton Rouge river people. And, I'm now told, the knife, called a push dagger, has also long been popular among those whose occupations were Mississippi River-related – warehousemen, keel boat men, riverboat gamblers, and the like."

My sister asked, "Why didn't Stacy find any evidence that Boyd Dupree had answered the internet ad placed by that tape-to-disk place you and your friends broke into?"

"She has now. But Boyd replied to an old ad that had been replaced by a newer one. Sebastian Sechrest answered the latest ad. Stacy didn't realize there had been earlier ads. So she didn't look for any residual evidence of such ads at the time she was digging into the ad that was still online."

"Interesting. By the way, will you be required to come back to testify?"

"No doubt."

"Here? Or in Tucson?"

"I don't know."

She said, "So those were Sebastian's computers under your bed?"

I acknowledged that they were. I had turned them over to Rollie Morton, who accepted them with a look that said many things at once. "I will assume you found these along side a road somewhere," was all that came out of his mouth.

I knew Gwen Dupree's lawyers would have a field day urging a jury to suppose any porno found by the police on Sebastian's computers could have been placed there after the computers were stolen. It would take an expert of Stacy's caliber to testify that such material had been scanned into the machines long before they were taken from Sechrest's home.

My sister thought for several moments, then said, "Poor Sebastian. He's free, and yet he's not."

"Stop with the 'Poor Sebastian' sentimentality. The man's an ogre," I said.

"He certainly won't teach high school anywhere ever again. That's for sure." Adelle put on her righteous-indignation look for me. Stern-faced, shoulders squared, her spine ramrod straight.

"I hope not."

Adelle said, "This will be very hard on Kristy, no doubt."

I said, "She'll likely have to testify against Sebastian. Whether in open court or not will probably be up to the judge. Perry Crisp and Juanita Bardella will likely be squirming for a while, as well. But Jason and Richie will probably not be dragged into the limelight."

"That would be a blessing. So what are you going to do with yourself now, Wiley?" she said.

"Drive home and hope I find a case that pays."

"And if you don't?"

"If I don't drive home?" I said, smiling.

"You know what I mean."

"I'll always find work in Las Vegas, Sis. The city is a magnet for confused, frightened, broken souls. So many new people. And, whether they are brimming with hope or drowning in despair, many of them will stumble. And the city provides so many rabbit holes to vanish into."

"And you chase after them."

"Someone has to," I said.

"Isn't that what the police are for?"

"You have to realize something about Sin City, Sis. A missing person in Las Vegas is like someone late for an appointment anywhere else. If someone fails to show up where one is expected, the police and everyone else assume that person has chosen not to show up; got cold feet and took off back to Poughkeepsie. Only if the person doesn't show up back where he or she started from within two or three weeks, then just maybe someone will overcome inertia and begin to give a shit. Or maybe not."

"Surely, you exaggerate, Wiley."

I shrugged. "Not by much."

49

Thursday

Bobby Shane Hollsworth had never liked betting the line, Fabian Maldonado had told me. Betting on a teaser spread made him feel unique, superior to, more knowledgeable than, those who wagered only in accordance with the odds those devious gambling gods in Las Vegas set forth and declared were without prejudice. However, those other Gods – the ones with capital G's – who actually determine the outcomes of athletic competitions, based, one must assume, on factors independent of such mundane considerations as spreads and odds, rarely seemed to favor Bobby Shane. And, in the end, the young man's ploys to wrench even better deals from his bookie, his photographer, and, most importantly, his plot to try to gain a financial chokehold on his videographer – cost him far more than any cash loss he had ever suffered. The premium he paid in hopes of dealing with the Duprees on more-than-equal terms was far more than any reasonable man would pay for such a hoped-for edge.

But, as often is the case, Reason is the unheeded voice at the table where the mind's debates take place. Greed whispers into Desire's ear, while Reason gapes into the Middle Distance, then mumbles some lame reply to Desire's picturesque proposals. In that regard, Bobby is at one with us all. Only Bobby's particular desires became a reach too far.

Over breakfast Adelle asked me if the cockroaches had really taken over my office. Not exactly an apt mealtime topic, but I didn't mind. I reluctantly confessed to my sister that I had been nowhere near my office on either quick trip back to Las Vegas.

"Then you don't really need an office, do you?" she said.

"Oh, but I do. Your ignorance of my profession rises to the top of the pond again, Dell. If you had watched as many grade B *noir* movies as I have, you'd know that vast numbers of the screenplays for those flicks call for the opening scene to depict a sultry seductress walking into a seedy detective's office through a frosted-glass door on which is stenciled 'Johnny Gumshoe, Acme Detective Agency'. Or something similar. The babe is wearing a mink coat, diamonds, and high heels. In one hand she's holding an unlit cigarette in an elegant cigarette holder; in the other she's clutching a small, bejeweled purse."

"A hat?" Adelle said.

"Oh, yes. I almost forgot. She has on a posh cloche with an embroidered rose on one side."

"Nice touch. A 1920's setting, no doubt."

"Sure. That'll do. Anyway, the seedy detective may or may not have a reception area. If he does, it's manned, so to speak, by a busty, gum-chewing, nail-filing secretary who looks like a Veronica Lake clone. The detective himself sits in a tiny office with his feet propped up on a messy desk. Overhead a ceiling fan turns slowly. The background music is a moody saxophone solo."

"I didn't know you had a secretary," Adelle said.

"I don't. That's because my screenplay writer is non-union. But the office part is mandatory. Can't be an authentic detective without one."

"Does Charlie Chan have an office?"

"Indeed. In downtown Honolulu. Why, did you know Charlie's character is based on a real detective? A Honolulu police detective named Chang Apana? Earl Derr Biggers met him while Earl was vacationing on Waikiki and before long wrote a novel about a cigar-smoking, panama-hat-wearing detective of Chinese ancestry."

"I didn't know that," she said. "So you're maintaining this office of yours in order to house cockroaches and to feed your fantasies."

"Basically, yes. But having nothing more than a virtual office and offering internet-only discounts just doesn't cut it, Dell. That violates the whole tone of the detective-client relationship."

"In this particular case you've just finished, Wiley, who is the sultry seductress who sashays into your tiny, no-receptionist office?"

She had me. I said, "In this caper I figure the opening scene for something a little different. I would probably depict a small, yappy dog running off-leash along a country club fairway ahead of his jogger-mistress. Suddenly the dog dashes ahead and begins barking. When his mistress finally catches up, the dog has found the murder victim around which the case revolves."

Adelle just stared at me for a moment before saying, "And you laugh when I suggest you need to be kept on a shorter leash."

Dante Foster called me at mid-afternoon. News of my success had somehow reached Glitter Gulch, where the farthest-most edges of the universe and Las Vegas' city limits are, by most locals there, thought to be one and the same.

"Congratulations, Wiley, my man. Jackpot! Three sevens!"

"So where's my pot full of nickels?" I said.

"I'm glad you asked."

For the next few minutes I listened to a tale of wonder almost equal to my own.

"The first piece of good news is that Jack has wiggled his fingers and his toes. His sister claims his eyelids fluttered, too. The doctors are using that copout phrase the always invoke."

"Cautiously optimistic?" I injected.

"You got it. You sure you weren't a doctor sometime in your past? Got your license revoked for refusing to speak exclusively in bullshit ambiguities?"

"It never happened."

"Have I ever doubted your word?"

"I'll take the Fifth on that."

"Allow me to continue. The second piece of good news is that last night Stacy and I revisited the illustrious Gem Depot. She let us in so we could satisfy our curiosity regarding what lay hidden inside that enormous safe."

I said, "Dead bodies? Did you think to take along a cadaver dog to warn you, just in case?"

"We should have," Dante said, chuckling. "In fact, the case did contain bodies. Lots of them, all named Benjamin."

"Jackpot yourself."

"Indeed! Stace and I walked away with thirteen thousand Benjamins. And, to spare your tired mind the math, that's one-point-three million dollars."

"Walked away."

"Okay. Staggered away, if you want to be picky," Dante said.

"Staggered in more ways than one, I assume."

"Yeah. We were definitely staggered. But we recovered quickly."

"And where do all these little green Benjamins reside now?"

"Right here in front of me. But don't worry. My office door is locked and the No-No Brothers are standing guard outside."

"So what now?" I said.

"That very question is the main reason for my call. Well, in addition to letting you know about the doctors' cautious optimism."

"Speak."

"As far as I am concerned, Wiley, all this money in front of me has been orphaned. It needs to find a good home. Or rather, homes."

"And what do you have in mind for all that poor, orphaned cash?" I said.

"I have a plan. Will you listen to it?"

"My ears are attuned."

"Attuned?"

"Attuned."

"First, I'm deducting my expenses. The eighteen-wheeler to Long Beach, the cruise tickets for six, pay for my crew, calculating their time and risks. And then –."

Miss Manners tells us that discussing people's incomes, especially one's own, in public is the very height of tackiness. It simply ought not to be done. So I will simply say that the million-three was divided according to Dante's plan. I had no quarrel with his sense of equitable distribution. After all, Dante is both an accountant and a wise investor.

Beyond that, I will reveal the following: After deducting Dante's expenses, he agreed to go, on his own, to the North Vista Hospital's chief administrator and attempt to negotiate a flat one-time payment that would represent an amount both he and the administrator would sign off on as a reasonable estimate of what Jack Stonecipher's total hospitalization costs would come to. That dollar figure was a gamble for both men. The agreed upon sum would represent much more than the current total Jack owed, but potentially far less than the final total. Dante's proposal, as he divulged it to me, was a mid-six-figure number. I thought his number to be a fair offer.

Dante said that the payment to the hospital would done *under the table*. One way or another. Perhaps in the form of *gift* from an anonymous *donor*. He didn't want even one of the myriad government bureaucracies to find out about the payment and wonder where such a large sum came from. And Dante supposed the hospital would go along, knowing it was going to reap an unexpected blessing.

Next, Dante gave me a bottom-end six-figure number he thought might be donated to local charities. He read me a list of potential recipients. I agreed with the money designated for innocents: dogs, cats, and small children. The Animal Foundation, Nevada SPCA, Heaven Can Wait, and BluSky's Rescue & Adoptions, all for four-legged critters; Sunrise Children's Hospital and the Fremont Children's Clinic for two-legged ones.

I objected to any money going to places and groups that help adults who had already had their chances in life and had blown them. The twelve-step folks, those who feed dumpster-divers, and similar charities. I had no problem with the existence of such aid groups. My opposition was in our giving money to them. Us, not everyone. Dante had no problem with that stance.

Before Dante continued, I told him I would like to add one item that he may not have considered. "Would you please send enough to Bobby Hollsworth's parents to cover his funeral expenses? I'd feel better if you did. His body will be released soon. You can make that contribution remain anonymous, if you like."

"I'll see to it. Ten grand, do you think?" Dante said.

"Funerals are cheaper than weddings, but they're not cheap. Twenty?"

"Done."

The remainder of the money – quite a lot, actually – would be divided four ways. Dante, Jack, Stacy, and I would get even shares. Dante said Jack's sister had been somewhat evasive on the topic of whether she had already quit her job in Denver and whether she planned to stay on through Jack's rehabilitation, whenever that might occur. Jack's share would allow him ample time to recover slowly, would provide sufficient income for both him and his sister to live in his apartment comfortably for quite some time. In my case, I would not have to return hastily to Las Vegas so that I could either find a paying client or else sit on the corner of Flamingo and Las Vegas Boulevard rattling a tin cup. For Dante and Stacy their shares simply represented supplementary play money. They stole it for the fun of stealing it, not because they had any need for it. One more stickpin in the Brent Karsgaard voodoo doll.

The final piece of Dante's good news came when he said, "The strangest thing happened soon after Stacy and I left the porn emporium. Arsonists came along and torched the place, Wiley. Can you believe it?"

"I can. And very fortuitous, I might add."

"How so?" Dante said.

I explained to him that I was worried Gwen Dupree's lawyers might backtrack the source of the tapes I had turned over to Chief Morton and discover my version of how I came by the disk may not jive with the clear fact that no one could tell just by looking at the store front what the business activity inside consisted of. There was no external indication that the place was a walk-in retail establishment. And, therefore, how would Jack have known to step through the door and browse?

"The store front signage was destroyed, wasn't it, Dant?" I said.

"Most definitely. The place was gutted. It would take a jigsaw genius to put that place's front window back together. And I don't think the fire department arson squad has anybody that good on its staff."

"What a blessing," I said.

"The gods work in mysterious ways, right, Wile?"

"And so do you, for that matter," I said.

"I appreciate the compliment. Oh, and a reminder. Because of our nation's glorious banking laws, I'm going to have to tease all our shares of the –."

"Windfall?"

"The windfall, yes. It will trickle into our accounts in amounts under the figure whereby the noble bankers must send Uncle Samuel a note reporting such deposits," Dante said.

"I understand completely."

"Nor would we want to draw the attention of Samuel's revenue–collection branch, would we?"

"Definitely not."

"The money is definitely not earned income. Nor do I see it exactly as a gift," Dante said.

"How about a dividend?" I said.

"Aw, Wiley, no. Dividends are taxable. How about we simply assume that every penny of this money is after-tax money. Surely, upstanding member of the national congregation that Mr. Karsgaard is, he has already tithed the Church of the Potomac the proper percentage. Don't you think?"

"A rock-solid assumption, my friend. I trust you on that. After all, you're the accountant," I said.

"In any case, Wiles, don't plan to come home and plunk down any sizeable sum on nineteen black very soon."

"I promise I won't."

50

In the early evening I drove Adelle to dinner at Jonathan's Cork on the northeast side of Tucson. I managed to sweet-talk Chef Jonathan into preparing his off-menu steak tartar for our hors d'oeuvres. Normally one is expected to order that specialty over the phone well in advance. However, I explained to the chef/owner that I had just flown in from Las Vegas to help celebrate my sister's fortieth birthday and had heard ever so much about how superbly he prepares that delicacy. I apologized for not having the time or foresight to phone ahead. Cheerful and accommodating fellow that Chef Jonathan is, he readily succumbed to my pair of white lies. Adelle was flattered enough that I had shaved two years off her real age that she kept mum.

Later, I chose the bison filet for my entrée, while Adelle decided to be adventurous by ordering char-broiled ostrich. A bottle of Australian merlot helped the meat slide down our throats and cleanse our minds of the earlier parts of the day.

The hour was late when Adelle and I arrived back in Arroyo Arenoso. Adelle went straight off to bed. I sat at her computer for an hour, and then I, too, retired and slept better than I had in almost two weeks.

Friday

My sister had left for school already by the time I got up, performed my ablutions, and dressed. Because the month was now May, Arizona's Mountain Standard Time was the same as Nevada's Pacific Daylight Time. I waited until I thought Stacy would be at work and then phoned her.

"Congratulations. I hear you got your man." She spoke in a monotone. No enthusiasm.

"Man and woman."

"Husband and wife," she said. Then added, "In their thirties. I bet they had sex together once in a while."

"Had. Not any more."

Her voice still flat, she said, "You shot the dude."

"'Twas me or him."

"That's not grammatically correct."

"So?"

"Don't set a bad example."

"To you?"

"Oh, I don't matter, eh? That figures."

"Well, you sort of do. Sometimes."

"Asshole."

"Is that any way to speak to the man who is going to whisk you away on a grand vacation?" I said.

Silence.

"Hello?"

"Is this just another one of your let's-play-a-cruel-joke-on-the-gook-girl games?"

"No."

"It's not? For real?"

"For real."

"I'm listening."

"Can you afford to take ten days off, starting Sunday?" I said.

"Afford? Yeah. Dante already told me I'm rich as Rockefeller. But does this mean we're going somewhere Dutch treat?"

"Not at all. Entirely on my dime."

"Where you taking me, Mr. Suddenly Nice Guy?"

"I bought you a first class ticket from Las Vegas to LAX for Sunday morning."

"Oh, shit. What is this gonna be? A one-way cruise from Long Beach to Singapore?"

"No, no, no. I'm going to meet you in LA. From LAX we fly first-class on Alaska Airlines to Cabo."

"You're making this up. I knew you were fucking with my head again," she snapped.

"Capella Pedregal. Five-star resort. Ten days. You and me."

"And ten nights?"

"We're not going to sleep on the beach, Baby."

"Hey, dude. Just because you're paying doesn't mean you get to treat me like your hooker. Okay?"

"Stace, I don't look at this at all as trying to buy your love."

I held the phone away from my ear as she broke into a chorus of "Can't Buy Me Love".

When she finished I merely said, "McCartney you're not."

"Capella Pedregal. Is that the place with mirrored bedroom ceilings?"

"I don't know about that."

"I think it might be." Pause. "This is for really real, right? Cross your heart and hope I won't kill you if you're lying?"

"Cross my heart."

"My God! We're leaving Sunday?"

"The day after tomorrow. We're meeting up at LAX."

"Shit! That only gives me a day and a half to shop for new clothes. I need a new bikini, a couple new dresses for going out to dinner, new shoes. Lots of new shoes."

"You'd better get started."

"Why are you doing this?"

"I owe you."

"You've owed me for months. For years."

"You did as much or more to solve this case than anyone."

"You're right about that. Stacy Park! She's a bloody genius! Go ahead. Say it."

I repeated her self-applause.

"Listen. Dante's not coming, is he?"

"No."

"How about Sheila?"

"No."

"She throws a boring hump, eh? Not so hot? Just lies there flat, like a starfish, does she? Lost interest in her already, huh?"

I said nothing.

"Go ahead. Say 'No', 'No', 'No', and 'No' again."

"I haven't even seen Sheila again," I said, which wasn't quite true. But almost.

"Jeez. You're weird."

"I may be. But check with my sister, Adelle. Just a few days ago she said to me, and I quote, 'Shagging coeds is not your style.'"

"She really said that? Hmmm. Okay. No Sheila."

"You're grandmother's not invited either," I said.

"Granny has good neighbors. They'll look in on her."

"Just you and me in Cabo, Stacy."

"Hey! Maybe we'll find a body on the beach. And maybe that body will have been murdered. And maybe in between… well, doing you know what…we can solve whodunit. Together, of course. I promise to give you some credit, too. Okay? Then you'll owe me another ten days somewhere. Bali or Tahiti or Rarotonga, huh?"

"Stace, in *Charlie Chan's Chance* the great detective claims, *'One at time is good fishing'*."

"Aw. Come on."

"Oh, all right. In *Charlie Chan's Murder Cruise* he allows that, *'Most happy to celebrate – even without reason.'*"

Stacy said, "Yeah. That's better. See you Sunday. You'll recognize me right away, because I'll be the one wearing –."

"No! Stop! Don't tell me."

"Okay. But why?"

"I love mysteries with surprise endings."

www.ingramcontent.com/pod-product-compliance
Lightning Source LLC
Chambersburg PA
CBHW072258020726
47501CB00002B/309